or *Unleashing Chaos*

loud at Desi's antics in the human world and her
fish out of water story and this delivered! Jace was
the perfect ... ective, mysterious, and a little broken. I loved the
twists and turns the story took and the ending caught me totally by surprise. This
is the perfect spicy book to curl up in a bubble bath with." —*USA Today* Bestselling
Author Ruby Dixon

"Fantastic spice, fabulous banter, and a great plot that grabs you from the very first
page and leaves you wanting more after the last. Five smoldering stars!"—*USA Today*
Bestselling Author Alexandra Silva

"*Unleashing Chaos* is a deliciously spicy, witty book that I couldn't put down. Desi and
the supporting cast were fiery and exactly the kind of paranormal romance I didn't
know I needed." —*USA Today* Bestselling Author Amanda Richardson

"Steamy and Sassy! *Unleashing Chaos* doesn't fail to keep the pages turning! Vaughn and
Johnson are quickly becoming my go-to authors." —*USA Today* Bestselling Author Sarah
Bale

"*Unleashing Chaos* is a sweet and steamy read with a fun twist on the seven deadly
sins." —Amazon Bestselling Author Jamie Applegate Hunter

Praise for *Spellbound*

"Crystal and Felicity have a magical way of telling enchanting romance stories that
submerge you in the plot and keep you grasping on for more! Unleash your wildest
romance desires and be prepared to be spellbound!" —*USA Today* Bestselling Author
C.C. Monroe

"Haunted hotel? Check. Hot twin ghosts? Check. Grade A spice? Check! *Spellbound*
was a fun(ny), haunting, chillingly good read, with awesome prose and great tension.
I couldn't put it down!! To me it was the definition of a paranormal romance: spooky
aspects with well-written romantic (& sexual) tension. This was my first time reading
Crystal & Felicity's work and it exceeded my expectations. I highly recommend it."
—Stephanie Rose, Wattpad Creator

"*Spellbound* is such a captivating read full of twisty secrets, the perfect haunted hotel
setting, and swoon-worthy enemies-to-lovers romance that is sure to have you turning pages long after you've said, 'just one more chapter.'" —Author Lilly Brooks

Also by Crystal J. Johnson and Felicity Vaughn

Spellbound

PLAYLIST

HURRICANE Luke Combs	**TENERIFE SEA** Ed Sheeran
LET HER GO Passenger	**8 LETTERS** Why Don't We
HALF HEARTED We Three	**STAY** Florida Georgia Line
FAR AWAY Nickelback	**THE NIGHT WE MET** Lord Huron
ELECTRIC LOVE Børns	**DIVE DEEP (HUSHED)** Andrew Belle
PERFECT STORM Brad Paisley	**IF YOU'RE GONE** Matchbox Twenty
HELL ON THE HEART Eric Church	**ALL FOR YOU** Cian Ducrot
YOUNG AND BEAUTIFUL Lana Del Ray	**BLEEDING LOVE** Leona Lewis
TAKE ME TO CHURCH Hozier	**WICKED GAME** Theory Of A Deadman
SOMEONE YOU LOVED Lewis Capaldi	**LOSING SLEEP** Chris Young
SWEET CREATURE Harry Styles	**RUNAWAY TRAIN** Soul Asylum
MESS IS MINE Vance Joy	**MIDDLE OF THE NIGHT** Loveless
SPEECHLESS Dan + Shay	**BEAUTIFUL THINGS** Benson Boone
ALL OF ME John Legend	**BEAUTIFUL CRAZY** Luke Combs
WILDEST DREAMS (TAYLOR'S VERSION) Taylor Swift	**LOSE CONTROL** Teddy Swims
WOULD YOU GO WITH ME Josh Turner	**NOT ANOTHER LOVE SONG** Ella Mai

For anyone who has ever felt like they don't belong:
Your "too loud" brings joy.
Your "too quiet" brings peace.
Your "too weird" brings beauty.
Your "too damaged" brings understanding.
Never fear unleashing your chaos; it can change the world.

ONE
DESI

A demon in the human realm is bound to cause mischief, but a demon princess house hunting with her voracious big brother and his equally snackish husband . . . well, that's pure chaos. And it isn't mayhem for the reasons you might think. I have standards. *High* standards. Ones that demand a great view, fashionable furnishings, and stainless-steel appliances.

I need a house that screams *I've got my shit together and you want to date me!* Seven houses in and I haven't found one that even slightly meets my expectations.

"At this rate, you're going to waste all your time visiting every rental in Denver," Mandis says as we walk down the steps of a brownstone.

"I can't help that I'm not willing to compromise my standards and settle for something less than ideal," I say, kicking a rock down the sidewalk as we make our way through the neighborhood and toward the closest bus stop.

"What was wrong with that one?" Glen asks, sliding his muscular frame between me and my brother and linking his bulky arm with his husband's.

"It just didn't have everything I was looking for," I hedge, not meeting my brother-in-law's hazel gaze.

"What was the problem? What was it missing?" Mandis asks and raises an eyebrow, awaiting my answer. I sigh and let my head fall back to stare at the late afternoon sky, my wild red curls cascading down my back. "The white appliances were ugly, okay?"

Mandis and Glen let out groans in unison. "Desi. You've made everything about this so diff—"

I hold up my hand, stopping Mandis from saying the same words he said after touring the last two rentals. "Please. Don't start. I didn't think it was too much to ask for a nice, modern house where it snows, but where it is currently autumn. I want to wear sweaters and scarves and drink those pumpkin coffees somewhere I feel comfortable."

"You want to be a basic white bitch," Glen adds, biting into an ice-cream cone with his pointy front teeth. An ice-cream cone he didn't have in his hand a minute ago.

I pull on the back of his shirt, making the buttons strain against his broad chest, bringing him to a stop.

"Where did you get that?" My gaze darts to my brother. "You didn't conjure that for him, did you? You know what Dad said about using your gift while we're here. You could ruin everything."

Mandis runs his hand down his neatly trimmed red beard and rolls his eyes. "Calm down, I didn't conjure it for him. Although I wish I had. Look how handsome he is feasting. My gluttonous little demon. The only thing that would look better in his mouth is my c—"

"Then where did it come from?" I demand, stopping my brother from steering this conversation to their notorious sex life.

"I took it from the freezer you so vehemently hated in that house," Glen says with a proud smile.

"You stole it?"

"I was hungry."

Panic surges through me. I glance back at the town house, and yank both demons into a brisk stride. My knowledge of humans is limited to the four family vacations we took in this realm when I was younger and human movies and TV shows, but I know they don't like when someone takes what doesn't belong to them. The human authorities put thieves in ugly orange jumpsuits and make them sleep in bunk beds. Neither of which fits the aesthetic I'm going for, not to mention that orange clashes horrifically with my hair.

"Give me that," I say, using my gift to yank the cone from Glen's hand and float it into mine.

"Good job keeping a damper on *your* power," Mandis grumbles, narrowing his bright-green eyes at me. "Next thing you know, you'll be telling every human that angels and demons live among them."

I shoot my brother the kind of glare that could kill. Of course I wouldn't confirm anything about our existence with a human. I'm no glutton for punishment; our father would never let me hear the end of it.

To spite Mandis, I shove half the ice cream into my mouth. A jolt of cold pain pierces my brain, followed by pure regret. I groan and press the heel of my free hand to my forehead.

"That's what you get for taking from my sweet peach," Mandis says with a cocky grin.

"Shut up, Gourmandise," I hiss.

Glen pats my back and slips the rest of the cone from my hand. "It's okay, Desi. I forgive you. That bite was impressive."

Glen feeds Mandis a bite of ice cream, who closes his eyes as if he is experiencing the height of bliss. That isn't surprising; overindulging is euphoric for him. He swallows before saying, "Don't call me that heinous name."

Our parents were . . . *creative* when choosing names for me and my six older brothers, and arguably, Mandis, prince of Gluttony, got the short end of the stick on that deal, since Mom had been obsessed with all things French in the human realm when he was born. I love using it against him. The flush that crawls up his face gives me the best kind of sisterly satisfaction.

"Now, now, Your Highnesses, no more arguing. Let's keep moving and find Desi the perfect bachelorette pad, yeah?" Glen interrupts, literally and figuratively steering us both back on track.

The three of us resume our stroll down the sidewalk, and after a few seconds, Mandis breaks the silence. "Why don't you just stay in a hotel? You have the money to pick the best one in the city."

My jaw drops and I place my palm against my chest with an over-dramatic gasp. "You can't be serious! I want all the luxuries of home. What if *someone* wants me to cook a meal? Besides, I want to prove that I'm reliable. Staying in a hotel says I'm here for the short term."

My brother and his husband share a glance, and Glen is the one to say, "But you *are* here for the short term."

"Not to mention, you don't cook," my brother adds.

"I am aware of that," I say with a growl. "But everyone else doesn't need to be."

Mandis unbuttons the front of his tailored suit jacket and pulls at the knot in his silk tie. I tried to convince him to wear something comfortable, but he refused. I'm not the only one who was raised to believe first impressions are important. Dad always used to tell us that you have to dress the part. If you want respect, dress respectfully. If you want to invoke fear, look terrifying. I suppose that's why my father carries a gigantic ax with him wherever he goes. The king of Infernis might be scary to some, but I know the loving demon underneath the leather and metal spikes. He is the one who gave me this chance to find something different.

"What about this one?" Glen asks, handing me his phone.

The first picture piques my interest. The modern façade is sleek with cherrywood trimmings and a limestone base. Tall windows look out on a sandstone walkway that leads to a black front door. The outside is perfect, and something tells me the inside is too. For the first time today, I'm excited about a house.

"Let's go," I say, bouncing on my heels and handing the phone back to Glen.

Mandis lets out a puff of air that makes his lips rattle. "Eighth time's a charm."

Glen calls for a car using an app on his phone, and within minutes we're driving to the other side of the city. It's strange how humans use their phones for everything. My brother, Lux, once brought me a phone after one of his trips to the human realm. He loaded some games, books, and movies on it, but it never worked like it does when it's connected to the service in this realm. I could only play the offline games, and after a couple of weeks I ended up placing it in my keepsake box. Now it's in my pocket and I'm using it again.

I take advantage of the drive, attempting to tame my curls and touching up my makeup. I clean up the eyeshadow around my green eyes and freshen up my lipstick. Out of all the houses we've toured today, this one makes me the most nervous. Something tells me it's the one, and I plan to put my best foot forward to impress my potential landlord.

We arrive, and my hand trembles as I open the car door. It's even better in person. We walk up the stone path lined with chrysanthemums. I take in the outdoor chairs and ottoman arranged around a copper fire pit to the side. The pictures of the outside didn't do justice to the enormity of the windows running from the floor to the ceiling. Bursts of giddiness pop inside me. This house will give the best first impression to my future partner.

"Hi there!" All three of us turn our heads toward the cheery voice piping up from the yard next to us.

Kneeling in the flower bed in front of an equally beautiful house is a petite woman. She looks to be around thirty-five, with shoulder length black curls, brown skin peppered with a smattering of freckles over her nose, and deep-brown eyes. She gets to her feet and brushes her palms off on her jeans before crossing the yard to us. "I'm Meredith. Are you guys here to talk to Jace about the room he's renting? I hope so; he's been wanting to get that room filled for a while now."

She places her hand next to her mouth like she's about to divulge a juicy secret. "Between you and me, I think he's lonely and using this as an excuse to make new friends. But he'd never admit it."

My brother and Glen exchange a quick glance, each with his eyebrows raised. "You don't think he's the kind of guy who makes 'new friends' and cages them in his basement in hopes of eating them for breakfast, do you?" Mandis asks.

Meredith playfully slaps my brother on the bicep. "I hope not. He has all that fancy workout equipment down there, not to mention the rec room. That would be one hell of a mess to clean up."

"I had a friend like that once. He caged his best friend, an imp—"

"Okay!" I cut Glen off before he scares the neighbor and she puts in a bad word about me. "It was nice meeting you, Meredith. Maybe if I get the place, you and I can grab a drink sometime."

"I'll take you up on that. It's been a while since I had a neighbor to gossip with."

We wave goodbye and walk to the front door.

"I like her. She seems fun," Glen says.

"Of course you do, my tiny macaron. She smells like strawberries and cream," Mandis says, brushing his thumb over his husband's cheek.

"Okay, okay, behave, please. Stop discussing people's scents. It's weird." I knock and smooth down the cashmere of my blue deep V-neck sweater.

Glen brushes my hands away from my chest. "Stop fidgeting. Your tits look great."

With a sly smile, I wiggle my eyebrows. "I know; that's why I chose this sweater."

"Don't encourage her, darling, or her ego won't fit through the door," Mandis grumbles.

"Okay, okay, I get it," I say, feeling guilty about how obstinate I've been all day. "I'm sorry I've been a beast, but I am so nervous about this. It's really important I find the perfect place, or you know that Dad is going to—"

I clam up when I hear footsteps behind us, and the three of us turn in unison.

A man in slacks and a button-up shirt walks up the path. His brown skin is smooth, and his hair is styled into mini twists that lie close to his head. He meets my gaze with the most breathtaking sky-blue eyes, and my knees go weak when his plump lips turn up into a smile. He may be the most handsome human I've seen all day.

"I'm here about the room for rent," he and I say at the same time.

I crinkle my forehead, and he cocks a brow. Seconds tick by as we stare at one another, waiting for the other to explain themselves. I take advantage of the quiet to size him up before he says, "So, you *don't* live here?"

"No. So *you're* not the landlord?"

"Nope."

I lift my chin and square my shoulders. "Well, I hate to break it to you, but that room is mine."

"A confident woman. I like that. But we'll see who gets the room. May the best man or woman sign a lease today."

He holds out his hand, and we shake.

"I'm Cannon, by the way."

"It's nice to meet you. I'm Desi."

He takes a step back and looks up at the modern exterior with its black shutters and wrought-iron fixtures. "This is a big place. It's hard to believe that there's only one room available."

"Maybe they have more than one," I say hopefully.

Mandis clears his throat and says, "We'll never know if no one knocks."

"Right," I say quickly, dragging my stare from Cannon's icy blue gaze to tap my fist on the door.

A man wearing joggers and a T-shirt with a short, green alien-looking creature printed on it stands on the other side of the threshold. His chestnut-brown hair is rumpled, and his angular jaw is covered in scruff. Black horn-rimmed glasses frame his light-gray eyes, and his rosy lips, with their predominant cupid's bow, rest in a scowl. He doesn't give off the kind of vibes I would expect from someone who lives in a house like this.

His eyes bounce between the four of us and for a moment confusion clouds his features. "Um, hello. Can I help you?"

For a split second, I'm struck silent by the combination of his voice, eyes, and mouth, but I collect myself quickly and say, "Yes, I'm Desideria. I'm here to look at the room for rent." Was it a dick move to pretend Cannon isn't even standing there? Probably. But was I here first? Yep. Am I desperate? Also yep.

"You must be Jace. I'm Cannon; we spoke a few minutes ago." My new competition for the single room wedges his way to the front of the group and gives me the side-eye. "I'm excited to see if the room you're offering will be a good fit for me."

The homeowner, Jace, looks between me and Cannon and then to my brother and Glen. "I only have one room available."

Mandis and Glen both hold their hands up in surrender. "We're just here for moral support for my sister," Mandis explains, nodding toward me. "You don't have to worry about us."

I bat my lashes, giving Jace my best puppy dog eyes. "I really, really need a place to stay. I've been house hunting for what feels like ages, and I just know your place would be *perfect*."

Jace releases a breath and steps aside, gesturing for us to enter.

"I'll let you two duke it out. Please take your shoes off before we go any farther," he says, pointing to the wooden-slat bench in the entryway.

"Your ad said you wanted to rent the room out to a guy." Cannon flashes me a million-dollar smile that screams he has an advantage over me.

"It's true; I'd prefer to rent the room to a man. No offense, Desad . . ."

"Desideria. Just call me Desi." My nostrils flare as I sit down to unzip my knee-high boots, then tug them off and push them under the bench. I get to my feet and move in front of Jace. Standing straight, I'm still about five inches shorter than him. "Why is that, by the way? Do you have a particular reason you don't want to live with a woman?"

"I'm attracted to women and don't want to complicate the situation." He tilts his head toward Cannon. "He's a good-looking guy but not my type."

"Well, as long as *I'm* not your type, I think we'll be okay," I joke.

He crosses his arms and steps back, never taking his eyes off me. His lips stretch as he runs his tongue over his teeth behind them. "A girl like you isn't what I'm looking for," he quietly says.

I can't hide the flinch at the obvious diss. Even Mandis lets out a low whistle, and when I hear a grunt from his direction, I know Glen has elbowed him in the gut. *Good.* "Well, all right, then," I murmur.

Jace removes his glasses and rubs his eyes. He takes what I imagine are several calming breaths before saying, "Look, it's nothing against you, and I'm not saying that it's impossible for a man and woman to have a platonic relationship. I just want to make sure this is a safe place for everyone involved."

My eyebrow dips and I push my hands into my back pockets. "What are you saying? You don't think you'd be safe around me? Or you don't think *I'd* be safe around *you?* Because trust me, I can hold my own. And I'd never hurt anyone." I shake off the embarrassment and clear my throat. "Regardless, I got here first, so I think it's only fair that I get the chance to have the room."

Cannon speaks up then. "But I called first. So I think that gives me first dibs."

"Dibs? What are we, five?"

"Listen—"

Glen steps in and holds up a hand to silence us both. "Hang on. Stop." He looks at Jace and says, "Man, you're telling me you don't have two free rooms in this house? Think about it, you could have double the extra cash. Because trust me, this girl right here is *not* going to give in."

Jace stares at Cannon's Italian leather boots lying haphazardly on the floor, but he doesn't answer Glen's question. "I'll take you both on a tour and explain the house rules. If one of you still wants to move in, we'll discuss it from there."

I grin and silently thank my mother for teaching me to always put my belongings away neatly. It might just help me out in this case. "Okay, sounds good to me," I say, clasping my hands in front of me. "Mandis, Glen, stay here, and we'll be back, okay?"

Mandis raises an eyebrow. "Sis, you might want to rein in your bossy side until the guy lets you sign the lease, yeah?"

I roll my eyes and discreetly give him a vulgar hand gesture.

"Ready?" Jace asks, and Cannon and I both nod.

Jace takes a moment to eye my brother and his husband like he's not sure if they'll stay put. He must notice they look too exhausted to rifle through his home because he leaves them alone and leads us into the kitchen. There isn't a white appliance in sight. It's perfect. I run my hand over the shiny granite countertops while eyeing the dark-brown cabinets and the stovetop built into the island in the middle of the room. From here I can see right into the living room, making it a perfect space for entertaining friends and family while cooking.

Jace points to the barstools and says, "Obviously, you can eat in here, but all dishes need to be placed in the dishwasher. If it's full, start it, and if everything in it is clean, put it away. I'm not picky about the food situation; just contribute and let me know if you take the last of something."

With a quick nod, I say, "Absolutely. No problem. I'd even do the grocery shopping if you needed me to. I'd contribute monetarily, in any way at all. I can promise you I'd be the model roommate." I hold my breath in anticipation of his answer; if I have to look at one more potential home today, I might just give up and let my father promise me to a demon.

"Noted," he says, before continuing his tour.

I don't see so much as a speck of dust on the wooden floor as we move through the open floorplan and into the living room. The only thing out of place is a game controller on the plush gray couch. The fireplace on the main wall is constructed of simple lines, and a stack of wood burns in the center. The high ceilings and windows make the room spacious yet cozy.

"All your belongings would need to stay in your room. No kicking off your shoes and leaving them in the middle of the floor. You can bring a blanket in here to watch television, but I expect it to be put away and the pillows on the couch straightened when you're done."

"That's not a problem. I appreciate a clean house," I say.

"Me too," Cannon pipes up, and I give him a dubious look. Anyone who *really* appreciated a clean house to the same degree as Jace would have never left their shoes in the middle of the floor.

Not that I'm concerned with being *that* neat myself. This house looks like it's barely been lived in. But with my powers, I can keep a house this clean with zero issues. As long as no one's looking.

"Dude, is that the new Spider-Man game you're playing?" Cannon asks, wandering over to pick up the case on the coffee table.

"Yeah, I just picked it up last night."

"I'm jealous. I was going to grab my copy yesterday but I had to work late. My job keeps me busy most of the time. Whenever I get a minute, I have my PlayStation controller in my hand."

The pair of them carry on a conversation that's like some secret code. They talk about graphics and movies and games they're looking forward to. I'm at a complete loss and feel my opportunity slipping through my fingers. I'm going to be booted for my lack of knowledge about human geek culture.

This isn't fair. Just because I don't know about spiders that turn into men or men who turn into spiders or whatever the hell it is they're talking about doesn't mean that I don't deserve a chance to move into this house that would be perfect for me.

I think about interrupting with a question or two to join the conversation, but I don't know where to start. So I just butt in to remind them of my existence.

"Hey, guys, I don't mean to interrupt, but can we continue the tour? I'd like to see the bedroom . . ."

The men stop talking, both looking a tad embarrassed for getting caught up in their own thing and forgetting I'm here. Jace clears his throat and says, "Yeah. If you'll both follow me upstairs, I'll show you the room."

Cannon and I walk a few steps behind, and he leans in and whispers, "You are diabolical. That conversation was my in."

I glance at him with a wink and murmur, "A little, but a girl has to do what she has to do. I'm going to get one of those rooms. No matter what. Maybe he'll take mercy on you and give you the other, but this body will be in one of these beds tonight. I can promise you that."

"If *he* isn't ensnared by your evil scheme, I'd be happy to have you in *my* bed tonight."

Damn, Cannon. That was unexpected.

"I—"

"This is the room," Jace says, completely oblivious to what he just interrupted.

It is the exact kind of room I imagined staying in for the next ninety days. It's open and sunny with a picture window that takes up the entirety of the side wall, looking down onto an inground pool and across to the other side of the house. The furnishings are modern and clean with lots of white and grays, and the bed is plush, king-size, like I have at home. There's plenty of closet space and a small en suite bathroom. The only thing that it *doesn't* have is a garden tub. It has a shower stall, which I'm not used to, but I am *not* complaining.

"It's perfect," I breathe, forgetting for a moment to be calm, cool, and collected; I'm looking at this room like it's the love of my damn life. "I only need the room for ninety days. Can't you let me stay in here, let Cannon stay in another room, which there *must* be in this massive place, and then I'll be out of *both* your hair in three months? I'll even pay extra rent. Anything you want, Jace. I just cannot bear to look at another house. Please. I'm begging you."

The two men exchange glances, and Cannon says, "I'm fine taking another room if you got one, but this is your place, so the call is up to you."

"Three months?" Jace asks.

My heart lifts. "Three months. Not a day more."

"No drama, keep my house clean, and you go in ninety days." Jace's firm tone sends a shiver through me. I'm not sure if I want to run or drop to my knees and say *Yes, sir*. Either way, he isn't messing around.

I find my voice, and when it comes out, it's raspy and low. "Absolutely. No drama, I'll leave everything cleaner than I found it, and I'll be gone before midnight on the ninetieth day." I take a step toward him and stick out my hand. "I swear it, Jace."

He moves to wrap his hand around mine and hesitates for a moment. When we touch, his skin is warm and the handshake firm. "You got a deal. Let me show Cannon his room then I'll take you both downstairs to complete the rental agreement."

With that settled, I'm free to turn my attention to the real reason I'm here.

I'm officially on the hunt for a human partner.

TWO
DESI

I thought coming to the human realm was going to be the solution to all my problems, that I'd just *know* how to attract the ideal eternal partner.

Wrong.

How foolish I'd been.

In Infernis, everyone is so chaotic. Demons don't follow the same type of social norms that humans do. We celebrate sexuality, especially in its rawest forms. All we require is consent, so seeing a demon walk up to someone they don't know and ask if they want to hook up is normal.

I may not be bold enough to operate the way everyone else does in Infernis, but at least I know *something* about the way the world works.

Here, I am *totally* clueless.

I heave a sigh and stare at my iPhone, which seems to be a good deal smaller than Jace's. He's been tapping on it between stirring an unknown concoction and taking sips of some drink he says is healthy. I think the juice looks and smells like liquified grass. Why humans choose to torture themselves by consuming disgusting beverages all in the name of fitness, I'll never understand.

I refocus on the problem at hand. Jace and Cannon always seem to be typing on their phones. Even Glen found this house using his phone. Maybe it has the answers I need. I stare down at the little rectangle in my hand and wish an onslaught of terrible things on my brothers. How could they let me come to this realm without teaching me more about the technology humans rely on?

"Can my phone help me find someone to date?" I blurt.

Jace drops what sounds like a large utensil into the sink and it clatters in the metal basin. He curses under his breath, clearly startled, before saying, "You mean like a dating app? I've never used one before."

I chew the inside of my cheek, feeling a little guilty for practically screaming at the man; we *have* been sitting in comfortable silence for over an hour now. But instead of apologizing, I crack a joke. "My bad, I didn't realize there was also a rule against talking between the hours of six and eight."

His shoulders relax and his face betrays the slightest hint of a smile. "Very funny. I have not imposed a no-talking rule." He glances at me from the corner of his eye. "Yet. I'm just still not used to having anyone around. And you've been so quiet all night." He grabs three dishes from the cupboard and spoons pasta into them. "Dinner is ready. Will you let Cannon know?"

I remove the blanket from my lap and fold it, wishing I could use my power. I hate manually completing all these small human tasks—folding, sorting, and placing. How do they have time for anything fun? It is such a waste of energy, but I can't upset Mr. Clean by leaving it balled on the couch.

Standing at the bottom of the stairs, I yell, "Cannon, dinner's ready."

"I'll be down in a second," he calls back.

Jace rolls his eyes and takes a deep breath as I hop onto the barstool next to him.

"What?" I ask with a shrug.

He doesn't answer but pushes my bowl in front of me. I peer into the dish, all thoughts of Jace's clear annoyance with me forgotten, and a bright smile consumes my face. Fettuccine alfredo. My dad *always* has the chefs cook it for our Friday night dinners even though he doesn't really like it. "Thank you. This is my favorite food. Look at you. You're already winning on the roommate front. Not that you have much competition. I've only ever had six brothers as roommates, and, well . . . anyone could win against them because they are the literal embodiment of—" I stop myself before I say too much. "Well, they're royal pains in my ass."

"Hey, Jace has *some* competition now," Cannon says as he enters the kitchen, settling on the barstool next to me and flashing a grin before digging into his pasta. "This smells fantastic, Jace. Thanks."

Jace twirls his fork, wrapping the fettuccine around it, and nods at Cannon before turning back to me. "Six brothers, huh? And none of them ever taught you about cell phones or dating apps?"

I nearly choke on the bite I'd just taken and wipe my mouth with my napkin before speaking. "Six *older* brothers. They're all sort of a big deal where we come from, so connecting with others was easy for them. I'm the only one on the dating struggle bus."

"I'm an only child. I'll never understand that overprotective big brother thing," Jace says.

"Oh, no, they're not overprotective. Far from it. Things are . . . *different* where I'm from."

"Isn't that the truth? I'm starting to believe you've been hidden away in some secret compound your entire life. I've never seen some-one our age so clueless about technology," Cannon says with a snicker.

I hate that he and Jace think I'm incompetent, but explaining my realm's technology to them isn't possible without blowing my cover. The last thing I have time for is house hunting again when they learn they're living with a demon *princess* who needs to find a partner to reign beside her for the rest of eternity.

I let out a nervous chuckle. "Right. So, these dating apps . . . you can really meet people on those things? It's not, like, some kind of scam or something?"

Jace snorts into his pasta and Cannon shrugs. "I mean, yeah, it could be a scam, but most of the time there's a real person behind the screen. Dating apps are designed to connect people with common interests. You know, farmers, lovers of hot sauce, gluten-free people, even clowns have a dating app. Some people even meet their person online."

Their person. That sounds like an eternal partner to me. "Their 'person.' Like, the person they want to be with forever?"

"If you believe in that shit," Jace mumbles before Cannon can answer.

My gaze darts to Jace, and he avoids my eyes. "Oh, and you don't?"

Jace grabs his empty bowl and stands. "There is only right now and the things you can control in this moment. Nothing else matters."

Without another word, Jace rinses his bowl and loads it in the dishwasher before walking out of the kitchen and down a hallway next to the dining room. Then a door clicks shut, and Cannon and I are left in silence. I clear my throat and shift my gaze to Cannon as I continue eating. "Well, that was awkward."

"That's what love can do, Desi. It can turn a man into a jaded human being," Cannon says, shoveling a forkful of pasta into his mouth.

I look down the hall to where Jace disappeared and then back at Cannon. "Wait, what? You think Jace had his heart broken or something, and that's why he feels that way?"

"I'd bet my Lexus on it." That's a steep bet considering Cannon's silver sports car is top of the line. I've never seen anything like it in Infernis, which is saying something because demons have an obsession with fast, decked-out cars.

"But *you* believe in love. Right?" I ask.

He sets down his fork and turns to me, his eyes bright as they search my face. "Yes, Desi. I believe in love."

A strange feeling gnaws at me, and I force myself to look away and back at my pasta to take the last bite. "I'm glad I'm not the only one. That would make doing what I need to impossible."

"And what is it you're doing exactly?"

I chew the inside of my cheek and deliberate about what to say. I can't tell him too much; I've only known him for a couple of days and there's no way I can trust him—or Jace—yet. So, I tell him a bastardized version of the truth.

"I need to find a person to bring home to my father, a person who is suitable for me to marry. Where I'm from, our family is . . . in the public eye, I guess you could say, and it's important that I—" I clear my throat. "Make a good match. And since I'm in sort of a time crunch, I'm only allowed to be gone a certain amount of time."

"That's right! That explains the ninety days. Sounds like something out of one of those chick-flick movies. Hold on, I bet you *want* me to think your dad is some kind of politician, but he's actually a *king* and he's going to bypass *all* your brothers and crown you queen because he wants his land to be run by a woman of grace and beauty."

"Aww, Cannon, you think I'm beautiful?" I say with an exaggerated sigh.

"No."

The flush deepens and I want to crawl into a hole and dig my way back to Infernis with the fork in my hand. "Oh, no, I know, I was just—"

"You're stunning, Desi. Absolutely stunning."

Now my face is on fire, and I'm not sure what to say to that. No one has ever said something so sweet to me, and when I think of the things I'd want to hear from a man . . .

That would be one of them.

I realize too late that I still haven't responded, and I finally say, "Thank you, Cannon. That's kind of you."

He shrugs and pushes his bowl to the center of the countertop. "It's true. Not to mention I understand what it's like to have parents who have high expectations for you. My dad puts a lot of pressure on me as well. Sometimes I feel like whatever I do it isn't good enough for him."

"Finding a husband is the only difficult thing my father has ever asked of me. I hate feeling like I'm letting him down."

He taps my phone. "Unlock the screen." I do and watch as he goes through a series of steps before a new icon pops up. "That's the most popular dating app. Just follow the instructions and you will be all set to peruse the internet for a date."

"Thank you."

"No problem. See you in the morning, Desi."

"Night, Cannon."

I sigh and get to my feet, pick up our dishes, and rinse them before putting them in the dishwasher, grumbling the whole time because I want to use my power. But it's still too soon. What if Jace comes out of his office? He'd hit the ceiling and then I'd definitely be out on my ass.

With that grueling task done, I settle back on the couch under my blanket and follow the instructions to set up my profile. It isn't long before I'm swiping right for guys who interest me. Most of the men I swipe right on return the gesture, which is a good sign.

For at least an hour I repeat this process, and before bedtime, I have a date set up for tomorrow night. I can't keep a goofy smile from spreading over my face. This is happening far faster than I could've hoped.

When I check the time, it's well past midnight, and my yawns are becoming more frequent. I stand up and reach for the blanket, but I can't help myself. I study the room as I hold my breath, listening for any indication that one of my roommates is coming this way. After waiting several seconds to make sure I won't get caught, I grin and curl my finger toward the blanket. The fabric swoops through the air, and I watch with satisfaction as it drapes itself over the arm of the couch.

My phone pings with another message from the dating app. I snatch it up, hoping it's not my date for tomorrow canceling already.

It isn't. It's a new, totally sexy guy I'd swiped right on, and the message is short.

Hey Desi. You're really gorgeous. Just wondering, are you DTF?

DTF? What does that mean? Racking my brain, I come up empty. I crane my neck up the stairs and see Cannon's light is off. I know he has to work early, so I don't want to bother him.

But Jace's light is still shining under the door down the hall.

Maybe he's working. Or playing more video games. Either way, he's still awake, and I need to know what this message means before I answer. I make my way down the hall and tap lightly on the door.

"Come in."

I crack it open and peek my head inside. Jace is seated behind a desk with a very large computer screen on top. His back is to a wall of shelves adorned with figurines of aliens, warriors, and superheroes. In the center of all his toys is a wooden sign with sharp-edged lettering that reads AFTERMATH DESIGNS. The rusted steel wall across from him houses a television, with a fire burning underneath. Two leather chairs sit across from his desk, but don't look as if they've ever been sat in. But it is the wall at the far end of the room that takes my breath away. A floor-to-ceiling window looks into the backyard, where the pool is lit in shades of purple and blue.

He looks up in surprise, his eyes wide behind his glasses. "What's up?"

I slide the rest of the way inside and let the door click shut behind me, then cross over to his desk and lean on the back of one of the chairs.

"Umm, well, I just got a message from a guy on the dating app I downloaded earlier."

"A suitor already?" he asks, sarcasm lacing his voice.

"Uh, yeah, for tomorrow, but this message is from a different guy. Anyway, he said something to me, and I don't know what it means. I was hoping you could help."

"Okay, what is it?" He doesn't bother to look back up from his monitor. With one hand on his mouse, he clicks away at the keyboard with the other.

"He asked if I was 'DTF.' What does that mean?"

Jace jerks his head up and the room falls silent. He holds out his hand and gestures with two fingers for me to pass him my phone. I give it to him, and he aggressively types away with a disgusted look on his face.

"Problem solved," he says, sliding my phone across the desk.

I snatch it up and read his response.

> Nope. I'd rather play in traffic. Next time, man up and ask a girl to dinner first. And I suggest you splurge to make up for the disappointment she's bound to have after she experiences your subpar fucking skills.

A snort escapes me, and I cover my mouth with my palm. "Jace! Okay, clearly it meant something vile, so I'm going to go ahead and thank you for the save there, but come on, tell me. What does it mean?"

"It means 'down to fuck.' I'm assuming you're not down. At least not directly after a hello."

My nose wrinkles and I shake my head, shoving my phone into my hoodie pocket. "No. Nope. Definitely not. That's—nope." My face is burning, and I push my hair behind my ears. "Thanks, Jace. I appreciate it. I'm glad I didn't just answer him without figuring that out first."

He gives a curt nod and I head for the door.

"Hey, Desi?" I spin around to face him again, and he says, "Be careful. Meet these guys in public places and don't go home with them until you're sure you aren't getting serial killer vibes."

I meet his gray eyes and notice that he's removed his glasses. Now they're even more striking. I've never seen eyes that color before. Shaking my head to clear the random thought, I say, "Right. Of course, sure. I won't do anything stupid."

"It may be a good idea for you to turn on your friend locator, so your brother knows where you are just in case."

I swallow and gnaw on my bottom lip. "Well, actually, my brother is—uh, out of the country. He and Glen left to go on a trip to eat food. Like, you know, one of those things where you just eat . . . *a lot.*"

His eyebrow dips and he drawls, "A buffet?"

"Like, on a global scale, sure. Point being, he won't be any help if I get into any trouble, and I don't know anyone here besides you and Cannon. Well, and Meredith, but we don't know each other like that y—"

"What about your other five brothers?"

Shit, why does he remember everything I say? "They're all there at the, uh, buffet together."

"Okay, that's weird. Get Cannon to turn his on." He pauses and wrinkles his nose. "Never mind. He has an Android."

I mirror his facial expression even though I have no idea what that means. "Yeah, ew."

Jace leans back in his chair, and it tilts with his weight. Folding his hands over his abdomen, he lets out a quick breath. "Put me in your phone and allow me access to your location. If I don't hear from you by ten tomorrow night, I'll shoot you a text, and if you don't answer, I'll send the cops to go find you."

Something about him caring enough to send the cops to look for me warms my heart, but then another thought occurs to me. "What if I'm . . . busy doing . . . *other things*, and that's why I don't answer? Wouldn't that be embarrassing?"

He shakes his head and rolls his eyes, turning his attention back to his computer. "Then I guess you better text me back before that happens."

"Fair enough. Good plan."

"Glad you approve. Good night, Desideria."

My heart skips a beat at the sound of my full name leaving his lips. He learned how to say it. I've heard it all my life from countless people, and never once has it captured my attention like it does now. Each syllable is like a smooth melody in a low octave. It vibrates through me in all the right places.

It takes the strength of a hundred demons to compose myself and say, "Night, Jace. See you tomorrow."

He nods, and before I can slip out the door, he says, "One more thing: next time you need to know what an acronym means, you know you can google it, right?"

I laugh and nod on my way out the door. "Right, of course. Google."

What the fuck is Google?

I press the heels of my hands to my eyes and lean against the wall at the other side of the hall. I'm ridiculous. Jace is not my type at all. Not to mention, he's made it clear I'm not his. I need to keep focused on those men who are interested in dating me, like the serial killers who require me to turn on my location tracker. I hope my date tomorrow doesn't end in disaster.

THREE
DESI

"I did not mean to buy this much stuff," I say as I drop bags of clothes, shoes, makeup, and hair products onto my bed. "But I left most of my belongings at my parents' house, so I think we can call this spree necessary." It's not untrue; I didn't want to haul all my stuff from Infernis, but as soon as I got here, I realized my mistake. All the items I went shopping for today are necessities if I'm going to be dating. And tonight, I have my first date with Kyle.

"Hey, a girl's gotta do what a girl's gotta do," Meredith says as she adds the bags she was carrying for me to the pile.

"Thank you for taking me to the mall. I would've had no idea where I was going. Back in In—" I stop short and clear my throat. "Back in my little hometown, we don't have all those stores. I'm not used to this kind of variety." I gesture for her to sit down in one of the plush armchairs across from my bed.

She sits and I do the same, crossing my legs under my butt. "Glad to help. It was fun to have a girl's day. I was serious when I said it's been a while since I had a neighbor I could gossip with. In other words, it's been a while since a woman lived next door. I've been stuck talking to Jeremy and our sons, and I'd be better off talking to a rock sometimes."

I grin. "Well, can I trouble you for a little something else?"

She clasps her hands. "Please. Anything to avoid going home to all the chores I have to do."

"I have this date tonight. I haven't been on a real date before, and I just . . . I need advice. How do I act? What do I say?" I have a million other questions, but I shut my mouth and let her think.

"Oh honey, you have nothing to worry about. He's going to take one look at you and be invested. But I guess the best advice is to be yourself, ask questions, and listen. Oh, stroke his ego by laughing at his stupid jokes. I don't know why, but men love it when you think they're funny."

"Okay, I can do that. And also . . . how do I know *for sure* if he's creepy? Jace had me turn my phone's location tracker on last night, which freaked me out a little. What if I read this guy all wrong?" Kyle's pictures had me weak in the knees based on his extraordinary height, ski instructor build, hazel eyes, and blond hair, but looks could be deceiving.

Meredith shakes her head, the dark curls whipping around her narrow face. "Always follow your gut. If he is giving you a bad feeling, then you run. Send me a text, I'll call saying you have a 'family emergency,' text Jace to come get you, and then you're out of there. But if you're *really* in a jam, you can always kick him in the balls. But you know there is a safer and perfectly scrumptious option in this house—every time I catch Cannon sliding out of that Lexus of his, I swear I drool down the front of my shirt."

"He *is* handsome, but I'm not sure it's the best idea to date him or Jace."

She snorts and tucks a curl behind her ear. "Please, you'd have a better chance at landing a date with a priest. Jace is damaged goods." My ears perk up at that; it reminds me of the conversation I had with Cannon last night, but before I can put too much thought into it, I glance at my alarm clock and nearly jump out of my skin.

"Oh my gosh, I have to get ready! He'll be here in an hour!"

Meredith stands. "Well, I'll let you get to it. I'll stop by tomorrow with some goodies so we can chat about how it went."

"Sounds perfect. Thank you for everything."

Meredith nods and slips out of my bedroom door with a wave.

Now that it's time to get ready, I feel sick to my stomach when I think about what I *didn't* ask Meredith. Kyle invited me to dinner, and then he said we'd just "see where the night takes us." I have a feeling I know what that means, and I'm nervous about it.

I don't have any intention of sleeping with a stranger on the first date, but it would be nice to be kissed, maybe even touched. But just the thought of it has my heart hammering, and as I apply my eyeliner, my hand is trembling.

The chances of me finding my perfect match on my very first date are slim to none. Kyle might as well be the appetizer to what could be a five-course meal. And let's face it, what I'm really looking forward to is dessert. The man I choose will have to be the decadent chocolate treat I crave when life is at its worst *and* its best, even if I might have to swallow a few bites of salad before I get to what I want.

Taking a deep, cleansing breath, I shake the nerves out and start again, feeling a little steadier as I finish my makeup and tame my unruly mane of curls. I slide the dress I decided to wear off the hanger and slip into it, smoothing the emerald satin over my hips and adjusting my breasts so my cleavage is fully on display. One thing I *do* appreciate about my realm is that we've never been encouraged to hide or be ashamed of our bodies. I choose a pair of stilettos, and when I check the final product in the full-length mirror, I take a note from my brother Fier and admit that I look pretty damn sexy.

Snatching my clutch and a black leather jacket off the chair in the corner, I make my way down the stairs. Jace is leaning over the island in the kitchen, flipping through a stack of papers. His hair is just as disheveled as yesterday, and he wears a plain black T-shirt and gray joggers. He's eating a bowl of cereal, the only snack I've seen him eat since I moved in.

"Hey," I say, walking across the kitchen, my heels clicking on the tile floor.

He glances up at me and stops with the spoon halfway to his lips. "Hey. You look . . ." He blinks and shakes his head before shoveling the cereal into his mouth. "Nice."

I raise an eyebrow and place a hand on my hip as I lay my jacket and purse over the island. "*Nice?* Are you sure you're not talking about that cereal you're currently stuffing into your face?"

"Nope," he says with his mouth full, pointing at the bowl with his spoon. "This is good, and you look nice."

That's okay. He doesn't need to say the words; the way his eyes roamed up and down my body the second he looked up said it all. Even now he continues to steal glances in my direction. My grumpy roommate thinks I look smoking hot. And I do, dammit!

"Don't you think your contacts might be overkill for a first date though? Maybe hold off on the sexy witch thing until the second date, when you strap him to the bed and sacrifice his poor soul to Satan," he says.

Satan. I nearly laugh out loud at the mention of the name, but more than that, the notion that I'm wearing contacts. "What are you talking about? These aren't contacts. This is my real eye color."

"No way. They practically glow. I've never seen eyes like that before." He steps around the counter and bends down until we're eye to eye, inspecting me as though he's never *really* looked at me. "Oh. They *are* real. Your eyes are amazing."

"Thank you," I manage to say, and clear my throat, unnerved by how close he is to me. "So are yours."

I don't mean to say it; it just rolls off my tongue. I noticed them the first time we met. Eyes like his aren't common in Infernis; nearly *everyone's* irises are green, red, or purple, and his are the smokiest, richest shade of gray that reminds me of a stormy day, perfect for staying inside and reading under a blanket with a mug of hot chocolate.

He stiffens at my compliment and takes a step back, returning to his cereal. "Thanks. When is your first victim supposed to be here?"

I bite my bottom lip and glance at the clock on the microwave. "Any minute now."

The front door opens and a cheerful voice asks, "Anybody home?"

"In the kitchen!" I call back.

"He's going to kick his damn shoes off in the middle of the entryway," Jace grumbles, shoving more cereal into his mouth, like it's going to cure his irritation.

I've noticed that Jace is especially irked by Cannon's lack of tidiness. He practically follows Cannon around the house, picking up dishes and lining his shoes up under the bench in the foyer. But even though he has little patience for Cannon's disregard for his rules, the two get along. They've spent the past two nights in the living room playing video games and talking about work over beers. I must admit that I'm jealous that the two have clicked so easily, while Jace and I are still tiptoeing around each other.

Cannon strolls into the kitchen, pulling on his tie. He stops and whistles. "Damn, Desi! That dress is sexy as hell."

I shoot Jace a glare as if to say *That's the reaction I was hoping for*, and then flash a smile at Cannon. "You think so? I just got it this morning."

"Green is *definitely* your color. Jace, did you have any clue that we were living with such a smokeshow?"

"None," he mumbles as he moves to rinse out his bowl.

Cannon chuckles. "I got to get our boy a new prescription for his glasses."

I roll my eyes and examine my nails before glaring at the back of Jace's head. "He's just irritable because that was his last bowl of peanut butter puff cereal."

Jace grunts and walks past us. "I have a proposal I need to finish. Enjoy your date, Desideria."

"I will," I answer in an overly chipper tone.

The doorbell rings, and Cannon grabs my shoulders, turning me to face him. Bringing a bunch of red curls over my shoulder, he says, "You got this. Smile and remember you look smoking hot."

I close my eyes and take a deep breath before going to the door and swinging it open. The man on the other side is just as attractive as his photos, and it's all I can do to keep my jaw from dropping.

His blond hair falls in soft curls over his forehead and his hazel eyes sparkle as he takes me in. "Hello, Desi, it's so good to meet you in person."

I grin and step back, opening the door wider and letting him in. "Thank you, Kyle. You too. Come on in and let me grab my jacket."

He follows me into the kitchen where Cannon is at the sink getting a glass of water. He looks up but doesn't say anything, just nods in Kyle's direction.

Kyle gives a polite nod back, and I feel the need to explain myself.

"Oh, this is Cannon. He's just my roommate. I'm not, like, married or anything."

Crap.

What if he thinks I don't ever want to get married now?

I backpedal. "Not that I'm opposed to marriage. In fact, that's what I'm looking for. Eventually, I mean. How do *you* feel about marriage? I think the possibility of being with the same person forever is romantic. I love going to weddings, and I've even planned my own just for fun. Have you ever thought about *your* wedding before?"

Cannon coughs and does a spit take into the sink, water going everywhere.

Kyle fidgets and looks around the room. "I . . . um . . ." He pulls his phone from his pocket and stares at the screen. "Oh, damn. I hate to do this, Desi, but I just got a text from my vet and my . . . um . . . my lizard isn't doing so well." He steps backward toward the door. "Maybe we can reschedule for another time."

"Do you want me to message you later?" I ask.

"You know, this isn't looking good for my, uh, turtle. He might need a kidney transplant. I'll message you when things have calmed down." Kyle runs for the door and slams it closed behind him.

I'm stunned. The message came out of nowhere, and he left so quickly.

"I thought he said his pet was a lizard," I say, my shoulders slumping just as I get my jacket pulled over them.

"I'm thinking it's more like a snake with an aversion to almost marriage proposals within two minutes of meeting his date," Cannon says.

Kicking my heels off and leaving them in the middle of the floor, I move next to Cannon. "What did I do wrong? I know I went on a bit of a ramble, but I'm just nervous. Was marriage not okay to mention? Where I come from people talk about all kinds of things openly, including marriage, and no one freaks out."

"Desi, I don't care where you're from; most guys younger than twenty-five are going to freak out about marriage. That's a conversation for, like, the twentieth date, if not the fiftieth."

I prop my elbows on the counter and thread my fingers through my hair, gripping it at the roots. "I clearly have no idea what the hell I'm doing."

"You need to relax. Remember, these guys are just as nervous as you."

I snort and open the fridge, snatching a can of soda from inside. "Yeah, right. I am such a damn mess. You've been on dates before. How do you know what to say? When to say it?"

"Treat your dates the way you're treating me right now."

"That won't work. I'm only like this with you because you're so easy to talk with."

"You're overthinking this." He tips his chin at my shoes and says, "Throw those back on and let me at least take you out for some appetizers and a beer. You look too good to let this go to waste."

A smile sneaks onto my face and I let my shoulders relax. "All right. Like a practice run so this humiliating situation doesn't happen again?"

He holds his arm out to me. "Sure, if that's how you want to think of it. I just figure this is my chance to wiggle my way in for a short date."

"Wait. Are you considering this a real date?" I ask, grabbing my purse off the counter and slinging it over my free arm.

"A mini date," he says, with a flirtatious wink.

We stop at the front door where Cannon's shoes lie nowhere near the bench. He puts them on, and we step outside. The sun is low in the sky and the air is brisk. Goosebumps form on my legs, my dress doing little to ward off the cold. Cannon opens the car's passenger door, and I climb inside. He speeds down the road, shifting gears and tapping his fingers to the music.

I can't stop myself from sneaking peeks at him. A light dusting of black stubble graces his jawline. His skin is perfect, not a single blemish. I want to touch it and see if it is as soft as it looks. And those dimples, they might charm me more than his words. Meredith wasn't joking when she called him a scrumptious option.

It isn't more than five minutes before he pulls his Lexus into the parking lot of a hole-in-the-wall bar. He guides me in with his hand at the small of my back. His touch makes me a little nervous, yet at the same time it's calming, which is good since the place is packed. Businessmen in suits and a cluster of women holding fruity drinks congregate around the bar. Even with everyone absorbed in conversations and the dim lights, I feel a little too dressed up, but Cannon doesn't seem to mind as he flashes a smile at a group of people dressed in sports paraphernalia and leads me to an empty booth.

"This place is busy," I practically yell to Cannon across the table.

"Yeah, they have good everything, but their fried pickles are my favorite," he says, pulling two menus from behind the napkin dispenser and handing me one.

My eyebrow dips. "Fried pickles? Like, pickles you put on a burger? Fried?"

Cannon's eyes widen. "You don't know what fried pickles are?"

I lift one shoulder in a shrug. "I take it they're delicious?"

"That's the understatement of the year," he says as the server comes over.

He orders us some, himself a beer, and a margarita for me. As we wait for our drinks, I look at Cannon and chew on my bottom lip before saying, "Thank you for taking me out tonight. I would've sat at home and sulked for the rest of the evening if you hadn't."

"Not a problem. I've wanted more time to get to know you, just the two of us."

My heart pounds against my rib cage at the thought of us alone. "Yeah? I'd like to get to know you better too." My nerves are rattled, and I take a drink of the margarita as soon as the server brings it out. "What do you want to know?"

"Let's start with the basics. I know you're under pressure to find a partner, but why look for a potential husband in Denver? Wouldn't it be easier to find someone closer to your home?"

I take a long sip of the frozen drink and choose my words carefully.

"My hometown is small and there aren't a lot of men to choose from. I went out with a few guys, and none of them were what I was looking for. I needed to get away, get out on my own. And this seemed like the kind of place I wanted to be."

"And were you looking for a ski instructor? Is that the career of choice for your future boyfriend?"

I cock my head to the side and stick my tongue out. "Apparently not, at least not one with a pet lizard."

He laughs, and it's a hearty sound that warms my insides. Cannon is like a summer breeze; he emanates light and makes every situation comfortable.

"Tell me what a man has to bring to the table to make you swipe right."

"You talking physically or emotionally?"

"Either. Both?"

I shift and lean back casually against my seat, trying to play cool. "As far as looks go, I like it when a guy is taller than me, which isn't always easy, considering I'm not exactly petite." I let my gaze travel over him, from his face down to his arms. "I'm a bicep girl. I like it when, you know, a guy's arms sort of . . . bulge out from under his T-shirt sleeves." My eyes flick up and I continue. "I like broad shoulders—even though I can take care of myself, I also like to feel protected." Meeting his bright-blue stare, I add, "And light eyes get me every time. Personality . . . funny, sweet, calm, collected."

"So, when do you take me home to meet your dad?"

My cheeks heat and I push my hair behind my ear. "My dad is a little intimidating. Why don't we start with finishing this date and then a second one before we start talking about that?"

"Just joking, Desi. I only want to spend time with you. I definitely don't want scary dad brought into the mix."

"I know. I was kidding too," I say, taking another long drink of my margarita, nearly draining the glass. I haven't eaten all day so I could fit into this dress, and my alcohol tolerance isn't very high as it is. I can already feel my eyes glazing over and my head spinning just enough to loosen my nerves.

"Do they dance at this bar?" I ask, looking around to where the band is playing near the front of the room.

"I don't know, but I do know that I don't dance. Ever. Never. If you need to move, we can go for a walk." He stands and grabs my hand, pulling me out of my seat playfully.

"No, no, no, sir. I don't think so. I'm not going to miss the magical pickles. You hyped them up too much." I shove him gently back into the booth and slide in next to him, leaning in against his side, soaking in his warmth. "And what do you mean you don't dance? That's a travesty."

"I'm terrible at it. I even ditched those slow dances where you just spin in a tiny circle with your partner."

"Ohh," I say in an exaggerated tone, resting my head on his shoulder. "That makes sense. I'll give you a pass then. But maybe you'll let me teach you one day? Just you and me at the house?"

He glances down at my face and cracks a smile. "We'll see."

His hand drops next to mine on the seat, and his thumb traces zigzags over my knuckles. It's a sweet gesture that makes me flutter with excitement. I sweep my index finger over his in a small confirmation that I approve of the touch.

"You're soft," he whispers against the crown of my head.

Heart racing, I lift my eyes to his. "Cannon—"

"Here you guys go," the server says in a cheery voice as she slides a plate of pickles in front of us and we break apart as if electrocuted.

"Thank you," I say, turning to face the table, grabbing a pickle, and dipping it in the ranch dressing before cramming it into my mouth as she walks away, her face flushed with the knowledge that she just interrupted something. What, I have no idea. But it was something.

"What do you think?" Cannon asks, eating a pickle chip.

I swallow and nod as I snatch another one from the tray. "Delicious, actually. I'll admit I was a little unsure. But there's something about them that's addictive. I think I could eat this whole damn tray. I can't believe my brother has never conj—I mean, has never cooked these for me before," I say, hoping he didn't catch my almost slip. The word *conjure* in relation to food really doesn't make much sense and would no doubt lead to some awkward questions.

"I'm guessing you've never been to a state fair. The fried possibilities are endless."

"Never."

"We'll have to add that to our list of potential dates."

"Sounds like a plan to me," I say, shoving another pickle in my mouth.

He grins and I lean back against him, and we spend the next couple of hours talking about anything and everything from favorite foods to favorite colors to most hated movies and pet peeves, and before I know it, I'm yawning every other minute, and the three margaritas I've had are slurring my words.

"Desi, I think it's time I take you home," Cannon says with an amused expression. "You look like you're feeling a little *too* warm and fuzzy."

"I'm good," I say through a yawn, and I cover my mouth sheepishly. "Well, I might be just a li'l bit tired." I hold my index finger and thumb up to show just how tired I am, which is not a lot. Which happens to be a total lie. I'm exhausted, but also feeling brave. I turn to him in the booth and run my fingertip down the center of his chest. "Did you have fun tonight?"

"I did. I think I achieved what I set out to do. I've learned more about you and have you cuddled right next to me. This was a good start in my opinion."

It's not just a good start, but a phenomenal one. After having my first date run out on me, Cannon is the reason my night was salvaged. Despite the drama it could stir in the house, I wouldn't mind having another night like this with him.

I get to my feet, and he stands up right behind me, placing his hand on the small of my back. When we get home, he helps me to my room.

"Oops, I didn't take my shoes off," I sing with a giggle as I plop down on my bed to remove them. "Jace will be mad."

"Jace clearly has issues with giving up control. This place is staged like a model home. He needs to let go and live a little," Cannon says, turning down my blankets.

I start to climb into bed but shake my head. "Whoa, no way am I sleeping in this dress." I hold up one finger. "Be right back." I make my way to the closet, swaying a bit as I walk, and shut myself in.

I lean against the closed door, shutting my eyes and taking a deep breath. Cannon is a great guy—sweet, polite, funny, handsome. But he's the first guy who's shown me attention. I have to slow down; there's potential here, but I just got to the human realm. I have more to experience, more to see.

I slip out of the dress, hang it up as neatly as I can manage in my condition, and slide into a pair of flannel pajama pants and a baggy T-shirt, something that shouldn't give Cannon the wrong idea.

"Okay," I say, coming back to bed and climbing into the spot he's made for me. "Thank you, Cannon. For everything."

"I had fun with you tonight. Thanks for indulging me. Is there anything I can get you before I leave?"

"A glass of water maybe?"

He nods. "Coming right up." He disappears into the hallway and comes back a few seconds later with an ice-cold bottle. "Here you go."

"Thank you. I appreciate it. And thank you for showing me how to act on a date. Next time I have one, I won't bring up marriage. I swear."

"Just be yourself, Desi. I'm sure you'll charm the right man." He leans down and kisses my forehead. His lips are soft on my skin, giving me a giddy feeling. I close my eyes and bask in the sensation. My bliss is short lived when he pulls away and turns off my light before leaving.

I stare at the ceiling and replay my time with Cannon. Every conversation, every touch, every tingle that coursed through me. I had fun, a little too much fun thanks to the margaritas, but fun all the same.

A flicker of light catches my attention, and I turn on my side to look out the massive window . . . and straight into Jace's room.

My jaw drops. How did I not realize this before?

The decor is much like the rest of the house: simple, clean, and comfortable. He steps around his bed and takes off his glasses, setting them on the nightstand. He looks slightly different without the distraction of the black rims on his face. Even from here I can see the strong line of his jaw and the scruff that lightly covers it. He grabs the back of his shirt, his biceps flexing with the movement, and my eyes go wide as he takes it off. Holy shit, he is ripped; his abs could have been chiseled by a world-renowned sculptor. His chest is broad, the perfect complement to the muscular arms I already knew he had. And every inch of him appears to be soft tan skin.

His body is gorgeous.

I feel creepy watching this private moment, but I can't tear my eyes away. In fact, I want to get up and move closer to the window to check if I can see any better. But I don't. I just hope he doesn't take off any more of his clothes.

Or hope that he does. I don't know. I'm so confused right now.

Jace acts like he can't stand me half the time, and I can barely stomach him either. Yes, he's organized and there doesn't seem to be one aspect of his life that's run by chaos, which is what I want, right? But he's cold. His practical take on everything makes him seem boring and unapproachable. Play video games, eat some bland, healthy food, load the dishwasher, work, run, work some more, maybe eat some peanut butter puffs if he has had a bad day, and go to bed. I'd have more fun, and a better conversation, with a bucket of rocks.

Yet here I am, still half-drunk on tequila, watching my rigid, type-A, apparently jacked-as-hell roommate get undressed for the night, like a stalker in some horror movie. I guess it just goes to show that my limited experience with a male of any species has left me easily excitable.

I wonder if Jace gets excited about anything. My dress, which I *know* was hot, didn't have much of an effect on him. He spared me a couple of glances before a "You look *nice*."

Nice. Pfft. He probably doesn't even jerk off.

Jace snaps the button open on his jeans.

Jeans! He's actually wearing something that isn't loungewear. I wonder if he went out tonight. Did he have a date too? I don't get the chance to ponder the thought further because he pulls down the zipper and tugs the jeans down, revealing skintight boxer briefs and a set of strong, powerful thighs, and I nearly implode.

"Oh, oh, no," I say out loud, covering my mouth with my palm. "I didn't mean to manifest that shit . . . *shit!*"

Thankfully, Jace disappears into his bathroom. Although there is nothing more to see, I don't turn away. Images of his perfect body are seared into my head: rippling muscles, tanned skin, and those stormy eyes. My thighs clench, and I jerk my hand away from where it's toying with the waist of my pajama pants.

"No. Absolutely not." I fold my hands on the outside of my

comforter. "Forget what you saw, brain and hormones. Go to sleep. We are *not* getting turned on by Jace Wilder. Not happening."

But my eyes don't listen and sneak one more peek into his room just as all the lights go out. I bet he has an entire bedtime routine and has never felt conflicted about anything. I snort at the thought. That's absurd; of course he's been conflicted. I bet he contemplates what he loves more—peanut butter puffs or Spider-Man?

FOUR
DESI

After that night with Cannon, I met a few guys from the dating app, and while none of them held my attention for long, I didn't scare any of them away or send them running to the vet to tend to their dying pet reptile. They're all handsome and perfectly nice, but not one intrigued me enough to arrange a second date. So far, the one good date I've had was the practice one with Cannon.

I finish my after-dinner treat—a bowl of chocolate chip cookie dough ice cream mixed with the brownies Meredith brought over this afternoon—and when I pull the dishwasher open to put my bowl in, I groan. It's full of clean dishes.

If I were at home, all it would take is a snap of my fingers and all the dishes would be put away in seconds flat. I glance over my shoulder to see Jace sitting on the couch watching a documentary about the evolution of sci-fi movies. I can't risk him catching me in the act of using my divine power, so I heave a sigh and unload the dishes the old-fashioned—normal—way.

When I get to the cups, I open the cupboard and wrinkle my nose. All of them are sitting with the inside exposed to the elements. I peek around the door to make sure he isn't looking and tap my finger to the shelf. In the blink of an eye, they've all flipped upside down. With a satisfied grin, I continue my work.

"Umm, what are you doing?"

I rise onto my tiptoes and slide the last cup into the cupboard before closing it and turning around. "Unloading the dishwasher so I can put my dirty bowl in. What are you doing?"

"Watching you put the cups in the cabinet the wrong way. You're putting the part that touches my mouth on the bottom," Jace says.

I roll my eyes and place my hands on my hips. "If you leave them right side up, all the dust that floats around in every cabinet is landing *inside* the cup where you put your drink and then you're *drinking* it!"

He gives me a pointed glare and his voice is a low rumble as he says, "Desi, put the cups the right way."

I want to fight, to push my point. His way of storing the cups is asinine, and it needs to be fixed. *You need a place to live, Desi*, I tell myself before I lose my temper. "Yes, sir," I mutter, turning away from him and opening the cabinet to please the man of the house.

"Thank you," he says, stepping beside me to rinse out his bowl.

I flip the last cup and say in a clipped tone, "Not a problem." I shut the cabinet with a little too much force and flee to my room.

This past week with Jace has been frustrating to say the least. There are times when I feel like I can do nothing right around him. Granted, tonight I pissed him off on purpose. But earlier in the week he got irritated when I didn't fold the blanket over the arm of the couch and left it on the back instead, and when I left a dryer sheet inside the dryer. Like, aren't there bigger things for him to worry about?

Not to mention, I feel incredibly creepy about watching him get undressed the other night, half-drunk on tequila or not. That's putting me on edge too. It's just an awkward situation, and I'm disappointed in myself. I promised there would be no drama, yet I can't help but skate close to the line. The demon in me wants to flip his organized world upside and turn all the cups the *right* way.

I need to get out of the house and get some air. Keeping up

appearances is exhausting. Not to mention, Jace's rigid way of doing things goes against the core of who I am. I need to let loose and thrive in a little chaos. What better place than a nightclub? I just want to get a drink and dance. I consider texting Cannon to join me after he gets done with work but change my mind. He won't dance with me, and I don't want to leave him by himself while I'm off having fun.

Slipping on a low-cut purple halter, I pull my hair over my shoulders and paint myself into my skintight jeans. I do a quick smoky eye and highlight my cheekbones, the knee-high boots and leather jacket I'm wearing adding a certain edge to my outfit that I haven't shown on any of my dates. Maybe it'll keep the boring guys far away and bring on the more exciting options.

When I go downstairs, Jace is nowhere to be seen, and I'm glad. I don't want to answer any questions about where I'm going or feel like I'm being scrutinized for my decisions. I just need to get away.

Thirty minutes later, after using the Google Jace taught me about the other day, I'm at a club on the other side of town called Apex Fusion, and after showing the fake ID Lux had made for me and paying the cover charge, I'm ushered inside. The flashing lights, vape fumes, and thumping bass consume my senses, and I'm immediately in my element.

The dance floor is crowded, and so is the bar, but I make my way to the bartender and order a gin and tonic. Moving to a less crowded area, I lean against a high-top table and sip my drink, watching the couples dance and grind against each other, and my body itches to be on the floor with them.

A man with coiffed blond hair leans on my table, his brown eyes slowly skimming over my body. Unlike many of the other men here, he's dressed in a designer button-up and slacks that cling to his muscular thighs. I can almost count the bulging muscles through his clothes.

"What's a gorgeous woman like you doing watching everyone on the dance floor? You should be out there," he says, flashing me a wide smile.

I raise an eyebrow and set down my glass, mirroring his posture and propping my chin in my palm. "Well, maybe I was waiting for you to come ask me." I know I'm laying it on thick, but this guy looks like exactly what I'm searching for—outgoing, put together, and handsome.

"I'm Patrick."

"Desi."

He holds his palm out to me and says, "Would you care to dance, Desi?"

"I'd love to." I abandon my drink and follow him into the crowd.

Patrick places a hand on my waist, and the pulsating bodies press us close. His palm slides down my hip and around to the curve of my ass. Before I can even move to put space between us, the tips of his fingers dig into the plump flesh, urging me forward. His body sways to the beat, forcing mine to meet his movements, and his leg slips between my thighs. Leaning in until his lips brush my ear, he says, "You are hands down the hottest girl here."

My breath catches as he puts pressure on the apex of my legs with his thigh. Under different circumstances, with a different man who *asked* permission, I have no doubt it would feel good, but right now, it just feels . . . gross. This is not okay; everything in my body is screaming at me to get away from this guy.

I slide my hands up his chest and gently push against him, putting a little space between us as I mumble a thank-you. The dance floor is so crowded that I don't see any easy path away, so I settle for pulling my lower body back so his thigh isn't touching me anymore. But he doesn't seem to take the hint.

He slides his hands under my jacket, roaming freely over my rib cage. The space between us disappears again, and this time he leans in so close to me that his lips are dangerously close to meeting mine.

"I want to take you back to my place and get you out of these pants."

Anger at his presumption and, as much as I hate to admit it, fear bubble up within me. As a princess of Infernis I'd always been under a certain amount of protection, but now I'm on my own, not to mention I can't use all my strength if I am going to remain undercover. And I *must* remain undercover. I can't screw this up and get caught performing some superhuman feat.

I push him with a stronger hand and step away, bumping into the couple behind me. "Please don't touch me like that. I won't be going home with you," I say, turning away from him to walk off, but he grips my wrist and yanks me back toward him.

"I asked you to dance. You said yes. You wear these tight jeans, low-cut top that shows half your tits, and then you tell me you don't want me to touch you?" he hisses, his mouth against my ear again. "I call bullshit."

I twist my wrist, trying to pull it from his grasp, but he holds tight. "None of that gives you permission to grope me," I snap.

"I'm just dancing with you, sweetheart. Quit overthinking it." He wedges his thigh between mine again, and I swiftly draw up my knee, planting it dead center in the juncture of his legs.

Patrick moans and doubles over, his hand gripping his smashed testicles.

Meredith was right. That worked.

I push through the crowd and run to the back of the club. A blue neon sign over a hallway reads RESTROOMS. Before I duck inside, I glance over my shoulder and see Patrick charging through the crowd toward me, fury burning in his eyes.

Women stand at the sink playing with their lipstick and finger-combing their hair, but they pay no attention to me as I slip into the last stall and lock it behind me. My heart pounds so hard it makes my stomach churn. I lean against the wall and close my eyes while I catch my breath. In over a century of existence I've witnessed all kinds of debauchery, but none of it compares to what that man tried to force on me.

In Infernis, things like *that* simply don't happen. Demons and chaotic energies may get greedy and end up in trouble for petty theft, commit mischievous deeds when their pride is damaged and they just want to be a dick to the person they feel wronged them, or even get into fights in dark alleys sometimes when they let their wrath consume them. But never, *ever* does anyone put their hands on another being in an intimate way without permission. My father would never allow it, nor would his father before him, and back and back down the line all the way to the beginning of time. And he has taught Lux to abide by that law. Ever since I can remember, the prince of Lust has been taught the importance of consent. Any demon or energy who didn't follow suit would be damned to nothingness.

Having a man touch me like that without permission is a complete shock. Fight, flight, or freeze? I did all three tonight, I suppose, but now I'm stuck here in the bathroom because I can't go back out there; I know he'll be waiting.

Sliding my hand in my back pocket, I retrieve my phone and stare at the blank screen. I have three people I could call—one is annoyed with me, one is at work, and the other is having her *one* date night a month without the kids. I refuse to be the one to mess that up. Meredith has been talking about this date all week.

I take the most comfortable option and call Cannon, but he doesn't answer.

"Dammit," I mumble, firing off a text.

> Cannon, I know you're working, but I really need you to answer. I'm in kind of a bad spot and I need your help.

I stare at my phone for a good five minutes, but he doesn't answer. I wait, and wait, and wait, and eventually, I forget where I am and slump onto the toilet, my head in my hands.

There is only one other person I can text, and I *really* don't want to. Jace and I are hardly friends, and this is sort of a "phone a friend" situation. But Cannon isn't getting back to me.

Maybe Patrick isn't even out there anymore. Maybe he's given up. I start to come out of the stall when I hear two women enter the bathroom talking in hushed tones.

"Did you see that guy out there?"

"Yeah, he looks pissed."

"I think someone kicked him in the balls," the first one says, stifling a laugh.

"He probably deserved it. He looks like one of those tools who thinks he can touch *whoever* he wants *whenever* he wants."

So that's a thing that happens a lot here. That's unfortunate.

"He's clearly posted up waiting for someone."

Their voices fade as they head back outside, and I close my eyes, taking a deep breath before typing a text to my other roommate.

> Jace, are you awake?

He answers almost immediately.

> Yeah.

I swallow over the lump in my throat and tamp down my growing panic.

> I need you to come get me . . .
> I'm at a nightclub.

The three dots appear at the bottom of the screen and vanish. They start again and just as quickly go away. Several seconds pass before they return, followed by a message.

> Are you drunk or are they kicking you out for flipping all their cups the wrong way?

I freeze for a long moment, unsure whether to laugh or scream.

> Ha-ha. You're so funny, are you going on tour with your jokes? No, I'm not drunk, and no, I haven't touched their cups. This guy asked me to dance, put his hands all over me, he wouldn't stop when I asked him to, and he wouldn't let me go. I had to knee him in the balls to get away from him and now he's waiting outside the bathroom for me. I heard some girls talking about it. He's pissed, and I'm freaked out.

> Fuck. Sorry. They canceled my comedy tour, so I've got time to come pick you up.

A couple of seconds later, he sends another message.

> I just checked your location to put in my GPS. For fuck's sake, Desideria. Apex Fusion is a cesspool of assholes. Stay put. I'll be there in fifteen.

> Okay. Thank you.

Why is this so hard? Back home, demons find their partners—or whomever they want to date for the moment—every day. They do all the things the humans do—dinner dates, dancing, walks in the park hand in hand, but without the uninvited groping and coma-inducing conversations. Humans have always had their issues; I just never expected them to be so distasteful when it comes to dating and sex. Finding a decent human shouldn't be this difficult. I hate to admit it, but maybe I should have tried harder to find a demon partner.

Fifteen minutes later my phone vibrates in my hand, and I almost drop it in the toilet, I move so fast to unlock it.

> Come out of the bathroom. I'm right outside.

My heart leaps into my throat and I burst out of the stall, wash my hands, and open the door carefully, scanning the area for both the offending man and Jace.

The one I'm happy to see stands right next to the bathroom, just as he said, and I have never been more relieved to see another person in my life. He's wearing faded jeans and a half-zip pullover sweater that is the richest shade of burgundy. It's out of place with the sweaty shirts and bare skin around us, but it looks good . . . comfortable, safe.

All my earlier annoyance with him melts away. "Jace, thank you," I mumble, and before I can stop myself, I'm wrapping my arms around his waist and pulling him to me in a grateful embrace that surprises even me.

He goes stiff under my touch, but my relief won't allow me to let him go. After a few seconds, he relaxes and gives me an awkward pat on the back.

"Where is the guy that had you locking yourself in the bathroom?" he asks, his voice laced with anger.

I look up at him, still hanging on to his waist. "What?"

"The jackass trying to pass himself off as a human who was touching you without consent. Where the hell is he?"

His dark tone reminds me of the text message he sent that creeper who asked me if I was DTF the other night, and I don't know why I didn't predict that he'd ask me to point this guy out.

Trying to ignore the anger I can practically feel rolling off Jace, I glance around the club, but the guy isn't anywhere in sight. "I don't see him. I don't want you to start anything with him anyway. I just want to go home."

"Someone needs to say something—"

"Please, Jace."

He sweeps his eyes from the bar to the dance floor one last time and nods. "All right. Let's get you out of here."

We exit the club, the absence of the loud, thumping music a shock to my ears. I'm still holding on to his waist, and he drapes one arm around my shoulder, holding me close to his side.

The parking lot is littered with club patrons, mostly smoking cigarettes and pot, some of them just leaning against their cars and talking, but my heart drops when I see a familiar head of coiffed blond hair. He laughs at whatever the guy across from him says. As if he has a tracking device on me, his eyes catch mine and his smile fades. "Hey, does your boyfriend know you were grinding up on my dick on the dance floor?" he calls across the lot.

Jace stops walking and his fingertips sink into my shoulder. "Still want me to leave it alone?"

I don't get a chance to answer before Patrick takes another stab at me.

"Your girl's a slut, bro."

Jace moves like he's on autopilot and set to kill mode. In several long strides, he's in Patrick's space. He grips the front of his shirt and pulls him up until they are face to face. With eyes full of fear, Patrick struggles for his footing.

In a voice that would put any movie villain to shame, Jace says, "Fucking funny, *bro*. I heard you have a problem with words like *no* and *stop*. I suggest that in the future you respect someone's decision when they come to their senses about you and go fuck yourself instead."

Hades help me, but seeing Jace like this makes me view him in an *entirely* different light. He is beyond sexy right now; there is no way I could pretend to ignore it even if I wanted to try. I've never had anyone defend me like this before, and I won't be forgetting the feeling anytime soon.

"Desi, do you have anything you want to say to this tool?"

I step closer to Jace and look Patrick in the eye. I'm no longer scared of him. Jace has reduced him to a shaking, blubbering mess in a matter of seconds, and I see how weak he really is. This is a sorry excuse for a human.

"Yeah. When someone tells you no, you listen. Regardless of what they're wearing. And also, slut shaming is so last century," I spit.

Jace looks at me over his shoulder, his lips in a tight line as he fights back a smile. He gives a slight tip of his chin that says *you did good* and turns back to Patrick. "Tell the lady you're sorry for disrespecting her not once but twice tonight."

Patrick vehemently nods. It's clear he wants to get away from Jace. "Sorry for disrespecting you, ma'am."

Jace lets him go with a shove and grabs my hand. Without a word, he leads me to his BMW and opens the door for me. I remain quiet as he climbs in on his side and shuts his door. As soon as we're alone, he grips the steering wheel and drops his head to the center of it. I watch as his back expands with a deep breath and slowly deflates several times. Every muscle of his upper body is coiled tight, from his biceps to the cords running down his neck. With a final loud exhale, he sits up and turns on the ignition.

The car remains silent, nothing but the purr of the engine as he pulls out of the parking lot. His grip on the steering wheel doesn't let up, and not once does he take his eyes off the road. I'm starting to believe we're going to sit in awkward silence and never address everything that just happened when he finally says, "I know you're eager to meet people, but you've *got* to do a little research about the places you're going. Ask me or Meredith before you go to bars or clubs. Either of us can let you know if you'll be safe there, okay?"

I glance at him from the corner of my eye. He's not trying to lecture me like he was the other night; it's clear from his actions tonight that he was truly worried about me. "I will," I say quietly, and after a minute, I add in a whisper, "I didn't do that, by the way."

"Didn't do what?"

"'Grind up on his dick,' or whatever it was he said. I didn't do that. I didn't make him think it was okay to grope me like he did."

"It doesn't matter what you did or didn't do. He should have asked or waited for you to tell him you wanted his touch beyond dancing." His gaze leaves the road for a split second as he gives me a once-over. "Are you all right? He didn't hurt you, did he?"

"No, not really. He, uh, shoved his leg between my thighs and slid his hands under my shirt. Then when I tried to walk away, he grabbed my wrist and wouldn't let go before getting in my face and yelling at me. But he didn't really hurt me."

"Good. I wouldn't want to have to turn the car around and kick his ass."

My eyes widen. "What?"

"I scared the hell out of him for what he did, and the only reason I didn't beat the shit out of him right then and there is because you didn't want me confronting him in the first place. But if he injured you . . . game over. I won't stand for a man hurting a woman."

Of course he'd do that for anyone who was being harmed. Any decent human would. Jace is a decent human. It's not just about me.

I shake my head to clear my ridiculous fantasy. The delusion of having my "who hurt you?" moment with my grumpy roommate is destroyed. "Right. Well, I won't be doing that again, so you don't have to worry."

"You really need to take a friend with you out to bars. Someone to watch your drink and ward off any assholes. That's like woman survival 101. Where have you been living that you managed to miss out on the dating basics?"

It's right now that I realize I haven't shared anything about my situation with Jace. Each time the conversation about dating turned serious, Jace abandoned ship, and I was left with Cannon. I don't want to lie to Jace, not when he's here and actually asking me questions. I tell him the closest version of the truth I can.

"I didn't need 'dating basics.' Back home it was a big ordeal to date me because of how intimidating my father is. My first date was the practice trip to the bar with Cannon the other night."

The large touch screen in the dash casts a dim glow on Jace's face, highlighting the tight line of his lips. The tick in his jaw has calmed but his body is still stiff. I brush my fingertips over the edge of the soft leather seat to distract myself from my embarrassment.

Jace's voice is a low timbre as he asks, "I don't understand. Guys date girls with intimidating dads all the time and get over it. What's so different about yours?"

"It's a long story. Do you really want to hear it?"

"I asked, didn't I?"

"Fair enough." I let out a breath and tell him everything I told Cannon the other night.

His brows furrow and the streetlights draw dark shadows around his mouth and eyes. "Your father is *making* you find a husband?"

"A partner. They can be platonic, but I must take over my share of his business one day soon, and to do so, I must have someone I can always rely on. My brothers had to do the same. But I don't want to simply have a *platonic* partner by my side. I want that partner to be someone I *love* . . . and there was no one in my hometown who interested me, so I came here. That's why it's so important that I make some progress in the next couple of months. I don't have to be in love yet or propose to someone, but I need to show him I'm trying. And right now, I'm no closer than I was when I got here."

"You do realize that you have a choice. If your dad is involved with a cult or strong-arming you because of your culture, you can say no. I'm sure Cannon will help me get you out of it if you want us to."

I don't know what would be worse, me telling him I'm a demon from Infernis or him thinking my father is a cult leader. But one thing is clear, I don't think he'd ever understand how important it is that I step up as my Circle's leader. It's not only *my* realm that hangs in the balance, but the potential eternal home of his and every other human's energy.

FIVE
JACE

My life has been turned upside down and spun on its head since Desideria stepped through my door. I placed the ad for a roommate to ease my finances while I got my marketing design company off the ground. *One* roommate who maintained a civil environment, paid their rent on time, and followed my rules for a clean house. What I got was a fellow nerd who can't put his shoes away and a fiery redhead who seems to enjoy bringing me to the brink of a panic attack daily.

I was ready to turn Desi away. It was clear from the moment I met her that she's a magnet for trouble. And that was *before* I knew she was on the hunt for a potential husband. I've had my fair share of emotional turmoil, and I swore to never knowingly let it into my life again. My business is my focus . . . my future. Nothing, and no one, is going to derail me from making my dream come true. But god, those big green eyes framed with long lashes had me tossing caution out the window and letting Desi move into my spare room.

Now, Desideria sits at a high-top table on the other side of the restaurant. She fits in with the ritzy patrons, her curls piled on top of her head and a black dress that does her curves justice. She runs her slender finger over the strand of pearls around her neck and takes a sip of her third gin and tonic. Her gaze has shot to the front door every time it opens, only to be followed by disappointment. It wasn't my intention to watch her crash and burn tonight. Far from it. Given my anxiety, I usually avoid places like this, but after the other night, I pushed those feelings aside.

When Desi texted me to tell me a man had his hands all over her, it sent a mixture of anger and worry through me. I didn't think twice about grabbing my keys and driving across town to the shithole known as Apex Fusion. It was the first time I'd driven above the speed limit in years, and still I'd caught every red light, seemed to get stuck behind every slow-ass driver on the road, and had to pull over for an ambulance *and* two fire engines. For every minute that passed, my heart pounded harder and harder in my chest. By the time I reached the club I'd chewed my lip raw, and I was terrified at what I might find when I walked through that door.

Anxiety is no friend of mine, but I know it well. Situations like that one send me into a spiral that goes *deep*. I can't stop picturing all the things that could go wrong, may have gone wrong already, or could go wrong in the future.

What if she came out of the bathroom and that dickhead was outside waiting for her and I got there too late?

What if there's a girl inside who knows him and sends him a text letting him know Desi's in the bathroom and he corners her in the stall?

What if he'd already drugged her drink?

What if I get inside and I can't find her? What if I have to fight that guy and I get arrested?

I did end up confronting the guy, and I was actually proud of myself for the way I handled it. Desi got to tell him off, and I got the satisfaction of intimidating the asswipe who made her feel like her only choice was to hide. The entire situation was enough to make her hesitant to schedule another date for the next week.

But she doesn't have anything to worry about tonight. The man who was supposed to meet her over an hour ago has yet to show, and

I don't think he's going to. Based on the dejected look on Desi's face, she feels the same.

"Come on, man," I say to Cannon as I grab my beer. "Let's go put her out of her misery."

We weave through the maze of mahogany tables and black tie–wearing waiters. The closer we get to Desi, the clearer it is that she's crushed. Her chin rests in her palm, and she stirs her drink with a thin, black straw. If she understood how foolish her quest to find a husband is, she'd save herself a lot of heartache.

Cannon places his hand on her shoulder and gently asks, "Did that asshole stand you up?"

She looks up at him and one side of her mouth lifts in a sad excuse for a smile. "Yeah, looks like it."

I slide into the chair next to her, and Cannon sits across from us. My plan is to let him handle the relationship stuff. It was obvious the night I told Desi what I thought about falling in love that I wasn't cut out to help her. I can be the voice of reason—the one who reminds her to google where a guy wants to meet her before going—but I'm not the one to give her encouraging words when a jerk leaves her hanging.

"So much for y'all watching one of my dates from afar to tell me what you think is going wrong—or to make sure he's not a creeper. He didn't even have the common decency to show up." She downs her drink like a champ and clanks the empty glass on the table.

"I have to admit that I wasn't really down with spying on your entire date anyway," I say, rolling up my shirt sleeves and setting to work on my beer.

Leaning on an elbow and cocking her head to the side, she says, "Why did you agree to do it, then? You don't seem like the kind of guy who goes along with things he doesn't want to do. In fact, you seem like the total opposite."

She isn't wrong. And trust me, I struggled with whether or not I should tag along. I would have loved nothing more than to stay home and lose myself in a video game or my latest design for my company. When Cannon suggested we come along to make sure she was all right, he woke up that little nagging voice inside my head. It started giving me one horrible scenario after another. No matter how much I tried to counter it with reason, it kept going. I had to stop it before it spiraled out of control, and the only way to do that was to make sure Desi's date didn't get out of hand. Of course, I'd never tell her that.

I shrug and say, "It was a long day of reading contracts and starting a new project for a client. I was hoping the next guy's lame-ass excuse to get out of a date with you was because he had a pet llama."

"You're such a dick, man," Cannon says, glancing at Desi. "The woman asked us to help. How can you say no to that face?"

Desi scoffs and raises her glass to the bartender, who gives her a sad smile and a nod, as if he'd been serving her drinks for hours and knew her whole unfortunate story. "Looks like Hunter did."

"Desi—"

"No, seriously," she says, nodding her thanks when the server brings over her next drink. "What is wrong with me? I'm the common denominator here."

"It's not you, Desi. You're looking for it too hard. Good things have a way of finding you when you least expect them," Cannon says.

I fight the urge to roll my eyes. Cannon seriously should be a motivational speaker with all this hopeful, "let's look on the bright side" nonsense. When it comes to love, at least from what I've seen, there is no bright side.

Desi sighs and sits back in her chair. "I guess I'm going to just cool it with the dating for a little bit; maybe the right guy will just march up to me at the mall and tell me how gorgeous he thinks I am," she says with a breathy laugh, taking another sip of her drink.

I pull my lips between my teeth and stare at the bubbles floating up from the bottom of my glass. Desi is stunning. There is no question that she can find someone who would want to be with her just for that. But she deserves better. I've lived with her for going on two weeks and every day I'm unpacking a new Desideria mystery. Ninety days isn't enough time for anyone to fully know her, and it doesn't give her a fair chance to know them either. How the hell is she supposed to dedicate her entire life to someone she just met?

Taking a deep breath, I face her and say, "I don't understand why it's so important to your father that you get married. People run successful businesses and hold it together just fine without a partner. You said the other night that your dad would settle for you picking a friend. Why don't you go that route? Wouldn't it be easier?"

"Sure, it would be easier *now*, but if I did that, I would never be able to go back and change my mind. Whatever we choose is for eternity."

I raise an eyebrow. *For eternity? What a strange way to phrase it.*

Her cheeks flush and she continues, "For *life*. And then I'd never be able to marry for love. And I want that too much to settle."

I cock my head to the side and nudge her with my shoulder. "I don't know where you're from, Desideria, but your family has some strange customs. Around here, half the relationships don't last five years, let alone a lifetime."

"Trust me, I know it's strange. Which is why I'm really enjoying my time here. Thank you both for being my friends, honestly. I couldn't do this without your help."

It's clear she's feeling down and stressed about this whole situation. There's no need to keep harping on it.

Leaning in, I drape my arm over the back of her chair and stage-whisper, "You're not going to ask us to join your bizarre *family business*, are you?"

She laughs and elbows me in the side, to which I respond with an exaggerated *oof*. "No. You're safe from my father's brand of strange."

Damn, that bright smile and laugh. It's been a long time since someone genuinely laughed at one of my stupid jokes. I would sit here all night acting a fool just to see and hear that again.

"Jace! What a surprise to see you here."

At the sound of a familiar, yet out of place voice, I swivel in my seat. A man with salt and pepper hair wearing a suit claps me on the back.

Matt Brown. The one investor I am *dead set* on bringing onboard to financially back Aftermath. I don't trust many people in our industry. I've seen ideas stolen and projects swept out from under a designer after they've done all the legwork. But Matt is an anomaly. Not only does he care about the integrity of his personal reputation, he has the capital to help fund my company, *and* he's an incredible graphic designer. Scratch that, he is the *god* of graphic design. I've admired his art for years. If he believed in my work and what I'm doing, it would validate every dream I'm chasing.

"Hey, Matt. It's good to see you," I say, rising to push my chair back so I can stand to shake his hand.

"No, no," he replies, gesturing for me to remain seated. "Don't get up. You look cozy." A good-natured but teasing smirk turns up the corner of his lips. "Who's this beautiful woman you have with you?" he says after leaning over the table and exchanging a quick introduction with Cannon.

My cheeks heat from the implication that Desi is *with me*. "Oh, this is Desideria. She's my—"

"It's a pleasure to meet you, Desideria. I'm Matt Brown." He brings Desi's knuckles to his lips and places a light kiss on them. "Your date is one hell of a graphic designer. He's one of the best I've seen in a long time. This guy has talent seeping out of every pore."

Wow. I never realized Matt was such a flirt. He's way too old for Desi, and I'm pretty sure he's on his fourth marriage, but he's laying it on *thick*. It's clear she's already enchanted him, and he's only just met her. And my *date*? What is he talking about? Why would he automatically think I'm her—*oh*. My arm. It's draped over the back of Desi's chair. Shaking my head, I stifle a laugh. *This should be interesting.*

Desi flashes Matt that same smile I was admiring, slides her palm onto my thigh and squeezes, saying, "Doesn't he, though? I've never seen someone who can just . . . *envision* something and then turn around and create it so easily, just like that." She snaps her fingers and turns her head to look at me adoringly. "Not to mention he's the best human I know."

Well, then. The woman can beat Matt at his own game. I shouldn't be surprised. Desi's always quick on the comebacks. I was shocked to hear she put her foot in her mouth before she had a chance to leave the house with her first date. She's blunt and never afraid to ask a question, but she has this charm that gets to me even when she's infuriating me.

Matt chuckles. "And I thought *I* got a hard-on from *your* work. I think Desi is outranking me as your number one fan."

I open my mouth to downplay the compliment, but Desi beats me to it, saying, "I'm pretty sure Jace is just as turned on by your work. He practically has a shrine to you in our hallway."

And there it is, Desideria's blatant charm. I search for the nearest table to hide under. This is going to be bad. He's going to think I'm some kind of pervert. I'll have to close the business. My career is going straight down the—

Matt quirks a brow. "Your girl is good. I just might write you a check right now."

My jaw drops, and Desi pinches my knee, bringing me out of my shock. I've been working for months to get a reaction out of Matt. Detailed proposals and insight into new accounts, I've done it all. He's responded to each effort with a simple: *Thanks. I'll take a look when I can.* If I'd known all I needed to do was tell him his work turns me on, I would have sent him a dick pic a long time ago.

Desi leans into me and rests her head on my shoulder. "I guess Jace better keep me around, huh?"

"He better," Matt says, giving me a pointed look. "He's going to need you the week after next at the charity dinner I'm inviting you both to. Some other well-known designers will be there with their pieces up for auction. It'll be a good networking opportunity for him, and I'm sure you'll be amazing at winning them all over."

Charity dinner? Matt's never so much as invited me out for coffee before, and after one meeting with Desi, I'm in with the bigwigs? Is this girl working some sort of witchcraft? I slide my hand into hers where it still rests on my knee.

"Sounds like a good time," I say, looking down at Desi. "You up for it?"

She glances up at me, those green eyes twinkling with mischief as she winks. "I'm up for anything, Wilder."

Matt claps his hand against my shoulder. "Good. Let's see how you do with a roomful of your peers. If you can win those cocky bastards over, I have to believe there's nothing you can't do." He tips his head at Desi, saying, "It was a pleasure meeting you. Cannon, keep an eye on your friend; he has his hands full with this one."

"Will do," Cannon responds, lifting his drink to his lips to hide his smile.

Once Matt is out of sight, all the stress disappears. I sink back in my chair like a human Jell-O formation. "Holy hell. That's the best conversation I've ever had with Matt. Even during my business presentation he didn't interact with me that much."

Desi props her elbow on the table and rests her chin in her palm. "Yeah? I wonder what the difference was . . ." She purses her lips and looks up at the ceiling in mock thought.

She was fantastic. I've spent months trying to figure out an in with Matt, and she wins him over during a brief introduction. Her intuition is impeccable. I've never seen anyone read someone the way she did.

"Where is that confidence on your dates? If you brought that to the table, you would be irresistible," Cannon says.

Desi tosses her hands in the air. "I'm trying, but these guys aren't making it easy when they run off before the date starts or don't show up at all."

"Hey, you have a willing second date right here, just tell me when you're available."

My eyes dart between them, and a heavy feeling spreads through my gut. My roommates hooking up is bound to lead to issues in the house. Just the thought of them together while I'm in the next room. . . I drain the rest of my beer and slam my glass on the table.

It's a childish move. One that draws their attention and makes me feel like an asshole. Why should I care if they get together? They're adults and what they do is none of my business.

"Are we good to get out of here?" I ask, jumping to my feet.

Cannon stands and holds out his fist. "Yeah, man. I believe you and I have a campaign to finish tonight."

"I've been thinking about it all day," I say, bumping my knuckles with his.

It's a lie. Every thought I had about video games and work vanished earlier tonight when Desi came downstairs in that little black dress. I couldn't take my eyes off her during the Uber ride here, or while she sat alone waiting for her date. No matter how hard I tried to steer the conversation to one of the many hobbies Cannon and I have in common, I couldn't stop thinking about the swing of her hips or that shade of pink on her mouth. And now I can't stop thinking about how jealous I am that Cannon will take her out on another date.

SIX
DESI

"Luke, I am your father," Cannon drones in an exaggeratedly deep voice with his fist over his mouth.

Jace turns in his seat and his fork clatters onto his plate, then he holds his hand out toward Cannon's throat. "Force choke!"

Cannon pretends he can't breathe, clawing at his neck.

"Bro, did you know that's not actually the line?"

Cannon freezes, his jaw dropping like Jace just told him his puppy died. "What? You're lying."

My eyes bounce back and forth between the two of them, wondering who the hell Luke is and why his father is so important.

Jace goes back to stabbing his chicken parmesan, shoveling it into his mouth. "Yeah, it's like, the most misquoted line ever. It's actually, 'No, *I* am your father.' Isn't that crazy?"

Cannon shakes his head. "I am *shook*. I feel like my whole life is a lie."

"I know. I felt the same way when I found out."

"I feel like I need to . . ." Cannon jumps off his stool and grabs the baguette from the basket in the middle of the island. "Challenge you to a duel." He makes a strange noise with his mouth and holds the piece of bread in front of him like a sword.

I scoot away from them with wide eyes. "What the—" I start, but of course, no one is paying attention.

This is my new normal. The men of the house have their own language, their own routine, their own friendship, which doesn't include me. I should be used to it. Growing up with six brothers also made me the odd one out. It wasn't that I'm a girl; they couldn't care less about that. I'm the baby. The one who never understood their inside jokes or wasn't there for many of their favorite moments. It wasn't so bad when I was in Infernis. Over a century of life meant I had friends to run to when I was lonely. I'm getting there with Meredith, but it's not the same. I don't know her as well yet, plus she has kids of her own.

Jace snatches a ladle from the utensil holder by the stove and echoes the noise Cannon made, and they begin some sort of deranged sword fight, bouncing around the kitchen and living room.

Cannon finally stabs Jace in the abdomen with the baguette and Jace falls backward onto the couch, writhing in imaginary pain.

"*Star Wars* night!" Cannon chants, holding the bread in the air and pumping his fist.

Jace bounds off the couch and mimics his movements with the ladle. "*Star Wars* night! *Star Wars* night!"

I lean on the counter and bite my thumbnail, watching them parade back into the kitchen. What in the hell is going on? What has happened to my two grown-ass roommates? They must have gotten some new video game they plan on playing tonight. They're always doing something, whether it's a video game, computer program, or movie premiere . . . and I just go to my room and read or watch chick flicks and reruns. I'm tired of playing third wheel.

I get up from the barstool and rinse my plate, placing it in the dishwasher. Wiping down the countertop where I was sitting, I push my stool underneath the island. "Okay, clearly I'm out of the loop. Again. See you guys in the morning," I mutter, and I'm pretty sure neither of them hear me or even notice as I head up the stairs.

I grab a spicy novel that's the newest craze from my dresser and fall back on my bed. Staring at the cover, I sigh. Stories like the one in my hand had to be inspired by some real-life event. And if that's the case, why is it so easy for the main character to find her perfect match? Neighbors, childhood friends, even enemies can be "the one." But I can't so much as go on two dates with the same person. The women in these pages have everything I want. Hell, I'm even living vicariously through them in order to have a sex life. They have the perfect person, and I have their erotic love scenes and a drawer with three battery-operated friends. Pathetic.

I crack the book open, ready to return to the steamy moment with the characters that led to last night's solo moment of pleasure. Marco is about to get his second wind when a light tap comes from my open door. I look over the top of the book to find Jace leaning against the door frame with his hand in his pocket.

"It's *Star Wars* night. What are you doing?" he asks.

I lay my book face down on my chest and intertwine my fingers on top of it. "Reading. Why would I want to sit and watch you guys play yet another video game I know nothing about?"

"It's *Star Wars*."

When I lift my brows and shrug, he opens his mouth, closes it, and looks around my room. His face contorts like he's pondering one of life's biggest questions. I'd jump in and give him some insight, but I'm not sure I would have the answer. Especially if it's regarding Luke, his father, or sword fighting with kitchen utensils.

Jace runs his fingers through his hair, and his gaze returns to me. "How do you not know what *Star Wars* is? We are talking about one of the greatest movie series ever made, Desideria."

"It's a movie? I—I thought it was a video game." I feel like an idiot. "You guys are always playing those fighting games, and given the bread and spoon battle, I just thought . . ."

He walks to my bed and holds out his hand to me. "Stop talking and get up. I'm second-guessing my choice to let you move into this house more and more by the second. I can't live with someone who doesn't know what *Star Wars* is."

I stare at his hand for a moment, shocked at the gesture. "You want me to come watch it with you?"

"Yes. I—" He puffs up his cheeks and directs his attention to my window. After taking several deep breaths, he sits next to my hip on the mattress. "I know it can't be easy living with the two of us. Cannon and I have a lot in common, and you're stuck listening to us go on about nerdy shit. I want—*we* want—you to feel included. So we came up with movie night. Once a week when we're all home we'll just chill together."

I perk up and prop myself on my forearms. "That's a nice idea. Will I ever get to pick the movie?"

"Sure," he says, not even trying to hide the hesitation in his tone.

The man is a control freak. Just the thought of me picking a movie makes him sweat. What does he think I'm going to make him sit through? He's talking about an entire *series* of movies. Multiple movies. I'm asking for the chance to pick one two-hour film. He takes neurotic to an entirely different level.

"I'm asking for *one* movie of my choice and for you guys to watch it with me," I say.

"I know, and that's fair, especially after what you did for me at the restaurant the other night." His features sober, and he meets my eyes. "Thank you. I should have told you how much I appreciated it. I just got sidetracked. Matt is still talking about how amazing he thought you were."

I wave my hand in the air. "It was no big deal. I didn't say anything that wasn't true. You're a huge fan of his, and you work your ass off day in and day out. Plus, it sounds like I even get to go to some fancy party."

"You don't really have to go to that. It's going to be a bunch of elitist assholes in suits pretending like they care about a cause, but they just want to one-up each other. I can make up an excuse for you."

"No, I want to go. It sounds like fun." I pause and cock my head to the side. "Well, not the way you just described it, but the way I had dreamed it up in my head. I've never been to an event like that before where I'm not the daughter of the guy in charge. In other words, I've never been with a date. Even if it *is* a fake one. So let me help you finish sealing this deal."

"Are you sure you want to do this?"

"Yes, Jace. I'm sure."

"All right. I'll take you on one condition."

My heart drops to the pit of my stomach. I'm sure this is going to be some stupid stipulation about passing an exam on when to use the proper cutlery. Sarcastic comebacks are already racing through my head, and this fake date is bound to be over before it starts.

"What's the condition?"

"You watch *Star Wars* with us. I can't have a girlfriend, even a fake one, who doesn't know about Jedi mind tricks. You'll be too susceptible to the dark side."

I laugh and shake my head. "Okay, okay," I say, holding my hand up in surrender. "I'll watch *Star Wars* with you." We both stand and I leave my book on the mattress, pulling a hoodie over my head.

Before we leave my room, I say, "Jace?"

"Yeah?"

"Thank you for including me. It means a lot."

He gives a curt nod. "You're welcome, Desideria."

Besides Cannon and Jace's constant back and forth and the references I don't seem to understand, the movie isn't bad. The guys make me a deal that I can choose the next movie once we've finished the series. What I don't learn until later is that I have *eight* more movies to go. I've already decided that I'm picking the sappiest, most romantic movie I can find, and those two will endure my torture.

SEVEN
JACE

My eyes spring open as a shout pierces the quiet. I snap up in bed, straining to see what made the noise. There's no one hiding in the corners or creeping through my closet. All I find are the remnants of a recurring nightmare floating around in my head.

I clap my mouth shut and fall back on the mattress. Laying my palms flat on the sheets, I focus on my breathing and count through each inhale and exhale.

It's been a while since I had the dream. Through the practice of mindfulness, Dr. Holloman has helped me work through the memories that plague me. We designed a routine of healthy eating, exercise, and daily planning that helps me feel secure. He also taught me how to divert my negative energy and thoughts into my art. It took some time for the new habits to calm what sometimes feels like a constant raging storm inside me. And then I had to throw everything off balance by inviting strangers into my home.

They say you have to sacrifice for your dream, and I'm offering up my mental health to make it a reality. Not that everything is terrible with Cannon and Desi around. Living alone had a downside—the smallest sounds, like the freezer dropping a batch of ice, used to set my heart racing. I was talking to myself more than I was to actual people. Now I have two people to eat dinner and watch movies with. I didn't realize how lonely I was until I wasn't anymore.

I turn to my side and tuck my comforter under my arm. Staring out the window, I watch as the sun peeks over the rooftops. The sky glows in shades of orange and pink. Clouds streak through the colors, and I can't help feeling like they represent me—thousands of shades of gray in a world alive with vibrant colors. I've existed in monochrome for so long, playing it safe in the neutral tones. That is, until recently.

My attention drifts to the window directly across from mine. Desi lies curled on her side, her fingers gripping the edge of her blanket. I have a bad habit of letting my eyes wander in her direction. I should turn over and let her have her privacy, but she makes it too easy to admire her while she's sleeping. She only pulls her curtains closed when she's dressing. As soon as she's ready to crawl into bed, she opens them again. I'm always up for the day before her, and I wonder if she takes the same precautions in the morning. No doubt her freckled skin would look amazing in this light. And her hair . . . those wild red waves would look like fire. I bet her skin is soft and warm when she wakes up. It would be tempting to glide my hand under those blankets and find out if I were lying next to her. I could wake her up with a kiss on her shoulder, her neck, her lips. She seems like the type of woman who would moan her consent. But I'd want to hear the words, just a quiet *touch me*, and my hands would be all over her.

My hand slides down my stomach until my fingers graze my hard cock through my underwear. I press my hips forward into my palm, and an image of Desi's elegant fingers wrapping around me plays in my head.

I jerk my hand back and shake my head. No! I'm not doing this. Desi is my roommate and I'm not crossing that line. A very creepy line I might add, watching her while she sleeps and jerking off. I need to let off some steam, and this is *not* how I'm going to do it.

Throwing the covers back, I jump out of bed and march to my bathroom. I spend less than five minutes throwing on a pair of joggers and a hoodie. After brushing my teeth and tying my running shoes, I head out.

Every morning I go for at least a two-mile run, but this morning I opt for four of my usual laps through the neighborhood to double my time out of the house. There's no way I want to go back too soon and end up running into Desi in the kitchen still sporting a goddamn semi.

I do have to admit, though, it is a bit of a relief to know that I can still get it up like that first thing in the morning for an *actual* woman, and not just the idea of one. At twenty-nine, I'm in my prime. I should get it and take it whenever and however I can. It's what most guys my age do. But after everything that happened, I have no desire to take that route again.

I've spent my fair share of time acting like the biggest jackass when it came to the opposite sex. I was going out with a different woman every other night, sleeping with her, and never calling her back because I was too busy on a date with the next. The carnage of broken hearts I left behind was a mess. I was careless in an effort to dull my pain. When I realized what I was doing, the guilt ate at me.

I'm better off on my own.

But this morning, seeing Desi in her bed, so peaceful, beautiful . . . it woke something up in me. I wanted to touch and be touched, to experience the high that comes with bringing someone the most blissed-out feeling.

Until I remembered that underneath that gorgeous face and fiery personality she has the capability to crush me from the inside out. And I'm not the kind of man she's searching for. The only thing I'm committed to is my business and working through everything in my life that left me fucked up.

When I finally get back to the house, I'm a sweaty, disgusting mess, and all I need is a hot shower. I'm walking up the stairs when my phone rings. I dig it out of my pocket and when I see Matt's name on the screen, my mood lifts. He must want to talk about the proposal I'd emailed him.

"Hey, Matt," I answer, pulling my shirt up by the hem and wiping my face. "How's it going?"

"Jace, I'm good. And you?"

"I'm all right, just finished up my morning run."

"Damn, talented *and* in shape. Not fair," he quips, and I just shake my head as he continues. "I wanted to see that design you talked about in your email. Can you send it over?"

My heart pounds in my chest, threatening to break right out of it and flop onto the floor. "Of course. What's up?"

"I have a friend who is looking for some marketing material for a business she just bought, and your style would work perfectly for her."

"That's amazing, just give me five to shower and change clothes."

"No problem. Jace, this is exactly why you're invaluable. I know I can count on you."

I can't help but beam from ear to ear as I enter my bedroom. "Thank you. You don't know what that means to me."

"Of course. Talk to you soon."

I say goodbye and set my phone on my dresser. Walking to the bathroom, I reach behind me, grab my collar, and pull my shirt over my head.

"Jace, wait!"

I yank the wet fabric from my head and stand stunned in the doorway of my bathroom. Desi is sitting in my bathtub with bubbles foaming over the top. Her eyes are wide, and she grips the side as if she is about to stand. Rays of sunlight shine through the frosted window behind her, and I learn firsthand what her hair looks like in the early morning light. The shock of finding her like this is accompanied by the pure panic of knowing she invaded my personal space without asking.

"What are you doing in here?" I ask, my voice deep and ricocheting off the walls.

She just stares at me, her bright-green eyes trailing down my body and back up until they land on my chest, and I have a feeling it isn't because my pecs are ripped. But she cuts her gaze from my scarred flesh, still struck silent.

"Desideria!" I snap, trying to pull her from whatever stupor she's stuck in.

"I am so sorry!" she blurts, shaking her head and drawing her knees up in front of her chest. "I woke up and I was going to get ready to go grocery shopping, and I could tell it was cold outside, and one thing I miss so much about living at home is taking baths, and, well, I just thought I could borrow your huge tub this once and you'd never know." She hangs her head again and buries her hands in her hair. "The more I talk, the worse it sounds. Look, I'm *really* sorry."

I run my palm over my chest. It's just as much to calm my frazzled nerves as it is to hide the gnarly scar on my left pec. I don't miss the way she sneaks a peek at it, hiding the action behind a failed attempt to seem casual. This is a feeling I despise. I'm in the one room in the house that no one enters without my permission. Desideria hasn't just come into my room without me knowing; she's seeing parts of me I'd rather keep hidden. Anger builds inside me, searing through my veins until I've reached my boiling point.

"I'm starting to believe that you enjoy irritating me," I say through gritted teeth. "First you mess with the cups in my kitchen, putting them the wrong way. Then you call me to rescue you from a shithole nightclub after I warned you to be careful. Now you're moving in on my personal space. I don't think you're sorry at all."

Her jaw drops and she lets her knees slide from her grip. I feel like a hypocrite; for all my talk about privacy I can't help my gaze sliding down to where the bubbles are starting to dissipate around her curves. But her sharp tongue sends my eyes back to hers real quick. "We already discussed this. I do *not* put them in the wrong way. And as far as you 'rescuing me,' you didn't have to come. I could've just sat in the bathroom stall all night until they closed and then made a run for it and hoped that the guy wasn't waiting for me outside. And, yeah, I guess I did invade your space today. What else do you want me to do besides say I'm sorry, Jace? Get down on my knees and beg your forgiveness?"

God. The mental picture is so clear. Desi on her knees, looking up at me through those long lashes. I'm rattled just thinking about it.

"Don't tempt me, Desideria," I say, clenching my jaw closed too late. I'm losing all common sense talking to her while she's naked.

Her eyes widen and her plump lips part. "What was that?"

I should man up, take responsibility for the reckless things coming out of my mouth, but I don't. "You're putting your mouth on the part that touches the cupboard shelf. Something could have crawled around on that shelf, or there could be dust sitting on it. It's the *wrong* way."

She cocks her head to the side and narrows her eyes. "That is absolutely *not* what you said, but that's bullshit anyway, because if the cup is facing up, then the dust is falling *into* the cup! So either way, the dust is getting in, genius!"

I slide my palm over the back of my neck and look at the ceiling. I can't do this with her. Not when those bubbles are evaporating and threatening to give me a glimpse of her breasts. It takes several deep breaths to get my heart rate back to normal and calmly say, "Finish your bath and wipe down my tub when you're done. Don't come into my room again without asking first."

I grab two clean towels from the drawer by the door, tossing one onto the bathmat for her. Without another word, I slam the bathroom door behind me and stalk to the guest bathroom that Cannon uses.

The hot water relaxes me, relieving the tension in the back of my neck. I hate when my plans are derailed. My expectation was to take a shower and get that project off to Matt. Finding Desi in my bathroom did more than divert me; she sent my thoughts right back to the places I didn't want them to be. She's taking up space in my head that I purposely designated for other things . . . safer things.

I flip the water to cold, hoping it will freeze the thoughts, and my hard-on, away.

Desi doesn't cross boundaries; she decimates them like a wrecking ball. She's unadulterated chaos, wreaking havoc on my sanity. She's also the vibrant morning sky, bringing shades of electric green, fiery red, and passionate purple to my monochrome life. All her innocent discretions, as irritating as they are, make me feel alive.

By the time I dry off and wrap a towel around my waist, I know I was in the wrong with the way I reacted. The new plan is to send the project to Matt, make Desi an amazing lunch, and apologize for overreacting.

"Jace!"

Desi's scream sends me into a panic. I leave my dirty clothes on the floor and race down the stairs, holding the towel at my waist so it doesn't fall. She stands next to the kitchen counter, a pile of jeans resting on top and a pair in her hands. My heart continues to run when my feet have stopped. I look her over, searching for blood or a broken bone. She's wearing a midthigh length nightshirt with a sloth hanging from a tree on it. Bare legs, bare arms, and nothing out of sorts. But based on the way she screamed my name, there must be.

"What's wrong?" I ask through labored breaths.

She looks at the jeans in her hand and back at me a couple of times, her eyes wide as if I should know exactly what is going on. When she realizes that I clearly do not, she says, "My jeans, Jace. Why did you put my jeans in the dryer?"

"Because you left them in the washer last night. I believe the words you are looking for are *thank you*. I also folded them, by the way, so you're welcome."

"'Thank you'? For what? For ruining my brand-new clothes?"

"How the hell do you dry them then?"

"Meredith said *not* to dry them! That they would shrink if I did! That I had to hang dry them. And she was right. Now they're all about two inches too short!" She holds up a pair to her waist, and I look down at her ankles. I cringe because even I can tell they're shorter than they're supposed to be. "And what started as a size fourteen is probably now, like, an eight and I won't be able to fit one thigh in them!"

"How the hell was I supposed to know that some rocket scientist made women's jeans different from men's jeans? You clean them, dry them, put them away, and wear them."

"They aren't different, but these fit me perfectly. Meredith and I spent hours going to stores. I tried on several pairs to find these. It's not easy to find jeans that are long enough *and* fit my hips and thighs." She slaps her hands down on the top of her legs to make her point. "And these jeans need to hang to dry."

Hang drying jeans and secret bubble baths, it's too much. "There's a simple way to avoid this—don't leave your jeans in the washer."

She grits her teeth and closes her eyes for a split second. When she opens them, I swear, the green is brighter than ever before. Stepping forward, she takes the pile of jeans from the counter and tosses them at the couch without even looking, where they bounce off the cushions and land haphazardly on the floor. Taking one more step toward me, she says, "You are so damned condescending."

I step forward, leaving mere inches between her and my chest. "And you are so spoiled."

Her lashes flutter and her lips part. My teeth ache to bite into the plump, pink bottom one. The heat radiating off her is tempting me to pull her close and see what her skin feels like against mine.

"I'm not spoiled. I just know what I want, and I'm willing to go after it, even if I'm not sure how to make it mine," she whispers, focusing on my lips looming above hers.

I struggle to maintain control. Just one tilt of my head and I'll know if her lips taste as sweet as they look. God, I want to know. Keeping my voice a low rumble, I say, "You aren't as clueless as you let on, Desideria. You know exactly what you're doing."

"And what's that?"

Dozens of answers fly through my brain. *Sleeping with your blinds open. Standing too close to me on purpose like you are right now. Pissing me off just to make me squirm. Making me hard every time you come into a room.*

My last sliver of control vanishes, and I eat the remaining space between us. My bottom lip brushes hers as I rasp, "Just pick up your jeans."

And as the realization that I've nearly kissed her sets in, I jump back as if she's burned me, wipe the back of my hand over my mouth, and turn away to the stairs before she can say a word.

EIGHT
DESI

The last two days have been utter hell. Jace refuses to look at me, and, if I'm lucky, he might grumble a *good morning* or an *excuse me* as he maneuvers around me. Beyond that, our communication is nonexistent, and I'm tired of this game.

"Why is it you can leave your shoes scattered about or forget your cup on the coffee table, but I rearrange the pillows on the couch, and Jace loses his shit?" I ask.

Cannon peers around the refrigerator door and cocks a brow. "You act as if I'm a complete slob."

I lean against the island and cross my arms over my stomach. "Well, compared to Jace's ridiculously high standards, you kind of are," I say, and when he looks at me with an offended expression, I raise my hands in defense. "Hey, it's not your fault he expects something so far beyond perfection that it's impossible."

"True. One bowl in the sink will not cause the world to crumble around him." Cannon returns to the counter with all the fixings for turkey sandwiches. Without getting a plate out of the cupboard, he prepares our lunch directly on the granite—an act that would send Jace into an epic meltdown. "Why don't you just talk to him? The man is a pretty good listener, not to mention really funny."

I've seen Jace's funny side a couple of times, and it's a side I really, really like. But ever since we argued and nearly kissed—or whatever the hell happened—he hasn't shown me any side except the angry one, and it's intimidating as hell.

"I've tried to talk to him. I've tried opening up to him. It's like we take one step forward and two steps back. I just think that somewhere deep down, or maybe not so deep down, he doesn't like me. That there's just something about me he can't stand. He likes you. Me, not so much."

Cannon sets the used knife on top of the jar of mayo and slaps the top slice of bread over the meat and cheese. He grabs two plates from their shelf and tosses our food on top. "You're overthinking this, Desi. You've had guys walk out on you, never call you back, and stand you up, but you're here worrying about Jace. You need to do something to get your mind off him."

I pick up the sandwich and tell him thank you before shoving a bite into my mouth. I haven't eaten all day, and I am what Glen likes to call hangry.

"You're right, you're right. I just hate that he's my roommate and we can't seem to get along for more than a couple of days at a time," I say after swallowing and taking a drink of tea. "You're right, doing something else sounds fun. But what? Ideas?" I take another bite of my sandwich and drum my fingernails on the countertop.

"Do I have permission to cash in on that second date?"

I think for a moment. I don't want it to seem like I'm going out with Cannon because I'm pissed at Jace, because that isn't the case at all. Cannon is funny, sweet, sexy, and he wants to take me out and show me a good time. Isn't that what I'm here for?

"Absolutely."

"I feel like you've got a little aggression you need to work off. Dress warm and comfortable and meet me down here in twenty. I'm going to take you somewhere that you can pretend you're sticking it to Jace Wilder."

"Now that, I like the sound of."

Twenty minutes later, we're in Cannon's Lexus and he's driving us to some undisclosed location. I am questioning my choice of clothing when he keeps talking about how cold it is outside.

"Did I dress warmly enough?" I ask, looking down at my black yoga pants, purple puffer jacket, and the white running shoes I've finally broken in. "You keep mentioning the cold, and I'm getting paranoid."

"We are going to be outside, but don't worry, I'll make sure you stay warm."

We drive to the outskirts of the city and Cannon pulls into a dirt parking lot with a wooden sign advertising archery. My insides roll at the thought of me using a new weapon. My father and brothers are versed in all manners of combat, but I never found joy in it like they did. So I was taught the basics of self-defense and left to lounge by the pool or spend time with friends.

Cannon opens the passenger-side door and holds his hand out to me. "You ready to burn some energy by shooting things with arrows?"

I take his hand but hesitate before moving to get out of the car. "I—uh, would you believe me if I told you I've never shot a bow and arrow before? I have no idea how to do it."

"Maybe that's all part of my devious plan to get close to you."

I smile as I climb out of the car and let him pull me against his side. I don't let go of his hand as I say, "Well, please, continue. I'd love to see where this plan takes us."

I glance at Cannon from the corner of my eye as we walk into the building to rent bows and arrows. He looks good with his gray hoodie and black jacket, but it's his joggers that send my mind to deep, dark places. They remind me of the joggers that sit low on someone else's hips.

"Ready?" Cannon asks, snapping me out of my wandering thoughts.

I literally jump and hold out my hand for the weapon. "Yep. Yep. I'm ready. Let's go pretend the target is Jace's grumpy face."

He shakes his head and laughs, leading me to the back of the building where several individual shooting ranges are lined up with targets at each end. We set down our quivers and Cannon walks me through some basics. He's a great teacher—patient, descriptive, and very hands on when he shows me how to nock an arrow.

"This is going to take some upper body strength, so don't get too frustrated if you fall short the first few times you shoot," he says from behind me, helping me aim at the target.

I hold back my grin. Even without regular exercise, I have upper body strength for days compared to a human, but I do have a feeling my aim *is* going to suck. I let him guide my arm to assist with the aiming. When I let go of the arrow, although it's nowhere near the target, it hits the board with a loud *thump*.

I look over my shoulder at him and smile. "What were you saying about falling short?"

He holds his hands up and smiles. "Not a damn thing. You might be a natural at this. Let's just hope that you're not begging for your arms to fall off tomorrow."

I give him a wink and ready the next arrow. He moves behind me again, adjusting my stance. I shiver when his hand grips my hip and turns it a bit. The small liberty he takes sends my insides fluttering. "Just pretend the middle is Jace with that exasperated look on his face when you don't do something just the way he likes it, and let it fly."

I snort and say, "All right. I think I can do that." I draw my elbow back, and when the arrow is ready to fly, I release it, and this time it sails all the way to the board and hits the bottom of the target.

Cannon laughs and wraps his arm around my waist, pulling me against him. "Well, at least you shot him in the balls."

"So, you think I'm a threat with a bow and arrow?"

"Oh, you're absolutely a threat. There's something hot about a woman who can wield a weapon."

My face lights up at the compliment. When I was younger, my brothers were always faster and stronger. I remember my father patting them on the back when they perfected more complex training moves. It was hard not to feel jealous in those moments. For the first time, I feel like I could receive that same praise from my father.

"I just might start walking around with a quiver and bow. It would be pretty badass."

Cannon raises an eyebrow and chuckles. "That would be intimidating to future suitors. Which might not be a bad thing for me; I'd have a clear path."

"You're the only 'suitor' who hasn't ever stood me up or gone running for the hills. Or wasn't boring as hell."

He purses his lips and lifts his fingers to a curl that hangs in front of my eye. Brushing it back he says, "It's a shame for the other guys. They have no clue that they're missing out on spending time with an amazing woman. Have I told you how much I like being around you?"

My skin flushes and I reach up to capture his fingers with mine. "A time or two. But I wouldn't mind hearing it again."

"I like being around you, Desi. It doesn't matter what we do, just being in your presence is enough. Watching movies, eating dinner, shooting arrows into fake Jace's junk, it's all fun."

He's right; it is fun. Hanging out with Cannon is like spending the day with my best friend. It's comfortable and easy. We can talk about anything or nothing at all and never have an awkward moment. It's been a while since I felt that way around someone.

"I know what you mean," I say, taking a seat on the bench against the wall and resting the bow between my knees. Cannon sits down beside me and places his hand on my leg, his thumb moving in comforting circles. "You like hanging out with me better than Jace?" I lean into him, shoving his shoulder playfully.

He rolls his eyes, seeing my question for what it is. I'm feeling a little down after my fight with Jace, and I just need to know that what went on between us isn't because I'm unlikeable. It's stupid and childish, but I can't help feeling that way.

"You and Jace aren't on the same playing field. In fact, you two are very different pastimes. He's LARPing, and you're ice skating, with tight outfits and extremely entertaining maneuvers. Both are fun to watch and keep me intrigued."

"LARPing?"

"It's people in costumes pretending—it's nerdy, very nerdy."

"So I'm just not as nerdy as he is?" I tilt my head back and forth. "I guess I can go with that." I sigh and lay my head on his shoulder. "I just wish he weren't so angry all the time, ya know? There have been a few times when we've all gotten along so well, and I've had so much fun with *both* of you. I wish it could be like that all the time."

He stretches his neck so he can see my face. "Is that a hint of longing I hear? I'd almost venture to say you like Jace more than you're letting on."

I chew the inside of my cheek as my face heats. "I—well, that didn't really come out right. I didn't mean, like, in *that* way. I just meant—"

"He *is* good looking."

"You're good looking."

"He owns a business and drives a BMW."

I flick my wrist at him and shake my head. "Not that either of those things matter, but you drive a pretty killer Lexus."

"He watches you whenever he's eating that sugary cereal he loves."

"Peanut butter puffs." I jerk my head away from his shoulder. "I know because he asks me to buy them whenever I go to the grocery store."

Cannon hums and crosses his arms. "I get it, Desi. Like I told you from the very beginning, he's been hurt. I understand not wanting to get involved with his personal turmoil, but it doesn't mean you're not attracted to him."

I'm still stuck on what Cannon said. *He watches you whenever he's eating that sugary cereal he loves.*

"What do you mean?" I blurt, unable to stop myself. "What do you mean, he watches me? I'm not just going to let you speed right past that one."

"I mean, maybe he freaks out on you because he's scared to like you. Maybe Jace Wilder is just as confused about you as *you* are about *him.*"

No way is Jace conflicted about me. We spend too much time driving each other up the wall. He's organization and healthy foods and caution. I'm chaos. He didn't even want me to move into his house. I begged him until he couldn't say no.

"And what about you?" I ask. "How do you feel about all of this?"

He licks his lips and pivots his body toward mine. "I like you, Desi. A lot. But I understand that dating is new to you. I'm not looking to make you choose. You do what makes you happy. If you like spending time with me like this, then let's continue to do it. And if you decide you want to take things further, know I'm a willing participant."

Is it really that simple? After all the terrible dates, men standing me up, the run-in with Patrick at the club, Cannon is willing to just let me run the show? Let me make the decisions? Maybe this dating thing isn't so hard after all.

"Okay. That's fair." My stomach rumbles, and I place my hand over it with a giggle. "But right now, can we go get food? I'm starved."

"Deal. Let's go find some fried pickles."

NINE
DESI

I lean back in the lounger and take a sip of my wine. The trees surrounding Jace's backyard wear half their leaves in burnt orange. The other half litter the ground or blow in the late fall breeze. Today will be one of the last days to comfortably sit outside and watch the sun set. It won't be long before the mornings are frosty and snow covers the ground. It will be like the chill I've felt from Jace over the past week. We haven't spoken more than a few words, most of which are *Can you get cereal at the store?* or *Please turn down the TV*. And to make things more awkward, Cannon has been in and out of town for business, so our buffer is gone.

"And then she got in her face and had the nerve to tell her if she didn't like it, she could take her ass home. Can you believe—" Meredith's eyes go wide and her mouth drops. It's the first time she's stopped talking in the past twenty-five minutes. "Oh wow. Where is that little beefcake off to tonight?"

I look over my shoulder just in time to see Jace rounding the corner toward his BMW. I turn back to face her and cross my arms over my chest, pretending I don't notice how delectable he looks in his suit. "I don't know, and to be honest, I don't really care."

"Oh no. Is there trouble on Fantasy Island?"

I snicker at Meredith's ridiculous name for the house. She says I'm living the dream of millions of women—a clean house, no kids, and two hot single men under one roof.

"Oh, no, everything is peachy. If you don't count the fact that Jace is a type-A, overbearing neat freak who has ridiculously high standards that *no one* can ever live up to. We got in a fight because I used his bathtub without asking—which now that I say it out loud does sound kind of bad. After that, he shrank all five pairs of the new jeans you helped me pick out. And then, he and I almost—" I stop and shake my head. "He's just been a jerk, and I'm sick of it."

Meredith takes a sip of her red wine. "I'm trying to live vicariously through you, and you're destroying my fantasies. This domestic situation of yours is starting to sound like married life."

"Sorry," I grumble, pulling my chunky sweater closed. "He's impossible."

She picks up the wine bottle between us and tips it upside down. Not a single drop falls out. "And to top it off, we're out of wine."

"Oh no, not tonight. That is unacceptable." I hop up from the lounger and beckon for her to follow me through the French doors. I have every intention of raiding Jace's liquor cabinet when I stop short. A large white box sits on the counter. It wasn't there when Meredith and I went outside earlier.

When she stretches on her tiptoes to look at the top of the box, her shirt lifts and I spy a telltale mark that's hidden halfway under the waist of her jeans. My eyes widen but I don't have time to confirm the design before she exclaims, "Hey, it has your name on it!"

Sure enough, my name is written in neat handwriting on the tag stuck to the top. I set my glass on the counter, lift the lid, and move the tissue paper to reveal what's underneath.

Seven pairs of jeans. The first pair I pull out is a size fourteen, curvy, long length—the exact size and measurements I need. My jaw drops as I inspect each pair, finding that every one of them is the right size, and each one is a different wash; the two extra ones are new washes I hadn't even seen before, both extremely flattering and exactly something I'd wear.

I draw my bottom lip between my teeth as I pick up the white card at the bottom of the box.

> Desideria,
>   I'm truly sorry about your clothing. It's been a while since I had a woman in my house, with all the rules about laundry and such. I was honestly just trying to help, and I fucked up. Please accept these as a replacement, plus two extra for my general dickishness.
>   I left you a bottle of wine on the counter. Enjoy a quiet night to yourself—or share it with Meredith. I'm sure she'd be up to hanging out tonight.
>   Jace

My lips part as I wordlessly hand Meredith the card. I lift the bottle he left for us and inspect the label. It's too expensive for just sitting around and getting drunk. This is the kind of wine people drink on special occasions.

"Oh yes, Fantasy Island is back in full swing. Jeremy would have just handed me the credit card and told me to buy new jeans. This boy did it for you. If I were single and he would give dating a chance again, I'd be all over him."

"I—"

Dating Jace. Yeah, right. The only kind of dating Jace does is fake dating to impress potential investors at charity dinners.

Oh no.

Tonight is the charity dinner I was supposed to attend with him as his *charming girlfriend*! No matter how pissed I am, I know how important this is to him; there's no way I would purposely screw this up.

"Meredith! I was supposed to go with Jace to a charity thing tonight for his business! An investor invited me week before last when he saw us out at a bar—it's a long story, but that's where he was going earlier!"

"Are you telling me you have a fake date to attend?" I nod and she grabs my hand, pulling me to the stairs. "This is Grade-A romance novel stuff. You are going to that ball, and I'm about to be your fairy godmother."

I don't even have time to think about the fact that Meredith might actually be my *demon* godmother before she whisks me up to my room.

An hour later, I'm strolling into one of the nicest hotels in downtown Denver wearing the green silk dress that Jace thought looked *nice* on me; tonight, I hope it elicits a bigger reaction. My red curls are piled on top of my head, and my makeup is impeccable. Tonight, I want to impress Jace's colleagues, make it up to him for not being here from the start.

He extended an olive branch; now it's my turn.

At first glance, I don't see him anywhere. The room is packed with men in suits and women in elegant gowns. I scan the crowd again, looking for a head of messy brown hair. What if he was embarrassed to show up alone after the fuss Matt made about him bringing me? It'll take a long time to forgive myself if I let him down.

I slide through the crowd, hoping that he didn't pass up this opportunity. Tables with floral centerpieces and fine china are situated around the outskirts of the dance floor. I take in each face until my gaze falls on a man with his back to me. He nods at the others seated at the table with him, and I suck in a quick breath when he turns his head to the side, giving me a glimpse of him.

Jace's hair is combed away from his face, and he's not wearing his black-rimmed glasses. The men carry on a conversation while he nurses a beer, disengaged from the discussion. Gathering my courage, I sneak up behind him and trail my fingers along his shoulder and across his back.

"Hey, baby, fancy meeting you here," I murmur.

He spins around in his seat and his stubble-covered jaw goes slack. His slate-gray eyes sweep over me from head to toe. This time I don't have to ask him what he thinks about my dress; it's clearly doing its part. "Desideria, I thought—"

"My plans fell through, and now I get to be exactly where I want to be tonight."

He opens and closes his mouth before shaking his head like he's clearing the cobwebs out of it. "Gentlemen, if you'll excuse me," he says, standing and looping my arm in his. "What are you doing here?"

"What do you mean, what am I doing here?" I ask sweetly, running my palm up and down his arm. "I'm your girlfriend, how could I miss this?"

"The jeans weren't meant to bribe you. I really am sorry that I lost it on you the other day. It was a dick move, and I wanted to replace what I ruined. I told you before that you didn't have to come tonight, and I meant it. You don't need to fake that you're my girlfriend."

I take his hand and tug him out to the dance floor, folding myself in his arms and gazing up at his face. "Thank you for the jeans. I didn't think they were a bribe, I thought they were a sweet gesture and a heartfelt apology." I adjust so we are in a more traditional dancing position, and his hand slides to my waist as I settle my arms around his neck. "And as far as 'faking' being your girlfriend, I guess you're an okay guy *some* of the time, so it won't be *that* hard to do. Plus, I said I'd help you, and I intend to keep my word."

Jace falls silent and grips my waist tighter. "I don't deserve it after the way I reacted. Thank you."

Before I have a chance to reply, he takes my hand, lifting it over my head, and sends me into a spin. When I'm back in his arms, he leads me in a smooth box step to the beat of the seven-piece orchestra. I wasn't expecting him to actually be able to dance. Cannon acted like dancing was some kind of plague to be avoided at all costs. Being less outgoing than Cannon, I assumed Jace would feel the same, but once again, he surprises me.

"Where did you learn to dance like this?" I ask. "I thought I was a decent dancer, but you make me look like a toddler on wobbly legs."

He laughs and the sound vibrates through me. I haven't heard that sound nearly enough. I like it. Judging by the goosebumps on my arms and the sudden ache between my legs, I like it a little *too* much. I force the sensation away and focus my attention on him.

"My mother owned a dance studio in Colorado Springs. I spent my summers helping her with classes. A lot of the time there wasn't a boy to dance with the girls, so I got *volunteered*."

The image of a younger version of Jace being told to dance with random girls for the purpose of teaching lessons makes me smile. "That's pretty cute," I say as he twirls me around the dance floor.

I'm so lost in thought and distracted by my body's reaction to his proximity that it takes me far too long to notice that no one else is dancing. Instead, a large group has gathered to watch us.

"Oh shit," I mutter between clenched teeth, my face flaming. "Everyone is watching us."

Jace glances around and cocks a brow. "Not us, *you.*" I sweep my gaze over the delighted faces studying us and open my mouth to tell him he's exaggerating, but he continues talking. "I can't deny that there's something otherworldly about you. The magical glow of your eyes, your striking red hair, and Cannon was right, you do look stunning in this dress."

I'm surprised. Not just surprised but floored. All those nights ago when I thought he wasn't really paying attention, he was. It appears my dress had made an impression on him, and it's doing the same thing tonight. I should pat myself on the back for finding the courage to wear it again. I almost bypassed it for something more muted, but I threw caution to the wind and snatched it from my closet.

"You know no one can hear us, right? You don't have to lay it on quite so thick," I say, keeping a smile on my face.

"I'm not. This is my moment of truth with you. Let me have it."

I swallow and say, "Okay. I will. And thank you."

As we continue to move around the dance floor, I can't ignore the warmth radiating from him or the hard muscles under his crisp white shirt or the way his slacks hug his legs. Everything from the way his suit fits to the innocent brush of his hand on my lower back reminds me that the last time we were this close was during a highly charged moment—we exchanged heated words, we invaded each other's personal space, and we almost kissed. Our lips brushed—soft, rosy lips that are now right in my line of sight. A mouth that has piqued my curiosity. Can Jace Wilder kiss as well as he dances?

The song ends and the crowd erupts in applause. I step out of the circle of Jace's arms and shove my renegade thoughts into the dark corner of my mind. I slam the door shut on them and double lock it. It is one thing to admire Jace's body, although that was a creepy accident, and another to imagine kissing him. It's a line I don't believe he wants to cross with me, no matter how much he stares at me while eating cereal.

Jace and I both give our audience shy smiles and move to exit the floor.

He leans into me and whispers, "I'll be right back, okay?"

"Okay, I'll be here." An upbeat song I love starts playing and I sway my hips to the beat as everyone else moves back out. "Right here, dancing!"

He nods once before rushing off in the direction of the bathroom, leaving me to wonder if I did something wrong.

But instead of stressing about it, I just close my eyes and let the music sweep me away.

TEN
JACE

The door to the men's room hits the wall as I barrel through it. A man at the sink stares at me in the mirror while washing his hands. I flash a tight smile his way, masking the anxiety that's tightening my chest, and lock myself in the last stall. As soon as I'm alone I push out the air I was holding in my lungs. My hand fumbles with my tie, and I release the top button of my shirt. Why is it so hot in here?

I press my ass to the wall, bend at the waist, and grip my knees. So many eyes on me, watching my every move. They must know Desi and I are faking it. What would a woman like her be doing with me? They're going to tell Matt, and he's going to be pissed that I didn't tell him the truth. He's going to pull the funds.

Deep in the back of my mind I know every single thought I'm having is irrational. No one out there knows anything about my dating life except for Desi. She's here for me and has no intention of letting them in on our secret. But none of those rational thoughts are as loud as the ones sending me into a panic.

"Breathe," I tell myself, doing my best to bring myself to a place of peace, planting my palm on the wall across from me.

I count inside my head, not wanting anyone to walk out of here talking about the weirdo who likes to count while he's shitting in the last stall. With each number, my breathing evens out and my muscles relax.

My panic had been mounting ever since I left the house. I was walking into this dinner without the reason I was invited in the first place. Small talk, especially with strangers, isn't my thing. Add in the pressure I was feeling to fit in and impress, and I'm surprised I didn't spontaneously combust the second I set foot in the ballroom. All the stress that had me teetering on the edge evaporated the moment I saw Desi. It was such a relief that I almost burst into tears. Like she knew exactly what I needed, she brought me onto the dance floor, and every negative feeling faded away. I was captivated by her—the way she felt in my arms, the playful smile on her lips, how her body moved with mine. For a brief moment, it was just her and me . . . until it wasn't.

I release a gust of air that rattles my lips, stand up straight, and exit the stall. At the sink I wash my hands and splash cool water on my face. Ripping two towels from the dispenser, I dry off before meeting my reflection in the mirror.

"She's got this, just follow her lead and everything will be all right," I say, straightening my shirt and tie.

Feeling like myself again, I head back out.

When I reach the edge of the dance floor, there's an upbeat song playing, and more people are back out there, most of them with ridiculously silly moves that look like something out of a comedy sketch.

But in the middle of them all, spinning in circles with her dress fanning out around her legs, is Desi. Her curls have fallen out of her bun and fly behind her as she dances, joy radiating from her face and laughter spilling from her lips at something the person next to her just said.

She's stunning. Right then, the realization that I'd like to be the one to make her that happy hits me square in the chest, and I want to capture this moment forever. I slide my phone from my pocket and snap a photo of her at the perfect time. Her head is thrown back and she's laughing, the green of her dress bringing out the ginger freckles peppered all over her skin.

Before I can think better of what I just did or convince myself it was too weird, I shove my phone in my pocket and make my way back over to her, gently pushing through the crowd.

"Hey, sorry," I say, running my fingers through my hair. "I just needed a little air."

"That's okay," she says, her voice breathy. "Are you all right?"

"Yeah, I'm good now. I think you deserve a drink after that dance." I hold my arm out to her, and she loops hers around it.

We walk off the dance floor, and she continues to smile. I thought for sure she would sober a bit once I led her away. It's a boost to my ego to know she's happy to leave with me. I'm steering her toward a server holding a silver platter of cocktails when Matt steps into our path.

He wears a wide smile and his hazel eyes crinkle at the side. "Jace, who knew that you could cut a rug? I guess with a spectacular woman on your arm all things are possible." He leans in and presses his cheek to Desi's, kissing the air. "Desi, I'm glad you came and made sure our boy got out of that comfortable shell of his."

She moves away from him and snuggles in at my side. "Are you kidding? I wouldn't have missed this for the world. And besides . . ." She drags her finger all the way down the lapel of my suit coat and traces the waistband of my pants. "I'd never miss a chance to see my man in one of his sexy tailored suits."

If I thought I was going to pass out earlier, I was mistaken. Desi's fingers roaming close to my zipper makes me light-headed. This is not the time for me to faint or to physically show Matt how turned on I am. I give Desi's side a firm pinch and plaster a smile on my face, saying, "The lady has a thing for a man in a suit."

"As she should—you're going to be wearing them more often if you want to build this company. I heard that Bryce Edmonds kid down at Rhode Island School of Design is looking to sign with a smaller firm. He doesn't want to work his way up with the big guys. Your art is gritty and edgy, and he would complement you with his clean lines and bold color choices. That kid is hella talented and could be just what your company needs."

I'm familiar with Bryce Edmonds. Everyone in the industry is. The kid is a genius with a stylus and an iPad. I've spent hours watching the videos he posts on social media of him working. Even the designs he created back in high school were impressive.

I rub my jaw and let my thoughts spill out of my mouth. "Edmonds knows he's good. I've seen him talking in a few digital art forums. He isn't going to settle for a start-up salary even with the potential of becoming a partner in a few years. I'll have to sell my BMW *and* a kidney to afford him."

"Or you can bag him and get yourself a guaranteed investor who'll help with the cost."

"Are you saying—"

"I'll sign the deal if you bring on Edmonds. The two of you together would blow these old assholes out of the water."

It sounds so simple. One person straight out of college. He should be chomping at the bit for any opportunity to work in the industry. But this kid is like a first draft pick for the NFL. Why the hell would he settle for my small design firm?

Desi shakes my arm, her voice brimming with excitement as she says, "Jace, you have to talk to him. He'd be lucky to work with you."

"Listen to her. She makes a lot of sense," Matt adds.

"All right. I'll schedule something with him in a couple of weeks, a video conference first, then later if all goes well, we'll meet up at your office in New York. No matter what it takes, I'll make it work."

Matt holds out his hand. "I look forward to seeing the return on my investment."

I grip his fingers and we shake. "I look forward to making you an even richer man."

He chuckles and gives Desi a mischievous glance. "Treat him good tonight. He deserves it."

She matches his expression and winks. "Don't worry, I'll make sure he's taken care of."

The innuendo sends all kinds of images of how she could do just that racing through my head. God, how I want to act on them and take this charade a little further. My entire body is buzzing, dying for physical attention. I want skin on skin, her mouth, her hands. Nothing but her can sedate the need she's brought to life in me.

"You two have fun. And no more dancing, you stole all the attention from me," Matt says over his shoulder as he walks away.

I slide my hand into my pocket and ensure I'm not showing the entire room how turned on I am. When I'm satisfied that nothing is tenting, I turn to Desi and say, "You're too much, but damn if Matt didn't like it. You just locked down that deal for me."

She snatches a drink from a server and takes a sip. "Nah, you locked down that deal with your reputation and talent. I'm just arm candy."

It's not true. She is so much more than that. But I'm not about to verbally duel it out with her. We already know our arguments tend to get heated.

I take her hand and run my thumb over her knuckles. "Thank you for coming tonight, Desi. I was lost before you got here."

"Of course. I wouldn't have missed it."

"Now, I know Matt said no more dancing, but one more for celebratory purposes won't hurt. May I?" I ask, pulling our clasped fingers to my chest.

She nods with a bright smile, and I sweep her out onto the dance floor.

One dance turns into several. I spin her around and hold her close while she helps herself to a glass of champagne. If I had my way, we would dance all night. I have a reason to have my hands on her and press my body to hers. The minute we walk away, I know I'll never touch her like this again. When the crowd thins, and her dance moves are a little unsteady, it's time to call it a night. We say good night to Matt and the rest of the suits she charmed and make our way to my car.

She giggles as we walk across the parking lot, and I can't help but wonder what's going through her head.

"What?" I ask.

She loops her arm with mine, like she's done all night. "Did we really waste an entire week giving each other the silent treatment over shrunken jeans and the imaginary soap scum you assumed I'd leave in your tub?"

The muscles in my cheek twitch as I fight the urge to laugh. "I'm irrationally disgusted by a ring around my bathtub."

"If you had checked your tub after you yelled at me, Daddy, then you'd have seen that it was perfectly clean and clear of any sign of me," she says sweetly.

I swallow and pull on my tie. I've never asked a woman to call me anything but my name. But the acts that go along with the term *daddy* . . . those I enjoy partaking in.

No, Jace. Keep it light and fun. Desi is your friend. Just your friend.

I open the passenger door for her and say, "Daddy, huh? Keep it up and sneak into my bedroom again, and I'll show you how *daddy* I can be."

"Oh, we're making jokes now?" she says, a throaty giggle escaping her lips. "Don't threaten me with a good time."

Before I shut her door for her, I say, "Yeah, yeah. Remind me to hide that bottle of 'I'm sorry' wine I bought you when we get home."

When I get into the car and shut the door, she grins over at me. "Not a chance. It's already in my special hiding place with my other special . . . *things*."

"Are you talking about the bag of Oreos you hide behind the pots? I've already helped Cannon sneak into that stash a couple of times."

She feigns an offended gasp. "What?! Thief!" Her voice changes to a more serious, deadpan tone. "But, no. I'm talking about my vibrators."

I fight to keep my eyes on the road, gripping the steering wheel so hard my knuckles turn white. Clearing my throat, I manage, "That's an interesting place to keep your wine."

"What can I say? Sometimes I like to feel some full body tingles with my . . . you know . . . *downstairs tingles*."

My heart starts to race, and all I can think about is how embarrassing it will be if I get a boner right here in the car with her. "Desideria, I don't—do you—I don't think this is a good conversation to have with me."

A little gasp of horror comes from her side of the car, and my eyes dart over to her, afraid that something's wrong, that she's somehow hurt.

But she's not. She's just looking over at me with sorrow etched on her features. "Oh, I'm sorry, Jace. I didn't mean to make you uncomfortable."

"I'm fine talking about sex. Despite the myths about nerds never getting any, I'm well versed in the subject. I just find that when that door is opened it's hard to close, and it could complicate situations. Especially when it feels like lines have *already* almost been crossed prior to talking about sex."

"So, we *did* almost cross a line. I didn't read too much into that."

I take a deep breath before speaking. "You were there, Desideria. We were emotional and struggling to rationally voice our frustrations.

I chalk it up to feeling like we lost our minds for a moment. I want you to know that I'd never cross that boundary with you, not when you're looking for the type of relationship I can't give you."

"Of course," she mumbles. "You don't believe in commitment. And that's exactly what I'm here to find. Not that I'd—never mind. You're right. I just want to know what it feels like."

"What?"

"I want to know what it feels like," she says a little louder, and without even looking I know she's turned her whole body to face me. "To be completely desired. Needed. To be kissed so desperately that I lose my breath. I want them to come back for more, desperate to kiss me again. And when they do, I want them in control, for them to tell me what would make them feel good. I don't want to be a fumbling mess. I just want to be theirs for that moment. You know what I mean?"

My blood stills. My heart stops for a moment. Everything freezes. I completely know what she means because that's where I thrive. So much in my life has been outside my control but sex is the one place—other than my art—where I can create an outcome where everyone is happy. It turns me on to dominate in those moments that bring a woman pleasure. But part of what she just said doesn't compute. There's simply no way it can be true.

"Back up a second. You've *never* been kissed? I know you said Cannon was your first date, but you've *never*—"

"I mean, when I was younger, yeah, but every time it was with some sloppy dem—*guy*—and it never meant anything. No more than a messy kiss on the lips with either hardly any tongue or *way* too much tongue. I've never been *really* kissed. Hence, the desire for someone to be in control."

I fall silent because I have no idea what to say. It seems truly impossible that this beautiful creature has not been kissed within an inch of her life. When I finally pull my car into the garage, I cut the engine and turn to her.

"Then I'm glad I didn't cross that line with you the other day. I would have let you down, and I don't want to be on that list of meaningless kisses from guys who never returned for more. You deserve better than that."

Her sharp inhale cuts me to the bone. She opens the car door and jumps out, pulling her heels off as she goes. "Thank you for tonight, Jace. I had a great time," she says, her voice suspiciously thick, as she runs into the house without looking back.

Fuck. Well, it's clear that she took what I said the wrong way. Like I wouldn't *want* to kiss her. Like I wouldn't *kill* to come back for more. When the exact opposite is true.

But she can never, ever know that. I won't hurt her that way.

Or myself.

I lean back against the headrest and close my eyes. This is the exact thing I never wanted to happen. When hormones and sex get involved, things get messy. People get hurt. I've spent my time on the receiving *and* the giving end of that pain. I swore I'd never get twisted in that kind of emotion after everything that happened to me, but it appears I'm the clown who's caught himself in that trap again.

ELEVEN
DESI

I feel so foolish. I should have never let the alcohol go to my head and flirted so much with Jace. I mean, yeah, he made the "daddy" comment, but he was clearly joking and of course I took things too far. And then to tell him I've never *kissed* anyone before?! Ugh, he probably thinks I'm such a loser. No wonder he felt like he had to let me down easy and tell me it wouldn't be a good idea for us to be more than friends.

I let myself into my room and swing my arm behind me, slamming my door shut with my power. With an aggressive sweep of my hand, my curtains race across the rod, colliding in the center. I kick my shoes off and focus on the zipper on the back of my dress. It slides down with little effort and my dress ends up in a pile at my feet.

It's a release to use my power. I've spent weeks bottling it up and acting like a human. My lazy nature isn't made for loading dishwashers and folding clothes by hand. I'm like a fish running on land when I thrive floating in the water. All that pent-up energy along with the sting of rejection is too much to contain.

It hurt when Jace said if he kissed me, he would never come back for more. Am I so easy to discard? The way all my dates turn out seems to say I am. My self-confidence is already raw, and with every word Jace said, he picked at the open wound until it bled.

After putting on a satin nightgown, I wiggle my finger at the clothes on the floor. My dress and undergarments float to the laundry basket, and my shoes slide across the carpet until they sit side by side inside my closet. I dust off my palms, like I've just spent hours tackling the dirtiest of jobs. Desperate for something to ease my stress, I will my oil diffuser to turn on. The room fills with the calming scent of lavender and a soft blue light. I fall onto my bed and motion for the lights to turn off.

When I'm as comfortable as I can get in my agitated state, my power pulls back the curtains. I turn on my side, my gaze drifting to Jace's bedroom. The light is still off, signaling that he either hasn't come upstairs yet or he already went to sleep while I was getting ready for bed.

I doubt the latter is true. I've been slyly watching him every night for weeks now, learning his routine, and there's no way he did everything he needs to do in that amount of time. He always turns his blankets and sheets down first, as if prepping his bed for his entry. Then he separates all his laundry from the day, takes a shower, does a set of stretches, and reads for a while before finally turning out the light.

He hasn't come up for the night. I wonder what he's doing down there. I hold back a laugh that turns into a snort. Probably sipping on disgusting grass juice and contemplating the next video game he should buy.

As if on cue, I hear his footsteps on the stairs. They're slow, almost unsteady, like he's trying to decide which way to go. I close my eyes and hold my breath as I wait for a knock at my door. I'm not sure why he'd come talk to me; I think we said all that needed to be said tonight. But then he starts walking again, heading across the house into his bedroom and shutting the door behind him. I exhale deeply and let my eyelids flutter open.

Covered by the veil of night, I watch as the light clicks on and he enters his bedroom. He's distracted by something on his phone and doesn't so much as spare a glance at his window. But that's no different than usual. He doesn't pay attention on a regular night; I'm not sure that he even realizes our rooms share this view. Unbuttoning his dress shirt, he walks into his bathroom.

But something strange happens after that. He comes back out a few seconds later in nothing but his black boxer briefs, running his fingers through his chestnut hair, causing it to stand in different directions. His thumb is still swiping across his phone's screen, which is highly unusual. He hasn't taken a shower, turned down his bed, or separated his laundry. I'm choosing to ignore how creepy it is that I know his routine that well.

My gaze drifts below his waistline, and my thighs clench with desire, a gasp escaping my lips. Jace's nightly routine has gone out the window because whatever he's looking at has given him a massive erection.

"Fuck," I whisper, drawing my bottom lip between my teeth.

He paces the room, and not once does he look up from his phone. He fidgets between slipping his hand down to adjust himself and rubbing his palm along the back of his neck. It's almost as if he's conflicted.

What's got you all riled up, Wilder?

The pacing stops and he stares down at his erection, which is still alive and well. I swear he tilts his head enough that he can see my window from the corner of his eye. Like he's made up his mind about something, he marches across his room and slams his hand against the light switch on the wall.

The room goes dim but not dark. The bathroom light is still on, casting everything in a buttery glow. He walks to the foot of his bed and tosses his phone on the mattress before falling back beside it. I lift my head from my pillow and examine the profile of his body. He lies there with his feet touching the ground and his arms at his side for what feels like several minutes. The screen goes dark, and I wonder if he fell asleep. All of this is so unlike him.

My question is answered when his head slowly turns my way. I drop down, landing in an awkward position. My heart hammers in my chest, and I freeze. He didn't see me. There's no way he knows I'm awake. My diffuser light isn't that strong, is it?

I inch my head in his direction, hoping his gaze has moved away. I suck in a sharp breath. He's still facing me, and his hand is drifting down his abdomen. I should turn my back and ignore what he's doing.

But I don't.

The overwhelming desire to match his movements has the back of my fingers brushing over the swells of my breasts. I take in a sudden breath when I feel how hard my nipples are through the satin, and I can't help but turn my hand over and pinch them once, my lips parting with a whimper. Keeping my eyes on him, I slide one hand down my stomach to match his, but instead of stopping, I slide my fingers just beneath the waistband of my lacy panties, running them over the silky, soaking wet skin between my thighs.

My breathing stops as I wait to see what he'll do next. He follows my lead. The tips of his fingers inch beneath his waistband. He swipes them back and forth, teasing himself before his entire hand disappears inside. The black material of his underwear leaves nothing to the imagination. His fingers curl around his hard length. He tips his head back, and I swear he lets out a drawn-out *fuck*.

I stop teasing myself and press my thumb to my clit, sliding two fingers inside my slick entrance, and I'm unable to stop the moan that slips from my lips. The need I'd been feeling for Jace boils to the surface and there's no more holding it back. Not when it feels like he's watching me as he pleasures himself.

Taking my bottom lip between my teeth, I rub harder and my back bows off the bed as my legs begin to shake. But I don't take my eyes off him. All I can think of is how I wish it was his hands on me, and that this is the first time I'm openly acknowledging that I have thought of him every time I've touched myself for the past three weeks.

He locks eyes with me, and the space separating us disappears. It's like the pool that our rooms overlook vanishes into a black hole. His window becomes my window, and we're right beside each other. The languid strokes of his hand pick up speed and his lips part. His mouth is so perfect, those sharp peaks of his cupid's bow. I want to know how his kisses taste.

His mouth moves and I hear the words as if he's whispering them in my ear. *Come for me.*

I can't stop myself from unraveling. I cry out as the little coils in my lower abdomen unfurl and every nerve ending in my body crackles with pleasure. But I don't close my eyes like I ordinarily would. I keep them on him and say his name. I *beg* him to let go.

Jace . . . please.

He curls into himself, his chin resting on his chest. The muscles in his abdomen flex and he grits his teeth. His hand stops on an upward stroke, and he trembles. It is so damn beautiful to see him falling apart.

Jace's arms fall lifelessly to his sides, and he stares at his ceiling fan. He remains like that, his chest rapidly moving up and down. When his breathing slows, he looks my way again and tips his chin. His mouth forms the words *thank you* before he stands up and vanishes into his bathroom.

He's thanking *me*? Damn, I should be on my knees—*well*, I'd like to be.

But I have a feeling what just happened between us is the closest I will ever get to touching him. And I'll just have to be okay with that.

TWELVE
DESI

Cannon and I sit across from each other at our favorite sports bar with a basket of fried pickles between us. He has this sixth sense when it comes to me needing some quality time with a friend. He barely had the words *fried pickles* out of his mouth before I'd grabbed my purse and was out the door.

The house was feeling stuffy with the lingering question of what happened last night. Jace went about his routine like it was no big deal. He drank his green vomit morning smoothie after working out and asked me if I had plans for the day. We exchanged small talk until he reminded me to rinse out my bowl and start the dishwasher before retreating to his office. At no point was there a good opportunity to work in a casual *Hey, did we watch each other masturbate last night?*

I'm wondering if my imagination was playing tricks on me. Because if it wasn't, how could he be so indifferent about it? When people talk about the elephant in the room, no elephant is bigger than watching your roommate get off.

"So, are you going to talk to me about what's bothering you?" Cannon asks, popping a pickle drenched in ranch dressing into his mouth.

"What do you mean?" I ask too quickly, cramming another pickle in right behind the one I just ate, washing them both down with a big gulp of Diet Coke.

He laughs and takes a swig of his beer. "You're inhaling those pickles like you may never see them again after tonight. And you've hardly said a word all day. Come on, tell me. You'll feel better."

"Okay, okay. So last night was the charity dinner with Jace, right?"

"Yeah, he said you two had a good time, really charmed Matt."

"We did. Matt basically said he'd back Jace's company if he signed this Edmonds guy, so it was a success."

Cannon stares at me blankly with a pickle dangling between his fingers. "So . . . I'm a little lost on what the problem is."

"Hold on, sir. Be patient."

Cannon sits back in his seat and devours the pickle. "Yes, ma'am, please continue."

"Jace and I had a really good time. . . we danced. A lot. And we drank. No wait, he didn't drink, but I did. I had a little too much champagne."

"Desi?" he says, lifting his brows in a way that tells me to get to the point.

"We were flirting, and it sort of got a little bit out of control."

Cannon sits forward, his blue eyes lighting up. "Oh? Wait, wait. Are you about to tell me I was right? That Jace is attracted to you?"

My face reddens and I look down at the table, suddenly very interested in the place mat. "I—"

Cannon's chuckle has a devious tone as he slides over to my side of the booth and tips my chin up with his finger. "Spill it."

"Basically, I made it clear that I wanted to kiss someone, and I wanted it to be him. And *he* made it clear that would never happen. I was embarrassed, ran upstairs to my room, and went to bed. But then . . ." I take a deep breath and continue. "I noticed that when he came to bed, he didn't follow the same routine as—"

Cannon cuts me off. "Wait. Are you saying you can see into his room?"

"Yeah," I say with a sheepish shrug. "He can see into mine too . . . that's what this is about, actually."

"How so?"

"I . . . I think . . . I think Jace and I used each other to get off last night, and not just with mental images. I think we watched each other through our bedroom windows," I blurt, all my words running together. As soon as I finish the sentence, I drop my head into my arms on the table, mortified.

"Oh!" Cannon stares straight ahead and eats another pickle.

"Oh? Oh!" I throw my hands up, catching his attention again. "Come on, Cannon. I need some help working through this. The man is acting like nothing happened. I'm starting to think something was in my drink last night, and I made it all up."

He stays quiet for a moment and from the lines on his forehead, I can tell he's really thinking it through. After taking a gulp of beer, he says, "What did you expect him to do this morning, come downstairs, give you a kiss, and say thanks for the peep show?"

I open my mouth to come back with a snarky remark, but snap it shut. What *did* I expect Jace to do? He didn't make it awkward. He just didn't bring it up, but neither did I. If I couldn't find the right moment, maybe he couldn't either.

Propping my chin in my palm, I toss another pickle in my mouth. "I don't know. It's just weird that he would turn me down for a kiss but want to share something so intimate with me."

"I don't think he planned it, Desi. The urge hit him, and you happened to be watching."

"But he watched me too. And it was . . . it was more than just watching. It was like we were following each other's leads. Like we were actually together. I could see his mouth moving, and I could tell what he was saying. And he was telling me what—" My voice cracks and I clench my thighs under the table. "He was telling me what to do."

"I can't speak for Jace. All I can say is welcome to the complexities of men."

"But I know you would have said something to me, so it can't just be the 'complexities of men.'"

He nods like I've made a good point. "Let me rephrase. Welcome to the complexities of damaged people."

I groan and press my fingers to my eyes. I don't have time for complicated. Especially from a man who isn't even in the running to be my eternal partner. What I need right now is honesty and clear signals. Jace shouldn't be taking up space in my head.

"Why can't these guys be more like you? You're not damaged."

"Trust me, I have my issues." Cannon runs his hand back and forth over my shoulder blades. "Talk to him, Desi. I still stand by my belief that he's reasonable. Get it off your chest and move on."

I lay my head on his shoulder and sigh. "Fine. I'll talk to him. But only because I want us to move on from this so that I can continue doing what I need to do."

"I hope that isn't peeping through *my* window," he says, lifting one side of his mouth in a playful smile.

I scrunch my face in embarrassment and groan, "It's not."

"Good. Let's get out of here. I have to get up early for a business trip."

He throws a wad of money on the table, and I hold out a neatly folded bill to pay for my portion. He swats my hand away, refusing to let me pay again. It's sweet, but nights like these aren't dates. We're friends chatting about life, and it feels wrong not to contribute in some way. I slide the money into the side pocket of my wallet, deciding that I'm going to keep it for a day when I can treat him.

Once we're in the car, I realize I've never asked Cannon a really basic question. "What is it you do for a living? You're *always* working, whether at the office or out of town on a business trip."

Cannon turns the radio to his favorite '90s station and says, "I help people organize their business."

I bite my lips between my teeth and nod, holding back my laughter. Cannon has a difficult time following the basic rules in the house. It's hard to believe that my disorderly friend advises others on how to keep their business organized.

"I know what you're thinking and stop. I'm on my way to becoming the top dog."

"The king of organization. How fitting." This time I do laugh.

Cannon rolls his eyes, but he smiles at the same time. "It's going to happen. It's the reason I rented a room from Jace. Once I'm at the top, I most likely won't stay here. Off to bigger and better."

When I get myself under control, I say, "That's honestly impressive, Cannon. You certainly deserve whatever promotion you're working toward because you're always busy doing something for your career. I commend you on that. All I do is unload the dishwasher and look for a boyfriend."

"I'm sure all the chores and man searching will lead to bigger things. It sounds like your father will be happy if you pull it off."

"*He* will be, but the question is, will *I* be happy?"

"I think that's solely up to you, Desi. No one can control your happiness but you."

If only I could have control over my whole life. If every decision I ever made could be my own. But that will never be the case. I'll always have to play by my realm's rules.

And right now, those rules are really messing with my future.

When we get inside the house, I say, "Thank you for taking me to eat and getting my mind off everything for a little bit. I needed that advice from you too. It's a little embarrassing how clueless I am when it comes to all this stuff."

He smiles and pulls me in for a hug. "No need to be embarrassed,

Desi. You'll figure out how to navigate it all. You're just in an atypical situation. Cut yourself some slack."

"Yeah, I'll get right on that," I say under my breath, and Cannon just chuckles, kissing me on the forehead.

"Get some rest, Desi."

"Yeah, you too."

After Cannon goes to bed, I look around with a sigh. It's my week to clean the living room and do the bathroom and kitchen laundry, and I haven't gotten around to either yet. It's late, but my nagging thoughts will make it impossible to sleep. Since Jace and Cannon are both in their rooms for the night, I can get things done the easy way and burn off some steam.

After changing out of my jeans and into more comfy clothes, I plop onto the couch with my phone and begin my chores.

I point at the vacuum on the stairs with one finger, sending it back and forth from one step to the next. With my other hand, I use my thumb to scroll through my favorite clothing website while barely lifting my index finger to take care of the bath towels in the laundry basket. They float in the air, folding themselves into squares and dropping into another empty basket one by one. I sway my foot gently through the air, directing the feather duster over the TV and electronics.

At this rate, my chores will be done in five minutes flat, and I can go upstairs to—

"What in the fucking magical ass Mary Poppins trippy shit is this?" Jace's voice floats in from the kitchen, and my heart stops.

I spring to my feet, and the towel drops back into the basket, the vacuum topples down the stairs, and the feather duster falls to the floor with a clack, my concentration broken. "I—uh—I—what are you doing? I thought you were in bed?" I croak.

Jace rubs his eyes with one hand and tugs at his hair with the other. "Do I look any kind of off to you? Is my skin a sickly color? Do you think someone spiked my drink? Fuck! How do I tell a client that one of their employees slipped me a hallucinogen?" Jace falls onto one of the barstools and yanks on his tie, as if it's strangling him. "Their marketing director gave me the creeps. I should have changed seats. Fuck. Fuck. Fuck. I *drove home* like this." He pulls at the collar of his dress shirt and several of the buttons pop off. His face has now turned a sickly color and sweat beads his brow.

I toss my phone to the couch and rush across the room. I have no idea where he's been, but I know he needs to calm down. "Jace, I need you to breathe," I say, invading his space and placing my palms on his knees. "You didn't get drugged. You're fine. I promise you, okay?" He doesn't meet my eyes, and I place two fingers under his chin and lift his gaze to mine. "Do you hear me?"

"I can't . . . I can't go through that again. And if I hurt someone . . . I can't, Desi."

My eyebrows knit together, and I forget my situation for the moment. "Go through what? Jace, what are you talking about? You didn't hurt anyone," I whisper, sliding my hand from his chin up his cheek and into his hair. He shakes underneath my touch, and I shift so I'm a bit closer to him. "Jace, talk to me."

"I can't get into a car accident. I couldn't live through that again."

My skin tightens and my heart squeezes. Before I know what I'm doing, I'm reaching out and brushing my fingers against the material on his shirt, right over where I know the scar is. I didn't have much time to think about it the day I first saw the mangled skin. Everything got out of hand so quickly. But the seconds I spent looking at it were enough to know something terrible happened to him.

"This scar. It's from a car accident?"

He nods while gulping down air. His eyes are rimmed red with tears waiting to fall. I've never seen him so freaked out before. Up until this moment, I believed that Jace Wilder was unshakable.

His breathing isn't getting any steadier, and my worry is mounting. "Slow down your breathing, Jace. You're scaring me with how much air you're gulping down. Do you want some water? What can I do for you? I don't want to crowd you. Some people want someone close to them in times like this, some people don't."

He takes my hands and presses my palms to the back of his head. "Rub. Slow."

While my fingers graze his scalp, he rests his forehead to my chest and presses his hands flat to my back. His breathing slows as does his trembling. We remain like that for several minutes before he takes a deep breath and says, "I'm sorry."

"No. Don't apologize, Jace," I say, continuing my scalp massage. "I want to be there for you. You've been there for me when I've needed you; let me return the favor."

He lifts his head and the crease between his eyes is so deep. "Tell me what the hell is going on. What I saw can't be real."

I close my eyes and take a step away from him, dropping my hands to my sides. I can't tell him what I am. My father was *very* clear about that before I left. He gave me permission to tell one human, and that person had to be my eternal partner. It made sense at the time. He would have to know what I am and where he'll spend the rest of eternity. Angels and demons may influence humans to see the value in what we can offer after this life, but we should never do something that jeopardizes them making the decision for themselves. Telling Jace that I'm a demon could put his eternal happiness at risk.

"I don't want to put you in a panic again," I say in all honesty.

"Desideria, I *will* spiral again if you don't give me an explanation. Don't let me make up my own. I don't want to feel like a fool when there's a simple reason why I saw what I did."

"That's the thing; there *is* a reason, but it's not simple. And telling you could have terrible repercussions on—"

"Just tell me."

The desperation in his voice is like a knife straight to my heart. He needs the truth to gain control of his emotions. If I don't explain what I am, Jace could end up in a worse place than he was a minute ago. I don't want to be the reason he endures that type of pain again.

"Okay. Hang in here with me for a second. Do you believe in angels and demons?" I ask.

He bolts from the stool and shuffles around in the cabinet next to the sink, pulling out an orange prescription bottle. After a short struggle with the childproof cap, he shakes a pill into his palm and slips it under his tongue. Several long seconds pass, and he remains as still as stone. Afraid he's gone into shock, I ease forward but stop when he turns back to me with a steely expression. He crosses his arms and takes several deep breaths, filling his lungs so much his shirt strains against his chest. "Don't fuck with me right now. I'm not in a good place."

I want to square my shoulders and match his demeanor but going head-to-head with him isn't going to make this situation any easier. I'm pretty sure he just had a panic attack. There's no way I can add to his stress. He needs to know that he wasn't seeing things, and that everything will be all right.

I sit on the stool he vacated and fold my hands on the counter. "I'm not fucking with you. I need you to answer the question."

He tosses up his hands and scrunches his nose, clearly not understanding where this conversation is going. "I don't know. I don't discredit the possibility of beings that oversee humans. They haven't been proven, but they haven't been disproven either."

"What if I told you it's not about *overseeing* humans . . . but letting humans prepare to choose what they want for eternity—chaos or peace? Angels are representatives of peace, demons are agents of chaos." Jace just stares at me, so I keep talking. "What you saw when you came in . . . that was me using the power I've been given. Jace, I'm a demon princess from Infernis—sort of like the realm humans call Hell." I hold my breath, waiting for the explosive reaction that is sure to come.

"Perfect. Because I'm the one who will bring balance to the force. Vader is my father."

I roll my eyes when I realize he's referencing *Star Wars*. "No, Jace. This isn't a fantasy movie. I'm telling you the truth."

He paces the length of the kitchen, running his palm over his face. "You sound ridiculous right now."

"Then you tell me what you thought you saw," I say, sweeping my hand in front of me and giving him center stage.

"I don't know!"

"You do. I just told you I have powers!"

"If you're a demon, where are your horns and tail?"

I scoff. "I didn't take you for someone who makes judgments based on stereotypes. Not all demons have horns and tails. But I'll explain—my family and I are High Demons. We don't have them. A couple of my brothers' eternal partners do, though. What else can I do to prove it to you? Do you want me to use my powers right here?"

He leans against the counter and crosses his arms and ankles. "Sure. I'd love to see what you can do, *demon princess*."

It's written all over his face; he thinks I've lost my mind. He's waiting for a subpar illusion that he'll analyze in order to put me in my place. And then he'll send me packing. I either scare the hell out of him with something amazing and risk him asking me to leave, or I give him what he's expecting, and he gives me the boot because he's scared I'm going to chop him into little pieces while he sleeps.

I place my hands on my hips. "Just so you know, the Circle I'm set to rule isn't exactly the coolest or most badass. I'm basically the princess of the laziest demons and energies in Infernis. So it isn't like I can start fires with my hands or blow things up. But I *can* do this."

I stand straight and turn toward the living room. Raising my hands, I will the 72-inch flatscreen television to come to me, slowly, so he can see exactly what's happening. The wires snap out of the back, left like discarded strings sprawled over the entertainment center. And since my power hasn't failed me once, the TV floats toward us at the desired speed, only coming to a stop at the island, where I set it down behind where Jace had just been leaning so smugly, waiting for me to prove myself.

"Proof enough for you?" I ask, resting my hands back on my hips and lifting my shoulders in a shrug.

He doesn't answer me but asks a question of his own in pure awe. "You can levitate shit?"

"It's more about moving things in my line of sight. You know, not having to lift a finger and all."

"Do it again. But this time can you hook all the wires back up?"

I snort. Not even my powers can take his focus away from a tidy house. I send the television back and the wires move like vines until each is in their designated place. "Do you want to watch me vacuum, dust, and fold again?"

"No, I'm weirded out enough for one day." He steps closer to me. "What about the story about you needing to find a husband? Is that true or do you have a sinister reason for being here?"

I stay rooted to the spot, letting him make all the moves. I don't want to scare him any more than I already have. "That's absolutely true. No sinister reasons whatsoever. It's a long story. Are you sure you want to hear it?"

He doesn't take his eyes off me as he says, "Absolutely."

"Okay. So like I said, I am set to rule my own Circle in Infernis— Sloth, obviously. Things have become more hectic over the millennia, and my dad, Chaos, can no longer rule alone. One of his stipulations for us taking over our own Circle is that we have an eternal partner. They don't have to be romantic or a particular gender. It just takes two to rule—a buddy system if you will."

"Even for your brothers?"

"Yes. They all have an eternal partner. Most of them are spouses, but a couple of them are platonic. They all found their match in a fellow demon. Some have been together for centuries, some only for a decade—my brother Fier is so proud that it took him a long time to find someone he was willing to share power with. You've met one of my brothers and his partner. Mandis, the one who came here with me the first time, he's the epitome of gluttony. He overdoes *everything*—food, drink, love, all of it. He and Glen, his partner, are disgustingly in love. And Lux . . . can you imagine being the prince of Lust and having to commit to one person for the rest of eternity? He and Bernadette are still practically newlyweds. So it's not like I'm *that* far behind, but now they're waiting on me."

"And you don't think you could find a demon like they did?"

I shake my head. "All six of my brothers, and my parents, they're all so chaotic. All the demons are, even me. But I need something different. I don't think I can rule effectively with another demon because I need someone who complements me. Not someone who's the same. I can't imagine being with someone like me *forever*. And when a member of the royal family says forever, we mean it. When you choose an eternal partner, that's it. It's for all time. And I don't want to choose an eternal partner who's platonic or just someone who's a viable leader. I want to marry for love. I want someone who, like me, wants more of a balance in life. So my dad thought I might be able to find someone in the human realm since I wasn't having any luck with the demons. He sent me here and gave me ninety days. If I don't succeed, he's picking a demon for me. And I'll be stuck with them."

Jace cocks a brow. "You have ninety days to find someone to be your forever? Most humans can't handle a lifetime after dating for five years."

"Yeah, well, that's not how it works for me as the future queen of Sloth. I don't get to follow human rules. Honestly, I don't think my father thought this through. But regardless, that's what I have to work with, and now I'm almost down to sixty days. Any day now one of my brothers—or who knows, Chaos himself—will pop up to check in and make sure I'm making progress. Because if they think I'm just screwing around, they'll pull the plug and it's an arranged marriage for me," I say, running my hand through my hair and gripping it at the roots, feeling the walls start to close in on me.

I've tried not to let the stress of this situation get to me, but now, sharing it with someone else, it's become more real. And I'm terrified.

"How would that work between a demon and a human? Aren't you immortal, or at least live a thousand times longer than us?"

Jace's entire attitude has changed. He's propped his elbows on the counter, and just the way he listens tells me he's enthralled. I can't help but smile when I answer.

"We're immortal. And if I choose a human, he'll have to become immortal as well."

"How is that possible? Are we talking like, how a vampire turns a human, or elixirs? Do you cast a spell on him?"

"One big revelation at a time. I'm scared your brain will combust and your heart will stall out if I give you all life's secrets."

He looks off into space, pulling at his bottom lip. I wonder if he is trying to figure out the answer himself. No doubt he's diving deep into fantasies about radioactive spiders and superhuman aliens. I'm just becoming familiar with his creative brain, but I know it's marveling at all the possibilities.

He turns his attention to me and says the most unexpected thing.

"You know I'm giving you my day for chores now that I know you just have to twirl your finger around to get things done."

I laugh, and it feels good. Part of me was scared that I'd lost all the ground I'd gained with him. "That's a fair trade after I freaked you out, and probably took a decade off your life."

"It's worth it. I like knowing humans aren't alone."

"Just think of us as your friendly guides to selecting the perfect afterlife for your energy."

"But if you don't find a partner then there might not be a place for the lazy energies to live out their eternity."

"You catch on quick," I say with a wink.

"All right, guess we need to get to work finding you a man to drag kicking and screaming to hell with you."

"Very funny," I say.

His smile fades, and he gets that disconnected look again. It's almost like his brain leaves for a few seconds. All the information I just gave him is a lot, and I worry he's going into shock again. In a matter of minutes, I've changed the universe as he knows it. I wonder if he regrets knowing what happens when his body and mind die.

He returns from his thoughts and locks eyes with me. "You're right. This is a lot for me to take in. Be patient with me as I navigate this, Desi. I'm sure I'm going to say the wrong things. I've had my near run-in with the other side, and I've got to admit that I'm a little freaked out about having it so close to home again. No pun intended."

"The car accident you mentioned earlier," I say, leaning against the counter next to where he stands. "Do you want to talk about it?"

"There isn't much to say." He walks to the refrigerator and removes a bottle of water. After taking a long chug, he continues. "I was driving behind a truck that was carrying metal piping. The company didn't secure it well and when the driver slammed on his brakes, the strap broke. A pipe flew through my windshield, sliced right through my chest, and went out of my back next to my spine. It nicked my lung, I spent almost four weeks in a coma, and with the damage to my nerves, the doctor thought there was a good chance I wouldn't walk again. I should have walked away with millions from my lawsuit—been set for life—but the guy with the most money is usually the winner. And that wasn't me. After paying the attorneys and medical bills, I had just enough from the settlement to pay off my student loans, buy my extremely safe BMW, and put a little into savings before getting Aftermath off the ground."

I'm speechless as I picture the scar on his chest. To think of Jace being in such a dire medical situation makes me feel uneasy. He's always so controlled, so put together; to know he almost didn't make it doesn't even seem possible. "That's terrifying. I don't blame you for not wanting another brush with death. But I can promise you this: I'm not here to hurt you, and I have zero say in when a human's energy goes to the 'other side.' Neither does my father. Do you trust me?"

He leans back on the counter and crosses his arms. The way he examines me makes me fidget side to side, much like the water bottle dangling from his fingers. I watch it brush back and forth against his ribs until he says, "I trust you."

I didn't realize how worried I'd been that he was going to kick me to the curb until he uttered those words, and I exhale in relief. "Thank you." I glance at the TV. "I don't know about you, but I'm wired. Do you want to watch TV with me? I don't think I could go to sleep now if I tried."

"You aren't going to turn me into some nocturnal ghoul, are you? I enjoy my early morning workouts."

I smirk and roll my eyes. "I'll try not to. The world might crash down on me if I disrupt your routine."

"It might. It's an important routine," he says with a sly grin.

After everything he went through tonight, I have a feeling that there's a lot of truth behind those words. I'm starting to understand his constant need for order. A little bit of control when you feel like everything is falling apart is important.

"You pick the movie while I run upstairs to change." He takes the steps two at a time then pauses. "And Desi?"

"Yes, Jace?"

"Don't pick something too sappy."

THIRTEEN
DESI

There is something comforting about finally finding my normal with my roommates. We move around the kitchen, each taking a task to hurry along cleanup after dinner. No bickering about who has the easier job or trying to weasel our way out of the chore. Jace stands at the sink, loading the plates into the dishwasher while Cannon wipes down the counters. I'm packing the leftover pizza into glass containers. I like when we fall into a natural groove like this.

Cannon moves beside me, running a wet dish cloth in circles over the granite. "Pardon me. I just need—" He presses his front to my back, maneuvering around me as he continues to clean.

"You just need me to move," I say with a laugh.

"Nah. I'm happy to have you in my way. It gives me an excuse to get close to you."

I look at him over my shoulder, meeting the playfulness in his eyes. "You just spent an entire meal rubbing shoulders with me."

"True, but I kind of like you trapped like this."

Cannon's words warm low in my stomach. He has never shied away from a chance to flirt, but my body reacts in a new way with him this close.

"Then by all means," I say, turning back to the counter and finishing my task, lowering my gaze to the granite with a smirk. "Trap away. I'm one hundred percent willing to be caught."

"So I've heard." He gives me a quick kiss on the cheek and continues on his way.

I place the pizza in the refrigerator and move to the sink next to Jace. "Mind if I wash my hands?"

He steps to the side, giving me room to reach the soap dispenser. "Cannon seems to be a good candidate for your . . . quest," he says, keeping his voice low so only I can hear him.

"Quest?" I say with a chuckle.

"Do you have a better name for it?"

"Not really, but quest makes it sound like some sort of noble cause that will save the universe."

Jace bumps my shoulder with his. "Think about it. It kind of is. You're keeping balance in the force. Good and evil."

I lift an eyebrow and quirk my mouth at the thought. It's a strange way of thinking about my attempt to find an eternal partner, but he's right. It kind of is a quest, minus the swords and horseback riding that come to mind when he calls it that. "I guess you're right. But it's not really good and evil. More like tranquility and mayhem." I glance behind me to see Cannon rummaging through the freezer. "And as far as Cannon goes, he's a possibility. I like spending time with him."

Jace shrugs and says, "He's an easy solution to your problem."

Solution to my problem? I don't like the way that sounds. In fact, there's a gut-roiling feeling just talking about Cannon as an option. Maybe it's because we're whispering about him when he's on the other side of the kitchen. Whatever it is, it doesn't feel right.

I turn to face Jace and open my mouth to tell him that maybe considering Cannon isn't the best idea. But the words never come out.

"Who's up for shots before we start movie night?" Cannon asks, holding up a bottle of amber liquid.

Jace and I exchange a glance at Cannon's random question. I wonder if his brain is going to the other night when he thought someone had drugged his drink. He was so worried about losing control. Come to think of it, I can't recall a time when he had more than one beer.

"Why?" Jace asks, drawing out the word.

"Just because. Haven't y'all ever done shots just because?"

"I mean, yeah, in college, but not in years."

"Desi?"

"Not really," I admit. "But I'm always up to try new things."

Cannon and I lock eyes and then drag our gazes to Jace, who just sighs.

"The shot glasses are on the top shelf in the cabinet next to the fridge."

Cannon gets to work setting up a shot for each of us before handing them out and lifting his glass. "To a random Tuesday night!"

Jace and I each pick up a glass and raise it. We clink them together, say "Cheers," and toss them back.

"Fuck!" I say, hissing as the strong, spicy liquid burns all the way down my esophagus. "What the hell is this?"

Cannon raises an eyebrow and turns the bottle around so I can see the name, and the laugh that escapes me is nearly hysterical.

The cinnamon whiskey has none other than a dancing red devil at the top of the label. What are the odds?

"What's so funny?" Cannon asks.

"Oh, I don't know, I—"

"Want another?" Jace interrupts, and I'm grateful.

I exhale and still feel the burn in my throat, but say, "Yeah, why not?"

He pours Cannon and me another shot but skips over his own glass. I hate that he clings to control even in the one place he should feel the safest. None of us would let anything bad happen within these walls, but Jace doesn't seem to trust anything or anyone but himself. And sometimes I wonder if he even trusts his own judgment.

Damaged. He is so damaged. All I can do is hope that he'll choose to repair the emotional hurt that accident caused him.

Cannon and I clink glasses and take the second shot, but before another can be poured, I put the bottle back in the freezer, rinse out the glasses, and set them in the dishwasher.

"What are you doing?" Jace asks. "You didn't have to—"

"I know," I say softly with a glance in Cannon's direction, hoping he meets me in the middle here. If he doesn't, it'll be a huge strike against him in the running for potential eternal partner.

My shoulders sag in relief when he says, "Yeah, man, I don't want to drink too much. You ever had a cinnamon whiskey hangover?" He blows out a breath that makes his lips rattle. "No thanks." He slides between us and throws his arms over our shoulders. "Let's go watch this movie."

Thirty minutes into what Jace dubs the "sexiest sci-fi film of all time," my head is on Cannon's shoulder and I am on the verge of falling asleep from pure boredom. This movie is terrible. The dialogue is cheesy, and I am convinced Jace chose it as a joke. I look over to tell him as much when I see him looking between me and Cannon with a pensive expression on his face.

"What are you looking at?" I hiss.

He clears his throat and crosses his arms. "I was just thinking that you two look comfortable."

Cannon's perfect mouth pulls into a wide grin. He puts his arm around me and says, "I'm cozy. Great movie, good friend, and a beautiful girl. It's a good night."

I snuggle deeper against Cannon's arm and place my hand on his chest. His white T-shirt is soft under my cheek, and I can't stop myself from taking a deep breath of his cologne. The scent of orange with a hint of spice reminds me of warm summer nights in Infernis.

It wouldn't be so bad to spend those nights with him. I could give him a chance. Couldn't I? There's no logical reason why it felt a little bit off when Jace mentioned it. It just . . . *did*. And that's not a real reason. So why not cuddle up to Cannon right now and enjoy tonight as *potentially* a little bit more than friends? *Potentially.*

"You smell good," I whisper against his T-shirt, nervous flutters making an appearance in my belly, as if I've never complimented the man before now.

"You always smell like sweet fruit," he says.

I cringe, burying my face against his chest. I'm sure he means it as a good thing, but it's awkward, like he was struggling to find something nice to say. It's so not like him. He normally lets the compliments roll off his tongue.

The unease is quickly swept away when he lifts a curl that has fallen across my cheek and wraps it around his finger. I watch as the red strands cover the warm brown of his skin. They complement each other so well. The slight tug on my hair sends a bolt of electricity through me.

It crosses my mind that maybe he's nervous too. We've been out together for appetizers, and out with Jace, but we've never been quite this close in a private place before. We were in a position sort of like this at the bar that first night he took me out, but we were surrounded by people.

Not here. Tonight, we're at home on our couch, and it's just us.

And Jace.

My eyebrow dips as I look at Jace from the corner of my eye. He's looking at the screen, but his fingers are drumming against the arm of the couch, as if he's pretending to watch the movie but really, he's waiting to see what happens next over here.

What is he thinking? Why do I care so much? He's not the one with his arm around me. Cannon's the one who's showing me affection and attention. Who's open enough to do more than lock eyes with me through an open window during a stolen moment of passion.

So I turn my attention back to Cannon and trail my fingertips from his thigh to his knee as he continues to twist my curl around his knuckle. His skin is soft, and I wonder if my touch is affecting him at all.

"What are you doing?" he asks, his leg twitching under my fingers.

"I just thought it felt nice to be touched, and you might like it too." I continue drawing swirling patterns on his thigh. He adjusts his hips and presses his cheek against the top of my head, planting a kiss there.

"It does feel good," he says into my hair.

I let my fingertips wander around his leg, exploring the strong muscles of his thigh and the dips on the side of his knee. Feeling a bit bolder, I inch my finger under the hem of his basketball shorts; with this innocent touch, I hope he'll take things a little further.

But he doesn't.

"Did Desi ever tell you that she's never really kissed someone before?" Jace says to Cannon, leaning forward so he can see his face. "She's hoping that one of the guys she dates will give her the kind of kiss that leaves her wanting more."

Cannon's fingers stop playing with my hair, and his heart beats faster under my ear. "Yeah. She might have mentioned that in passing."

I should be irritated at Jace, but I know he's just trying to help. Maybe reminding Cannon of that will be the push he needs to make a move. I mean, it's not as though he hasn't mentioned wanting to take me out and get to know me on another level. Here's his chance. I'm literally giving him an opening to take it.

I don't remove my hand from his leg. In fact, I amp everything up by moving my fingertips toward his inner thigh, and this time, I force myself to maintain a featherlight touch on his skin. When I hear his breath hitch, I glance up at him through my lashes to make sure he's okay with what I'm doing as I slide my hand back down to safer territory.

Jace keeps his eyes on the television and speaks like every word out of his mouth is an afterthought as he says, "I always took Desi for the kind of girl who would melt if a guy just placed his hand on the side of her face and rubbed his thumb slowly over her bottom lip."

My eyes widen as I lift one of my legs to the couch, pretending to readjust, kicking Jace right in the thigh while shooting him a look that screams *Too much help*. My nostrils flare as my friend just smiles and doesn't break his focus on the movie as he mutters, "I'm just sayin.'"

I part my lips to reply but don't get to because a warm palm is turning my face back toward Cannon, and when my eyes meet his, they're bright blue and laser focused right on me.

Cannon's thumb barely grazes my lip before he drops his hand to mine and moves it back to where it was before Jace's unsolicited advice mic drop. "Is it true, Desi? What he said? Would you like it if I did that?"

I suck in a breath before whispering on a shaky exhale, "Yes, Cannon. I would."

He leans down and brushes his lips against mine. His breath is warm, laced with the cinnamon from the liquor. The kiss is gentle and innocent, like butterfly wings fluttering past my lips. When he pulls away, I'm hungry for more. So much more. It's just a taste of what a real kiss can feel like.

I grip the front of his shirt and move a little closer to him, eager to feel his mouth on mine again. He brushes his thumb over my cheekbone, staring down at me. Seconds tick by but he doesn't come back for more. The warmth pooling in the center of my being begins to chill. Perhaps that was all he wanted.

"That was . . . sweet."

I tilt my head to look back at Jace. He no longer pretends that the movie playing on the television is more intriguing than what's happening beside him. His elbow sits on the arm of the couch with his chin resting on his thumb. His eyes are a deep ash as they lock with mine.

"It was sweet," I say.

"From the minute I met you, you were anything but sweet. You're fire and destruction and temptation." He looks away from me to Cannon. "She wants you to ruin her."

"She what?" Cannon asks in confusion.

Jace stands and grabs his bottle of water from the coffee table. "Don't hold back with her. Take what you want and show her what she needs."

My jaw drops like it is unhinged. Those words. Those words do things to my body that no person has done before. I ache in a way I didn't know was possible. If Cannon's kiss left me hungry for more, Jace just made me ravenous.

Jace climbs the stairs, and I continue staring long after he disappears.

Cannon places his hand on my upper arm and says, "Is that true? Is that what you want?"

My gaze slides from the stairs to Cannon, and I swallow hard.

Is that what I want? Do I want Cannon to "ruin me"?

If by *ruin me*, Jace meant a kiss that makes every nerve ending in my body crackle with electricity, turning me into a live wire, a connection that feels primal and raw in nature instead of tentative and sweet, a touch that scorches every square inch of my skin . . . then yes.

I nod and lift my hand to his, intertwining our fingers and bringing our joined hands to his thigh, resting them there as I say, "Yes. It's true. That's what I want."

"You're sure, Desi? So much of this is new to you. I don't want to overstep. It's all right to take things slow and learn what you want."

I appreciate Cannon's concern; younger me would have been

charmed by it. I'm years, decades, beyond that. I've spent countless nights fantasizing about what I want. I'm not naïve. I don't need to ease into experiences I'm ready to have. I want to dive in headfirst.

"I'm sure."

Cannon bites down on his lower lip and grabs my hips, arranging me so I'm straddling his lap. He cups my face again, but this time when his thumb traces my lip, it's more adventurous. The tip dips into my mouth and slides across my tongue. His expression darkens when I close my lips around him and gently pull away with a kiss.

"You don't know how long I've imagined this," he says, gliding his hand to the base of my neck and pulling me to him.

"I think I do. I started thinking about it the minute you propositioned me that first day," I tease against his lips.

He captures my mouth with his. There is no hesitation, no gentle, no sweet. His tongue seeks mine and he hums when he tastes me for the first time. My fingers dig into his shoulders as I give myself over to the sensation. His hand runs down my spine and stops at the small of my back. He pulls me so close that I can feel the hard hills and planes of his body through our clothes.

The kiss is everything I imagined a perfect kiss to be. The glide of his tongue playing with mine and the stings of pleasure when he nips my lip. His hands roaming over my back and sliding into my hair. It's passionate, hot, and . . .

Cannon slows the tempo, giving me two chaste pecks before pulling away. I move to sit beside him and catch my breath. I sit staring straight ahead at the now blank TV screen, my brain scrambled, bewilderment washing over me.

That had been *the kiss* I'd always wanted. The kiss Jace had described. Cannon had done everything right—the heat, the passion, even the sting of pain I'd only admitted I wanted in the deepest part of my heart—it was all there.

But I felt . . . nothing. Nothing besides the knowledge that *that* should have been a kiss that left my panties drenched and me desperate to bring Cannon to my room for the rest of the night.

I draw my bottom lip between my teeth and peer at Cannon cautiously. When I see the same expression on his face that I imagine is on mine, the knot in my stomach dissolves *just* a bit.

"Cannon?"

"Desi?"

"I—how was that for you?" I blurt, unsure of how to start this conversation.

I can almost see his brain search for the right words to say, the ones that won't leave me in tears. It makes me want to hysterically laugh. We've created a solid friendship, and he shouldn't feel the need to mince words with me.

"It was nice."

My laughter is loud and truly happy. "I couldn't have said it better myself. That kiss was everything I imagined it would be, but . . ." I let out a breath that makes my lips rattle and lift my shoulders in a shrug.

He chuckles and relaxes into the couch cushions. "It's strange that you and I get along so well, but there isn't an ounce of sexual chemistry. Not that you weren't a good kisser, you were."

"Please. You don't have to explain it. I was there," I say, holding up my hand.

"So now what?"

I shrug and lean into him. "We just enjoy each other's company. *And* we don't have to sit through another uncomfortable movie night with Jace trying to orchestrate a make-out session between us."

"That works for me," he says, wrapping an arm around my shoulder in a tight side-hug.

We fall right back into the easy friendship we've built over the last month. I'm happy that nothing has to change. I don't know what

I would do if I didn't have Cannon to share my frustrations with. Especially since most of those frustrations revolve around Jace.

Jace used to frustrate me with all his rules, but now I just find them endearing. Now he frustrates me because although it's clear to everyone else in this house and probably the old lady who lives across the street that he's attracted to me, he's pushing me and Cannon to share passionate, heat-filled kisses while he goes to his room alone.

Jace, who fucked his fist while watching me ride my hand through our windows and *told me to come*. And has *yet* to bring it up with me.

Yeah, it's safe to say that I have a bone to pick with Jace Wilder.

FOURTEEN
DESI

I've spent a week trying to corner Jace and have a conversation about what happened between him and me after the charity dinner. One thing after another got in my way. I wasn't going to bring it up the night of his panic attack, and the kiss setup with Cannon . . . well, that was just awkward timing. I thought I'd catch him at breakfast or dinner, but he always found a way to avoid the conversation. Tonight will be the night. Unless he tries to bail on our movie night because Cannon's out of town, but I have the ultimate weapon to prevent that.

I cue the movie up as he comes downstairs wearing sleeping attire, his glasses perched on his nose.

"I don't know if I'm up for movie night," he says, plopping onto the couch next to me.

"That would be a shame," I say, nodding at the television. "I figured we could just continue our *Star Wars* marathon now that we're done with the newer movies and it's time to go back in time to the '70s, apparently." I shake my head. "Still so weird how they did that."

Jace looks at me with something like admiration in his eyes. "I'm impressed. You're finally coming over to the dark side."

"I am, but if you don't want to be here to witness my downfall . . ." I say, grabbing the remote, "I can just go watch it in my room."

He reaches over me and snatches the remote from my grip. "No, I didn't say that. I'll stay. This will give me a renewed sense of energy."

I offer him a smile, but inside, my chaotic little demon soul is rubbing its palms together with sinister glee. I've got him right where I want him.

"Speaking of energy, do you want any snacks?" I ask as he presses Play.

"I shouldn't since it's so late, but I've only had two bowls of peanut butter puffs this week. I think I can handle a snack or two."

I give him a sly grin and look back at the kitchen. Like I'm directing traffic, I move my arms and call forth the foods that I've learned are his favorite cheat day items (besides the aforementioned puffs). A cup of ice and a can of Coke float out of the kitchen along with a bag of veggie chips and some gummy bears. My magic places the items on the coffee table, and a carton of Ben & Jerry's and a spoon drift into my open hands.

"So weird," he mumbles, grabbing the chips. "My very own demon Jedi."

Pride suddenly swells in my chest. I've never really been proud of my powers before; everyone in Infernis has some sort of power, depending on their rank. But Jace referring to me as *his* very own demon Jedi is, well, I don't know what it is, but it makes me feel like I belong here, which means more than I care to admit.

"That's me," I say, opening the ice cream and digging in. "Is this your favorite? You keep saying we haven't made it to your favorite movie yet."

I pull the blanket out from behind me and spread it over my legs, lifting it up and wordlessly asking if he would like to share it with me. Surprisingly, he takes it and drapes it over his legs as he speaks.

"It's top three but *Return of the Jedi* is my favorite. I should give some deep explanation, but if I'm being honest, it's for one stupid reason." He pops a chip in his mouth and stares at the screen.

Is he serious? He can't leave me hanging like that. I told him the biggest secret of my life, the one that could get me in *serious trouble* with my dad, and he can't share why a movie is his favorite? No. That will not do. The man owes me this at least.

I gesture for him to continue. "And that would be?"

His cheeks turn pink, and he grabs his glass of soda. Bringing it to his lips, he quickly says, "I may have had my sexual awakening because of that movie."

My eyebrows hit my hairline as I think about the dinosaur-looking creature, the gold metal man, and the one creepy guy with the red and black face. "Wait, what? With who? Jar Jar Binks?"

"What? No!" He sits up straight and tips his head toward the television. "Princess Leia."

"Oh," I say with a nod. "I see. Was it the space buns or the white robe that did it for ya?"

His eyes take on this dreamy glaze like he's picturing her in his head. "No. There's this one costume she wears that always took center stage in every wet dream I had from fourteen until, well . . . whatever age it stopped being acceptable to have wet dreams because that's *definitely* when I stopped."

I'm silent for a moment until laughter bursts out of me and I bend over, clutching my stomach. "Jace, stop," I say through my tears. "You had wet dreams over a *Star Wars* character?"

"Damn right I did. You don't understand, Desi. You haven't seen that costume. It's the epitome of sexy. It's the costume that puts every sexy nurse and French maid outfit to shame. I'd rather have a woman walk into my bedroom in that costume than *any* skimpy lingerie."

I stare at him wide eyed with my mouth open. "You are *passionate* about this subject."

"I'm passionate about many things. That costume just happens to sit high on the list."

"Fair enough," I say, leaning back against the arm of the couch.

This is the perfect opportunity to bring up the other night. I take a deep breath and sit forward, placing the ice cream on the coffee table and replacing the lid. "Jace, I need to ask you something, and I need you to be honest with me."

He pauses the movie and tilts his head to the side as he looks at me. "Of course. When have I ever not told you the truth?"

I ignore the gnawing feeling in the pit of my stomach and decide to be as blunt as possible. "The other night. After the charity dinner. Did you . . . I mean, did we —"

His eyelids drop slightly, making his gaze dark and hooded as he says, "Did we what, Desideria? Say what you need to say."

"Did we touch ourselves while watching each other through our bedroom windows? And tell each other when to come? Or did I imagine that, and it was just a one-way street? In which case I look *really* foolish right now, and I'd like to crawl in a hole and disappear," I ramble, wringing my hands in my lap. My heart is racing, my blood throbbing in my veins, and I have to press my thighs together the moment I ask the question.

"Does it matter what happened that night? I think it's safe to say we've moved on."

In what way does he think we've moved on? Asking the question is proof that it still lingers in my head. I can have the smuttiest book in my hand or be folding clothes and the image of him watching me with his dick in his hand creeps in. I haven't moved on from that night at all.

I hold back the derisive laughter that's threatening to bubble up. "Yes, it does matter. It matters to me. And no, it's not 'safe to say we've moved on.' How can we move on if I wasn't even sure it had actually *happened* until just now? I need to talk about it, Jace. Please," I murmur, hating the way the word sounds on my tongue, so desperate and needy.

But I am, I guess. I need to talk about it. I want to talk about it.

He removes his glasses and rubs the bridge of his nose. "Okay, let's talk about it. I'm not sure what you want me to say. You saw it happen."

I clench my jaw and turn to face him, crossing my legs underneath me. My knees rest on his thigh and I don't bother to move. "I want you to tell me *why* it happened. Why that happened and somehow the idea of kissing me is just too disgusting to consider!" I blurt, my face heating and chest rising with the frustration building inside me.

Jace springs up from the couch and his glasses hit the coffee table with a *clank* that makes me jump. "Where did you get that I find the idea of kissing you disgusting? When did I say that?"

"You didn't have to, Jace!" I exclaim, getting to my feet so we are closer to being eye to eye. "I all but offered myself to you on a silver platter, and you turned me down! Then you pushed me to make out with Cannon. Why else would you do that when you knew I'd *gladly* have made out with *you*? You can't have any desire to kiss me, or you wouldn't have done either of those things."

He points a finger at me. "Fuck that. I'm not talking to you about this."

"Why not?"

"Because what you and Cannon do is your business. I was just trying to help you both out. But I see I shouldn't have gotten involved. You guys would have figured it out."

I snort and look up at the ceiling. "Yeah, we figured it out, all right," I mutter, flinging myself back down on the couch, snatching the blanket and covering myself up with it again.

Jace looks down at me with narrowed eyes, and while I can tell he's tempted to turn around and walk out of the room, he can't help himself. He sits back down and tucks himself back underneath the blanket next to me and says, "What are you talking about? Didn't y'all kiss last week?"

With a sigh, I nod. "Cannon and I may be best friends, but sexual chemistry we do *not* have. It was a good kiss, I could tell it was everything I had wanted. Everything you described. But I felt nothing. Nothing at all. And neither did he. In fact, I felt ten times more in that moment with you after the charity dinner, and we weren't even in the same room."

"Fuck, Desi." He slides his fingers through his hair and falls back against the cushions. Staring up at the ceiling, he watches the fan rotate in slow circles. I'm convinced he's hypnotized himself until he says, "It's not that I didn't want to kiss you. Obviously, my actions after turning you down prove that the thought turned me on." He sits up and his gaze travels over my face, soaking in every inch of me. "I was thinking about you even before I noticed you watching me."

My breath catches and I swallow before admitting a secret of my own. "I think of you every time I touch myself."

He lifts a brow and one side of his mouth lifts in a smirk. "Every time?"

"Every. Single. Time."

"Since we're being honest about what we do alone, that wasn't my first time thinking of you either."

Desire courses through me, hot, wild, and nearly uncontrollable, but I manage to stay on my side of the couch and keep my hands to myself. "Really? And what exactly is it that you think about? Because I can tell you that just the *idea* of you pleasuring yourself to thoughts of me gives me more pleasure than that kiss with Cannon. There's no telling what knowing details would do."

"Are you asking me to add mental images to go along with your secret drawer of sex toys?"

"Maybe."

"I'll let you fill in the blanks, but I will say it has to do with my bathtub and a lot of bubbles."

I cover my mouth but a giggle escapes even as my core clenches. That's a perfect example of what Jace does to me—makes me laugh and turns me on in the same damn breath. How is that possible?

"You're turned on by the thing we had our huge argument about?" I tease, scooting back to my original spot on the couch so my legs are resting on his again.

"Come on, Desi. I had a gorgeous woman naked in my bathroom. Was I happy that you went into my room without asking? No. Did I get turned on by finding you in my tub? Absolutely."

Jace said the night of the charity dinner that he wasn't afraid to talk about sex. I never thought it meant he would be so candid about his fantasies. He's so careful about everything else in his life, but he acts carefree when it comes to this subject. It's a huge turn-on to see him release the tight grip he has on everything else.

"Well, while we're confessing things, that's also not the first night I've watched you from my bedroom window," I say, covering my eyes when I realize how creepy that sounds. "I mean, I've never seen anything like *that*. I assume you usually do that in the bathroom. Anyway, I know your whole nightly routine by now. Only because I sleep on my left side, and when I turn over, I can see right in. I know I could close my curtains, but you've never closed yours. And I guess part of me hoped you were watching me too."

He pulls my hands away from my face and flashes me a dimpled grin. "Don't close your curtains unless you want to. It would be a shame for everyone involved."

My lips part in surprise. "Wait. You *were* watching me?"

He takes the remote from my lap and before he presses Play, he says, "You need your spank bank material and I need mine. No harm in that."

It turns out that luring my roommate into an uncomfortable

conversation with *Star Wars* movies is very beneficial. I got more than I bargained for, but I think he did too. And like he said, there's no harm in what we're doing. We're both attractive people spending day in and day out with each other. There's bound to be sexual tension— sexual tension that just reached new heights.

The movie carries on and the next thing I know, I'm running the back of my hand over my closed eyes and the sun is beaming through the living room window. I wiggle my toes and brush against something hard and hairy. Inching my eyes open I find Jace asleep on the other side of the sectional couch. I glide my foot up and down again and realize our legs are tangled and I'm touching his calf.

I start to disentangle our limbs, but I can't find it in myself to do it. He looks so peaceful—his eyelashes so long that they're grazing his cheekbones, his chest rising and falling in a gentle motion. There's something about his skin against mine that is so sensual. It makes goosebumps rise on every inch of my body, and I thank my lucky stars that he's still asleep because I'm sure he would be able to feel them against his leg.

That ache returns, the one that was ignited during last night's conversation. I can't believe we fell asleep so close to each other. I swallow hard and gnaw on my bottom lip. Turning my face into the couch cushion to try to calm myself, I—

The doorbell rings and Jace and I jump up from the couch, nearly kicking each other in the face. Jace lets out a shout, looking back at the door. "That scared the hell out of me."

"Me too," I pant, still startled by the sensations being so close to him had sent through me. "Who's here this early?"

"I don't know. I'll get it," he says, pulling down the leg of his joggers where it's bunched below his knee.

He walks to the foyer, tugging at the front of his pants, and I try not to notice. Don't most guys have to *adjust* in the morning? It's natural and not something I should overthink.

After I hear the click of the door, a moment passes before Jace calls, "Desi, you have a visitor!"

Jumping up from the couch, I tug my shorts down and pull my hair over my shoulder, trying not to look like I just woke up.

Rounding the corner into the foyer, I stop short and almost run into Jace when I realize who's here.

Not my favorite brother, the one who brought me here to begin with, the one who understands me, knows how to listen, and gets what I'm doing.

But my second oldest brother, the one who can call bullshit at every turn, and knows the ins and outs of love and lust better than anyone in this realm or any other.

Lux.

"Desideria, sister, I hope you're well," my brother says, looking around Jace's house approvingly. His red hair falls over his forehead and his green eyes, identical to mine, are bright and curious. Clad in a monochromatic suit as always, he is 100 percent overdressed for a casual visit.

"Lux, hi. I didn't know—what are you doing here?"

Jace gestures down the hall with his thumb. "I'll be in my office if you need me. It was nice to meet you, Lux," he says, shaking hands with my brother.

"Likewise, Mr. Wilder. *Extremely* nice to meet you," Lux says, and my eyes widen as my brother unashamedly checks out Jace's ass as he makes his way down the hall.

I slap him on the forearm. "Um. Hello? What are you doing here?"

Lux shoves his hands in his pockets and strolls past me. He lifts his chin and turns in a circle between the kitchen and living room. After several deep breaths, he says, "This place smells just like my den of lust after a long night of orgies."

My mouth opens and closes several times before I say, "What? No! We haven't—Jace and I are just friends. There's no lust here."

"Is that right? And I bet you've taken up ironing and grout cleaning as your new favorite hobbies."

His gaze falls on the rumpled blanket on the sofa and the out of place couch cushions. He turns to me with a raised eyebrow.

"Stop it, Lux. Jace and I were watching a movie and we fell asleep on the couch. That's it."

He picks up the blanket from the side Jace was sleeping on and brings it to his nose. All humor drains from his face and his eyes roll in the back of his head. "Your loss, sister. His pheromones are divine."

"Pheromones? No," I squeak, bringing my palm to my collarbone and nervously running my fingers over it. "He was asleep until you rang the doorbell." I lower my voice to a hiss. "Are you insinuating that he was *turned on*?"

A sly grin pulls at Lux's lips. "I guarantee you that the human was on the verge of losing it in his joggers. Too bad that delicious smell is tainted by your lust."

"*My* lust?!" I whisper-yell, my gaze darting down the hall to ensure Jace's head doesn't pop out of his office before I lower my voice. "You're not listening; I don't have any lust for Jace!"

It's a lie. I'm all but clenching my thighs together right now to relieve the throbbing between them. My brother knows *everything* about how humans function, but even if he didn't, I know my conversation with Jace last night affected us both. It was too flirtatious and way too descriptive. We journeyed into dangerous territory for people who are just supposed to be roommates.

"That's a shame. I was hoping that morsel of muscle and sex would be the human you bring to meet Father in two days. He's eager to see how you're faring in your search for an eternal partner."

My knees go weak, and I grip the back of the sofa for support.

"Excuse me. What? Two days? I have to come home in two days? And bring my . . . bring a human? You've got to be kidding me, Lux."

"It has been over thirty days since you left. You should be making some headway. Are you telling me that you aren't narrowing down your options?" Lux clicks his tongue and wanders to the front of the house. "So I should tell Father you're in the same predicament as when you left Infernis?"

Panicked, I let go of the sofa and follow him. "No. No. Don't tell him that. I'll bring Jace. You were right," I say, my words coming out in a rush before I can stop myself. "I like him, okay? I've even told him what I am. I just—" *Desi, what are you doing?* I don't want to lie to my brother, but I can't let him tell our father that I've made no progress. I'll be so screwed. "I still need to give him the rundown on the family. We're a lot for someone like him to handle, but I swear, I'll tell him tonight."

Lux spares a glance down the hallway and smiles. This demon is shameless in his quest to satisfy his sexual appetite. And if I'm being honest, I don't blame him for being attracted to Jace. I clearly struggle to keep it under control when he's nearby.

"I look forward to getting to know him, and I'm sure our brothers will feel the same."

All I can do is nod and say, "I'm sure they will. I'll see you in two days, Lux."

"Don't be late," he says, and on his way out he flashes me another sly smile over his shoulder.

When the door closes, I collapse back onto the couch and bury my face in my knees. *What the hell am I going to do now? It hasn't been that long since I told Jace what I am, and now I have to convince him to come with me to Infernis?*

I hear Jace's soft footsteps and the cushion next to me sinks with his weight. "Desi?"

I groan in response, leaning back against the couch and tangling my fingers in my hair.

Jace crosses his arms and sits back. He remains silent as the tension in the room grows. Every passing second adds to the weight of what I have to do. And it isn't until my bones ache and it's hard to breathe that he says, "I'm sorry if that visit didn't go the way you hoped. Do you want to talk about it?"

"Yes. In fact, I need your help."

Cautiously he says, "Let's hear it, and I'll see what I can do."

I exhale slowly and wring my hands in my lap. "So remember when I told you that my dad was going to send one of my brothers to make sure I was making progress with finding a partner?"

Jace nods and then his eyes widen behind his glasses. "Oh. *Oh.* Lux was checking up on you."

"Yes. And it's time for me to go home to check in. And Dad expects me to bring home my boyfriend. In two days. And—" I inhale sharply. "Lux assumed that boyfriend is you."

"And you told him I'm not. Right?" When I remain silent, he presses again. "Desideria, tell me you set him straight."

I close my eyes for a moment and when I open them, he's still staring right at me. "Jace, I tried. I tried to tell him we're just friends, but he wouldn't listen. He can te—"

Jace leans forward. "What? He can what?"

I thread my fingers through my curls and tug them at the roots. "I didn't mean to say that," I mumble. "Too late now, I guess. Lux is the prince of Lust. He can sense lust and sexual desire. He could smell it all over the place. And he knew who it belonged to. There was no convincing him differently. It's his expertise."

Jace removes his glasses and rubs his temples. "I consider myself an intelligent human being, but I need you to dumb this down for me. What did he smell?"

My entire body heats and my face turns scarlet. "I assume you know what pheromones are, yes?" He nods and I continue. "Well, he can detect them in the air. Not only can he detect them, he knows who they belong to and who they're directed toward. Don't ask me how. It's like asking me how I can levitate the TV across the room. It's inexplicable. It's just the powers we were given. As far as *what* he smelled . . . the, uh, the blanket we slept with last night."

Jace runs his hands over his face and falls back. "So because our bodies had a chemical response to being close, he thinks we slept together?"

I chew my bottom lip and adjust so I can bring my knees to my chest, tightening my core. "Actually, no. I panicked when he said he was going to tell our dad that I hadn't made any progress, so I stopped trying to tell him we were just friends. I changed gears and instead told him that you know what I am. I wasn't supposed to tell anyone but the person I picked to be my eternal partner. So, yeah, there's that."

"So now your brother thinks you chose me. What happens when they find out I know about you and I'm not your eternal partner? Do I get cut into tiny pieces and become shark food?"

"My dad isn't unreasonable. I'll tell him I took a chance telling someone but they chose not to come with me in the end. I just needed to buy myself more time. I technically have sixty more days, but if I go home right now for this check-in with *no one*, my dad is going to make me come home for good and marry me off to a demon and it's game over. This is just a stopgap measure. That's it."

Jace stands and paces the length of the living room. The only time I've seen him more out of sorts is when he had his panic attack. His reaction makes a lump grow in my throat and my heart sink. I should have thought this through, and I most definitely shouldn't have put him in the middle of it. But here I am with my future in his hands.

"You know how much the *other realm* stuff freaks me out, Desi.

How does that even work? Do I walk out in front of a car and then have one of those moments where I see the light at the end of a tunnel? Then we spend days in your realm until I hear a voice saying my time isn't up. When I return, it's only been seconds here and now I've had a near-death experience? I don't know if I can do that after what I've been through."

I stand and move in front of him, grasping his shoulders to stop his pacing. "Jace Wilder, you've seen one too many movies. It wouldn't be like that at all. We'd go through a portal, come out in my realm, spend no longer than forty-eight hours there, get back in the portal, and come back here. Two days pass here, two days pass there. No space-time travel stuff." I squeeze him in what I hope is a comforting gesture. "But I get it. You don't have to do it if you don't want to or don't feel comfortable. I completely understand."

"Forty-eight hours?"

"That's all the time a human can spend in Infernis or Pax while in their body. One visit in a lifetime, for no more than forty-eight hours. Any more time than that and you would become very sick. If you passed in a realm that wasn't meant for your energy, it would be devastating. Once an energy has entered our realms, it can't go back. It's the reason that some energies stay here; they can't make the choice between peace and chaos."

"Ghosts," he says. His face lights up when he realizes that ghosts are real.

"We consider them undecided energies."

"Fuck," he breathes and begins pacing again.

I need to convince him to help me. He's my only shot at buying another two months in the human realm. There's one thing I know— Jace is attracted to me. What I'm about to do will have an effect. Will it do what I need it to? I don't know, but I have to try.

Grasping his wrist, I pull him to me and press my body against his, looking at him from under my lashes. "Jace, listen to me. Think of this as a mini vacation. All you have to do is act like my boyfriend for two days. There are some pretty amazing things to see in my realm, and it might be fun to play pretend, don't you think? We did have a good time at the charity event."

His voice is a deep, serious rumble as he says, "Playing pretend for an investor and dancing, Desideria. We're talking about tricking the devil himself into believing we're a couple."

I grin and slide my arm around his waist and rest it on the small of his back. "My father isn't the devil. He's just Chaos. And my brother knows *far* more about lust than he does, and he's already convinced that we're hot for each other. He was certain that we were both two seconds away from coming undone, and that he'd interrupted some intense moment. This will be easy peasy."

"No death?"

"None. You just slip through the portal with me and we're there in the blink of an eye."

He shakes his head, which is a complete contrast to the words that flow from his mouth. "All right. I trust you to bring me home in one piece."

I bounce on the balls of my feet. "Oh my gosh, Jace. Thank you so much." I fling my arms around his neck. "You don't know what this means to me. I owe you *so* big. What do you want me to do for you? Anything you want. It's yours."

"Keep your lust-smelling brothers away from my house. And—"

"Done. And?"

"Finish watching *Star Wars* with me. I'm going to need a distraction to keep my mind off the wild agreement we just made."

I pull him down onto the couch with me and click on the TV, throwing the blanket over our laps. "Consider it done."

FIFTEEN
JACE

I pull my BMW up to a deserted bus station at the edge of town, narrowing my eyes as I put the car in Park. The blue and white awning over the front entrance is sun bleached and ripped to shreds. What used to be a glass door is boarded up with plywood and cracked open. The only redeeming quality about this place is the neon-colored graffiti marking the dingy exterior, the purple and green horned demon with a pointed tail being my favorite of the edgy art pieces.

"You're sure this is it?" I ask.

"Yep," Desi says, looking down at her phone and the instructions she got from the medium yesterday.

"If this isn't some seedy shit, I don't know what is," I grumble, jabbing my finger against the ignition button.

"At least it isn't the last stall of a rest stop in the middle of nowhere. That's how Mandis, Glen, and I came in."

I wrinkle my nose as we get out of the car and unload our two suitcases. "Disgusting. I do *not* like the sound of that. In fact, that would have been when I bailed."

"Yeah, you would've had a meltdown for sure," she teases, bumping me with her hip. She looks up at me, and in the predawn light, her freckled face is pinched with worry. "Hey, are you okay? You sure you still want to do this?"

"I'm scared as hell, but I trust you. This'll be fine."

I'm not lying. I do trust her.

But I'm putting on the bravest face I can because I don't want her to think I'm a coward. My anxiety already puts me at a disadvantage, keeping me from the social events and experiences that it seems every guy my age has. Others see it as weakness. Something I should just get over. I say screw that; it's pure self-preservation.

I dread panic attacks—the anxiety over feeling anxious. The tight feeling in my chest and the fight to take my next breath. Sometimes I think I'm on the verge of death when it crashes down on me. I drown in a sea of hypothetical scenarios, each growing worse as my mind spirals. Sometimes I drift in the stormy waters for hours. Desi was my lifeline the other night. She eased me back to the surface and stayed with me until I caught my breath. Not once did she make me feel like less for losing control.

"Will it help if I explain what's about to happen?" she asks, holding her hand out to me. Her slender fingers wiggle, urging me to take hold.

Butterflies. Goddamn butterflies beat their wings in my stomach and my palms become sweaty. *For fuck's sake, Wilder. Get it together. You've held her hand in public before. You've danced with her in front of a big crowd while they all watched and applauded. What's the big deal now?*

But that was before.

Before we locked eyes through our bedroom windows and crossed whatever invisible line we'd drawn.

Forget crossing the line. We'd obliterated it.

But I agreed to go with her to her home realm and convince her family that I want to be her eternal partner. If I can't even hold her hand in an abandoned parking lot, I'm definitely going to fail.

And I will *not* fail her. Not when she's come through for me every single time.

I wipe my palm on my jeans and slide my hand into hers. The

second she touches me, my mounting worry slowly recedes. She grounds me to the here and now. I fall into step with her as we walk toward the bus station.

"Do you want me to explain it?" she asks again.

"Yeah, it will help. Kill the element of surprise."

"The medium is like a ticket agent. Their job is to make sure no one enters or leaves this realm without being approved. They're like the guardians of the gates."

"Does this medium need to think we're together too?"

Desi nods. "Yeah. All the mediums think as one being. If one of them realizes we're faking it, all of them will. And it could get back to my father."

"Wait, one being? What do you mean?"

"Think of it like this: the mediums all share one conscience, they share thoughts, function as one. Don't let them fool you—they may look human, but they aren't."

I just shake my head as we enter the station; I have no idea what to say to that. Inside, everything is covered in dust—the counter, the linked plastic chairs in the waiting area, even the floor. We leave a trail of footprints as we walk through it, kicking up particles that catch the light. Desi guides me to a dark hallway in the back of the building. An exposed lightbulb hangs in the middle of the ceiling, with two steel doors on either side of the hallway. A hum of electricity comes from behind one, while the other is silent.

She nods to the quiet room, and I open the door. Bright light greets us along with a curvaceous blond wearing a low-cut shirt. The blond sits behind an oak desk with a large computer screen. They smack on a piece of gum and examine their pink, talon-like nails. "Can we help you?" they ask.

"I need to return to Infernis," Desi says, and for the first time, her tone carries the air of a royal.

Their big brown eyes framed with false lashes ping-pong between us. "Papers."

Desi digs out her identification and hands it to them. They set to work, pulling up her credentials on their computer, their nails clicking on the keyboard.

I lean in and drop my voice, saying, "Demons have passports?"

"How else would they identify angels and demons?"

"Of course," I murmur and wonder what other wild discoveries await me.

The medium returns the identification card. "It says here that you have clearance to bring one human with you. Is this him?"

"It is," Desi brightly says, holding up our clasped hands between us.

"You know the rules, he must return to this realm in two days." They turn their attention to me. "This is your one and only chance to visit outside your realm while you are alive. Anything you see beyond this point must be presented as a dream or a near-death experience when speaking with other humans."

"Yes, Desi explained everything to me," I say, recalling the hours she spent giving me a crash course in Infernis customs and traveling between realms.

"All right, if you will follow us this way, we'll open the portal for you."

The medium opens a tall, steel cabinet. At first glance it appears to be storage for mops and brooms. But when they wave their hand, the cleaning supplies vanish. "Enjoy your stay in beautiful Infernis."

Desi looks at me expectantly, and I sweep my arm out in front of me, delaying my entrance to the . . . *portal* for as long as possible. "After you," I say. "I insist."

Desi's bottom lip disappears between her teeth, and I know she's trying to keep herself from laughing as she steps inside the cabinet, holding her hand out to me.

"Come on, handsome. It's a tight fit in here, so it's a good thing you like me." She gives me a wink and pulls me flush against her. "Hi," she murmurs, sliding her arms around my waist, her fingertips slipping just under the hem of my shirt to graze my bare skin.

"Hello," I reply, hoping she doesn't notice the tremble in my voice. It's difficult to keep my wits about me with her proximity and the feel of her skin on mine. I place my hands on her hips, doing my best to not let them wander. But she is so soft and warm in my arms. And when our gazes connect for a split second, I swear there's fire in her eyes. Damn, I want to know what that burn feels like.

"No monkey business unless you're a two-pump chump. It's not a long ride," the medium says before closing the door.

Everything around us goes pitch black, and my stomach flutters like I'm being dropped. I grip Desi as tightly as I can without being too rough, but when bright multicolor bursts flash all around us like stars exploding in a night sky, I groan as my stomach starts to turn.

I drop my head to her shoulder. "What are those? Stars?"

Desi's voice is quiet and calm. "The energies of angels and demons. The In-Between is their final resting place when they choose to end their time in Infernis or Pax." As though she senses my panic, she slides her hands up my spine and places her palms on the back of my head, rubbing my scalp slowly and gently. Just like she did the night I found out she was a demon and she found out I'm a ball of anxiety. So even in this moment when I feel like everything around me is impossibly overwhelming, she brings me back to a place of calm.

I lift my face and a sound that I can only describe as pure childlike wonder escapes my lips. I'm aware that I probably sound and look a little ridiculous as I gape at the spectacular sight around us. This is incredible. And I thought sci-fi movies had the best CGI. They have *nothing* on the In-Between.

With a shudder everything vanishes, giving way to a man in a suit. A toothy grin spreads under their well-trimmed mustache. "Welcome home, Princess Desideria."

"Thank you," she says, guiding me forward with a hand on my back. I look behind us, expecting to see a battered storage cabinet standing in the open. Instead, I find a free-standing, arched door at the curve of a horseshoe-shaped driveway.

"What happened to the ugly cabinet?" I whisper.

Desi laughs, and the sound is like wind chimes echoing over the breeze. "This is Infernis. We don't need to hide the portals."

"That makes sense," I say, trying to find anything that signals I'm no longer in my realm. Nothing is out of sorts. Grass, trees, a small creature scurrying up a trunk, we could be anywhere.

Desi lifts her bag but I wave her off, laying it sideways on top of my rolling suitcase. When I intertwine our fingers again, my skin tingles at the touch, and I swear I feel her shiver. But I don't look at her to confirm. I can't.

It's about to be a *long* two days.

She turns to the medium guarding the portal. "Did my father send transportation for us?"

They nod and gesture to the gilded carriage turning into the driveway. "There it is now."

When the driver hops out of the carriage, I take a step back. The creature is unlike anything I've ever seen before. It has a long tail and skin with a greenish hue. The demon is humanlike and at the same time not. It flashes Desi and me a smile, showing off two rows of pointed teeth, before loading our luggage.

Realizing I'm staring, I release a long breath and take in more of this new place. The stars shine brightly in the sky and the cool breeze rustles the red and orange leaves on the dogwood trees across the street. A quick hum of wonder vibrates in my throat.

"Are you okay?" Desi asks, her curls whipping around and nearly hitting me in the face.

"Yeah, it's just—" I struggle to put my thoughts into words. "I expected this place to look ridiculously different from home. But it doesn't. It's just . . . *enhanced* somehow, I don't know."

It's not the only thing that's enhanced. Ever since we stepped out of that portal something about Desi has been different. I've told her before that she's gorgeous, and I meant every word. But here? Here she's resplendent. Everything about her is brilliant and dazzling. Her hair, her eyes, her—

Desi laughs as the driver opens the back of the carriage and we step inside. "What, you mean because we are about to take a horse and buggy to the palace instead of a car like normal people? And yes, we do have cars. My father is just extra AF."

I smile at the human slang she has picked up since moving in with Cannon and me, attempting to focus on it instead of how radiant she is in the moon's glow. "You have cars. That's unexpected. Is it always night here?"

"It's not night. It's quarter 'til five in the morning. It only took us a few minutes to travel through the portal."

"Right. Does your Circle look like this?" I ask, watching the scenery pass by. Antique light posts and storefronts with hand-painted signs line the cobblestone street. It's like something out of a Charles Dickens novel.

"No. My father has a thing for nineteenth century New York. Each of my brothers has made modifications to their Circle to reflect their personal taste. Some are what humans consider futuristic and others very medieval."

I turn to Desi, interested in her answer to my next question. "Then what will your Circle look like?"

She smiles and leans her head back against the seat, not taking her eyes off me. "Honestly, I haven't let myself give it a lot of thought. I want my eternal partner to be able to help me decide so that he's happy too." She bites her lip, and that simple little action does something to me. Something that is going to make being close to her this weekend really damn difficult. "What do you think about a space-themed Circle? Or maybe something modern, like a graphic designer would envision?" She gives me a wink and I swallow hard, forcing myself to stay with the conversation.

"A *Star Wars* themed Circle?" I ask, keeping the mood light.

"It's possible."

"Wild." I shake my head, soaking in the architecture and flora outside the carriage window.

It isn't long before we're pulling up in front of what appears to be a palace. We climb out of the carriage, and my jaw just about hits the ground as I look up at the building looming in front of us. It's constructed with black and gray stone, with turrets and spires, and stained-glass windows depicting dark but oddly beautiful scenes from what must be Infernis's long and storied history. No doubt it has countless rooms inside, and I want Desi to take me on a tour of every single one.

"My god," I mutter, eyes scanning the massive home and everything around it. "This is incredible. This is where you grew up?"

The grin that spreads across Desi's face is wide and proud, and I know immediately the answer is yes.

"Wait until you see the inside." She grabs my hand, guiding me to the front steps. "Come on, handsome. Let's go meet the fam."

"Wait, wait. Desi?" I pull her back, nearly causing her to bump into me. "Am I underdressed? I feel like I need some tights and one of those ruffly dog collar things."

She snorts with laughter. "Hades, no. Trust me, no one wears tights. Much less a Shakespearean shirt."

"You know who Shakespeare is?"

She ignores my question. Her gaze travels up and down my body, taking in my tailored black slacks and the fitted no-tuck crimson button-down. "You're perfect, Jace."

Her compliment makes my insides do some weird melting thing. I'm not sure whether to fear the outcome or revel in the feeling. It's something to analyze later.

"Do I bow when I meet your mom and dad? Should I pledge my allegiance to hell? Will they expect a blood sacrifice at dinner?"

"You're stalling."

"I'm *nervous*."

She leans into me. "Have you never met a girl's parents before?"

"I have. My ex's mom hated me, and her dad barely acknowledged my existence. It was one of those moments I'll never forget and never want to experience again. Hence the no serious relationship rule."

It's the most I've ever shared with her about any of my previous relationships, and the curious way she looks at me shows that she recognizes that. "I see. Well, clearly, she wasn't the one for you." Nearly cutting off her own sentence, she quickly backpedals and continues, "Not implying I am, just saying—don't compare her rude-ass family to mine, because mine may be a bunch of literal demons, but they're awesome. Now come on."

She tugs me up the stairs and through the doors as the doorman ... doordemon ... doorbeing. What is a demon with a face like a warthog and the body of a jacked-up bodybuilder that opens doors called?

"You don't have to bow, a handshake will do. Don't pledge your allegiance to anything. And the blood sacrifice won't be necessary. Not until the third meal," she says with a playful wink.

We enter the foyer, and I crane my neck back to admire the enormous chandelier dripping with black and clear diamonds. We climb the imperial staircase and weave through hallway after hallway. I slow her down as I examine every painting hanging on the walls and ask questions about them. It isn't until we reach a pair of black doors with snarling gargoyle heads carved into the wood that I fall quiet except for one question.

"Is this your father's office?"

She lifts her fist, wiggles her eyebrows at me, and knocks. A muffled command comes from inside, and she opens the door. The chance to show my nervousness is over. From here on out, I am the man who has vowed to be Desi's eternal partner.

The king's study might be the closest depiction to what I pictured when Desi told me where she was from. The skulls of countless creatures act as bookends on the floor-to-ceiling bookcases, and I can't help but wonder if Desi's father has some sort of fixation with biology or anatomy and physiology. A fire burns in the onyx fireplace and mounted above the mantle is the stuffed head of some vicious-looking creature that I cannot identify. The room is terrifying, but it doesn't compare to the being sitting behind an ebony desk in a high-backed chair.

Desi's father is a beast, but not like the demons with sharp teeth and scaled skin roaming the halls of the palace. No. The ruler of Infernis is every blue-blooded man's worst nightmare when meeting a girl's dad. He is the biker gang leader, the Mafia crime lord, the overprotective father who will break every bone in my body if I hurt his little girl. He wears fighting leathers and a crown of bones rests on his shiny, bald head. He gazes at me with a murky green stare, assessing me from head to toe.

Desi urges me forward, saying, "Father, it's good to see you."

"Desideria, I'm pleased you're here, and not alone."

I freeze, fixated on the giant ax sitting in the center of his desk like a menacing paperweight.

Desi nudges me, breaking my trance. I lock eyes with her, and my heart stutters and restarts in my chest when I see the adoring, loving expression on her face. "It's good to be home, and I am especially happy to introduce you to Jace Wilder, my boyfriend." She says the words with such confidence, they roll off her tongue so easily, that I have to remind myself that this isn't real.

"Jace," the king of Demons says, extending his hand.

I tap into that reassurance Desi gives me with her touch and extend my hand, my fingers trembling. "Mister . . . Your Majesty . . . Lord . . ."

So much for playing it cool.

"Chaos. You may call me Chaos."

I finally make contact with his palm and my face is on fire. "It's nice to meet you, Chaos."

"You as well. I've had your room readied for you, and your luggage should already be there. Go ahead and get freshened up, I have a big day planned for us. My wife and I will take you and Desi to visit her Circle today. The boys will be here for dinner with their partners. I'm sure they'll get rowdy as they always do." He releases my hand from his iron hold, and I flex my fingers to get the blood moving again. "Desi, I was thinking you could spend tomorrow showing Jace your favorite spots in Infernis and let him get acclimated to the way demons do things."

"That sounds like a plan to me," Desi agrees, then looks at me. "What do you think?"

I give her an enthusiastic nod. "I'm ready to see more of this place already. The small amount of architecture I saw during the ride here was so diverse. The planning sessions for them must have been intense," I muse, sharing the thing that has intrigued me the most since arriving in this realm.

Desi laughs. "Jace is a graphic designer, so he's enthralled with all things art and design related."

Chaos raises a dark brow. "Well, he's in for a treat, then. We'll head out and show Jace more once you're both settled."

"All right. Ready, handsome?" Desi asks.

"Absolutely. Again, sir, it was great to meet you, and I can't wait to see more of your realm."

Chaos nods his dismissal and we leave his study. As soon as the doors shut behind us, I let out a huge breath. Desi grins, placing her hands on my biceps.

"You did so good!" she says, shaking me gently.

"Thanks. But that was the most terrifying meeting of my life. Did your dad have a huge ax lying on his desk?"

We turn and walk, and she snorts, saying, "Yeah, but usually it's strapped to his waist, so . . ."

"The hell equivalent of a dad with a shotgun. This is definitely scarier."

"It's just for looks."

A humorless chuckle escapes my mouth. "Sure it is."

After taking countless winding hallways and staircases, we finally stop at a door. When she opens it, the sensual aroma of jasmine and vanilla greets us. Embers crackle in the fireplace, casting a soft glow on the ivory flowers etched into the mantle. The plush white settee is angled to capture the light shining through the lace curtains framing the window and the warmth emanating from the fire. There are pops of deep purple thanks to the decorative pillows and the comforter covering the four-poster bed in the center of the room. The *singular*, king-sized bed.

"Fuck me running. This should be interesting," I say, running my hand over the back of my neck. I don't know why I assumed they would separate us. We're adults who are supposedly in a committed relationship.

Desi's face flushes and she busies herself with a loose string on the sleeve of her jacket. "I didn't think about the only having one bed thing. I can go see if I can find an empty bedroom to sneak you into; I just worry that someone will notice and think it's strange we aren't in the same place at night," she rambles, her skin getting redder and redder the more she speaks.

I know what she's thinking about, because I'm thinking about it too: the night we spent on the couch and what Lux had sensed the moment he entered the house. That was one night *accidentally* sharing the same space. Sharing a bed on purpose . . . every demon will sense my desire for her whether they have the power to scent lust or not.

"Or I can sleep on the settee. It's just not the most comfortable thing in the world and *definitely* not long enough for you," she continues, capturing my attention again.

"No way!" I'm surprised how quickly I speak. Wanting to play it cool, I sit on the mattress and bounce a couple of times like I'm testing it out. "We got this. It's just sleeping. That is unless your father has some high-tech security devices in here that will make sure we consummate the relationship."

"I don't—he wouldn't . . ."

"It's a joke, Desi. But if you're uncomfortable sharing a bed with me, I can sleep on the floor."

"I'm not uncomfortable! I mean, I don't mind sleeping with you . . . oh, kill me now," she groans, burying her face in her palms and sinking onto the bed next to me.

I wrap my arm around her and rub her back. "Shhh, you're fine. I can't imagine the stress you're under. Don't let it get to you. You're not in this alone. Granted, my track record for impressing parents is zero to one, but maybe I'll do better this time."

She drops her hands and smiles. "You already have. I can tell my dad likes you. I'm not worried about that for one second."

"I don't think that was hard to do. Your dad seemed overjoyed that you brought a real-life human man with you. I think the only requirement was a pulse."

"Not at all. If my dad thought you were a tool or a douche, he would've given me *the look*. I've seen it many times, trust me. As long as my mom likes you, you're in."

"No pressure at all." I think of the last mother I had to impress. That was the beginning of the end, the first sign that our relationship wouldn't withstand harder times. It should have been clear to me, but it was her mother who caught on first.

"Is there anything I should do to win her over?" I ask.

Desi thinks for a moment, and her face turns that pretty shade of pink again. "Treat me like a goddess you can't get enough of and show how much you adore me. My mother is a sucker for a great love story."

I run two fingers over my lips and look her up and down, no longer able to contain how attractive I find her. I mean, I shouldn't hold back, should I? Isn't that why we're here? To convince people we're together? I can play into all the reasons I'm attracted to Desi. It will be the truth and buy her the extra months she needs to find a real partner.

"I can handle that," I say.

Her hand next to mine on the bed twitches, and I hook my pinkie around hers. When I lift my head, she's gazing at me, and she inches closer until her other fingers slowly entwine with mine. "I have a feeling you'll be really good at this," she whispers.

"Is that so?" I say, but the words come out more like a growl, sending a heatwave through me that there is no way she can't feel. Every inch of me is going up in flames, and the only thing that will soothe the burn is pressing my body to hers, and not just in a ballroom at a dance in front of a crowd of hundreds. I need her naked, curvy body underneath me.

What is wrong with me? I'm doing her a favor, playing a game. I need to keep focused and not let my dick take control, no matter how much it reminds me that it would like just that. That door should remain closed, but I inched it open the night I watched her come undone in her room. If I swing it wide open, I'm going to have a hell of a time closing it again.

"Yeah, that's so," she murmurs, scooting closer to me and shifting to her knees. I lift our clasped hands and rest them on her thigh, and I feel her shiver at that tiny bit of contact. "You're already making me believe you want me, and we just got here."

"That's because—"

Three firm knocks come from the door.

Desi and I jump away from each other, and she hurries to her feet, clearing her throat. "What is it?"

"Sorry to bother you, Your Grace, but your parents asked me to inform you that they are waiting for you and Mr. Wilder. The carriage will be here shortly to take you on the tour of your Circle."

"Thank you, tell them we'll be there in just a moment."

"Yes, Your Grace."

I stand and run my palms over my face. I can't let myself get out of control. Not in private. Not when it's not for show. Because then I have no excuse. And that's when my heart is in danger. Desideria's the kind of woman who will walk right through that open door and steal every last piece of me. She's hard to resist, though. Her face, her laugh, her body, her eyes, her skin . . .

"What's wrong?" she asks. "Why are you looking at me like that?"

I blink several times and shake my head. "Nothing's wrong, Desi. I just . . . you look different here. Your hair is redder, and your eyes are greener. And I swear your skin is glowing."

She doesn't even look down at herself; it's like she knows exactly what I'm talking about. "Both angels and demons are more . . .

luminous, I guess is the right word, in our home realms. No one has ever had a reason to notice before, though."

Something about her in that moment seems so vulnerable, so precious, like a rare gem I need to protect. "You're beautiful. I mean, your skin takes well to your natural environment." I smack my hand to my forehead. And there you have it everyone, Jace Wilder at his finest, complimenting a woman with what sounds like scientific bullshit.

A grin spreads over her face, and she reaches up, taking my hand off my forehead. "That was quite possibly the most adorable compliment I've ever been given."

Adorable. That's great. I'm sure that'll win her mother over. We might as well wrap a bow around my neck and walk me on a leash. I work hard to stay in shape; maybe her mother will appreciate it if I get down on all fours and wiggle my ass for her.

"Adorable is what I aim for," I say, taking her hand and leading her out of the room.

Her parents are waiting for us inside the carriage, their gazes filled with good-natured accusations as we climb in and sit across from them. Of course they think we were caught up in some heavy make-out session. Little do they know that the man Desi's passing off as her potential partner hasn't so much as kissed her.

Although he's starting to forget all the reasons why . . .

"Mother," Desi says, giving her a warning stare. "This is Jace. Jace, this is my mother, Athena."

The queen of Infernis is graceful, with her pointed chin held high and a diamond and ruby crown perched on her head. Her red hair spirals down her back in thick curls, and her skintight silk gown hugs her hourglass figure. If it weren't for her amber irises flecked with blue, Desi would be the spitting image of her.

I hold out my hand and grasp her delicate fingers. "Athena? As in the goddess of war?"

Her heart-shaped lips lift slightly at the corners as she says, "Not that Athena, but her story is notorious in our realm and her name a popular one."

"Don't let my bride fool you, Jace," Chaos says, bringing Athena's knuckles to his lips. "She causes wars in her own way. One being the pounding battle cry of my heart when she steps into a room."

Chaos's words are admittedly cheesy, but the sentiment behind them is pure truth. Anyone can see that he's madly in love with Athena, and the affection he showers upon her is the kind of romance Desi reads about in her romance novels. No wonder she has such high expectations for love.

"Ugh," Desi groans, rolling her eyes. "You two are so nauseating. Sorry you had to witness that, Jace."

"It's nice to see two beings so dedicated to each other and in love."

Athena smiles and leans forward to pat my knee. "You don't have to look far. The attraction you and my daughter have for one another might rival what Chaos and I share."

Desi looks at me with wide eyes, but I just lock my fingers with hers and give her mother a bright smile. "I suppose only time will tell."

"Indeed," Chaos and Athena say at the same time.

Desi may think I'm oblivious to the wiggled eyebrows and her mother mouthing that I'm *really handsome*, but I see them gently teasing each other. However, most of my attention is on the passing scenery and the questions I'm asking Chaos about his architectural taste.

When we reach Desi's Circle, we stroll the grounds, and I listen to a detailed explanation about what it will take to run the Circle she'll inherit. The landscape is simple—grass for as far as I can see with a sprinkling of leafy trees. And energies everywhere. They glow in pinks, blues, greens, and yellows while relaxing under the sun or soaring in the air on swings hanging from branches. The energies don't have human forms but there is a humanlike quality to them, a head and limbs, but without facial features or hair. Chaos says they mostly stick together, communicate telepathically, and feed off the energy created by this realm.

"I think these guys need a lazy river that runs around this place," I say, remembering the waterpark staple I used to frequent as a child.

Athena stops stroking Chaos's forearm and spares a glance at me. "A lazy river?"

"Yeah. In my realm, they're found at waterparks or resorts. It's a river that runs in a circle, and humans sit in flotation devices and just float. I think these energies would enjoy it."

"Already making plans," Chaos says, giving me a firm pat on the back. "I like him, Desideria. He is already considering those under your keep."

The show of praise by Chaos creates a lump of emotion in my throat. It's been a long time since I had a parental figure give me any attention. My last acts as a son went unnoticed. It didn't matter that I was a kid taking on an adult task; no one told me *good job* or so much as patted me on the back. It feels good to be seen like that again.

Desi smiles and nudges me with her elbow. "He's a creative genius, always thinking two steps ahead."

My cheeks heat, and I shake my head. "Hardly, I'm just a graphic designer."

"Stop it," she chides me, pressing her index finger to my lips and turning to her parents. "Don't listen to him. He's not *just* anything. He's so talented—he started his own company from the ground up."

Chaos stops walking and sets his mouth in a firm line. He looks me dead in the eyes and says, "You know, if you ever need help, I can pull some strings . . . for a small price."

I take a step back. "You don't mean . . . Desi said you don't do that. I mean, energies and souls . . ."

Chaos roars with laughter, and Desi's mother whacks him on the arm. "Chaos, you almost gave the boy a heart attack."

"Come on, Athena. It's all in good fun. You have some preconceived notions you'll need to overcome, but I got a feeling you'll get there, son."

Son. I let it sink in and bask in the sudden swell of pride it brings me. It's nice to feel like part of a family again. A good family that loves each other unconditionally, that would stick it out through the tough shit. It's a change from what I'm used to when it comes to my own family.

Desi's parents look at her with such adoration, like they would turn a realm on its head if it made her happy, like they would set aside their self-preservation if it meant seeing her smile. I get it. That smile might not be mine for eternity, but it's mine for the next two days. And I plan on being the reason for it until I have to let her go.

SIXTEEN
DESI

As we walk back to the carriage, Jace laughs and slings his arm around my shoulders. "Desi, are your brothers going to tease me like this too?"

"Of course they are. Father is a cupcake compared to them. They're relentless. So get ready for it," I say, turning and placing my palm on his chest, peering up into his face.

I'm playing the game, letting my parents see our affection in action, but I can't help feeling guilty. They've accepted him so easily. I was sure my father would wear a hard exterior up until the end of our visit and my mother would treat him with that haughty royal attitude she dons just for dramatics. When I come back home for good without Jace, they're going to be very disappointed.

Jace nudges me with his hip. "If I didn't know better, I'd think you're going to enjoy them giving me a hard time."

"I have to admit, it's fun to see you get all flustered. It's not like it happens that often, so it's sort of like seeing a shooting star or something."

"Trust me, you get me flustered too," he murmurs so quietly I almost don't hear him.

"What'd you say?"

"I—"

"It's almost time for dinner, so we better get back to the house," my father interrupts, and I could strangle him. "Jace, did you know that Desi gets irrationally angry when the family is even five minutes late for dinner?"

Before Jace can answer, I laugh and say, "When's the last time anyone was just five minutes late? I'd be *thrilled* with five minutes instead of twenty!"

Jace flashes a million-watt smile with dimples and all. "That must be why we get along so well. I have a thing for punctuality too."

"Just another reason you're good for each other," Mother says and climbs into the carriage.

I turn my face to the side and cringe. Our plan is working too well. My mother is practically etching our names into the his-and-her items she'll buy for our home. I wouldn't be surprised if she's imagining what her future grandchildren will look like.

The ride back to the house is full of lively conversation between Jace and my father, but Jace remembers what I told him before we left; he doesn't take his hands off me the entire time. He's either running his thumb over my knuckles or smoothing his palm over my thigh. When we pull up to the front door, he helps me out. We follow behind my parents, making our way to double doors that encompass an entire wall. The armored demons standing at each side pull on the iron door handles and reveal the dining room. Surprisingly, all six brothers and their partners are waiting for us.

"Well, I'll be damned," I say as Jace and I make our way along the stone-topped table to the two empty high-backed chairs in the middle. Doing my best to keep my composure, I glance at Jace from the corner of my eye. I'm sure a room with six red-headed demon princes and their eternal mates is quite the shock. Leather and chains, fine silk and suits, the other six future rulers of Infernis are intimidating to say the least.

"Good evening, my dear family," my father says, his voice reverberating off the walls.

"Good evening, Father," everyone replies in unison, my brothers keeping their dayglow-green eyes on my "future eternal partner."

Jace doesn't so much as flinch under their scrutiny. He studies the two enormous Gothic paintings on the walls, while keeping a firm grasp on my hand. I wonder what he thinks of the art that pays tribute to our realm's influence on bloody human wars, and the array of naked beings in compromising positions giving in to their carnal desires. I bet the seven deadly sins never felt as real as they do now. He is literally going to sit with the incarnation of them at the dinner table.

As my parents make their way to the head of the table, I study each member of my family. Tall, short, midsized, plus sized, slim, brawny, white, brown, Black, tailed, and without, my brothers' eternal partners add spice to our family dynamic. Each chose a demon whose unwavering support will make them a strong lord over their Circle. Some bonded themselves with their best friend, and others found the love of their existence. But all of them are pure chaos.

"I can't believe all of you are actually on time," I say, tapping my fingernail on the table.

"Of course we are," Avaros says, straightening his leather jacket over his bare, sculpted chest. "When Lux came back and told us how positively delicious your man was, we all wanted to be here to get a look as soon as possible." His gaze travels up and down Jace's form. "He wasn't wrong. I would want to keep him for myself too."

Jace's cheeks and mine turn the same shade of red. "Oh, for fuck's sake," I mutter. "Please stop it."

"Little sister is getting greedy," he says, taking a long sip of wine.

"He's just as delectable as I remember, Des," Mandis chimes in.

Glen crosses his arms and pouts. "What about me?"

"Do not worry, my succulent little peach. I can gorge on both of you."

"All right," I say with a clap. "Let's try to pretend we're a normal family for just one meal."

Jace meets the gaze of each of my brothers and says, "I'm flattered, but I think I already chose the sibling I like best."

My lips turn up in a smile and I slide my hand into his under the table. "Yeah? Well, that works out because I'm pretty sure she kind of likes you too," I say, leaning over and planting a kiss on his cheek, pushing back the fluttering wings in my belly.

"How many times have you bitched at me for showing affection at the dinner table?" Lux asks, while his wife's long spiked tail slithers up to where the buttons are open on his shirt, stroking his exposed chest.

I roll my eyes and shake my head. "That's because you and Bernadette would go for it in the middle of the table if someone didn't stop you. I'd like my dinner without either of your bodily fluids involved, thank you."

Jace chokes on his drink and pounds his fist to his chest to get it down.

Fier straightens his tie and brushes the lapel of his suit jacket. "Spill it, Jace. What was your first impression of our little sister?"

Everyone leans in, their undivided attention on Jace. This is the moment of truth. What he says next will determine if they're buying what we're selling. If one of them believes we aren't completely in love, I will be marrying a demon of my father's choosing.

Jace looks at me and smiles. "I won't lie. It's hard to look away when a fiery redhead with green eyes that almost glow walks into the room. Not to mention, she was wearing this blue sweater that displayed one of her many fine assets. She was so damn determined to be my roommate. But the last thing I wanted was a woman in my life, human or demon. I enjoy my freedom and having control of the things around me. But Desi upended it all." His voice drops, and it's like everyone has vanished and it's just him and me. "She's a little hurricane, leaving mayhem in her wake. But in the eye of her storm, there is a sweet moment of calm. She is the most beautiful chaos."

A chorus of *awws* and gagging noises—I'm pretty sure those are from Mandis—go up around the room, but they may as well not even be there.

He remembers everything about the day we met, down to the sweater I was wearing. But it's what he said last that has my heart in my stomach.

She's a little hurricane, leaving mayhem in her wake. But in the eye of her storm, there is a sweet moment of calm. She is the most beautiful chaos.

Is that just Jace playing the fake dating game for my parents' benefit? Or is that vision of me as true as the rest of his speech?

I have so much to say, but all I can manage right now is, "Is it really?" He glances down at me quizzically and I clarify, "The chaos . . . is it beautiful?" The look I give him lets him know that I'm not asking as part of the game.

He tucks a rogue curl behind my ear and the gloomy hue of his eyes brightens, turning almost a shimmering silver. "Desideria, your chaos is so fucking beautiful that sometimes, I wish it would devour me."

My lips part and I'm engulfed in flames, consuming every inch of my skin. I don't know what to say, and even if I did, I wouldn't be able to speak over the gigantic lump in my throat. I settle for leaning in and tangling my leg around his under the table, just wanting to be close to him.

After we stuff ourselves with three courses of gourmet foods, my father dismisses everyone, and Jace and I head up to my room. As soon as the door closes behind us, I plop on the bed face down.

"I am so full," I moan into my pillow. "I never eat as much as I do on family dinner nights."

"I never eat this much, *period*," Jace says, lying down next to me, his hand brushing my thigh for a fraction of a second. "But that food was amazing. You guys must have the best chefs in all three realms."

I can hardly think of anything except the spot where his unintentional touch still lingers. "Yeah, we do. Dad is extra about a lot of stuff, including his food." My heart bangs against my chest and I feel like I'm about to crawl out of my skin. "I'm going to change clothes," I yelp, jumping up and shuffling into the closet, shutting the door and leaning against it.

Closing my eyes, I mumble, "Get your shit together, Desi." It's just Jace. Why am I in such a mess over him *accidentally* brushing my freaking leg with his fingers? He held my hand and swiped curls from my face all day. But now we're getting ready to go to sleep. In the same bed.

With a deep breath, I change clothes and re-enter the room. Jace is still lying in the same spot, propped against the headboard. I smile, probably too brightly.

"Hey, sorry, just had to get out of those clothes," I say, sitting next to him, leaving a respectable distance between us.

We glance at each other from the corner of our eyes, and Jace licks his lips and tucks them between his teeth. "Is sleeping with me making you nervous? Remember, I can take the floor if that will help."

I turn to him. "No. I'm not nervous. Really. Are you?"

He tilts his head side to side, pretending like he's conflicted. But the sparkle in his eyes tells me he already knows his answer. "I don't know. Are you going to grope me in my sleep? Am I going to wake up with you wrapped around me like a koala?" He leans forward so our eyes meet. "Are you going to want to cuddle?"

The tension in the air evaporates, chased away by his humor. I'm glad he isn't taking this seriously because I feel a little stupid for not considering the sleeping arrangements before we got here. Demons don't care about modesty or stifling their desires. My parents wouldn't have expected us to worry about those things if we were truly dating.

I scoot toward him and say, "I'm big on consent, so I won't grope you. But I might tangle my legs with yours. We did that on the couch that night. I don't know if you know that."

"I know *and* I remember how your legs felt."

My head snaps in his direction and my cheeks redden. "What? You were awake?"

He lifts a brow and asks, "Weren't you? Because if you were, I think my legs deserve an apology. I don't recall you asking permission to give them a massage with your toes."

I groan, falling face down into the mattress. "I didn't even mean to! I was trying to figure out how the hell we ended up in that position and what body parts were where." My voice is muffled into the pillow. "I'm sorry, Jace, I didn't mean to grope your shins." A snort escapes me as I hold back hysterical, unhinged laughter.

He laughs with me. "Would it make you feel better to know I liked it and the lust your brother sensed when he walked in the house *was* mine?"

My laughter stops and I gnaw on my bottom lip. "It does. I mean, I already knew it was yours—Lux had no problem sharing how 'delectable' you smelled. But it's nice to know it wasn't *just* a chemical reaction, that you actually liked me touching you," I whisper.

"Don't get too confident in your footsie skills. It's been a while since I woke up with a woman. I'd forgotten how good it feels to have warm, soft skin next to mine."

"I'd never known what it was like to wake up with someone beside me. You're the first person I've ever slept next to," I admit, chewing the inside of my cheek.

Jace eases down onto the mattress next to me, and the warmth radiating from him drifts to my side of the bed. It takes every ounce of my willpower not to move closer, to rest my head on his chest and trace my fingertips over his pecs. Just his presence has me acting out of sorts.

"How did you go so long without simple physical joys? You've got a good century on me, and you've experienced so little."

I adjust on my side so I'm facing him and tuck my hands under my cheek. "There's just no one I've ever wanted to share that stuff with before. I've had plenty of chances. But there's been no person I've looked at and thought, 'Yep, I want to sleep in the same bed with him and wake up with tangled limbs the next morning.' Not until—" I stop and clear my throat. "Anyway, I'm ready to experience some things for sure."

"I thought you were going to check off a few of those things with Cannon," he begins, almost tentatively, like he's afraid I'm going to shut him down. When I don't, he continues. "You're sure you don't want to explore that? Cannon's a stand-up guy. He's smart, driven, funny . . . respectful. He'd be good to you, Desi."

"Cannon *is* a good guy, you're right. But even he admitted that he didn't feel anything. And I don't think that's going to change."

Jace's brows tick upward. "Cannon said that?"

"Yeah, he agreed with me one hundred percent. That it was *nice*, but there were no fireworks. That we were better off as friends."

"You two shouldn't give up because of one kiss, Desi. A relationship is about way more than the physical. Sparks can ignite over time. It's more important that you find someone who will always have your back—a true partner."

"I understand that, but I want it all. The kiss with him was a *fine* first *real* kiss, but I've been more turned on by the spicy books I read. And like I said the other night . . . by what you and I shared through the window." My face immediately flames with the mention of that night. "I need that kind of out-of-this-world chemistry too."

"I think I need to take a look at these books you're reading."

"You should. They're lifesavers on lonely nights. Or nights when there's nothing going on across the way in your bedroom," I tease.

Jace shoves me playfully and then gives a thoughtful hum. "I can't believe that was your first real kiss. I can understand if you were from my realm why you might avoid acting on your sexual needs, but you're from a place that's so free with everything that humans are taught is wrong. How were you able to stifle that desire for so long?"

If I had been around a being I was as attracted to as I am Jace Wilder, I never would have been able to hold back. But that's not how it's been for me. "Because no one in Infernis has made me want to explore that part of myself. I don't know, it's like . . . like I'm waiting for that one fire that I can't put out. And I hadn't even seen a spark of it here. So, it wasn't worth it to me. Which means that I am a very inexperienced demon," I say with a sheepish shrug.

"I can now see why sleeping in the same bed as me might be a little unsettling." He lifts his arm and pulls me in next to him. "But I promise I'll behave and meet your need for cuddles. You have nothing to worry about, Desi."

I snuggle into him and tuck my foot underneath his leg. "And just what do you think I might be worried about, Mr. Wilder?"

"That I might lose control and ravish you."

I know he's joking, but my breath still catches in my throat, and my gaze meets his. "And how do you know I wouldn't welcome that?"

"You don't want that, Desi. I have a track record of fucking and never calling a girl back for a second date. Nothing I can offer is romantic, or lasting, for that matter."

I want to tell him that doesn't sound anything like the man I know. He's a reliable friend and passionate about his work. Hell, the man is even dedicated to his video games. But I don't want to ruin what we have going on here. I like being this close to him, being in his arms like this.

So instead, I just say, "I'm not worried, Jace. All I want is to lie like this. It's enough."

His grip tightens on me, and he places a kiss on the top of my head. I soak up his body heat, letting it lull me to sleep. When I'm in that cozy place between awake and asleep, I swear Jace's chest rumbles and he whispers, "I'm scared it won't be enough for me."

SEVENTEEN
DESI

Fingers caress my temple, sliding curls away from my face. I savor the touch, keeping my eyes shut and remaining in my sleepy fog for a moment longer. I hate to think that if I inch my eyelids open, I'll realize this is just a dream that feels real. It very well could be some cruel trick of my sleep-deprived imagination. I woke up several times during the night to make sure I was still wrapped in Jace's arms. Every time I stroked my fingers down his chest, he grabbed them and held them to his heart.

Another featherlight touch traces the slope of my nose to the indentation above my lip. My heart flutters knowing he's watching me while I sleep.

The way he touches me sends electric currents running through my veins, and I don't know how much longer I can stay still. When his fingertips lower to my lips and trace the outline of my cupid's bow, I can't help it.

Our eyes meet, and the gray in his isn't stormy, but warm and cozy.

"Good morning," I rasp, biting my bottom lip shyly and releasing it as I search his face for what he's feeling as he gazes down at me.

He pulls his fingers away, curling them into a fist. "Good morning. Sorry if I woke you up. You just looked so . . ."

I shake my head and put my hand on his, opening it and

intertwining our fingers. "Don't do that, don't apologize. And please, finish your sentence. I looked so . . . ?" I offer him a smile that I hope tells him I'm truly curious and not making fun of him.

"You looked peaceful. The way your eyelashes rested on the tops of your cheeks and your lips puckered was innocent. It was like nothing bad plagues your dreams. I bet you dream about organizing cups the wrong way while floating on fluffy clouds."

I scoff and shove him with my free hand. "I do *not*. Especially because I happen to organize the cups the *correct* way. But I *did* dream last night. About you."

He quirks a brow. "Oh? What about?"

"Exactly where I want to take you on an adventure today. I can't believe I didn't think of it before now."

"You dreamed about taking me on an adventure? Is this going to be the eighth circle where they pull out toenails and plunge hot pokers into eyes?"

I wiggle my eyebrows and tickle his ribs. "No, that's where my dad is taking you before dinner tonight. This adventure is here. Within walking distance and everything. You want a hint?"

"Yeah. I'm intrigued."

"It has to do with the thing you love the most."

"Quiet afternoons and peanut butter puff cereal?"

I roll over and cross my arms on top of the cover. "Come on. Think a little harder. Although you could enjoy this thing on a quiet afternoon . . . and I suppose you could eat your peanut butter puffs while looking at it or designing it."

"Digital art. Is your dad looking for someone to design the new neon sign to hell?"

"You are full of jokes this morning."

He releases a long breath and looks up at the ceiling. "What can I say, I'm in a good mood. And now I'm eager to see what you have planned. Come on, little hurricane. It's time to start my last day in this realm."

My heart skips a beat at the term of endearment. I've never loved a nickname more in my life. "All right, give me a few minutes and I'll be ready to go."

Twenty minutes later I've showered, changed out of my pajamas and into a sundress, and Jace and I are walking down the cobblestone streets of the town square. Our fingers brush each other every so often, pulling my attention to him. He greets the variety of demons who acknowledge him—big, small, hairy, naked, terrifying, and humanlike, his interactions with them are no different than if they were beings from his realm. It wouldn't surprise me to learn that many of the demons don't realize he doesn't belong among us.

"So, where are you taking me?" he asks, looking down at me with a curious smile on his face.

"Uh-uh. I'm not telling you. It's a surprise. You could threaten me with one of Dex's never-ending speeches about the importance of demons and angels in the human realm, and I *still* wouldn't tell you."

Jace's forehead crinkles. "Dex?"

"You've never heard of Dex? Iudex?"

His features wrinkle more with confusion. "I don't know who that is."

"She's the most powerful being in all the universe. She judges all angels and demons when we step out of line and is the one who grants us entrance to the In-Between for eternity when we're ready to no longer exist in this state or banishes us to the Perpetual Torment if she deems us unworthy of existing any longer."

"You mentioned that earlier. It's interesting that you can *choose* when to no longer exist. What if you just want to live forever?"

I give him a sad smile as memories of my grandparents and old friends flash through my head. "Every lifeforce eventually craves rest.

My father wasn't the first to rule this realm. And his rival Angelo wasn't the first to rule Pax. Lucifer, Lilith, Hades, Beelzebub, they have all chosen to go to the In-Between. The way it's been described to me is something beyond peace. It's perfection."

"All of those demons, they were . . ."

I chuckle when I recognize the fear in his eyes. Those are scary names in the human realm. "They were all my grandparents and their parents and so on."

Silence stretches between us for a moment before Jace takes a deep breath. "And Dex has a tendency to prattle on, I take it."

"That's a nice way of putting it," I say.

"Torturous," he murmurs, wrapping his fingers with mine and swinging our arms between us as we walk.

The gesture is so natural, so smooth, that it nearly takes my breath away. I need to calm down; the theatrics of this are getting to me a bit. Because the truth remains; this is all for show. When we return to the human realm, things will go back to normal. No more kisses on the cheek or little stolen touches. We'll return to amicable roommates who happen to peep at each other while satisfying our own needs.

I nod toward the giant structure in front of us. "We're here," I announce, forcing myself away from my thoughts.

The pyramid covered in mirrors is unlike anything else in Infernis—a building clear as day and yet not. It reflects the midday sky and surrounding structures, blending in with the motif my father prefers while remaining unique.

Jace cranes his neck and shields the bright sun with his hand. "What is this place? It's not a tomb of dead demon rulers, is it?"

I snort and bump him with my hip. "Absolutely not. I won't take you *there* until our fifth date. Come on."

Keeping hold of his hand, I lead him through the revolving doors and into the lobby of the pyramid. An imp sits at the welcome desk, and she smiles brightly, her white, pointed teeth sparkling in the mid-morning light.

She rushes out from around the desk and curtsies deeply, her tail swishing around her. "Your Highness, Princess Desideria, welcome to L'Arte del Peccato. We are so thrilled you've decided to grace us with your presence today, and that you've brought Mr. Wilder with you."

"Please, there's no need for all the formalities." I check her name tag. "Sila. Thank you for being here and keeping this place running; I can't wait to show Jace everything it has to offer."

She beams and directs us into the first exhibit. "Enjoy yourselves. Please know the pyramid is empty besides you and the artists and will remain so until you are finished with your visit. Take all the time you need."

"Thank you."

As we walk toward the first exhibit, Jace looks down at me in wonder. "L'Arte del Peccato? The Art of . . . ?"

I grin and push open the red door. "The Art of the Sin. First up, Wrath."

A large demon with tusks and gray skin bows as we enter and points us to the center of the room. We walk up to the peak of a small hill, illuminated by a single light. The space is a void with black walls, and even the sound of our footsteps vanishes. When we're in place, a single drumbeat fills the room. It grows louder and louder, a battle cry. The demon sweeps his hands in front of him and a splatter of red runs across the walls, and he goes to work. As if he is conducting a symphony, the demon paints a picture of a battlefield. Soldiers lie lifeless on the ground. Occisor demons with massive, bulky frames dressed in armor wield their weapons, blood dripping from the blades.

Jace sits on the top of the hill, his eyes wide and mouth open. "It's digital art," he says.

I sit beside him. "It is."

"But how does he control the color with just his hands? And the lines are so precise."

"It's similar to virtual reality. The cuff on his wrist is programmed to respond to certain movements. He can change the colors by just pointing a finger."

The battlefield morphs from reds and blacks to orange flames that engulf the devastation and the sky above us turns into plumes of smoke. The artist takes us through a moving vision of wrath in some of its most threatening forms.

When the room descends into darkness again except for the single light where we sit, Jace turns to look at me with countless emotions written on his face. "Desi, this is amazing. I've never seen anything like it in my life."

I smile and get to my feet, holding out my hand to him. "I knew you'd love it. Come on, there are six more rooms to go."

The next room we enter is flooded in a deep green glow, and immediately Jace whispers, "Envy."

I hum confirmation and we go to the place the tall, statuesque demon is indicating for us to sit, a bench in the center of the room. We settle down, and Jace drapes his arm over my shoulders.

This exhibit is more abstract than the first—this artist is using every shade of green imaginable to create swirls of color around us that somehow make me feel like I'm caught in spirals of jealousy. I can't explain it, but the sensation is so real that I feel myself turning inward toward Jace in an inexplicable overprotective position. And when my knees meet his, I realize it's having the same effect on him. Our eyes meet and dart away from one another instantly, and we focus again on the bursts of jade, clover, lime, emerald, and mint that surround us.

When the colors fade, we move to the next room. The air in here is heavy and perfumed, and the walls are peppered with soft pinks and reds.

"Is this . . . ?" Jace asks as the door slides shut behind us.

The corner of my mouth turns up as the curvaceous blond demon up front beckons us to the blanket in the center of the floor.

"Lust," I say, my voice a husky rasp, and I rub my thumb over the center of his palm, completely ignoring the fact that there's no one here to show off for.

With a rich and smoky voice, the demon says, "I suggest you touch during my exhibit. Rest your head in his lap or lie next to each other. Whatever makes you comfortable. But I've been told that the physical interaction heightens the experience."

Jace sits down and spreads his legs before pulling me into the space he's made. He arranges me so my back is against his chest and his arms are wrapped around my waist. "Is this okay?" he asks.

"It's better than okay," I murmur. "I really, *really* like being close to you." *Why not be honest? I have a feeling this exhibit is about to make things awkward in here.*

"Good to know."

Jace rests his chin on my shoulder, and the demon sets to work. Like the artist before her, she also uses abstract images, but hidden in each are the curve of a hip or the swell of a breast. Bodies in human and demon form in the throes of passion. Some pairings are innocent, a stroke of a hand or lips pressed to a cheek, and others are completely lewd. But it doesn't matter what she paints, each stroke of her hand sends a flurry of warmth through me.

I'm not the only one affected by the art. Jace can't seem to stay still. His fingers sweep over my stomach, back and forth. Each stroke gets lower, moving over my belly button and onto the tops of my thighs. His chest expands against my back and his breathing turns shallow. But it's the growing hardness at the small of my back that captures my attention and causes me to lose focus on the art.

Jace wants me. Right now. He couldn't deny it if I asked him. This knowledge multiplies my desire and I shift between his legs, fighting a moan as I feel him twitch against me.

My center throbs and my skin aches to be touched. His hands on me feel so good, but I long for them to be under my dress, on my skin. I fight the urge to crawl into Jace's lap and feel him pressed against me. My nails bite into my palms, and I chew my bottom lip, using the pain to keep me in place.

He sweeps my hair away from my neck, and goosebumps cover my arms when his lips brush the shell of my ear. "I'm so fucking turned on."

If I thought feeling the proof of his need was sexy, hearing the words is enough to make me lose it. His lips on my neck set my entire body aflame. My brain chants that it's just the exhibit making us feel like this. The sexy, entwined images are arousing us, invoking a response from our bodies. If we were sitting like this anywhere else, we wouldn't feel the same.

But my heart and soul know better. At least for me.

I rest my head back against his shoulder and close my eyes, exhaling a shaky breath. "Me too," I murmur. "I've never seen the lust exhibit before; it's the only one of the seven I've never visited. I've heard what it—how it can affect you, but I've never experienced it firsthand." I clench my thighs together and watch his fingers as they play with the hem of my dress. "This is intense."

"That's an understatement," he murmurs. His fingers inch higher under my dress. Skin on skin, hot, smooth, needy. "What if I told you that I want to touch you?"

My breath catches. I can't let myself believe that he means what I think he means, because if he doesn't, I don't know if I can handle the disappointment. So I whisper, a smile in my voice, "You *are* touching me, Jace."

"I want to make you come on my fingers," he groans, moving dangerously close to my center. "Let me touch you just once."

"Fuck," I gasp, pressing back against him, discovering that he is even harder than he was a few moments ago. If that's possible. "Please, please, Jace. Touch me."

I unhook my ankles and bend my knees. Jace's palms glide from the tops of my thighs to the insides, easing my legs apart. He toys with me, drawing figure eights as we watch the art materializing on the walls. Each image is more erotic than the next. The indiscernible shapes have given way to clear pictures of demons in one sexual act after another.

He inches toward the part of me that's been craving him for weeks. My heart feels like it is going to burst from my chest, and each rotation of his fingers makes my breath hitch. It's not until he brushes the wet fabric between my legs that I stop breathing.

"Is it the art or me that makes you wet, Desideria?"

I nearly come apart at his touch and at his words, and I can hardly speak, but when I finally answer, my voice is hoarse with desire. "Both."

It's a lie and the truth. The art stirs something that has sizzled inside me for weeks. Ever since he was there for me when I needed to get away from that club, ever since he took his shirt off that night when I realized I could see into his room, when he almost kissed me. I could go on and on. Every night I dream about touching him, putting my mouth on him, but I've stifled that need. But in this place made to intensify desire, I'm all out of fight. I want to know what those fingers will feel like inside me.

I slide my hand between my legs, placing it on top of his. With a racing heart that makes me tremble, I guide him to move my panties to the side. "Please touch me," I beg.

Jace's fingers glide through my slick center, and he hisses, "*Fuck*, Desi."

The kisses he peppered along my neck and shoulder have turned into sucking and biting. He finds that sensitive part of me that aches for his attention and presses circles to it. Every rotation is gentle and slow but with just enough pressure to have me lifting my hips for more.

I know I should conduct myself like a princess of this realm. But I can't stop chasing that feeling that makes my skin tingle and the muscles in my abdomen tighten. I want to come apart, even with an audience.

"Please," is all I can manage. I can't wait any longer; every nerve ending in my body crackles with pent-up energy, and if he doesn't give me what I need, I'm going to explode.

Not only that, but I want to touch him. I love the position he has me in, at his mercy, but I want to put my hands on him. I grip his thighs, wishing with everything in me that I could feel his skin under my fingertips.

"What are you begging for, Desideria?" His fingers slow. It feels good, but it's not enough. Not even close.

"You. I need you to make me come. Don't tease me anymore, Jace," I whisper, rolling my head toward his neck, kissing up toward his jawline.

He doesn't take his gaze away from the violet, pink, and red images. He studies every brush stroke and mimics them between my legs. His free hand slides up my torso, leaving a trail that burns through the thin fabric of my dress. He grips my neck before easing his two middle fingers between my lips. "Suck," he commands, and the domineering tone in that one word nearly unravels me.

I draw his fingers into my mouth and brush my tongue along the undersides. A moan rumbles in my chest and I suck harder. The strokes under my dress become bolder, faster. His thumb rubs me in a way that my own fingers fail to do, and he dips inside me.

"You're so warm and tight. Can you do it, little hurricane? Can you come for me like this?"

I groan and nod, tightening around his finger in answer, lifting my hips to push it farther inside me. There is something so damn sexy about the way he's using me as his canvas to re-create the art that is being fashioned around us, and it makes me feel like the most desirable creature to ever exist.

As he rubs my clit harder, I shift against him, wishing so badly that I could wrap my hand around the length that I feel at the small of my back. I whimper as he stretches me, adding a second finger. Sucking harder, my cheeks hollow out and I fantasize it's his cock I've got my lips wrapped around.

As if she is inspired by the reaction of my body, the sweeps of the artist's brush move faster and the color shifts from the romantic pastels and reds to bold, bright splatters. My skin pebbles and my core winds tight while chasing the release it so desperately needs.

"That's it. Let go and come for me," Jace says, his voice deep and dripping with his own desire.

The longing in his tone is my undoing; I can't hold back another second. The coil inside me unfurls, my lips parting, his name rolling off my tongue like a prayer. His hand down my neck, across my collarbone, and into my dress. My nipple is already hard, but when his fingertips brush over it, it tightens to the point of pain.

"Jace," I gasp, lifting my hips and writhing against his hand, losing all regard for where we are and the fact that we aren't alone. All I care about is chasing the high he's giving me, giving in to the lust I've been feeling for weeks, and basking in the knowledge that he wants me too.

Everything slows and the warmth of the afterglow settles upon me. I turn to my side and rest my head on Jace's chest, his heart pounding under my ear. He brushes back the damp curls around my face, and I meet his gaze. Holding my stare, he brings the two fingers that filled me to his mouth and sucks them clean.

"Is that what you've been chasing after with that drawer full of toys?" he asks.

"Uh, yes. Suffice it to say, I never catch it. Not like that," I murmur. "Why don't you let me—"

The clicking of heels echoes through our moment, and I find the beautiful demon placing her sketching device on the hook by the door. She bows her head and says, "You may stay and enjoy my art if you like. Thank you for giving me the inspiration to create it."

I soak in the final results. She felt the sexual tension between us, and as it mounted, the wild, sexy painting on the walls and ceiling came to life. The art is an expression of exactly what she felt radiating from us.

"You're welcome. Thank you for sharing it with us," I say.

"It was my pleasure."

She slips out of the room, and Jace slides out from behind me and stands. He crams his hands in his pockets and strolls the perimeter of the room, admiring our collaboration with the artist. "Did she physically feel what we did, or is it just the emotion that she could interpret?"

"Just the emotion. Only Lux can tap into someone's lust in a truly invasive way."

He continues to walk, and I can't help but notice the strain of his jeans over his erection. He was just as turned on as I was, yet he never sought his own release. It must be uncomfortable to walk in such a state. I know I can't stop thinking about how slick my inner thighs are after what happened between us.

I was about to ask if he'd let me touch him when the artist stopped painting and packed up. I wish I had been able to get the words out. Now the spell has been broken.

"That was intense," I say, walking up beside him, my fingers brushing against his. "I'd heard about how it could affect you, but I'd always thought people were exaggerating."

Jace nods and hooks our pinkies together. "The art in this room is powerful, to influence us to give in to our body's impulses in such a way."

"Especially after we just talked about how we could never—" I clear my throat as we walk to the door to the next exhibit, sure that he understands what I'm getting at.

He stops in his tracks and my pinkie slips from his. Running his fingers through his hair, he says, "Trust me, I enjoyed it too. I'm sorry if I crossed a line. I didn't mean—"

"No. You didn't cross a line. I wanted it to happen, but I know we shouldn't do it again."

"We *can't* do it again, Desi."

I hear the words, but I also see the conflict in his features. This isn't how I want to end our time together. We have more to see in the gallery, and I don't want one moment of overthinking to ruin it. I hold out my hand and wiggle my fingers. "Come on. Gluttony uses smells in the exhibit. I really hope it smells like fresh brownies."

He smiles at that, and the worry melts away. "Peanut butter cups. I hope it smells like peanut butter cups."

I grin as he intertwines his fingers with mine. "Compromise: peanut butter brownies."

EIGHTEEN
DESI

After our last meal in Infernis, my entire family accompanies us to the portal. My brothers and their partners spend more time saying goodbye to Jace than they do me. They've created little inside jokes with him, and he and Glen even made up a handshake that ends with them licking what I believe symbolizes an ice-cream cone for Jace and a certain part of my brother's anatomy for Glen, and all of them say they can't wait until he's here for good.

I've just helped my family fall in love with a man they'll never see again, because he'll never be my partner.

Father moves beside me and wraps an arm around my shoulder and lowers his voice, saying, "I want you to know that what I've asked of you and your brothers is more important than my ongoing rivalry with Angelo. Although I do enjoy gloating that more energies have chosen Infernis as their home than Pax."

"I know that. No demon ruler has been responsible for the happiness of so many energies before. I imagine that stress is a lot for you," I say, patting his hand.

He grunts as he watches my brothers and Jace. "Your happiness is important to me too. The job you will take on ruling the Circle of Sloth won't be easy. Your mother has been my rock, just as your grandmother Persephone was Hades's. Your brothers have found the beings who will support them through the good and the bad. I want that same kind of devotion and companionship for you. Someone with a good head on their shoulders to help guide you when I'm no longer here."

My head snaps up and I search his face. No one is as strong as my father. He's carried the Seven Circles for centuries. Under his rule our realm has flourished, and he's won the ongoing gentlemen's bet with Angelo for decades now.

"We have time, Father. I'll figure it all out eventually."

"I must admit that I had my doubts when you left, but Jace is a perfect fit for you, Desideria. I'm proud of you for stepping up to the plate, but even more than that, glad that you've found someone who makes you happy."

My heart sinks to the pit of my stomach and I've never felt so guilty in my life. "Thank you," I murmur, leaning into my dad's embrace and hugging him around the waist. "But, Dad, he hasn't agreed yet, so don't—"

He waves me off. "Yeah, yeah, it's only a matter of time, though. I can see it in his eyes. He loves this place almost as much as he loves you."

My heart leaps back from my stomach all the way into my throat.

Jace could never love me. Jace doesn't believe in love. We're roommates, friends . . . apparently with a few benefits. But he's not in love with me because he's made it clear he'll never let himself love anyone again.

That thought makes me sad. I push it away to finish up the show for my family.

"Desi, come on, the medium is ready for us," Jace calls, holding out his hand to me.

"All right, I'm coming," I say, turning back to my parents and wrapping my mom in a hug before addressing everyone. "I love you guys, and I'll see you soon, okay? Thank you for being so kind to him."

Julius and Lux exchange wicked grins. "That fine specimen of human better return with you," the prince of Lust says with a wink, and suddenly I hope that he doesn't have some kind of weird connection to everything that goes on in the Museum of Sin. I shudder to imagine it.

I roll my eyes and wave over my shoulder. "Okay, on that note . . . bye!"

I take Jace's hand, and after going through the motions with the medium, we step into the portal.

"You ready to go back to reality?" I ask, giving his hand a squeeze.

"Yeah, it's time. My stomach isn't feeling well and I'm starting to feel light-headed. I guess my time in hell is officially up."

"Oh no," I say, placing my palm on his forehead and checking for a fever. I let out a relieved sigh when I find his forehead a normal temperature. "Okay, no fever, you're fine. You'll be good as soon as we get back to the human realm. Close your eyes, I think we're about to—"

And with that, we're off. A few moments pass and we're back in the broom closet in the bus station, being greeted by the gum-chewing blond.

Jace still looks a little woozy when we reach the BMW, so I pull a bottle out of my purse and shake a pill onto my palm.

"Here, take this," I say, handing it to him with a bottle of water.

"What is it?"

"Devil's claw root. It's only found in the human realm, but my mom keeps a stash of it. It's the only thing we've ever discovered that helps humans when they've stayed a little too long in Infernis. I grabbed some before we left just in case this happened."

He nods and swallows the pill before helping me load our suitcases into the trunk. He hands me the keys, and I drive us home. I realize then how sick he must feel if he's letting me drive. Jace follows all the traffic rules; he even holds the steering wheel at ten and two.

It's another thing he never gives up control over. I'm so grateful we left when we did.

My brain buzzes with thousands of thoughts. I think about my family's reaction to Jace, the responsibility of my Circle, but mostly, I think about the man next to me. Jace's hands rest on his stomach, his eyes closed, and soft snores drift through his lips. I wonder how things will change between us now that he knows everything about me, about where I come from . . . and after what happened between us in the lust exhibit.

It was an effect of the art; it played on the tension that had been building between us. But will it change our dynamic? Will it make things feel awkward around the house? I hope not.

When we get home, Jace carries in our bags and kicks the door shut behind us. The sheen of sweat is gone from his skin, and it has returned to its beautiful tan tone. He doesn't wait for me, taking the steps two at a time and heading for my room. Keeping some distance, I wrap my arms around my stomach and watch as he heads for the door. My heart sinks and I fight back the sting in my eyes. Everything is awkward. We've crossed a line we shouldn't have and now he can't even look at me.

He stops at the threshold and glances at me over his shoulder. "Thank you, Desi. I'm honored that you trusted me with such an important secret and that you let me help you with your family."

It surprises me enough that a tear I'd been trying to hold back nearly slips down my cheek. I wipe at my eye and step toward him. "No, Jace. I should be thanking you. You trusted me with your life, something you've come close to losing in the past, and I can't put into words what that means to me."

He drops his bag and turns to face me. Leaning against the door frame, he cocks a brow and says, "Come on, you let me bring you to an orgasm in the same room as a demon artist. Once in a lifetime experience."

And there it is. The playfulness and humor he shows when he lets his guard down. I was so close to thinking I'd never see it again, that we ruined what we built with one moment of uncontrollable passion.

I cover my face with my palms and laugh, sinking down onto the mattress. "I mean, there was no way I was getting out of that room without having an orgasm. I was just glad you were the one to give it to me. It was by far the best one I've ever had."

His gaze darts to my bedside table and the drawer in the top. "I'd hate to think I've put some expensive toys out of business."

I clench my thighs together and my face heats. "Even my clit-sucking toy has nothing on you, Jace Wilder."

He blushes. Blushes! Rubbing the back of his neck to hide his face, he says, "And with my newly inflated ego, I apologize for clearly putting a favorite device to shame, and wish you good night, Desideria."

I smirk and bite my bottom lip before nodding in his direction. "Good night, Jace. See you in the morning."

I contain the giddy laughter that bubbles in my chest as I enter the house. Jace and I finished another *Star Wars* movie, completing his favorite three. To celebrate the occasion, I ordered him a gift, and it arrived today. Jace has been stressing out since we returned home. He jumped back into his proposal for the guy Matt wants him to hire. Late nights and early mornings have ruled his life, and every minute in between is spent behind a computer screen. He carved out two hours last night for us to finish the third movie, and I'm excited to offer him another small reprieve.

I fumble with Jace's gift as I shut the door and maneuver through the entry. It's long, awkward, and bound to bring chaotic joy to his day. I step into the kitchen and find him sitting at the counter with a bowl of cereal, his laptop, and his glasses sitting high on his nose. This is perfect timing. He is clearly moving toward stressed out.

He glances at me from the corner of his eye and mumbles, "Another busy day at the mall, I see. That has got to be the strangest pair of shoes you've ever bought."

"Although I looked at several pairs of shoes today, this didn't come from the mall. It was just delivered to the house." I place the box wrapped in black paper in front of him. It stretches from one side of the kitchen island to the other.

He picks the gift up and studies it. "This is normally where I would make some ridiculous guess about what you bought, but I'm at a loss."

"I guess you'll just have to open it then."

His attention splits between ripping the paper and watching me. He looks hesitant, like I've wrapped a boa constrictor in a box and handed it to him with the hopes that it will curl around his body and put him out of his misery. The nondescript box comes into view, and he pries open one end. He looks inside and just as quickly closes the flap.

"No way," he says with wide eyes.

"Yes way. Take them out."

Jace opens the box again and removes two lightsabers. He hits the button on one and it lights up with a deep, electric drone. The red light reflects off the steel kitchen appliances. "Oh my god."

"The other one is Luke's," I say.

He turns on the other lightsaber and jumps to his feet. "Desi, these had to cost a fortune."

I shrug one shoulder. "Eh, my dad has no real concept of human money, and he's given me *way* too much as an allowance. I suppose I could have told him, but instead I decided to spend some of it on my friend. Dad has been saving his fortune for like, eight centuries now, so I think he can spare it."

Jace hands me Darth Vader's lightsaber and he takes Luke's in his other hand. "All right, I recall having a lightsaber fight once in this very room, and you had no idea what the hell was going on. And now, not only do you know what's going on, you bought me my very own weapon. It's time for a duel."

I grin and back up to the other side of the kitchen with the lightsaber in hand. "Join me and together we can rule the galaxy."

"Never." Jace swings and the glowing green light streaks before him with a sound that matches.

We spar and every time we hold our weapons together, they crackle with electricity. Our duel leads us around the kitchen and into the living room. Like children, we stand on the couch and jump off, bringing our lightsabers together again. I make a move to land my blade across his stomach, but Jace spins out of my way. The determined gleam in his eyes tells me that he won't let the dark side win.

I move around the coffee table, hoping to gain some of the space I lost. Jace bolts the other way and grabs my wrist. My lightsaber ends up on the floor and my arm behind me. He pulls my back to his chest and holds the lime-colored light to my throat.

"Surrender," he says against my ear.

My stomach clenches, my skin prickling with the awareness of how close he's pulled me against him. I don't think he intended to make this moment sexual, but I've gone from playful to horny in five seconds flat.

"I will if you will," I whisper, all thoughts of the duel out of my brain. I'm thinking with a *different* body part now.

He holds my wrist a little firmer and pushes the blade against my skin. "You give in so easily. If only you knew the depraved things I want to do to you, princess."

I'm not sure how he turned the tables. He was the good guy, and I was the bad. Now, I'm not so sure. I shouldn't let my mind run away with this thought. I shouldn't picture the wicked things I want him to do to me. But the husky sound of his voice won't allow me to ignore them.

Even though I know I shouldn't, even though I know it's going against everything we agreed on before we left Infernis, I push it just a little further.

"I can only imagine," I say, bumping my ass against him to see if he's as turned on as I am. Of course he is, and my panties are immediately soaked at the feeling of his erection. "But even better? I'd like to feel them."

His grip on me wavers, and he takes a step back. I'm afraid I've taken things too far. But when I turn around, Jace flashes me a smirk and replies, "Too bad I'm not prone to fraternizing with those who are on the wrong side of the Force. No matter how stunning they are."

Relief washes over me and I stoop to pick up my lightsaber, switching it off and setting it on the island. "Okay, what about now? I'm no longer on the wrong side," I say, holding up one hand in surrender and placing the other on my hip. "Now I'm just stunning." I lift one side of my lips in a grin that I hope tells him I'm teasing.

"I should reward you for coming to the right side of the Force, but seeing you wield a lightsaber was really sexy. I know, let me make you dinner. Fettuccine alfredo?"

I can't argue with that. "Sounds perfect, Skywalker. Don't let your guard down, though. I might switch sides at any moment. You have to keep your eye on me."

His laughter fills the kitchen as he moves to get the pots from the cupboard. "Keep swaying your ass like that when you walk and I'll have no problem keeping an eye on you."

I raise an eyebrow and stroll past him, swatting him on the ass.

"I'm built a certain way, so I can't help the way I move, *but* I will admit . . . I sway it a little extra when you're around."

"What a coincidence. I shake my ass more when you're around too. Tell me my efforts haven't gone unnoticed." He grabs the firm globes of his rear and looks over his shoulder. "I've worked hard for these buns of steel. I want to know someone in this house appreciates them."

"You aren't kidding. You've got an ass to die for. I absolutely appreciate your efforts *and* your rear end. And don't worry, I notice when you shake it. You do it when you pour your peanut butter puffs. It's like you're dancing out your bad attitude because you know your cereal is coming."

Jace pulls ingredients out of the refrigerator. "I'm getting ready to put twenty cups of sugar straight into my veins; of course I'm happy when I'm making my cereal."

"Fair enough. Do you need any help?"

"Nope. I told you, I'm doing this for you. Go sit on the couch and relax while I do all the cooking," he says, and the sloth in me has no problem obliging.

After running upstairs to change clothes, I'm lounging on the couch, my pajama shorts rolled up a little too far to be considered decent, my tank top dipping low in the front, and my hair falling wildly over my shoulders when Cannon strolls in from work.

"Good evening, roommates," he greets us, lifting his chin as he enters the kitchen. "Jace, are you making alfredo *again*?"

"We've got to keep our princess happy. Besides, check out what she bought me." He tips his head toward the counter. "I'll be making her dinner for the next year."

Cannon picks up one of the toys and whistles. "What did you do to get this?"

"Apparently she has a thing for me shaking my ass."

Jace flashes me a cheeky grin, and Cannon gives me a surprised raise of his brow and asks, "What were you two up to while I was gone?"

"Nothing really. It was like a trip to hell without you here," Jace answers.

I clap my hand over my mouth, smothering a giggle. The way he talks about my home realm is so tongue in cheek, but I don't miss the adoration in his eyes. He enjoyed his time with my family. A week ago he asked me to explain my family line and some of the legends of my realm. In exchange, he told me about his career and his decision to become a business owner. The give and take of our conversations has become one of my favorite things. Besides giving his ass a little swat.

Cannon comes over to the living room and flings himself in the chair across from me. "So . . ."

I lift an eyebrow and repeat, "So?"

"I have this friend who has two tickets to a concert downtown Saturday night. His date bailed on him, and I thought you might want to go."

A chuckle rings out from the kitchen, accompanied by the tinny sound of a wooden spoon sliding in circles inside a pot. "Real smooth, bro."

Cannon cranes his head over the chair back, looking in Jace's direction. "I have the balls to ask the lady out on a date if that's what I wanted to do."

I cover my mouth with my fist. It's a clear jab. Cannon has been saying for weeks that Jace has a thing for me. Now I know he does, but he's dead set on not acting upon it. Shots have been fired, and Cannon took no prisoners.

"I don't date," Jace grumbles.

"Your loss, man." Cannon shakes his head and hands his phone to me. "His name is Seth. Cool guy. Totally chill. I think you would have a good time with him."

I look at the picture of a handsome guy with light-brown hair and hazel eyes, a smattering of freckles across his nose. He wears a base-ball uniform with a field behind him.

"Is he really a baseball player?" I ask, unable to hide my excite-ment. One of my favorite rom-com actresses was in a movie about baseball. It was hard not to drool over the men in formfitting pants swinging at a ball with some kind of barbaric club.

"He is."

Jace drops a pan in the sink with a loud *clank*. "Don't set her up with a jock."

I twist around on the couch so I'm facing my roommate, whose skin has suddenly taken on a slightly green hue. Well, it might as well have because he looks so jealous that I wonder if my brother Julius rubbed off on him while we were in Infernis.

"Oi, you over there, shut up," I say with what I hope is a light, carefree tone. "I happen to like baseball."

"Yeah, man, baseball players barely even qualify as 'jocks.' They're not nearly as meatheaded as some of the other athletes I've known," Cannon adds. "Seth's a good guy."

"I just think Desi needs . . ." Jace yanks open the refrigerator and pulls out a carton of heavy cream. "Someone who'll put her first. Do you really think this guy is going to give up his baseball career?"

Cannon and I lock eyes. The exasperation on his face indicates his frustration with Jace. They always get along about everything. I hate to see a disagreement about my dating life putting a kink in their friendship.

"She's running out of time, Jace. At this point, every decent guy should be a possibility."

Jace fills a pot of water and slams down on the faucet handle to turn it off. He was in such a good mood a few minutes ago. I don't understand why this conversation is getting to him. He doesn't want to be one of my possibilities. He can't possibly believe that I wasn't going to come back and keep looking for a real partner.

"I mean, yeah, you're right," Jace says, mixing up ingredients for the sauce. "But shouldn't we try to at least, I don't know, make sure that we're helping her choose men who are actually viable options? And not ones who are probably playboys who can't commit to a cologne, let alone a woman for et—the rest of his life."

I shrug and glance at Cannon. "That's a fair enough point, but . . ." I look down at the picture of Seth again and wiggle my eyebrows at Cannon. "You went through all the trouble of setting this one up so I might as well, right?"

"You should. And you never know, maybe you and Seth will have a life-changing connection, and it all works out."

Handing his phone back to him, I say, "Will you send him my number so we can work out a meet-up spot?"

"Absolutely."

"Make sure your tracking is on. We don't want another issue like the one at Apex Fusion," Jace mumbles, adding more spice to the sauce.

"I will," I say.

While Jace finishes dinner, Cannon gives me all the information about the singer performing Saturday night. He plays me their music and shows me footage from one of their concerts. We remain huddled on the couch until Jace calls us to eat.

The mood doesn't change much at the kitchen island. We sit side by side, Cannon and I holding all the conversation while Jace focuses on eating. He finishes before us and rinses off his plate.

"Cannon, you got the dishes tonight?" he asks.

"Yeah, I got it."

"Thanks for dinner," I say in a quiet voice.

Jace gives a curt nod and heads to his office. "I'll be finishing up a project for the rest of the night. You two sleep good."

Several quiet minutes pass by after Jace disappears. The air is thick with tension. It's so uncomfortable that Cannon and I scratch at our arms and necks, never making eye contact. Whatever is going on with Jace has the potential to change the dynamic in this house.

NINETEEN
DESI

It's after midnight when I ease the front door open and step into the foyer. I sit on the bench and set to work unbuckling the multiple straps wrapped around my ankles. The heels were a sexy choice but not practical for standing and dancing for hours. However, they went perfectly with my little black dress, and I don't regret wearing them.

Not only was my date handsome, but he was smart and funny and very polite. Seth opened every door and thanked our server at the restaurant before we left for the concert. He even politely declined to give an autograph, letting his fan know he didn't want to be rude to me. His taste in music was fantastic, and he didn't shy away from singing along at the top of his lungs and shaking his hips. This date would lead to a second if it weren't for one major factor.

I didn't so much as feel a spark of passion toward him.

I'll admit I wasn't in the best frame of mind. It's been three days of awkward exchanges with Jace. He hasn't hung out or eaten a meal with me. Cannon has been away on a business trip, and I've attempted to consume every free moment Meredith has away from her husband and kids. It's been miserable around here.

After lining my heels up with the other shoes, I stand. The house is dark, forcing me to feel my way to the stairs. When I reach the top, I turn to go down the hall to my room but stop. The tension in this house has gone on long enough. If I have to eat another meal alone or watch Jace rush past me to his office with a mumbled greeting, I'm going to scream.

I march in the direction of his room. When I see a sliver of light shining beneath his door, my heart speeds up. I should walk away, wait until I'm not so worked up. But this can't wait. If I go back to my room I'm just going to toss and turn all night. But if I confront him tomorrow, I'll be sleep deprived and angry. I can spare him a fraction of my wrath by handling this now.

I knock on the door but he doesn't answer, so I take a chance and just walk in.

"Jace, can we talk?" I ask in a gentle tone, even though my voice is shaking with the effort of holding back my anger. I walk toward his bed and plant my hands on my hips.

Even as I stare down at him, he doesn't answer me, doesn't so much as flinch. My nostrils flare and my anger bubbles up inside me. I fear it won't be held back much longer.

"Jace!" I yell with an odd mixture of sternness and apprehension.

It's hard to both fuel my fury and keep my gaze from traveling down his naked chest. It's like he already holds an advantage, and we haven't touched on the root of the problem.

Finally, he lowers the book he's reading. His smoky gaze drags up to my heated face. "I don't know why you're asking the question when you've already barged into my room, intent on doing just that. I can't promise you I'm in the mood to talk, but you can say what you need to get off your chest."

I start to roll my eyes but instead I just close them and take a deep breath. "Fine. I just want to know why you've ignored me since that night I gave you the lightsabers. We went from having a good time laughing and dueling to you giving me the silent treatment for days on end. What did I do wrong? Help me out here."

Jace removes his glasses and sets them on his nightstand. He rubs his temples like just my presence is giving him a headache, but I know that's not the case. He's fuming because I'm confronting him, bringing the drama straight to his bedroom. But there would be no drama if he hadn't started it.

"You've done nothing wrong, Desideria. I've just come to realize that I can't help you. Dating isn't my thing. I'm not good at it, and I don't have anything to add to the discussion. That's what you're here to do, so I'm going to erase myself from an equation I don't fit into."

"You were fine helping me with it when you thought I was going to date Cannon," I say, crossing my arms over my chest and refusing to back down. He's not telling the whole story. There's something else going on with him. "Why is it that when another man got involved, you lost it?"

"I know Cannon. He would treat you right, wouldn't take advantage of what you're offering him. The assholes on dating apps and pretty-boy baseball players don't deserve to lay a hand on you when all they see is a beautiful face and a sexy body."

I rear my head back and nod slowly. "Oh. I see. That makes sense. I suppose that's why someone as intelligent and sophisticated as you couldn't be with someone like me—nothing but a beautiful face and a sexy body." He opens his mouth to respond, and I hold up a hand, running my tongue over my teeth. I'm on a roll now, my anger unleashed, and I won't be interrupted. "No. I'm not finished. But I was good enough for *you* to put your hands all over, wasn't I? Even though you had no intention of taking things any further. You fingered me on the floor of an art museum and never looked back. But those men are worse? Not good enough for me?" I scoff and shake my head.

Jace flies off the bed and stands on the other side facing me. "First, don't come into my room spouting some bullshit about how I supposedly think you are just tits and ass! You deserve a man who's intelligent and worships the ground you walk on. Not for one goddamn second did I believe you were worthy of anything less." He stabs his finger into his chest and continues. "I'm the asshole. I don't begrudge you the pleasure of pointing it out. What I did was a dick move. I placed you between my legs. I told you I wanted to touch you. I fucked you with my fingers. And I knew the entire time that it was wrong. I knew it, and I didn't stop myself. So, yes, I think I'm a fantastic judge of character when it comes to the men you should stay away from."

My face is blood red for about five different reasons, and I clench my jaw before I speak. "Come off it, Jace. Perhaps I should've known better, but you ignoring me for three days hasn't really helped matters. I was merely repeating what you said—that a man would automatically only see a beautiful face and a sexy body. Is it such a leap that I thought for a second that maybe that's all you saw too?" I move closer to where he stands and he takes a step back. "And don't pretend that you don't know that I wanted you to touch me. That you don't know I've wanted you to touch me for weeks." I keep walking toward him until I'm rounding his side of the bed and he doesn't have anywhere else to go. "That I want you to touch me right now," I whisper. "When are you going to get it, Wilder? I don't *want* to stay away from you."

He swallows and squares his shoulders, his stormy gaze blazing into mine. "I don't want to touch you again."

Those seven words are worse than a knife plunged into my heart and twisted. Tears sting my eyes and my chin trembles. "You're a coward and a liar."

He shakes his head, but the flex of his jaw holding in his words says it all.

I take another step forward, obliterating the space between us. "The idea of another man's hands on me makes you jealous, and instead of taking what I'm so freely offering you, you're lying to me and to yourself. It's a shame that you'll never grow a pair and take what you want."

I turn on my heels and leave the room, slamming the door behind me. I storm across the landing to my room and repeat the childish action. Gritting my teeth against the scream that's threatening to erupt from my throat, I practically rip my earrings out of my ears, remove my necklace, and jerk the cover down on my bed. I start to unzip my dress and turn to the window, staring out into Jace's room, where his curtains are wide open.

He's sitting on the edge of his bed with his fingers tangled in his hair, and I feel some satisfaction knowing that I've gotten under his skin because Hades knows he's under mine.

Unzipping my dress, I step out of it and kick it across the room. I reach around to unhook my bra and lift my gaze to the window, only to see Jace looking in my direction. Narrowing my eyes, I continue what I was doing, unsnapping the clasp and dropping the bra to the floor, leaving me in my bright-red thong.

I don't have to look back to know he's watching me. Every cell in my body buzzes to life, like his gaze is his fingers trailing down my spine. I continue to prepare for bed, using my powers to hang up my dress and pull out the pins that held my curls in place. Sauntering through my room in my thong, I create menial tasks—straightening a picture on the wall, leaning into my mirror to check if I have something in my teeth, and picking up a tiny scrap of paper from the floor. After my little show, I spare a side glance out the window.

Jace throws the book sitting next to him across the room and bounds to his feet. I expect him to march into his bathroom, but he flings his bedroom door open. I freeze, my heart so heavy in my chest that it weighs down my feet. Footsteps pound down the hallway, their beat oozing with pure determination. I wait for the sound of a fist hammering against my door, but it never comes.

I sigh and turn back toward the bed, about to give up on a second confrontation with him. I don't know where he's going, but it's clear he isn't coming into my room. It's not like he can go far. He's shirtless.

And that's when the door bursts open and Jace hisses, "Fuck it. I lied."

He closes the distance between us in two quick strides. His eyes burn into me, setting every inch of my naked skin on fire. I search for my voice, fighting for the words to ask him what he's doing. But he cups my face in both his hands and presses his mouth to mine.

Every muscle in my body relaxes and I melt into him, wrapping my arms around his neck. I realize as I part my lips and open to him that he hadn't kissed me in the art exhibit that day. I'd wanted him to ever since we stood toe to toe and argued over the laundry—when his mouth brushed mine and I felt those live sparks for the first time.

This kiss is everything I'd been waiting for. His lips move with mine like they were sculpted to fit together, and when our tongues meet, it nearly takes my breath away. He tastes like spearmint and smells like soap and sundried laundry. He is warmth and strength, and I could spend hours lost in his kisses.

"How is it that you infuriate me and turn me on all in the same breath?" he asks in a husky voice.

I gasp for air and say against his lips, "You have the exact same effect on me. That's why I couldn't stay away from you any longer."

"And this little striptease you just performed, what were you hoping would come of that?" His hand slides down my spine and pauses on the small of my back. My next words will determine what he does next. Will this moment just be a kiss, or will I tell him that he needs to turn it into something more?

I don't look away from him as I say, "This. That you would be brave enough to come in here and show me what you *really* want from me, Jace."

He scrunches his face and his fingers fist at my back. "This is a terrible idea, but I'm tired of fighting it."

Jace's mouth falls upon my skin again and his palms slide down my ass, pulling me closer. He's rock hard, the length of him digging into my pelvis. I follow his lead as he steps forward, and I step back. My fingers grip the hair at his nape, using it to steady my trembling legs. I fear that I'm going to stumble and rip his lips from my neck, breaking the spell he's under. It doesn't happen. The back of my legs hit the mattress, and he follows me down onto the fluffy blankets as I move up toward the headboard.

He holds himself over me, one arm on either side of my shoulders. Pressing against the juncture of my legs, he creates a steady rocking that hits me in just the right place. I move with him, needing that sweet friction to push me closer to the edge, to that place where I fall into oblivion and fly.

Jace kisses from one side of my neck, across my collarbone, and back up the other side. He takes his time showing attention to the sensitive spots that have me arching into him. Pulling away from my neck, he takes my breast in his palm, stroking my nipple until it's so hard it throbs. When the stimulation becomes too much and I whimper, he drags his tongue over the peak. The warm, slick sensation drives me wild, and I grip the back of his head. He understands my silent direction and draws my nipple into his mouth.

As he sucks and nips at the delicate skin, I tug at his hair with one hand and drag my fingernails down his spine with the other, pressing him closer to me, if that's even possible. He is everywhere all at once, consuming me until I know nothing but him. He lets go of my nipple with a pop and moves to the other. Lifting his free hand, he massages the abandoned breast, rolling the hardened peak between his thumb and forefinger.

"Fuck, Jace," I gasp, rocking my hips with his, harder and faster by the second. My release is building so fast that it's almost embarrassing, but I have wanted this for so long. Ever since that night after the gala, it's him I think of every time I slide my hand between my legs.

This is everything I fantasized it would be.

"I need to taste you, Desi. Tell me to make you come with my mouth." His words are a desperate command, spoken with a gruff voice.

I'm not sure how long he's thought about putting his mouth on me, but it's clear he wants nothing more in this moment. And he isn't the only one who needs this. I am throbbing to know what it will feel like to have Jace Wilder kiss me in the most intimate of ways.

I don't even hesitate before tugging his hair until his gaze lifts to mine. "Put your mouth on me, Jace." I take his hand in mine and slide it between us so he can feel just how much I want him. "You do this to me. Every second of every day. I want you to taste me."

"Fuck." One word with so many meanings—a grateful prayer, a passion-fueled moan, a promise of what's to come.

Jace kisses his way down my body, hooking his fingers into the sides of my panties. The closer he gets to my center, the lower the lace slides down my legs. He settles between my open thighs, kissing the inside of each before placing one leg over his shoulder. With his gaze trained on mine, he glides his tongue along my seam. Never has a toy made me feel what that single stroke does.

I let out a shuddering breath and grip his hair tighter, my other hand clutching the bedsheet next to my thigh. He doesn't take his eyes off me as he slips his tongue in a little farther, and when my lips part on a silent gasp, his mouth turns up into the sexiest smirk.

He brings one finger to my center and runs it through my slit. "God, you are so wet. Do you have any idea how sexy you are when you're like this? Your legs spread for me, fingers in my hair, back arching off the bed every time I touch you?"

Before I even have a chance to answer, he dives between my legs without warning and puts his mouth on me, his tongue sinking deep inside. I squeal without any regard for how out of control I might sound; all I care about is how he's making me feel—like I'm invincible, like my body is on fire in the best possible way.

Jace hums his approval as he devours me thoroughly. The tip of his tongue glides back to my clit, and he fills me with two fingers, reaching that place deep inside me. I break, his name flowing from my mouth, my body gripping him tight. Without missing a beat, he helps me ride out my high until I have nothing left to give.

I sink into the mattress, working to catch my breath. Jace remains between my legs, bathing me with his tongue and pressing kisses to my lower stomach and thighs. He is so attentive; I hardly have a chance to bask in the aftermath of the most intense orgasm I've ever had when that needy ache returns.

He's lapping at my center again when I tug on his hair until he looks up at me with lust shining in his gray eyes. "Jace."

He plants another kiss on my inner thigh. "Yes, little hurricane? You're interrupting my dessert, so it better be good."

I clench my core and tamp down the mounting desire building within me. *Damn, this man is going to take me out.* Thankfully, he gives me a reprieve. Jace licks his lips and rises to his knees. I glance down at where his cock is tenting his pants. He's still as hard as he was when he came in here, and I want to help him find his release, just as he did for me.

"Let me touch you. Please."

He reaches into his pants and lowers the waist, revealing his hand wrapped around himself. Not in all my decades have I seen anyone look so otherworldly. His chestnut hair perfectly rumpled, his cut abs like something chiseled by a sculptor's hand, and his cock . . . seeing it under his boxer briefs had *nothing* on this. His body is flawless. Even the gnarly scar on his chest is sexy.

With lazy strokes up and down his shaft, he says, "Tonight, on your date, you didn't—" He shakes his head like he's trying to dislodge the thought. "Have you ever touched a man?"

"You know the answer to that question, Jace."

"Do I?" he murmurs, shifting closer to me.

I rise to my knees but don't move any closer to him, letting him come to me. "You should. I didn't feel a spark of electricity with my date, Jace. No part of me wanted to touch him. In fact, all I thought about the whole time was what you were doing and if tonight *might* be the night you spoke to me again."

"Let me hear it. I need you to say it."

"No. I've never touched a man . . . not like that."

He stares at me with pure wonder in his eyes, like he's been given the most precious of gifts.

"Come here and give me your hand, Desideria."

The command in his voice makes my heart pound against my chest and my mind reel with provocative scenarios. Does Jace only enjoy giving orders or do his sexual tastes venture into more salacious types of play? I'm desperate to know, so with no reservations, I offer him my wrist.

"Open it for me," he murmurs, and when I unfurl my fingers, he brings my palm to his mouth and licks it, sending a shock wave of desire between my legs. He closes my hand around him, and his eyes flutter shut, his perfect lips parting, a groan escaping from low in his throat.

I move my hand slowly up and down. The sensation of his skin in my palm is addictive, and I can't help but tighten my grip on him. I enjoy the way he pulsates in my hand, and I steal glances at his face. He's always handsome, but it's impossible to stop staring when he's like this—his eyes hooded, jaw clenched, chest heaving.

"Is this okay?" I whisper, moving closer to him so our legs touch.

He releases my hand and combs his fingers through my hair. "Yes. Don't stop. I'm already close."

His touch and words drive me forward, and I speed up my strokes. With each pump, he grows harder. I marvel at his response, at how his body is so different from mine. Hard and soft, chiseled and curved, and all of it desperate for more.

"Come for me, Jace," I murmur.

"Fuck, Desideria," he gasps. His desire spills from him onto his stomach and over my hand. I draw my bottom lip into my mouth as I watch the milky liquid run onto my pale skin. If I thought watching Jace's desire was hot, the sight of him losing himself is off the charts.

Lifting my fingers to my mouth, I put my first two between my lips and suck, closing my eyes as the salty taste of him hits my tongue. I hum my approval and flash him a smile. "You taste good," I say as he reaches over to my nightstand for the tissue box.

"You're a wicked thing, and that's bound to get me hard again."

I smirk and lie back against the pillows with my hands folded behind my head as he gently wipes between my thighs before moving next to me. He doesn't lie down, but just moves my hair out of my face. The tips of his fingers fall to my chest and the crescent moon surrounded by seven pointed rays marking my sternum. It has an iridescent sheen, making it slightly paler than the rest of my skin.

"What does this mean?" he asks.

I shiver at his touch and say, "It's the mark of a demon. Every being not of this realm has one. Demons bear a moon and angels a sun with the same pointed rays, but not every mark is the same size or on the same part of their body. When angels and demons are in this realm, it's impossible to tell us apart. Unless I saw the mark, I wouldn't recognize a fellow demon since only those who have a humanlike form are sent here. It's believed that the creator marked us so we could identify each other and focus on humans when we're sent to guide them."

"It's beautiful. *You're* beautiful."

I press my lips to his and whisper against them, "So . . . you lied." He groans and a giggle escapes me. "You really thought I was going to let you slide right past that?"

The playful upturn of his mouth returns. I've missed that barely there smile these past few days. "I was hoping that my mouth between your legs would act as penance and that you would forgive me. Do you forgive me for being a jealous, lying coward?"

I smile and pull him down next to me. "Hmm . . . all right. I forgive you. But just so you know, you aren't going to be limited to doing that only when you screw up, okay?"

He falls back on the mattress, his arms spread wide. "Oh, the torture you inflict upon me, you evil demon queen. How will I ever survive having to taste you on a whim?"

I cackle and climb on top of him, straddling his waist and leaning back on his bent knees. "And now you see my true plans. 'Future queen of Sloth, too lazy to find a husband, shacks up with roommate instead.'"

Jace snorts and rests his hands on my hips. "You're funny. That's another reason you deserve to have the man of your dreams. You're too much fun to settle for anything less than perfect."

Lying forward on his chest, I take a deep breath and rest my chin on his pec. "That's just it. I'm actually afraid that at this point my father is going to end up choosing for me. You and Cannon have both said it yourselves; I'm running out of time. And when they find out you and I aren't going to 'work out' after all, he's going to lose patience with me. I just know it." Meeting Jace's gaze, I add in a whisper, "So that's why I'm going to ask you something, and I want you to hear me out."

Jace sighs and runs his fingertips up and down my spine, the motion both comforting and arousing. "All right. I'm listening."

I sit up, tugging him to face me, my legs wrapped around his waist. "My date tonight was confirmation that I'm not going to find someone who wants to go back with me from this realm. The time I have left just isn't enough to convince someone to give up their life here. I'm coming to accept that. My father will make a good choice for me. I'm sure my partner will step up when I need help ruling."

"You shouldn't give up. There is someone out there. Cannon—"

I place my finger over his lips. "You're listening, remember?" He sighs, clamps his mouth shut, and I continue. "I want to use the time I have left to have these kinds of experiences . . . with you. I trust you and you know what you're doing. I don't want to waste what's left of my freedom fumbling around with someone."

He slides his palm across the side of my neck and tilts my head back with his thumb. "Are you saying you want me to be your plaything while you explore your sexuality?"

I smirk and run my tongue over my top lip, keeping my eyes on his mouth. "That's absolutely what I'm saying, Jace Wilder. Are you up for it?" I ask, tightening my legs around his waist and grinding against his growing length.

Jace tilts his head back, his eyes darting across the ceiling. He's so practical. I can almost see him sifting through all the things that can go wrong and right.

"I'll agree on one condition," he finally says.

"What's that?"

"You stay open to finding someone yourself. You're too strong to roll over and let your dad choose for you. And if you find that someone, you have to let me know."

"I can do that."

"All right. You're going to have to explain what you expect of me. I wouldn't want to cross any hard lines for you." His fingers trail down my spine until he reaches the small of my back. He pulls me in tighter until his hard cock is trapped between us.

A whimper escapes my throat as I arch my back to create more friction between us, and a satisfied smile crosses my face when a hiss slides past his lips. "What if I told you I didn't have any hard lines? I am open to anything when it comes to you. I trust you that much."

He licks a path up the column of my neck and presses his lips to my ear. "I'd say you better pray I don't ruin you, Desideria."

I tilt my neck to signal that I want more of that, tangling my fingers in his hair.

If only he knew he already has.

TWENTY
DESI

"So, you're telling me that Harry Styles is a demon?" Jace asks.

Pointing at the pantry, I open the door from across the room and float a bag of pasta to my outstretched hand, then pour it into the boiling water on the stovetop. For the past twenty minutes, Jace has flipped through pictures of celebrities, searching to see if they have a mark.

"You tell me. Do you see a mark?"

"It's well hidden in his tattoos, but it's there. That dude seems way too nice to be a demon."

I feign offense, placing my hand over my chest. "Pardon you, sir. But I am a very nice demon."

"That you are. Keep your eyes on the sauce and make sure it doesn't burn."

Not only is Jace scouring the skin of this realm's most famous beings, but he's also overseeing my first attempt to cook him dinner. I don't blame him for questioning my skills in the kitchen; cooking is hard work. Stirring, boiling, simmering, it's difficult to remember it all. Thankfully, my power is handy when it comes to preparing food.

I twirl my finger and the spoon stirs the red sauce.

"Whoa!" His excited outburst makes me jump. "Snoop Dogg? An angel?"

I laugh as I wave my hand over the ladle stirring the noodles. "For real? Wait, I saw a demonic mark on Martha Stewart the other day on her cooking show. It's on her wrist of all places. And they're like, besties."

"Angels and demons could be friends then?" he asks.

"I wouldn't have thought so. The energy we create clashes. We would never so much as step foot in the other's realm. The results would be devastating, throw everything off kilter. Not only would the energies be at risk but so would the beings that originated there. But I guess it's possible when we're here. Actually," I say, leaning forward on the counter on my elbows, "that makes me think that maybe Meredith *could* be an angel."

His eyes widen. "Wait, Meredith, our neighbor Meredith?"

"Yeah, I know for a fact I saw a mark on her back a few weeks ago, but I couldn't tell which one it was. I figured she *had* to be a demon because we got along so well, but now that I know about Snoop and Martha . . ."

Jace just shakes his head as he gets up to grab some plates.

"I'm surprised you're shocked that demons and angels can be friends. Didn't you tell me that your dad and the ruler of Pax have a gentlemen's bet? That sounds pretty friendly to me."

"There's nothing on the line but bragging rights, but it's also more than that. What ruler doesn't want to have the bigger kingdom?" I look over my shoulder and raise my eyebrows. "Demons and angels have dick measuring contests too. Anyway. At the end of every century, they compare numbers. Whoever has the most new energies wins. Angelo has always had the upper hand, but now that humans have become more technologically advanced, it looks like Dad might win for the first time."

With the plates laid out, Jace moves in next to the stove. He crosses his arms and ankles, leaning against the counter. "Please don't tell me that technology is the root of all evil. It would be devastating to my career."

"Don't worry. It's not," I tell him, tapping two fingers against the worry line between his eyebrows. "It has actually made life for most humans easier. No more hunting for what you eat and spending hours sewing fabric into clothes. Humans aren't as weary as they once were. For the most part, having a peaceful life in this realm makes them crave a little chaos in the next."

Jace rubs his jaw and looks up like he's scrolling through all the new possibilities in his head. "That's interesting. I always thought that once you live this life, you want a little serenity. RIP and all."

"Angelic concept. It is one of the many desperate measures Angelo has turned to in efforts to swing things in his favor."

I hold up a spoonful of sauce and raise it to his lips. He hums his approval before asking, "Isn't that sort of dangerous, infringing on human free will?"

"Yeah, it could be. You know the drill. We need balance in the Force."

Jace laughs and says, "I am *so* rubbing off on you. So, which are you, Desideria? The dark side or the light?"

I move to the sink to strain the noodles. "Isn't it obvious? I'm the dark side."

"I thought you said something about being a nice demon," he says, moving behind me and slipping his arms around my waist, sliding his fingers under the hem of my shirt.

I swat at him. "Hey, now. I'm trying to cook your dinner without 'burning the sauce.' If you get me going like that, we might burn the house down."

He laughs and slaps me on the ass as he makes his way back to his stool. "After dinner then."

"It's a deal." Stepping to the sink to wash my hands, I'm drying them off on a hand towel when one of my rings flies off my finger and rolls under the refrigerator. "No!" I drop to my knees to stop it, but it's too late.

"What happened?" Jace asks, squatting down beside me.

"My ring . . . it slipped off my finger and rolled under there."

"Oh, no big deal, I'll just pull it out. Here," he says, ushering me aside.

I grin at him. "Move aside, big boy. I got this." With both index fingers, I pull the fridge away from the wall, and Jace gasps behind me.

"I'm telling you, I'll never get over it," he whispers.

Grinning, I glimpse the piece of shiny silver and stoop down to get it. I pick it up, and right behind it is a photo, face down in a pile of dust bunnies. Cocking my head to the side, I pick it up and turn it over. What I see shocks me to my core.

It's a photo of Jace and a beautiful blond, arms wrapped around each other, faces close . . . a *definite* couple's pose. This looks like a relationship *way* too serious for Jace. At least the Jace I know.

I slide the photo into my back pocket while I replace the fridge, and then turn to him.

"Did you get your ring?" he asks, not looking up as he serves our food.

"Yeah. I found something else back there too," I say, taking my seat beside him.

"I bet. Probably some spiders and dust. I may like a clean house, but even I have a little bit of sloth in me when it comes to cleaning behind appliances."

"Dust, definitely, but . . ." I slide the picture across the counter with an impish grin. "Who's this? Your high-school girlfriend?" I make a kissy face and give him an overexaggerated wink. "You two look very cozy."

His jaw drops and he inches his fingers toward the image. "No, she wasn't my high-school girlfriend." Lifting the photo, he studies it for a moment longer before crinkling it into a ball.

"Wait!" I say, putting my hand over his. "Who was she? What happened?"

"Hannah. My ex-fiancé." Jace sinks into his stool like the picture sucked all the life out of him and shuffles the food around his plate. "We were together when I had my accident. When they cut me out of my car with two feet of pole still lodged in me, she's the one they called. Other than a couple of work associates, the contact list in my phone wasn't long."

I lift my hand in wide-eyed shock. "Wait. What about your parents? Didn't they come to the hospital to take care of you?"

"No." He falls silent, gnawing on the inside of his lip. "My dad died a long time ago. And my mother . . . she didn't care enough to hang around. Left me with a ton of mommy issues to take up with a psychiatrist."

"I'm sorry, Jace. If I'd known, I wouldn't have brought it up."

He shrugs. "It is what it is. Those mommy issues seemed to play out in my relationship with Hannah too. From what I could tell from the letter she left on this counter with her engagement ring, she couldn't handle me being in a coma. The doctors were talking about spinal damage when I woke up. And just like good 'ole Mom, when shit hit the fan, she bolted. Story of my life." He ends by shoveling a large bite of food into his mouth.

The matter-of-fact tone with which he speaks about these two life-altering events stuns me. First of all, Jace had been *engaged*? And to a woman who left him when he was in a coma? And his own mother abandoned him before that. No wonder the man doesn't trust anyone anymore.

I pluck the photo out of his hand, toss it across the room into the sink, and flip on the garbage disposal with a snap of my fingers. "Damn, Jace. What a heinous bitch," I blurt, and my face flushes. "Sorry. I just felt a wave of wrath my brother would've been proud of."

A quiet chuckle comes from him. "Don't worry about it. I thought I erased her existence from this place. Turns out it's not so easy getting rid of your ghosts."

I hop off the stool, all thoughts of dinner forgotten, and hurry to his side, pulling him to face me. I position myself between his legs and place my palms on his cheeks. "Listen to me, Jace. It all makes sense now, why you don't trust people, why you don't do relationships, don't let yourself get attached." I run my thumb over his bottom lip. "But I swear to you, I am here for you, and the only time I will leave is when I physically can't stay any longer." Tears fill my eyes at the thought of my friend lying alone in a hospital bed because his bitch of a fiancé couldn't handle the possibility that she'd have to actually be there for more than just the fun stuff. "Do you hear me? You can trust me. Okay?"

"I hear you, Desi."

It's a start. I don't expect him to let go of that fear overnight. He said himself that he's sought professional help to deal with it. He's been hurt in ways I don't understand. I have both parents, and they would sever limbs for each other—and for me—if that's what it took. My brothers and their partners are devoted until the end. Jace doesn't have any examples of unconditional love left in his life. And it's heartbreaking.

I lean forward and brush my lips against his. "But do you *believe* me?"

"I want to, but that's going to take time. Be patient with me when it comes to trust."

"I can do that."

He tilts his head at the empty stool next to him. "Sit down and eat before we have to trash your masterpiece and order takeout."

I climb onto the stool next to him and pull my plate in front of me. "Is it actually good?"

He smiles and nods. We eat in silence for a few minutes, and after I take my last bite, I ask, "What are you doing tomorrow? We should do something. I feel like I've been cooped up in the house a lot lately."

"Have you ever skied before?"

I snort. "I don't know if you've noticed, but I'm not the most ath-letic person."

"True. How about sledding?"

I grin. "That's more my speed. If I fall, it's a far shorter distance to the ground." I bounce in my seat and clasp my hands to my chest. "I happened to buy cold weather clothes the other day at the mall, just in case I got to do something fun like this!"

"Oh, a trip to the mall. That's new. If you break that closet with all your clothes, you're not getting your deposit back," Jace says with a laugh while gathering our dishes.

"Ha! You're funny." I stand, and as soon as he places the dishes in the sink, I snap my fingers, washing and putting them away. He pivots around with a smile. I close the distance between us and push him gently against the edge of the counter. Running my finger down the center of his chest, I say, "What can I do to thank you for planning such a nice day for us tomorrow? I feel like I need to show you my appreciation." My fingers drift to his waistband and trace over his belt buckle.

He slides his fingers around the back of my neck and pulls me close, my lips a breath away from his. "I can think of a few things, but they're going to have to wait. Edmonds got the proposal and he has a couple questions for me. Can I take a rain check?"

Disappointment blooms in my chest, but I push it down. "Sure. Just come wake me up tomorrow when you want to go, okay?" I back off and walk to the stairs.

"Hey!" Jace jogs after me and grabs my wrist. He pulls me against him and lowers his lips to mine. The kiss isn't as heated as the other night, but it is sweet and feels just as good. I'm questioning if Jace Wilder is bad at anything.

With a final peck, he pulls away and says, "Thanks for everything you said. You didn't have to get upset about Hannah and my mother, but it was nice to know you were."

Any disappointment I felt a few moments ago is long gone with that kiss and those words. "You're welcome. But, yeah, I did have to get upset. They did you dirty, and you didn't deserve it. No one deserves such a dick move, but *especially* not you, Jace. You're a good person. The best I've ever met. Human or demon."

"I can say the same for you, Desideria." He kisses me on the forehead and disappears down the hallway leading to his office.

TWENTY-ONE
DESI

Something slips out of my fingers before warm knuckles caress my cheek. A low, sexy voice breathes against my ear. "Hey, we got to get ready if you still want to sled."

My eyes flutter open and I look around my room. Jace sits next to my hip, wearing a gray long-sleeved shirt and a beanie on his head. My gaze lands on his black joggers, then follow his legs down to his running shoes. He flips over the book I fell asleep reading and reads the description. "A haunted hotel and two brooding, handsome twin brother spirits. What more could a girl want?"

My face flushes and I snatch the book from his hand and fling it over to the other side of the bed. "You are nosy," I say in a gravelly voice. My eyes run over his form one more time. "Besides, you totally left me hanging last night. I had to take the edge off somehow." My tone is teasing, but the wink I give him is less silly than it is seductive.

"I'll make that up to you today with some cold weather and hot cocoa, but you have to get moving." He places a soft kiss on my lips and stands. "And you wouldn't be so grouchy if you hadn't stayed up late reading about beefy twins getting frisky with a hotel owner."

I grab a pillow from behind me and throw it at him, but he's too quick, slipping out the door before it reaches him.

With a whiny groan, I roll out of bed and jump in the shower. I twist my curls into two long braids that fall over my shoulders before digging through my closet to find a pair of thick ski pants that Glen insisted I buy when I decided to stay in Denver. Before I put them on, I layer them with a one-piece set of long underwear. I add a parka, waterproof boots, gloves, and a scarf. A quick look in the mirror reveals that I bear an uncanny resemblance to an egg.

"I'm ready," I announce, tugging a green stocking cap onto my head as I waddle into the kitchen under all my layers.

Jace is leaning against the island with a bottle of water in his hands. He unscrews the top and brings the bottle to his mouth. "You look . . . warm," he says, covering his smile by taking a sip.

He has added a jacket to his athletic ensemble and changed into snow boots. The fingers of a black glove hang out of his pocket. He doesn't look that different from when he goes running in the morning.

"Is it too much?" I ask, looking down at myself and gesturing to my pants and parka. "Should I ditch the snow pants?"

He sets down his drink and walks over to me. Helping me out of my jacket, he says, "We'll be in the car or moving, you won't get that cold. Did you get some fleece-lined leggings?" I nod and he continues, "Those will be better for this trip. The snow is solid where we're going, and it's a clear day. I promise we won't be in a blizzard."

Jace kneels before me to remove my boots and reaches for the waist of the bulky pants. He pulls them down and chuckles at the thermal onesie. Reaching around me, he feels for something just above my ass. When he comes up empty, he laughs. "At least you didn't get the kind with the drop seat in the pants."

I cock my head to the side and look down at him. "Ha-ha. You're hilarious. In case you didn't notice, we don't exactly have snow in Infernis, so I was just going by what I've seen in the human movies I've watched. Apparently, they're a little extra when it comes to wardrobe," I say as he gives the globes of my ass a playful swat. "I—" My words catch in my throat as he stands in front of me and traces the top button on the long johns before making his way down the center of my chest.

"The truth about everything is less is more." He pulls the fabric off my shoulder and kisses the exposed skin. "And the same goes for snow gear. If you wear too much, you sweat." The top of the onesie falls away, leaving me shirtless from the waist up. "Sweat cools the body. And when it's cold outside, the last thing you want is moisture eventually freezing." He cups my breasts, pulls down the thin fabric of my bralette, and lifts a peak to his mouth. After lapping at the now-hardened nipple, he says, "But there are other activities where sweat is very appropriate."

I gasp and lift my hand, gripping the back of his neck. "Oh, how fascinating," I manage as he kneels and slides the onesie a little farther down, exposing my lower abdomen and the black thong I chose this morning in the hopes he'd end up seeing it. "And what activities would those be?" I brace myself with a hand on his shoulder as he helps me step out of the garment that was already damp in places that would likely have been uncomfortable for the rest of the day.

He draws a wet trail with his tongue that starts at the waist of my panties and swirls around my navel. "The kind that will make us miss out on sledding."

I bite my lip and fight a battle in my head. I've never been sledding before, and doing that with Jace sounds like a lot of fun. On the other hand, his tongue on my skin is too tempting to resist. But he planned this day for us, and I don't want to derail it. There will be time for this later.

"Okay, okay," I say, tugging on his hair. "No more licking. Let me go get dressed."

"No more licking." He kisses the lace covering my center and stands. "Hurry before I change my mind."

I run up the stairs and tear through my clothes. I find my winter leggings and put on a tight long-sleeved shirt. Grabbing a puffer jacket, I return to the kitchen.

"Better?" I ask, holding out my arms and spinning around.

"Much. And I can see all those sexy curves now. Throw on your boots and let's get out of here."

After driving for forty-five minutes, we pull off onto a crude road in the middle of nowhere, and his SUV cruises over every bump. Snow covers the pine tree branches, and the sun beams down on an ivory blanket, making it look like a million diamonds on the ground.

We park on the side of the road next to several other cars. Children with sleds and snowboards zip down the sides of what appears to be a huge white bowl. Parents stand at the bottom with their phones out, capturing every moment. On the far side of the basin is a log cabin with smoke billowing from the chimney and people walking out with steaming cups in their hands.

"What is this place?" I ask.

Jace opens the back door to his SUV and pulls out the two sleds we brought from his garage. "It's private land. The owners were ski instructors at the top resorts for years. When they had grandkids, they wanted a safe place for them to learn snow sports. It's the perfect place for a beginner."

He picks up one sled and passes me the other, then holds out his hand to me.

I thread my fingers with his and say, "That's amazing. How did you know about it? It's way out here in the middle of nowhere."

His eyes scan the area, and I can tell the memory is bittersweet. "My dad used to bring me out here every year on the first good snowfall of the winter. It didn't matter if it was a school day. We dropped everything, it was just him and me. As I got older and had friends who wanted to learn to ski or snowboard, we'd head out here."

"I can't imagine how much you miss him," I say as we walk to the edge of the hill. "Besides Mandis, my dad was my best friend growing up."

"Yeah, he was the best," Jace says, and I can tell by the way he says it that he wants to change the subject.

I grip his hand tighter, and we both look over the ledge. The hill isn't the biggest one on the property by any means, but I've never gone sailing down a slope on a contraption made of wood and metal before, and I'm a little terrified. This just doesn't look safe; not that I'm the most careful being in the three realms or anything, but this seems purposely reckless.

The sled in my hand suddenly feels like lead instead of wood. I drop it to the snow and look at Jace with wide eyes. "I don't think I can do this."

"What do you mean you can't do it? You literally just sit down and slide."

I shake my head, staring down at the bottom of the bowl. Little kids jump off their sleds when they reach the end of their ride, cheering and running up for another go. But up here on top of what may as well be the new Mount Everest, I don't think I can do it.

I turn around at the crunching of snow and creaking of wood. Jace sits at the back of the sled holding out his hand to me. "Jump on, we'll go together."

With a deep breath, I nod and tuck our other sled safely under a nearby tree then settle in front of him. "Are you sure this is okay, us both being on here like this? I'm a lot heavier than these little kids," I say, my heart beating faster as he wraps his arms around my waist.

Jace scoffs and tightens his grip on me, moving my hair away from my neck. He plants a kiss on my spine and whispers, "Please, Desi. I could toss you around my bedroom without even breaking a sweat."

My lips part and I think I'll combust when I can't press my thighs together, but my misery is short lived because he takes that opportunity while I'm distracted to release me and press a palm to the ground, pushing us forward.

I scream as we fly down the hill, and Jace laughs as he holds me tight. The chilly wind whips at my face, and my stomach plummets. It's as if my entire life flashes before my eyes. At the same time, the thrill of the ride doesn't last long enough. We scoot along the flat ground, and Jace digs his heels into the snow to stop us.

Looking around my shoulder at my face, he asks, "How you doing, princess?"

I laugh and lean back against him, resting my head on his shoulder and looking up into his twinkling gray eyes. "Fantastic! Let's do it again!"

We run up the hill and slide back down at least a dozen times. Jace tries to get me to ride down by myself, but I refuse. I enjoy him wrapped around me as we laugh and scream. Parents waiting for their children at the bottom of the bowl are amused by us, but I don't care. His proximity is worth all the pointing and giggling.

By the end of our sledding adventure my leggings are soaked with melting snow and my teeth are chattering. Jace gathers our sleds and carries them to the SUV. He starts the vehicle and cranks up the heat before loading everything in the back.

Sliding behind the wheel, he asks, "Are you hungry?"

"Starved." I lift my sunglasses from my face and prop them on the top of my stocking cap. "Is there anywhere on the way home that we can get a hot bowl of soup?"

"Sure," he says, pulling his visor down and looking in the mirror. "Oh, I didn't put enough sunscreen on. I got a windburn."

My brows pull together. "Windburn? What the hell is that? Like a sunburn?"

He glances over at me, studying my face, his mouth twisted into a confused grimace. "Kinda. It's when the wind sort of chaps your skin—" He cuts himself off and reaches over to grip my chin, turning my face toward him so he can see me better. "How did *you* dodge the burn? Did you put on sunscreen this morning?"

I shake my head. "No. I've never worn sunscreen or taken medication in my life. I'm immortal, remember? Demons, and angels for that matter, don't get sick or suffer any kind of human ailment. That includes sunburns, windburns, acne, colds, anything like that."

"So you admit that you're always perfect. Humble."

"Shut up," I mumble. "I'm not perfect and you know it."

"Obviously. You get grouchy after staying up late reading sexy ghost books," he says with a snicker as he pulls onto the crude road.

I shoot him a glare and cross my arms over my chest. "And don't forget I'm hungry, so that probably isn't helping matters."

"So, you get cranky from not enough sleep *and* not enough food," he teases. "Maybe you aren't so perfect after all."

"Oh? Tell me, what else is wrong with me?" I ask, turning in my seat and giving him a smirk.

"You won't sled down a hill by yourself. You put the cups away upside down. You're known for sneaking into other people's tubs and taking a bath without permission. You're a bold exhibitionist who lures good boys down to hell to meet your demon family. And you thought I could help you find an eternal partner?"

The twinkle in his gray eyes tells me he's teasing, so I fire back at him. "Okay, first of all, in Infernis, there is no such thing as sledding, so I was a little scared, I can admit it. Second, I already explained why I put the cups away upside down at least fifty times. It makes perfect sense. Third, you're the only man whose bathtub I've ever snuck into, thank you very much. And as far as boys I've lured . . ." I slide my hand onto his leg and up his thigh until my fingers are nearly brushing the center of his pants. "Last I checked, I've only lured one boy anywhere, and that, sir, was you."

"Desideria." My name is a breathy warning on his tongue. He pulls my hand away and brings my knuckles to his lips, kissing them before placing my hand in my lap. "You don't know how flattered I am that you can't keep your hands off me, but the car isn't exactly my safe space."

I gasp and cover my mouth with my palm, turning so I can see his face. "Oh, Jace. I'm so sorry. I didn't even think of that." Swiveling in my seat, I press my forehead to the leather and pound it gently in a repetitive motion. "Stupid, stupid, stupid," I mutter, closing my eyes.

His hands remain on the wheel, but he glances at me from the corner of his eye for a split second. "Hey, don't do that. I'm not upset with you. But I do need you to turn around in your seat, so I know you're safe. I wouldn't fare too well if anything ever happened to you."

I can't argue with that, so I flop over in the seat and face forward. "Ugh, you know I'm not normally inconsiderate. I just—you make me lose control," I say, sliding down a bit and covering my face with my hands. "There are times—*a lot* of times—when all I can think about is you. And not just—" I take a deep breath and pause before I say anything else. Maybe I *shouldn't* say anything else. Maybe what I have to say will freak Jace out, and I don't want to push him away. Not when we've grown so close.

"Not just what?" he asks, and I realize I've stayed silent for too long, and now I have no choice but to say what I'm thinking.

"Not just what you do to me with your hands and your mouth," I say tentatively, bracing myself for his reaction. "I just like spending time with you. However I can get it."

The seconds tick by and I'm scared out of my mind that I've blown it. My mouth opens to begin an Olympic-sized routine of back-pedaling when he says, "Well, isn't this awkward?"

Fuck!

"A woman actually enjoys my company. I have to admit that I thought the cartoon T-shirts and the hours with a controller in my hand were some kind of lady repellant. It turns out that you, little hurricane, are attracted to nerds. Looks like you have another flaw."

The smirk he fights back is so charming. It might be *the* reason I can't keep my hands off him.

"You know I enjoy spending time with you too. You just might be one of my favorite beings," he says.

The relief I feel is immeasurable, but I can't let him see how nervous I was. So I just keep up the teasing. "*One of?* Who's your *favorite* being?"

"This is a hard one. It's a toss-up, obviously, between Luke Skywalker, Spider-Man, and Glen."

I'm not surprised that I'm competing against two fictional characters, but my *brother-in-law?*

"*Glen?!*" I exclaim. "Are you for real right now? Glen is above me on the list of favorite beings?!"

Jace turns a hand over on the steering wheel and flicks his fingers in a *what can I say* gesture. "I know what you're thinking. He tried to convince me that our handshake was about ice cream when it was really about blow jobs, but I'll give him a pass on that. He enjoys giving them and I enjoy receiving them."

I nod and purse my lips, and without taking my eyes off the passing scenery, I say, "Good to know. Maybe you can ask him for one next time you've got a hard-on. Ya know, since he's your favorite and all."

Jace makes a sound like what I said hurt. "You know. On second thought, Glen has sharp teeth. I've just promoted you to the toss-up list. Congrats."

I fling my hair over my shoulder and look at him from the corner of my eye. "Good boy. Now, where's my soup?"

"Don't worry. I know how you demons get when you're hungry. We're almost there."

Jace pulls into the parking lot of a little hole-in-the-wall café. The outside of the building is questionable—the cold winters have done a number on the teal paint around the windows and on the eaves. But as soon as he pulls open the glass door I'm hit with the scent of savory spices and fresh bread. The host leads us to a candlelit table near the corner and hands us menus.

When I can't decide between two different soups, Jace orders them both for me and two more for himself. We sit across from each other laughing and dipping our spoons between the bowls. He continues to tease me about not being able to sled alone, and I let him poke fun at me, adding my own jabs about his windburn, which makes him look like an inverted raccoon. We find ourselves in a hysterical fit of laughter more than once.

But about halfway through our meal, all that happiness fades when he looks over my shoulder. His eyes go wide and all the color drains from his face like he sees a ghost. I spin around in my chair.

A woman I've seen only once before stands behind me, staring back at him. Her blond hair falls over her shoulders in beautiful straight strands, and her blue eyes are shining with surprise. Her red lips pull into a faint smile before she says in a rich, soft voice, "Hello, Jace."

"Hey, Hannah."

TWENTY-TWO
JACE

One accident, one possible diagnosis, and one letter demolished a relationship I spent four years building. Hannah was my first attempt to trust someone after my mother bailed. It turned out I opened myself up to be betrayed again. I took those shattered pieces of my life and picked them up one by one with my bare hands and buried them. When I piled the dirt on top, I made sure to pack it down tight. It was a barren space; nothing would ever grow there. It was dead. Or so I thought.

Two words.

One woman.

And my past has risen from the dead.

Hannah looks the same. Her long blond hair rests around her face like a golden halo. The blue of her eyes is still captivating, like tropical waters on a sunny day. And that tiny beauty mark just off the side of her mouth tries to tempt me to kiss it. But I don't want to kiss her, I don't want to touch her, or talk to her, or see her. I wish she'd disappear like she did when I needed her the most.

"How are you?" Hannah is saying, but it's the feel of Desi's fingers wrapping around mine that brings me back to earth.

I look down at our hands and then up at her, our gazes locking. The green in her eyes is blazing, and I can practically feel the heat of her anger from here. I swear she's trying to send me a message telepathically, and I'm pretty sure I know what she's saying.

Show her what she's missing.

I don't know how good I'll be at this—acting like I'm not on the verge of a panic attack, like I'm not still angrier than hell at this woman who wrecked me when I was already destroyed, but I'll try. I have to.

"Good. I'm doing really good. I'm about to lock down an investor for my business. Now I'm just taking my girl out after an afternoon at Dulton Ranch."

Hannah glances down at Desi for the first time, her eyelids lowering as she takes her in. "I used to love when we went to Dulton Ranch." It's a lie. Hannah hated going there. She thought it was childish and preferred upscale ski resorts. I don't get a chance to correct her. "I don't think we've met. I'm Hannah. Jace and I—"

"Were engaged to be married until you left him to recover alone in a hospital bed after a traumatic car accident. I know who you are." Desi doesn't hold back, letting her voice seep with venom. It's all I can do to not utter an *Oooh, sick burn,* under my breath.

Instead, I place my index finger over my mouth, hiding my amused grin. "Hannah, this is Desi, my girlfriend."

Desi flashes Hannah a saccharine sweet grin and props her elbow on the table, resting her chin in her palm, but never letting go of my hand. Whoever started the rumor that demons are evil might have been onto something. Desi shows no qualms about sticking it to my ex.

Hannah blinks, her wide eyes shifting from Desi to me before saying, "I—nice to meet you?"

"I don't think I can say the same," Desi replies, matching Hannah's chipper tone.

"Babe," I say, lifting my brow. At the rate Desi is going I'm going to have to spring for an attorney to represent her in Hannah's murder trial.

"I'm sorry," she says to me without even acknowledging Hannah's presence, and when she leans over the table and wraps her hand around the back of my neck, I feel every nerve ending in my body crackle to life. Her mouth brushes against my ear and the rest of her words slip past her lips for only me to hear. "I'm sorry you have to be subjected to her presence, Jace. Let me protect you."

I chuckle at that, like I can stop her. I'm sure Hannah thinks my *girlfriend* is whispering dirty promises. If only she knew that the stunning creature across from me was the future queen of Sloth offering to be my emotional bodyguard.

Hannah shifts from one foot to the other. "Well, I just wanted to check on you." She points behind her. "I'm actually here with *my* boyfriend, and he's waiting on me to order."

The guy across the restaurant looks familiar—good looking, blond, built . . . with his finger in his ear. He studies his menu and only stops when he sniffs whatever lingers on his fingertip. I scrunch my face in disgust and make a choking sound when it dawns on me.

"Is that Stoner Zack from college? The one from your biology study group who left you hanging with all the labs?" I ask.

"Yeah. Science isn't Zack's thing. He's learning his dad's business and is set to take over in the next few years. We just moved in together. It isn't as nice as *our* house was, but we'll get there."

Uh-oh. Desi's fingers tighten on mine, and I brace myself for whatever she's about to say. I don't even bother to try to stop her, because if I've learned anything by now, you can't stop a hurricane.

"*Your* house?" Desi says, incredulity creeping into her tone. "Oh, honey, I don't think you have a right to *ever* claim ownership of that house or *anything* related to Jace. You gave that up the minute you left your ring on the counter and ran like a coward while he was in a coma." She scoffs, the derision seeping from her tongue. "*Our house.* As if."

I tuck my lips between my teeth and bite down, fighting to regain my composure. I almost feel bad for Hannah. Almost.

"Desi is protective about the things we share. Naturally, she's left her mark on the home she and I have created." I brush my thumb over Desi's knuckles. We may be putting on a show, but that's true. My house is different because of her.

"I better get back to Zack. It was good to see you, *Jace*," Hannah says, pointedly ignoring Desi.

"You as well, Hannah. Tell Stoner Zack that he should get the situation with his ears checked out."

"Yeah," Hannah says, turning on her heel.

Desi snorts a laugh before turning in her chair and calling, "Nice to meet you too, Hannah!"

I sink into my seat and release a long, audible breath. "Shit."

Desi lets go of my hand to cover her face with her palms, and I immediately miss the feel of her skin against mine.

No. That's not—she was just a comforting presence in a time of high stress. That's all.

"I'm sorry if I was too harsh. You don't grow up with six brothers who are the embodiments of the other *deadly sins*, a father who is Chaos personified, and a mother who *might* be the most dramatic creature who ever existed without retaining a little piece of each of them," she says, her voice muffled behind her hands.

"You have nothing to apologize for. If I was as brave as you, I would have said all the things I was thinking. You held me together through that."

She spreads two fingers and looks at me through the space between. "You thought I was brave?"

"I think you are many things. All of them are good. I've grown to have an appreciation for even those flaws I listed earlier. But I admire your bravery the most."

She drops her hands and tilts her head to the side, studying me.

"You were amazing," she whispers, taking my hand and bringing my knuckles to her mouth and kissing them, casting a quick glance over her shoulder to see if Hannah is still looking—which she is. "She didn't even deserve one word from you, and you were so put together and mature."

"Thank you, Desideria."

"You're welcome."

"Do you mind if we ask for to-go containers and get out of here? Stoner Zack doesn't have the best table etiquette, and I'm ready to be alone with you again."

Desi doesn't answer me. She just waves at the server and tells them we're ready for our check. After a slight argument over who'll pay the bill, I win and we're walking hand in hand out the door. I don't miss the way Desi wiggles her fingers at Hannah as we pass, making a show of us leaving. Desi wasn't kidding about inheriting dramatics from her mother.

The ride home is quiet, with only music playing in the background, and my thoughts linger on Hannah for a short time before wandering to Desi. She stares out the window with her hand resting on the console between us. She wiggles her fingers every once in a while, like she's tempted to touch something. I'm tempted for her to touch something too. I miss how soft and warm her hand was inside of mine.

With a mental pep talk and several false starts, I find the courage to overcome something that terrifies me. I take Desi's hand and place it in the center of my thigh. She watches me with wide eyes as I press her hand down, wordlessly telling her not to move it before I grip the steering wheel again.

"Is this okay?" I ask.

"Yes," she whispers, palming my thigh and running her fingers along the seam of my joggers. "It's more than okay."

Keeping my eyes on the road, I shake my head and smile. "Behave yourself, Desideria. I'm driving and I tend to get turned on by the smallest things you do. Don't make me regret this."

She laughs and says, "All right, but this is the second time I've been stopped from turning you on today. Am I going to get a chance to try again when we get home or . . ." I'm not even looking at her, and I can see the little smirk that's crossing her lips right now.

"Don't worry. Your drawer of toys is on hiatus until further notice."

TWENTY-THREE
DESI

When Jace and I get inside the house, I lean against the counter after tugging off my boots and socks. "Don't judge me, but my body hurts from going up and down those hills so many times."

He removes his beanie and neatly folds it before sliding it into his jacket pocket. "You took it like a pro today. I think you deserve a treat."

"Do I?"

"I don't suppose you bought a swimsuit during one of your many shopping sprees?" he says, cocking an eyebrow.

The thought of swimming in ice-cold water makes my body hurt even more. I'd do better running outside naked during a blizzard. I open my mouth to say as much when Jace flips a switch on the wall. Beyond the back porch the pool lights up in blue and purple, and steam rolls from the water.

"It's heated, and I cranked it up before we left. It should do the trick."

I nearly moan at the thought of hot water covering my tired muscles. "Oh my. You do realize this is sort of like a huge bathtub, right? You're giving me the ultimate reward. Are you sure I deserve it after borrowing your tub that one time?"

He steps closer and runs his thumb over my bottom lip. "I think you've already made up for that in more ways than one."

I nip at his thumb with my teeth and grin. "I'll be right back," I say and dart up the stairs to my room as fast as my sore body will take me, peeling off all my clothes as soon as I get inside. Rifling through my dresser, I pull out two bikinis: one is black and the other emerald green. Warmth blooms in my belly and I toss the black one back into the drawer and slip into the green one, which fits every curve perfectly. The cut of the top showcases my mark, and something about being able to show it off to Jace gives me butterflies in every part of my body. Not to mention, the color is almost identical to the dress I wore to the charity event, and I know Jace loved it. I hope this has the same effect.

Grabbing a towel and slinging it over my shoulder, I descend the stairs again to find Jace leaning against the island with one leg crossed over the other, looking down at his phone. He's wearing black swim trunks and no shirt, and I am struck once again by how perfect his body is. I suppose that's the result of not sleeping in, running, and spending an hour in your personal gym each day. I guess I'll keep my soft tummy in exchange for extra sleep.

"Hey. I'm ready," I say.

Jace sets down his phone and gestures to the back doors. My feet freeze and my skin grows tight just thinking of stepping out into the cold with so little on. I'm second-guessing my excitement for a swim.

"What are you waiting for? Open the door and let's jump in," he says, stepping beside me.

"But it's cold out there," I say in a small voice. "My feet are going to freeze before we get into the pool." I gesture to my body. "And in case you didn't notice, my swimsuit is kind of . . . skimpy."

"Oh, I noticed. And heaven forbid that the princess's feet get cold."

Without a warning he sweeps me up in his arms, like a groom carrying his bride over the threshold, and opens the back doors. My eyes grow wide when the edge of the pool gets closer.

I pound on his shoulder, screaming, "No, Jace. Please!"

"I'm not letting you back out of this."

I open my mouth to protest again, but he jumps into the air, and we're flying into the steaming water. As soon as it hits me, the tension in my muscles disappears. It's so warm and calm. I'm tempted to float to the bottom and melt, but the need to see Jace wet is stronger.

We surface at the same time. Brushing his hair from his face, he says, "Sometimes you just have to jump."

"Yeah?" I say, chewing on my bottom lip. "Well, I do have to admit that I'm finding that to be the case the longer I spend here. The best things seem to happen when we just let go." I tangle my fingers in his hair and pull him closer to me, kissing the corner of his mouth.

"And what is the next thing you hope happens?" He kisses my neck, working his way across my shoulder.

I lean my head to one side, letting my hair fall back over my arm, enjoying the feeling of his mouth on my skin. "I kind of like the direction this is going, what do you think?"

"I promised a reward for your obliteration of Hannah's ego at the restaurant, didn't I?"

"You certainly did. And on top of everything else, I wore this bathing suit just for you. Any idea why?"

"No clue." He tugs on the bow behind my neck before releasing the one at the center of my back. The fabric drifts away from us while he continues kissing and nipping at my collarbone. The warm water laps at my skin, and Jace cups my breast, kneading and stroking the hard peak. If I weren't already weightless, I would fall to my knees at the mixture of sensations.

"I—" Words try to flow off my tongue but it's nearly impossible to focus on forming a sentence as his mouth moves lower between my breasts, toward my mark. "Did the color look—" I gasp as he pinches one of my nipples before soothing it with a soft brush of his palm. "Familiar to you?" The last part of my sentence comes out as a squeak.

"It's that damn green. My new favorite color, but this is a very close second," he says, making a point of licking my nipple.

I lean my head back and offer him my other breast. "Perfect." I say with a wink as I meet his gaze. I hop up, wrapping my legs around his waist and hooking my ankles behind him. Running my tongue along his jawline, I kiss down the cords of his neck. "Can I ask you something?"

He looks down at me and raises an eyebrow. "Of course."

"Remember that night after the charity event when we . . ." I don't know why I'm embarrassed to say it when we're tangled together in a pool with his lips trailing over my bare skin.

"When we watched each other masturbate through our bedroom windows?" he fills in, planting more kisses down the center of my chest.

I try and fail to hold back a laugh. "Yeah. That. I've always wondered . . . what were you so engrossed in on your phone when you came in? What was it that got you so worked up?"

With a deep breath, he opens his mouth to speak but stops, and a bashful smile tilts his lips up. I'm really intrigued now. Jace is embarrassed.

"Um . . . it was you."

"What do you mean it was me? You were sporting that boner long before you knew I was watching."

I didn't think it was possible, but he turns another shade of red. "I got the *boner* while staring at a picture I took of you dancing that night."

I'm stunned into silence for a moment, struggling to find my words. "Wait. You took a photo of me that night and—"

"It wasn't a creepy picture. You had your arms up and that damn green dress was just clinging to every curve. I just planned to look at it once more and get ready for bed, but—"

I want to interrupt him before he can keep going, before he can work himself into a spiral of thinking he'd messed up, but I can't even think fast enough to form a coherent sentence. Finally, I blurt, "No—no, I don't mean it like that. I'm not creeped out, I—I'm just confused. I thought I was still just that irritating third wheel roommate you let move in because you didn't want to argue. But you were taking pictures of me because you thought I looked beautiful?" Tears spring to my eyes at the thought.

"At what point during that night did you think I wanted you anywhere but in my arms? I had to excuse myself after dancing with you to catch my breath. Your mere presence changed my entire night. You made everything so much better . . . easier. And that's not something I'm used to getting from another person. It overwhelmed me."

I rest my forehead on his shoulder. "That is honestly the sweetest thing you could have said."

"I'm glad you don't want to have me arrested for being a Peeping Tom."

It's my turn to blush. "Well, I'd be quite the hypocrite if that were the case," I mutter.

His eyes snap to mine. "What'd you say?"

I sigh and drop my legs from around his waist and disentangle my arms from his neck, standing to face him while I make what might be my most humiliating confession. "One night I was in bed, just minding my own damn business, trying to sleep, when you were freaking *undressing in front of the window*! I watched you. I just couldn't look away. I watched you undress like a creep, and it was all I could do to keep my hand out of my panties while I did it," I blurt, my words a long stream with basically no pause for breath. "I'm sorry." I cover my face with my hands and let out a groan.

He moves my palms away and grins. The flash of his teeth and the glint in his eyes speak volumes. I just have no clue what is going to come out of his mouth. "I could have closed the curtains, Desi. You left yours open, so I did the same. It turns out I was just putting on performances for you longer than you were for me."

I gape at him. "You knew I was watching you?"

"I had a feeling, or maybe it was wishful thinking. Either way, it was a rush."

Warmth floods from my face to my core and I jump onto him, wrapping my legs back around his waist. "I'm glad I could give you that. Watching you certainly gave me one. So how many times did you see *me* naked?"

"Naked?"

"Sure."

"Zero. I always looked away. I'd just watch you prancing around your room in your little thongs and bras. I didn't want to go full blown creeper. That is until the other night when you invited me to the top-less Desi show. Why? How many times did you see me naked?"

I blush at the thought of the skimpy nightclothes I wear in my room at night and meet his eyes as I drape my arms over his shoulders. "None. I swear. I'd never invade your privacy that way."

"So just some innocent admiring in private moments on both our parts."

"It sounds like it."

"I'm not interested in innocently watching anymore." He hooks his thumbs in my bikini bottoms. "Let me take these off."

My breath catches and I lean back to better see his face. "Please. But can I—" I untangle my legs from around his waist and stand in front of him, running my hands down his abdomen. "Can I take these off too?" I ask, dipping my fingers under his waistband.

"Fair is fair."

He helps me out of my bottoms and tosses them onto the deck of the pool. I follow his lead until we both stand in front of each other naked. I can make out hints of his body through the water. As the lights merge from one hue to the next, I sometimes get a better glimpse. It's enough for where we are in this thing we have going, yet it's not enough at all.

I drag my eyes back up to his face and push that stubborn strand of hair off his forehead again. "How is it possible that you are a human and yet so perfect, and I'm a freaking immortal demon princess and so imperfect?"

His lips form a firm line, and he shakes his head. "Nah. We're not doing this tonight or any night after. This, *you*, are gorgeous and curvaceous and soft and sexy. I won't accept anything else out of your mouth."

I can't help the smile that spreads across my face. "Yes, sir," I say, sliding my hands around his waist and pressing myself against him. "Has anyone ever told you you're extremely bossy?"

He glides his palm up my back and tangles his fingers in my hair. Pulling so my head is tilted back, he says, "Has anyone ever told *you* that you're spoiled and need someone to put you in your place?"

I whimper under the force, but I love the throbbing it sends between my legs. "Yes, *you* did, that day I used your tub. Is that still what you think?"

"Yes, it is. Go to the steps, turn around, and put your hands on the deck. Make sure your back is arched with that perfect ass presented to me."

"Okay," I whisper, swimming to the side and doing exactly as he said, gripping the edge and putting my backside in the air for him to do with as he pleases. My teeth chatter as the frosty wind nips at my exposed flesh, so I lower to my elbows. The warm water laps at my shoulders and the back of my thighs while the chilled air on my rear reminds me how vulnerable this position is. It takes everything in me to not look over at him.

The water stirs around me, and Jace's palms rest on my hips. With a solid stroke, his fingers graze along my sides and over my shoulders. His chest presses into my back, and his voice is a low rumble in my ears when he says, "I've never seen you look sexier than you do right now. And trust me, I find myself thinking you're sexy very often."

"Very often, huh? What do I have to do to change that to *all the time*?" I tease, wiggling my hips against him and running my tongue along my bottom lip.

He pulls away from me, and his palm lands on my ass with a wet smack. I suck in a breath at the sting and rub my thighs together. I've heard a little pain intensifies pleasure, but I never thought it would feel like this. It doesn't matter how Jace touches me—rough, gentle, taunting—I want more. I always want more.

"Keep grinding your ass on my cock like that and it'll be all I think about for the rest of my life," he says.

His words send heat through my veins and a shock to my heart. I tighten my grip on the edge of the pool, and a smile spreads across my face as I grind harder, hoping like hell that he spanks me again. "Yeah? I want that; I want to leave my mark on your memory so that every time you touch yourself, every time you touch someone else, you think of me," I whisper.

"Sweet Desideria. You have a filthy mouth, but it's nothing compared to the things I imagine doing to you."

Jace grips my hips, guiding them back until they're pressed against him. He's like smooth steel, sliding against me. My body aches to feel him everywhere, inside and out. The blissful sensation comes and goes too soon, replaced by another swift spanking.

"You look so pretty with my mark on you."

"Jace," I gasp. "I need more. More of you." I glance over my shoulder again and search his face to find his gray eyes blazing. "Please, Jace. I want you to fuck me."

He stills behind me. His eyes squeeze shut, and he releases a long breath. The way his body goes rigid and how he tilts his head side to side, it's like a man at the edge of destruction making the decision to step away.

"No," he says, but he doesn't move back.

In one swift motion, he spins me around and takes my place sitting on the steps. My stomach sinks when I think I said too much and he's done. But Jace pulls me forward and positions me to straddle him. His fingers move to my hair, sweeping the red curls from my face. "Keep grinding against me," he demands.

He doesn't have to tell me twice; I grip his shoulders and position myself on top of him, rolling my hips over his in a slow rhythm that has my heart thumping against my ribs and my core pulsating with the sudden need for release.

Jace wraps my hair around his hand and pulls until my chin tilts back, giving him a clear path to my neck. He places his lips to my pulse and says, "That's it, little hurricane, make us both feel good."

My skin burns under his kiss, and my whimpers grow louder with each roll of my hips. "Fuck," I gasp, when he brushes against my clit just right. I need him to feel the torturous pleasure I feel. My hips move faster, and my fingers slip into his hair and tug. "I know you want to be inside me, Jace. Why don't you just give in?"

"Because you deserve better than what I can give you." He glides his mouth over the swells of my breasts. "You're worthy of more than my damaged heart and a fuck in a pool."

I use my strength to pull my hair from his grip and pinch his chin between my thumb and forefinger, forcing his eyes to mine. "We're all damaged, Jace. Some of us just have deeper cuts than others. Don't think for a second that it makes you not enough. Got it?" I push him backward onto the stairs so I'm dominating him, at least for the moment.

The muscles in his cheeks flex as he fights back a smile, but it breaks through. He grips my waist pressing me down on him. All it would take is one slight movement and he would be buried inside me. "Yes, ma'am. You're sexy like this."

I smirk and lean forward, capturing his lips with mine. "So are you," I whisper against them, and when I grind against him this time, my body thrums with need. "You feel so fucking good."

He eases his hand between us, and his thumb presses to my center, massaging small circles. The throb between my legs morphs into hot need. And when he presses two fingers inside me, I moan his name. Moving back on his thighs, I take him in my hand and match his pace. Our breathing quickens and he grabs the back of my neck, pulling me into a kiss. Frantic tongues and muffled moans, we're on the brink of losing ourselves.

"Come for me, Jace. That's all I need to fall apart. That's what you want to see, isn't it? What you want to feel? Every bit of this desire flowing from me, all of it for you?" I murmur, nipping his plump bottom lip with my teeth.

"Fuck yes." His back arches and another finger slides inside me, stretching me in a way I've never experienced. My whimper of pain and pleasure is all it takes. Jace pulsates in my hand, his lips devouring mine with pure hunger. And he is off on that euphoric high.

That's all I need to come unglued. I whisper his name over and over as I ride his hand, wave after wave of pleasure racking every inch of my body.

His fingers don't let up until I fall limp against his chest. The gentle stroke up my spine and back again reminds me to breathe until my heart settles. "You're so perfect," he whispers into my hair before kissing the top of my head.

I smile and hide my face against his chest as I wrap my legs around his waist. "Will you take me upstairs and just hold me for a while?"

"Of course." Jace carries me out of the pool and grabs a towel by the back door. He wraps it around us and takes me to my room. We settle into my bed and our bodies return to one another like two magnets drawn together.

I burrow into him, and my eyes get heavy. I'm so sleepy, but I want him to stay. I have a feeling, though, that he won't. Not all night. The first time we messed around he didn't stay, and he only did in Infernis because he had no choice. So I force my eyelids to stay open.

"Thank you for today, Jace," I whisper into the dark. "I enjoyed every single second of it."

"You're welcome. Thanks for laying it on extra thick with Hannah. I know it's petty, but I enjoyed watching her squirm."

I grin and nip at his collarbone. "Making her squirm gave me a thrill that was probably a little sadistic, but what can I say? I am a literal demon with the prince of Wrath for a big brother. So I guess I have an excuse."

"I would have sworn Wrath was *your* Circle in that moment," he says, twirling my hair around his finger. "I like watching your demon side let go. You should give in to that chaos more often."

I raise an eyebrow and say, "Oh? You think I should be more chaotic than I already am? *You?* Mr. Neat and Tidy? I'm truly shocked."

"It's in your nature, little hurricane, not mine. But I'll admit I'm starting to recognize how much fun it can be."

"Fair enough." I place my palm on his cheek and bring his lips down to mine. "I promise to explore my more chaotic side if you promise to stop punishing yourself for what your mother and Hannah did to you," I whisper, biting the inside of my cheek and hoping I haven't said too much. "One day, Jace, please, let yourself trust someone. Or at least *try*."

He kisses the tip of my nose. "I'm working on it. You've made it a little easier to do. I know exactly what I'm getting with you. You're not meant to stay, and I already know how this ends. So I just bask in moments like this, knowing they aren't tainted with false promises of forever."

I swallow, and I'm suddenly glad this room is dark because I'm sure hurt just crossed my features. How can he say he trusts me if he thinks that during *any* moment with me I'd make false promises? My chest caves in on itself, and I genuinely have no clue what to say to that.

Doesn't he know that if he would give me a chance, I'd—

I shake my head and close my eyes. There's no point in even thinking it.

It can never be.

I even out my breathing and feign sleep because I have nothing more to say. If I open my mouth to speak, my voice is sure to crack, and tears will fall. He'll know he hurt me, he'll feel bad, and tonight will be ruined.

A few minutes pass before Jace eases out of my hold. He pulls the blankets around my shoulders, tucking me in like a small child. The touch of his lips on my brow kick-starts my heart. I want to pull him back in the bed with me, but I curl my fingers into the sheet below me and keep my breathing slow. I don't know why it's important that he believes I'm asleep, but something deep inside me demands that I don't so much as flex a toe.

He speaks in a whisper so quiet it's hard to hear him. But I make out enough of his words.

"I wish you'd come into my life earlier, when I still had half my heart to give you. It wouldn't have been what you deserved, but I would have loved you totally with that half. Now, I can't even gather all the pieces and put them back together. It's just a dark void inside of me that you've shined a little light into. Thank you for that, Desi."

Footsteps pad across my room and the door opens and closes behind him.

Now that I'm alone, I let the tears fall and wish with everything in me that things were different.

TWENTY-FOUR
DESI

The first of my mistakes was thinking I could curb the growth of my feelings for Jace while being physical with him. In my head, it was an excellent notion. People do it all the time with no problems. I'm just not made that way. My second mistake was ignoring Jace at all costs for the past two days. I've made things awkward in the house, and I'm not sure how to fix it. Thankfully, I have someone willing to listen and prone to giving good advice.

I sit across from Meredith at her immaculate kitchen table. Everything about her house is pristine, from the white leather couches to the bright flower arrangements. One would never guess that two children live here. Even the half-empty bottle of wine and plate of chocolate covered strawberries resting between us looks picturesque.

"I can't believe you did it. You've done the impossible and gotten under Jace Wilder's tough exterior. You've got to tell me. He's amazing, isn't he? He has to be. Ugh, I am so living vicariously through you." She sighs, leaning back in her white wooden chair like she's lost in a daydream. "Not that Jeremy isn't good at the bedroom stuff. But he's tired, and with the kids, it's hard to find time. I'm sex deprived."

My skin flushes at the memory of me and Jace in the pool, not to mention any of the moments that came before. "Yeah. He's phenomenal. Like, I have nothing to compare it to, right? But I somehow know that there's nothing better. And that's part of my problem."

"All right, we've established that the man is ruining you for all other men in the bedroom, but what's the bigger problem?"

I take a long swig of my wine. "It's nothing that the entire world doesn't already know. Jace is emotionally shut off, and I want more. And not because I'm selfish, but because he deserves more. He thinks he's broken but I'm starting to see that he inflicts most of the hurting on himself these days."

I hadn't even truly realized until Jace's whispered words the other night how much I wanted the chance for him to be my eternal partner. And to know that if the timing had been different, it might have happened? It was devastating in a steamrolling over my heart kind of way. I didn't expect to feel that pain. If what I felt was a fraction of what Jace's heart went through, I couldn't imagine functioning day after day.

"You can't force someone to heal and leave that pain behind when they aren't ready. Jace has never talked to me about what happened between him and Hannah, but I saw how he changed. The man who locks himself in that house and buries himself in work is the product of a broken heart and an accident that almost took his life. He's so guarded now. I don't think those walls he's built will ever allow him to love like that again."

The Jace Meredith describes might be the one he lets her see, but I know someone else. Yes, he's cautious about letting others in, but when he does, he's funny and kind and affectionate.

"I know what you're saying. And I agree with you to an extent. You can't help someone who doesn't want to be helped. But I know he's in there. I've seen it—who he is on the inside. And it's even more beautiful than he is on the outside, which, I know, is hard to believe." I offer Meredith a weak smile, and she reaches over and takes my hand.

"Okay, fair enough. But you don't have much time left to bring someone back to your parents, right?" I shake my head and she continues. "Then I think you need to consider the other option in front of you."

"Cannon."

"Yes. He's talked to me about it, and he cares for you. A lot. And I don't need to point out all his great attributes. You already know them. I think it's time that you seriously consider Cannon and quit getting hung up on Jace. Not when you and I both know it's not going to happen. I'm not trying to be—"

I hold up my hand. "I know, I know. You're right. But it's not like that with me and Cannon, Mer. He's . . . it's just different than it is with me and Jace. Cannon and I don't have that chemistry. He would tell you the same thing if you asked. We already tried."

"Something's so wrong with both of you," she says, biting into a strawberry.

The front door opens, followed by the sound of two bickering children. Meredith finishes her wine in one gulp, and my eyebrows lift.

"Don't judge. It's a little stress relief and makes me a better mom," she says, plastering on a wide smile as the kids rush into the kitchen. "How was school?"

"It was great until the end. Macy told everyone on the bus that I sleep with a teddy bear. They all laughed." Meredith's son, Marcus, drops his backpack on the floor and glares at his sister.

The beads at the end of Macy's braids clack together as she places a hand on her hip and says, "Well, you do sleep with a teddy bear. Bubba the Bear."

Before Marcus can rip into his twin sister, Meredith interjects, saying, "Are either of you going to say hello to Miss Desi, or is she going to think I spent six years raising rude kids?"

The twins turn to me with bright smiles and rush me, saying, "Hello, Miss Desi."

I laugh as they wrap their arms around me, fighting to get my attention. The twins are sweet, but competitive. They battle it out to get the best hugging position, pulling and shoving while I sit in the middle.

"Miss Desi. Miss Desi," Macy yells over her brother, pulling on the front of my shirt. The low V–neck stretches almost to my navel, giving everyone a view of my pink bra. I rush to pull up my shirt, but it's too late.

"Out!" Meredith says, her voice breaking through the chaos and bringing her kids to a standstill. "Grab a snack from the pantry and go have some 'you' time, please."

Marcus and Macy grumble apologies and follow their mother's directions. As soon as they're out of the kitchen, Meredith's astonished gaze falls on me.

"Well, well. This all makes sense now. The weird marriage customs, your lack of knowledge about dating human men. Your ability to resist my persuasion. You're a demon," Meredith says in awe.

I clench my jaw and nod, not even bothering to deny it. There's no use. I'd suspected as much about Meredith a long time ago. "Yep. That's me. Wait! You tried to persuade me? Please tell me that you didn't mess with my emotions."

"No! That's not my gift. I'm not a peace-bringer or a humbler. I'm a counselor. My job is to give certainty with sound advice. And you've resisted my advice about Jace left and right. But did I try?" She tilts her head side to side with a guilty expression. "Yes."

Taking a deep breath, I decide to just go ahead and spill it all. Why not since we're sharing secrets. "Not only am I a demon, but I'm one of the seven children of Chaos. I'm the future queen of Sloth."

Meredith's jaw drops, and I lean over to push her chin up playfully, closing her mouth. "Sorry," she breathes, moving over to the chair next to me. "I've only heard of Chaos. I've never known anyone who's actually met him."

I finally process her words regarding her job and realize she's not at all what I thought she was. "I can't believe you're not a demon. This whole time, I thought for sure I had you figured out."

"Nope. I'm an angel." Lifting her shirt and lowering the waist of her pants, she shows me the sun with its pointed rays on the back of her hip.

"So Snoop and Martha aren't a fluke?"

"No." She tilts her head back and laughs, her curls bouncing with the movement. "Your daddy doesn't let you out much, does he?"

I flop against the back of the chair and cross my arms over my stomach with a huff. "What was your first clue? The fact that I brought up marriage before a first date even *started* or that I didn't even know angels and demons could be friends?"

"A little of both." She sobers, resting her elbow on the table and her chin in her palm. "I don't get why your father is hung up on you finding a partner. Angelo rules Pax alone. There is no handbook that says you *have* to be married. If that was the case Angelo would be in a world of hurt. Rumor has it that the king of Angels can't keep it in his pants. Everyone is shocked that he doesn't have more kids than the one he keeps under lock and key."

I unpack the reasons why my father thinks it's important for us to have someone to rule with. When I talk about my brothers and their partners, Meredith hits me with a barrage of questions. She seems fascinated by my life in Infernis, and it's nice to talk to someone who isn't from this realm about these things.

Meredith dusts a crumb off the table and says, "It sounds like a good existence, just the kind of nerdy stuff Jace would eat up. I'm surprised he doesn't want to be your partner. Then again, I'm not."

"What do you mean?"

She just keeps talking like I hadn't even spoken. "That's some chaotic shit Jace has going on. Are you sure that's not why you're attracted to him? Maybe you feel at home with his energy."

"Jace? Chaotic?" I scoff. "You've lost your mind, angel. He's the furthest thing from chaotic."

But even as I say the words, I wonder if she's right. Is this just a different kind of chaos that Jace hasn't accepted? Did I come here looking for something different, only to find what I could've gotten from a demon this entire time?

The thought is sobering, and I meet Meredith's gaze with a sad smile. "It doesn't matter either way. You're right, I need to let him go. He's made it clear that he can't be my partner. What do you think I should do now?"

She rests her hand on mine. I recognize that laid-back, calming feeling she emanates. It isn't something I normally thrive on, but with the ache in my heart on the verge of debilitating, I can use a little peace. "I return to my first choice for you. You said some of your brothers have platonic partners. Asking Cannon has got to be better than going home and letting your dad pick for you."

I let her words stew. I've already come to terms with knowing that if my father picks for me, I will have a platonic relationship. If that's the case, why not do it with someone who has become one of my best friends?

))>———————— ♛ ————————<((

"Thanks for coming with me tonight when you don't even know what we're going to do," I say, looking over at Cannon as he speeds down the highway toward the surprise destination I'd researched after my chat with Meredith.

He meets my gaze and shoots me a dazzling smile that never fails to give me the distinct feeling that everything is going to be okay. I can only hope that feeling will last through the end of the night. Because what I'm about to reveal will be life changing.

"I know anything you have planned for us is bound to be an

adventure, Desi," he says, a teasing hint to his tone. "I wouldn't miss it for the world, but it would be nice to know where we're going."

"Uh-uh," I say, shaking my head. "It's a surprise. Besides, we're almost there."

"Have you been there before?"

"No. In fact, I've never even done this thing before."

He glances at me from the corner of his eye. "Oh jeez. You're taking me turkey shooting, aren't you?"

I whack him on the shoulder. "Cannon! No! That's horrible!"

"What?" he says, trying not to laugh. "Our first outing was an archery range. It seemed like the natural next step."

I shudder. "Absolutely not. No, no, there will be no animals harmed tonight. Or any night." I point to the left. "There, turn up there, and it's on the left."

Cannon does as I say, and when he realizes where we are, he parks the car and looks at me. "You've never been to a ski resort?"

"I've never been *ice skating*, and they have two of the prettiest outdoor rinks. I've always wanted to try, and I thought you might want to do it with me for the first time."

"I have to warn you, I'm an excellent skater. Double Axels and spins—we're talking gold medal technique."

"Well, who better for me to skate with for the first time than a would-be Olympic gold medalist?"

"No one, and I'll keep you from falling on your ass too much." Cannon gets out of the car and comes around to my side. He opens my door, holding out his hand. "Come on. Let's turn you into an ice queen."

I place my hand in his and hop out of the car. "I'm ready, but you should know that I'm a little clumsy, so be prepared to hang on tight because I might end up on my ass a *lot*."

"I'm aware."

Cannon folds my hand in his, and I expect it to feel weird, like we're trying to force something that isn't there. But it doesn't. I'm just walking hand in hand with my best friend, and it feels nice.

We stroll down the cobblestone walkway through a small village of shops and eateries. Freshly fallen snow lines the road and river rocks and slats of wood make up the buildings. It's charming and reminds me of pictures I've seen of the Swiss Alps. We enter the building to rent our skates, then head outside to put them on.

The enormous rink is surrounded by the hotel, and in the distance snowcapped mountains point toward the darkening sky. The breeze blowing off their icy peaks makes it much colder than I'm used to. Twinkling lights snake along the wooden railing around the rink and dozens of skaters glide in the amber glow. It's one of the most magical places I've been to in this realm.

"Are you ready?" Cannon asks, standing in his black skates and holding his palm out for me.

I get to my feet and am immediately off balance. I snatch his hand and fall forward into his arms, my cheek smashing against his chest. "Yeah," I mumble, my voice muffled in his ivory cable-knit sweater.

He laughs and pulls me upright, supporting my weight and slipping his arm around my waist, gripping my hip. "Off to a fantastic start," he teases, pushing my hair out of my face and tugging my stocking cap down over my ears.

"I warned you. I think you underestimated my clumsiness," I say as we make our way to the rink.

"Perhaps." He steps onto the ice with the grace of a ballet dancer, and I realize he wasn't overexaggerating about his skill as he executes some fancy jump and spin combo before beckoning for me to join him.

I clutch the railing and say, "You don't understand. I don't think I'm even going to be able to go a couple of feet without landing on my ass, and you're over here doing some freaking world champion moves!"

"I've seen you walk in some killer heels, you've got this."

I wobble across the ice to him with the grace of a baby giraffe on ice skates. He hooks my arm in his and I grip his sleeve as we inch forward. Actors make this look so easy in the movies. How humans don't suffer more tragic ice-skating deaths is beyond me.

"Stop overthinking it and relax. This is a peaceful sport. Look at this beautiful scenery and let yourself glide," he says, urging me to make bigger movements with my feet.

I let out a breath and relax my shoulders, mirroring him so that my feet aren't making tiny steps but longer strides, and it does feel more natural. "Okay, okay, I got this."

"See? Just keep it up, breathe in and out, don't panic, and if you go down, don't worry—I'll be here to help you up."

I try not to let that statement get me choked up, because he's only talking about skating. He doesn't even know what I brought him here to talk about, and I am so afraid that this favor might be the one that makes him say, *Okay, that's enough. You've asked too much this time.*

"Are you ready to take a little more risk and speed up?" he asks.

"I think so," I say hesitantly, but he doesn't give me time to reconsider before we're only holding hands as we pick up the pace. I yelp as we round a corner and I'm certain I'm going to bust my ass, but when I stay upright, he looks at me with an approving grin.

"I told you you could do it, Desi," Cannon says as we come up on the next corner. "Let's try again, just lean into the turn and—"

But I guess I lean in too far because the next thing I know, I'm on my ass on the ice.

And not only is it really cold, it's harder than a damn slab of concrete. "Ow!" I exclaim, staring up at him, my bottom lip protruding in a pout.

"Mistakes happen." He pulls me up and doesn't give me time to think about my throbbing backside. We're off again. He turns and skates backward, and, like the little kids around us, I use his hands as support. "You should have seen me as a kid. I would fall all the time, and my mom would help me up and tell me to work through it. The sooner I learned how to stay on my feet, the quicker I could get to the reward."

"Reward?" I say, my ears perking up. "What's the reward?" I hold his hands tight and glide along the ice, feeling a little more confident when I'm able to look at him as we skate.

He tilts his head to the sky, which is now black with millions of twinkling stars. "For you, it's that you're ice skating during one of the most spectacular autumn nights I've ever seen."

I look up and take a second to appreciate it. Ever since we'd put on the skates I'd been so worried about falling that I'd hardly taken a second look. It really is beautiful, with the dark sky blanketed with fluffy clouds and sprinkled with a smattering of stars.

"I've always liked when everything around me just goes quiet. Nothing but the sound of skates on ice. It's simple—peaceful. Also, it's the closest I've ever gotten to feeling like I'm flying," he adds, his voice quiet and pensive.

For someone who lives such a fast-paced life, I'm surprised to hear that he likes when things slow down. I've always pictured Cannon as a ball of energy who thrives on the madness. Shoes thrown around and dirty dishes left abandoned; he's a mess. Yet on the inside, he wants calm.

And calm is exactly what I need. It's what I *came here to find*. So why am I not trying harder to make this work? I like Cannon. I like hanging out with him. We can talk about anything and nothing at all. Were there fireworks when we kissed? No, but when he's around I have a feeling of warmth and *safety*. He makes me feel safe. I may not be in love with Cannon, but I love his friendship. We could have an eternity of inside jokes, joyous dinner dates, and long nights talking about our favorite things. He may never be my perfect eternal partner, but who would be? Nobody's perfect. But Cannon can be the friend who always has my back.

I can trust him to do what he says he's going to do. And if he says he's going to be there to pick me up when I fall, I know he will be. In fact, I trust him more than anyone.

Well, almost anyone.

We continue skating, Cannon taking the lead. He sets a fast pace that whips my hair around my face and creates frizzy curls. He, of course, is a marble statue of perfection with a bright, wide smile and shimmering blue eyes. We're a little bit of chaos and calm all rolled into one.

Cannon raises his palm to my cheek, and I'm so numb I can't feel his touch. "You're freezing," he says. "Let's go get some hot cocoa, yeah?"

I nod, and we exit the rink, stopping to remove our skates and put our boots back on. It feels strange to walk on solid ground again, and I feel a little light-headed from all the spinning. Cannon keeps me tucked close to his side, as if he can sense my instability. He settles me in a giant plush swing hanging between two massive trees and promises he'll be back with something to warm me up.

He walks off to the stand that advertises drinks and treats, and I pull my phone out of my pocket to check it. There's a text from Meredith asking how it's going. I can't report back to her that I chickened out. I have to tell Cannon what I am.

I slide my phone back into my coat pocket just as Cannon returns with the cocoa, handing me a steaming mug before sitting next to me. I snuggle in against him, relishing in his body heat. "Thank you," I say, taking a tiny sip. "That is the best hot cocoa I've ever tasted!"

"I got them to add some peppermint for you. I remember you said one time that you liked peppermint chocolate."

I did say that once. In passing. The fact that he remembered is incredibly sweet.

"Oh, I also got you a brownie," he says, handing me a small square wrapped in wax paper.

I dance in my seat and take the treat from him. "Ooh, you really *do* know what I like."

He shrugs it off with a smile.

Maybe it wouldn't be so bad to spend my life with a friend. Cannon is sensitive to my needs and always goes out of his way for me. I like to think I offer him some of that same emotional support. It isn't the happily ever after I wanted but it could be a satisfying ending.

"Cannon?"

"Yeah?" he asks, not looking at me, but scrolling through his phone while sipping his hot cocoa.

"I need to talk to you about something, and it's really—" I inhale a sharp, shaky breath, and Cannon's head instantly jerks up, his eyes wide with concern. "It's really important."

Slipping his phone into his pocket, he sets his cup on the table next to the swing and turns his body toward mine. "What is it, Desi? Are you okay?"

"Yeah, yeah, I'm sorry I scared you, I'm just nervous."

"Nervous? Why? It's me. You don't need to be nervous."

A giggle escapes my throat and I slide my stocking cap off my head, suddenly burning up. Wiping away the sheen of sweat that's appeared on my brow, I say, "I wouldn't be so sure about that."

"Were you lying earlier? Have you been out practicing your archery on small animals?"

"No!"

He pats my hand where it rests on my thigh. "Then you shouldn't be nervous. Nothing you can say will end our friendship. In fact, I wasn't so sure you and I would get along when I first met you. I thought we were too different. But here we are, finding common ground. So trust me when I say what I feel for you is genuine and not going to change."

I close my eyes and grab his hand before he can move it, gripping his fingers in mine. "Even if I told you I'm not exactly who you think I am?"

"What do you mean you're not who I think you are? You're not Desideria—" He stops short and his brows dip like he's thinking hard about something. "Wait . . . what is your last name?"

"Ironically, that's a great question and an excellent lead-in to this conversation." He just stares at me blankly, so I forge on. "I don't have one."

"You don't have a last name?" he asks, his expression perplexed yet intrigued.

I shake my head. "I—I'm not exactly . . . *human*, Cannon."

He sucks his bottom lip into his mouth and nods. There isn't exactly panic in his eyes. I get more of the sense that he's waiting for the punch line to the joke, or maybe he's thinking it over. To be honest, it's impossible to read him right now. But he isn't running away, so that's a good sign.

"If you're not human, then what are you?"

I look down at my lap for a moment before meeting his intense stare. I ask him the same question I asked Jace when he caught me levitating household items that night. "Do you believe in angels and demons?"

"I do," he answers without hesitation.

"Well, then maybe you'll have no trouble believing that they can be right here in front of you, and not just in some alternate universe. I'm a demon, Cannon."

He laughs so loudly that people around us stop what they're doing to look our way. "I get it. I really do. You tend to find trouble and get everyone a little worked up. But it's very hard for me to believe you're an actual demon."

"Jace didn't believe it either," I grumble. "I had to prove it to him. Do you want that too?"

"What have you got? Are you going to sprout horns or maybe set loose a deadly plague?" I can't help but laugh. He seems excited about the second option, which I can't do.

"I can't do either of those. I don't have horns because I'm what's called a High Demon—my father is the king of Demons, otherwise known as Chaos. I'm a princess . . . of Sloth, actually." I don't stop to let him ask questions. "My power is basically used to make things as easy as possible."

I glance around to make sure no one is looking, and when I see no one is paying attention to us, I lift my hand and reach toward his cup of hot cocoa. It lifts from the tabletop and sails right into my open hand. "Here you go," I say, offering it to him.

Cannon glances back and forth between me and the table. "No way. Do it again."

I float the cup back to the table, and end with a shrug.

"You're being serious," he says, picking up the cup and looking for anything that gives the trick away.

"I am."

"That is *wild*. I didn't know a demon could do that."

I cock an eyebrow and tilt my head to the side. "What, did you think they could only suck out your soul or cause bouts of sleep paralysis?"

"Something along those lines. Does Jace know what you are?"

"He does. He went home with me a couple of weeks ago when you were out of town."

Cannon lifts a brow. "I'm having a hard time wrapping my head around that. Going to your . . . home? That must have put him on edge."

"He actually loved it there. It was the calmest I've ever seen him, now that I think about it."

"And the whole story about your dad wanting you to find a partner?"

"True. It's the reason I took Jace with me. I had to buy more time. My dad has this rule that my siblings and I have to find an eternal partner before we can inherit our Circles. Infernis has too many energies for a single ruler. He doesn't want us to feel the stress he has, so he's implementing a new tradition with us."

Cannon leans back in the swing, folding his hands over his stomach. I copy his position and we swing back and forth for a few minutes. It's a lot to take in, and as much as I want to keep pushing the conversation forward, I know he needs time to process it all.

With a hum, like he's reached a conclusion, Cannon says, "So if you don't find someone here, your dad will really choose a partner for you?"

"Yep. It was part of our agreement before I came here. I was so certain I'd find what I'm looking for, and I just haven't." My voice cracks and I look up at the sky and then back at my clasped hands. "That's a lie. I have found it. He just doesn't want me. So my finding him is irrelevant."

"Desi." He says my name with such sadness while rubbing my shoulder. "It looks like Jace isn't the only one with a thing for someone."

We lock eyes, and I wish I were strong enough not to cry in this moment, but my chest burns with my next thought, one that I can't help but voice. "Whatever he feels for me clearly isn't enough, Cannon. He doesn't want me badly enough to even try." Tears slide down my cheeks and I swipe at them just for more to fall in their place.

"It's not that he wouldn't try for you, Desi. I believe he would, but I think Jace doesn't think he's worthy to try for himself."

The emotion building inside me feels like a boulder on my chest. It crushes me to think Jace believes he's undeserving of me. I wish I could change that, but this is his battle to win.

"Well, either way, as much as I wish it were different, it just isn't going to happen with Jace. And the thought of going home and getting paired with someone my *dad* chooses." I shudder. "I love my dad, but he'll probably pick someone boring who doesn't even like movies."

Cannon feigns a gasp. "That would be torturous."

"I know, right? So, you remember how I said a couple of my brothers have platonic partners? Well, I was wondering if . . . maybe you'd want to come back with me. To Infernis. And be my eternal partner."

My cheeks are on fire, and I can't believe I'm asking Cannon, a handsome, talented, witty, charming, successful young man, to leave his life and come with me to another realm to be the king of Sloth.

But I don't know what else to do. I feel like he's my one shot at happiness. I have to take it.

"I'm honored that you would even consider me." The sweet smile on his face speaks volumes to his sincerity. "But I don't want to be the reason you don't find what will make you happy, so . . . I'll be your backup plan. If all else fails, I'll go with you."

My heart swells, relief washing over me, and I can't help myself. I leap onto his lap, throw my arms around his neck, and nearly knock us both out of the swing. "Thank you so much, Cannon, you have no idea how much better I feel knowing I won't be facing eternity with a stranger."

"Anything for you. You're my best friend."

TWENTY-FIVE
JACE

Almost nothing centers me the way running does. The cold morning wind whipping at my face, my muscles burning as I press them to move faster than normal. I feel invincible when I go a little farther or finish a little faster. All the mental stress leaves my body. I'm clear-headed and in a zone where anxiety can't reach me. It's the only time that I feel like I have complete control. I'm superhuman.

I run up the path to the house, only stopping when I reach the porch. I open the top of the water I left on the front step and gulp down half of it before I enter. Everything is quiet this early in the morning, and I normally like the time alone, but today it reminds me that Desideria will continue to find a way to avoid me. It guts me to think that she regrets what happened in the pool the other day.

After removing my running shoes, I grab my protein drink from the refrigerator and head down to the gym, flipping the switch on the wall. The room lights up and my workout playlist of angry punk and contagious '80s rock music pumps through the speakers. After putting on my workout shoes, I begin my upper body routine.

Placing the weight to the heaviest I can pull down, I straddle the bench, grip the handle, and begin my set. I try to clear my mind and focus on controlling my muscles, but I'm haunted by the image of red waves of hair and soft skin. Even if Desi regrets what we did, how can she possibly hide from it? I think about it more than I should. And dammit if I don't crave that rush again.

I'm lost in thought and finally nodding my head along to the beat of the music, getting into the steady rhythm of lifting when I get that odd sense that I'm not alone. I glance up into the mirror in front of me and see Desi standing at the doorway, her hands tucked into her hoodie pocket . . . a hoodie that's so long it's covering the shorts she's surely wearing underneath.

Cannon's hoodie.

Ouch.

"Jace? Can we talk?" she asks, stepping down into the gym, and my heart immediately goes into overdrive.

Not only is someone in my sacred space, the one place in this house besides the bathroom where I can *truly* get away from all my thoughts, avoid the never-ending spirals, push away the anxiety even if only for a moment . . . but it's *Desi*. She's in my space.

I want her here.

I don't want her here.

I *can't* have her here.

"Yeah, of course," is what I say, though. Because of course I want to talk to her. I ease the bar back in place and pat the bench next to me after wiping it down with a clean towel. "Sit."

With a small smile, she sits next to me, leaving some space, but not much. That makes me feel a little better. Maybe she doesn't completely regret it. "Hey."

"Hey," I say, bumping her shoulder with mine. And because I can't help myself, because I *need* to know why, I add, "Nice hoodie. Little big for you." I throw her a knowing look for good measure.

Her face flushes and she shakes her head, turning her entire body toward mine, her knees brushing my thighs. "It's Cannon's, but it's not like that. We went ice skating last night and I got cold. I forgot to give it back, and what can I say, it's cozy. Give me something of yours and you'll never see it in your closet again," she teases.

Images of Desi wearing my button-up shirts, boxer shorts, and my favorite Spider-Man T-shirt flash in my head. I'm tempted to go pull them all out of my closet and hand them over to her. "I'll think about what I can spare," I say, hoping I match her playfulness. A few days without her and I missed our easy banter. "I'm taking it that you didn't come down into the *dungeon of self-inflicted torture*, as you once called it, to ask if you can borrow my evolution of the cyborg T-shirt."

That pulls a real smile from her. "You'd never give me that T-shirt. But I'd take it." She clears her throat and pushes a curl behind her ear. "No. I wanted to talk to you about something important. I think you and I need to cool it a little bit, put some space between us."

And there it is, another thing in my life that was too good to be true. I wasn't expecting forever with Desi, but I was hoping that she would want this with me for a little longer. Her line is so clearly drawn, and I won't push to cross it, but I want to know why.

"Can I ask what brought you to this decision?"

"Of course. You may not like it, but I'll tell you the truth because you deserve that. I'm going to be leaving soon, Jace. I've only got a little over five weeks left. And when I go, I won't be coming back. Ever. And the more I—" Her voice cracks and tears fill her eyes. I move to pull her into my chest, *something, anything* to make her feel better, but she stands and holds up one hand. "Let me get this out. The more time I spend with you, the more and more attached I am. And that's only going to make it worse when I leave. Do you understand? It's not—it's not anything you've done, I just—you've made it real clear that you can't be what I need. And if I have any hope of finding that in the time I have left, I can't spend every second with you. No matter how badly I want to." Her last sentence is a whisper, and when she looks up at me, her eyes are full of such profound sadness, it pierces my heart.

"I'm sorry, Desi. I wish—"

"That I would have come into your life sooner, when you still had half your heart to give me."

I flinch as she repeats the words I said before leaving her room the other night. My desire to confess my feelings while I thought she was asleep was so stupid. I should have kept my mouth shut.

"Desi, I didn't mean to hurt you. I wanted to tell you how much I care for you, but that wasn't the right way to say it *or* do it." I stand and move in front of her, but I don't touch her. Not yet. "But I don't want to lose you as a friend. Tell me that's not changing."

When did I become so needy? What has this chaotic demon-woman done to me? Nothing I would ever want to change, but it's not something I'm used to either.

"Of course not," she says, and she takes the tiniest step toward me. "I wish *nothing* had to change."

"Me too." I lift the hem of my shirt over my face, pretending to wipe away the sweat, but it's just an attempt to hide for a second. Everything I say feels wrong. Every thought I have is damning. I don't see how we recover from this. How do we go back to just being friends when I would bleed just to touch her one more time?

"So you're going to start dating again?" That question shouldn't hurt as badly as it does. I have to pull it together. I'm falling apart over a woman who was never mine.

"Not exactly," she says, pushing her fingers through her hair. A tiny bit of hope rises in my chest. Maybe I won't have to endure watching her fall for someone else. I don't know if I could handle it.

"Then what is your plan? It seemed like you were going to try—"

"I told Cannon," she blurts. "I told him I'm a demon, the truth about why I need to find a partner so fast, and I asked him to come back to Infernis with me if I can't find someone else. Because I don't want to marry a stranger my father picks for me. I at least want to be with someone I like. And he agreed." She takes a deep breath. "He agreed to be my 'backup plan' if I don't find someone else. But I know that may not happen. And to be honest, I can't even imagine search- ing for it again." She sinks down onto the weight bench and props her elbows on her knees, hanging her head. "I'm so lost, Jace."

"I'm sorry, Desi."

I'm sorry for so much that I can never say to her. I'm sorry I'm an emotional mess. I'm sorry I can't open myself up and be what she needs. I'm sorry that I've caused her an ounce of heartache. I'm sorry I let myself pretend for even the smallest moment of time that she could be mine.

I need to move, to refocus my thoughts. I'm two seconds away from growing my bangs out and spending my days wallowing in depressing music. I walk past her, but not before placing my hand on her shoulder and squeezing once, hoping it gives her some kind of comfort. It's not the touch I wish I could give her, but at least it's something.

"What can I do to fix this?" I ask, pacing the room.

She looks up at me and turns around on the bench, throwing a leg over either side. I struggle to keep my eyes on her face and my thoughts safely focused on the topic at hand.

"I don't know, Jace. Nothing short of—" She stops and shakes her head. "There's no use saying it because it's not going to happen. You've told me and shown me in every possible way, and I respect your deci- sion. That's all I'm trying to do." Getting off the bench, she meets me where I stand. For the first time since she came into the room she puts her hands on me, sliding them up my abdomen, over my rib cage, and around to the back of my neck. "Because if I continue to *spend time with you* the way we've been spending time together the last few weeks, well . . . I'm going to become one of those people who just keeps pushing for the answer I want. And I don't want to be like that.

I just can't leave this room with you thinking I don't want you or you did something wrong. Because it couldn't be further from the truth."

"Everything is so confusing about this. But I do know one thing." I cup her face in my hand and run my thumb over her cheekbone. "I meant what I said to you the other night. You deserve better than being handed my broken heart and my flimsy trust. I *do* wish it was different, Desideria."

The tears in her eyes finally spill over and she nods, swiping them away with the back of her hand. "I know you meant it. I think that's why it hurt so bad. Because it also enrages me to no end that Hannah and your mother wrecked your trust so much that you can't even let me all the way in. Not just me, but anyone. I wish you would've let me kick Hannah's ass the other day. I could've knocked her out with one left hook. And your mom. I don't even know the whole story about what she did but I'd—"

"She left a seventeen-year-old kid to figure out how he was going to pay for his dad's cancer treatments when she decided being a wife and mother wasn't her *thing* anymore. I was there holding my dad's hand when he took his final breath, and she was in Florida starting her new life without us. No one was there to comfort me through it. I planned the funeral, I paid the hospital bills, and I sent her what was left of the life they built together in a single check. She cashed it without so much as a thank-you. I gave Hannah part of me that I had protected against that hurt, thinking it would be enough. It wasn't, and when she left, she decimated that too." I stop talking and realize I'm out of breath. After everything she has done for me, I wanted to give Desi something. So I offered her the truth that I'd only shared with one other person, Dr. Holloman. It wasn't nearly enough, but it was a small token to show her how much she means to me.

Her lips part and without hesitation, she throws her arms around my neck and pulls me close to her. "Jace, that is . . . I don't even know what to say," she whispers against my ear. "I'm so, so sorry. You deserve so much better than that. I know that was hard for you to share with me. Thank you for doing that. It means more than you know."

I nod and pull her back to my chest. If this is it, if I never get to touch her again, I'm going to be selfish and make this moment last. The way her body fits against mine, the way she smells, the sound of her breathing, the feel of her skin, I'll take and take until she is done with me, because I don't want to be done with this little hurricane.

TWENTY-SIX
DESI

Jace's loud-as-hell yelling wakes me from a deep sleep, and I shoot up in bed, my hair out of control and my tank top twisted. I spring to my feet and without bothering to right my clothing, sprint to his room and fling the door open.

"Jace, what the hell happened? Are you okay?" I exclaim, my chest rising and falling as my panic mounts.

He's jumping up and down on his bed with his phone in his hand. His hair is standing in every direction, and he wears a smile so bright it's lighting up the room. "Edmonds is going to sign!"

He holds his hand out to me and I timidly place my fingers against his. The next thing I know, we're holding hands and jumping on his bed together. I've never seen him let his guard down and give in to his happiness the way he is right now.

This moment with Jace is so wildly different from the one we shared in the gym a few days ago. We've talked since, watched a movie or two, eaten meals together, but that moment where he held me close like he was never going to get to touch me again was the last emotionally charged interaction we've had until now.

"Jace, I'm so happy for you!" I exclaim, giggling when he pulls me against him and tickles my ribs.

"It's thanks to you, Desideria, I swear," he says, and our jumping slows until we're standing a few inches away from each other. "Matt never would have talked me up so much if it weren't for you."

I shake my head. "You did all the work. You deserve all the credit. Not me."

"But—" His smile falters a bit and the light in his eyes dulls just a shade. "I need one more favor from you."

"Okay?"

"Matt didn't just talk *me* up during our video conference call yesterday. He mentioned *you* to Edmonds. And he wants to meet you since Matt sang your praises. It looks like I'm going to need my girlfriend one more time."

"Of course I'll help. What day is your meeting?"

Jace runs his hand over the back of his neck and looks away from me. "We're signing the papers at Matt's office. Which is in New York. Next week." He looks at me and flashes an innocent smile that has me going gooey on the inside. "I know your time is running short, Desi, and I understand if you can't. Not to mention, you *just* drew your line in the sand, and here I am not only leaping over it but completely obliterating it with a long weekend in New York City."

"Jace, stop. I'll go."

He looks at me as if I just spoke a language he's never heard. "What? Just like that?"

"Yeah, you dork. Just like that. You're my friend. You've done more for me in the past two months than I can count. I wouldn't deny you this, not when it's the last step to making your dream come true! The big city, right? The one with all the tall buildings and the green lady with the torch?"

He laughs and nods. "That's the one."

"That sounds like fun. Will we have time to do touristy stuff too? You'll be able to take me places?"

His features soften and he nods. "We'll have time to do some sightseeing. I'm sure we can visit the green lady. So you're in? You'll pretend to be my girlfriend one last time?"

The words *one last time* open a chasm in my heart that I do

everything in my power to ignore. "Consider me your adoring signif-
icant other. It's not a hard part to play, ya know."

His cheeks turn a soft shade of pink and he clears his throat. "Oh,
also . . . if you want to get two separate rooms, we can. I don't want to
make you uncomfortable."

I know I should take him up on it, that it's the "smart" thing to
do, but I'd like to spend time with my friend and not sleep alone in a
strange city. "That's not necessary. We're adults who've spent plenty of
time together in intimate situations. Sleeping in the same bed won't
be a big deal. We did it in Infernis, we can do it again. Besides, it'll
ruin the guise of being boyfriend and girlfriend if we're caught going
to separate rooms."

"Thank you. Not just for this but for everything you've done to
help me. I promise to make the trip worth it."

I curse the fluttering that happens in my belly when I smile and
say, "I have absolutely no doubt that you will."

A week later I'm yawning and dragging my rolling suitcase down the
stairs at four thirty, silently cursing Jace for booking such an early
flight.

Speaking of, there he is at the island, eating a bowl of peanut butter puff cereal, looking bright eyed and awake behind his glasses. He's
wearing jeans that hug his ass and a tight red sweater that somehow
brings out the stormy gray in his eyes.

This is going to be a long trip.

"Good morning, princess," he says, raising his eyebrow, and I
don't miss how his gaze runs up and down my body. It's not just the
way he looks at me that sends shivers up and down my spine. He hasn't
called me princess for over a week. I missed hearing his endearments

for me, but there's one in particular that I miss. I wonder if he'll ever call me little hurricane again.

Even though nothing can come of it, I'm suddenly glad I went for the dressier outfit—my dark skinny jeans, ivory sweater with a V-neck low enough to show some cleavage, and boots that come almost to my knees. My curls are loose and wild around my shoulders, but my face is bare; no time for makeup before a flight this early.

"Morning, sunshine," I grumble, grabbing a bottle of water from the fridge and taking a sip. "You're awfully chipper this morning."

"What can I say, I'm excited." He may be excited but the bowl of peanut butter puffs instead of his grotesque morning concoction tells me he's nervous too. He swallows another big bite and says, "I could hardly sleep last night. I got up at three and went for a run."

"Sometimes I wonder about you, Jace Wilder."

"And in those thoughts, do I have my clothes on or off?" He scrunches his face and shovels a spoonful of cereal into his mouth. "Sorry. That was inappropriate. I got caught up in playing the part of adoring boyfriend."

We're going to get into *so* much trouble. Then again, isn't everyone in New York expecting to see a happy couple? I suppose it doesn't hurt to start acting the part now. At least that's what I'm telling myself.

I grin and lean forward on the island, my V-neck dipping low enough to show him my lace bra and a glimpse of my mark beneath it. "Off. Almost always off."

The relieved expression on his face sends a warm sensation through my bloodstream. "Exactly how I imagine you," he says with a wink.

Shaking my head, I say, "Come on, *babe*, don't you think we should be going now?"

Jace takes the last bite of his cereal, washes his bowl, and says, "Hold on, one sec. I have to brush my teeth first. I wouldn't want my

girlfriend to have to deal with peanut butter puff breath. Disgusting."
He disappears up to his room and comes back five minutes later with
a toiletry bag that he stuffs into his suitcase. "All right, I'm ready."

"Breath check," I say, putting my hands on my hips.

He steps toward me and kisses me on the cheek, his lips barely
brushing the corner of my mouth, the scent of peppermint filling my
senses. "How's that?" he whispers.

I'm speechless for a couple of seconds. "Perfect," I say. "Very
minty. You pass."

"Good. The Uber is out front. Come on, princess." He grabs both
of our bags and I sling my purse over my shoulder, following him out
to the car.

When we get to the airport, the crowd is much worse than I
expected. Granted, I've never been to an airport, much less flown in
a plane, but I didn't think it would be like this. "Do you think we're
going to make it?" I ask, worrying my lower lip, looking around at all
the people flitting in and out of lines and rushing to different kiosks
and service desks.

"You're starting to sound like me with the worrying. We have just
over two hours to get through security. We're fine. If we're going to
worry, it should be about your ID. Are you sure security isn't going
to flag you?"

I give him a pointed glare. "Are you kidding me? My father is
the king of Demons. They're everywhere in this realm, including the
government. My ID will be just fine."

Jace gives me an impressed nod and says, "Then we're good to go,
provided you didn't pack anything sharp in your carry-on bag."

"Damn, I guess we need to go back home so I can unpack my
machete," I quip, and even I know to say it under my breath. He scowls
at me, but I don't miss the glint in his eyes. I'm pretty sure that I could
tell this man that all the video game consoles in the universe were

damaged by a major virus and he would continue skipping through this day; even his anxiety has taken a backseat to his positive attitude.

After we make our way through security we stop at one of the markets to stock up on snacks. Jace even says I have enough time to look at some of the souvenir shops inside the terminal. When we get to our gate the attendant is calling for first class to board the plane.

"Keep moving, princess. That's us."

I look over my shoulder at him, my eyes widening. I may have never been on a plane, but I know from movies and TV that first class is only for the elite. "First class? Really? Isn't that expensive?"

He shrugs. "Yeah, but this is a special occasion and a reason to splurge a little. Besides, it's your first time on a plane. I wanted you to have a good experience. The seats in first class are so much more comfortable, you get champagne, there's more leg room, *and* you get a blanket."

Warmth blooms in my chest. Jace paid extra for first class tickets *just for me*. I loop my arm in his and look up at him, leaning my head against his arm. "Thank you. That's really sweet."

We board the plane and take our seats. Jace is the epitome of relaxed, scrolling through his phone. I, on the other hand, am staring out the window and playing with all the gadgets around us. This exceeds my expectations. Or maybe it's not truly the plane that has me in awe but the man sitting beside me. It's incredible to me that just a few days ago I was letting him down gently, putting some space between us because I'm trying to protect my heart, essentially telling him it was "me, not him," and now here we are in first class seats he bought just for me. Who does that?

He glances up from his phone and smiles. "Are you all right? Do you need anything before we take off?"

I chew the inside of my cheek and pretend that I wasn't just thinking about how phenomenal he is. "No. I'm just a little scared. There isn't a reason for planes when you have portals," I say, wringing my hands in my lap and laying my head back against the headrest, letting my eyelids flutter closed.

Warm fingers slink beneath mine and curl around my thigh. I crack my eyes open and watch as Jace's thumb rubs calming strokes against the outside of my leg. The gesture is innocent, but my body doesn't see it that way. I fight the urge to inch my thighs apart and feel him touch me more intimately.

"As soon as we're in the air, I'll order you a drink," he says, letting his fingertips travel up and down my inner thigh.

I swallow hard and nod. "Okay," I whisper. "As long as you don't stop doing what you're doing right now, I'll be good to go." My voice is shaky and my heart beats hard against my rib cage. I could pretend it's because I'm scared of takeoff, but that's probably only 20 percent of my problem right now.

"I'm not going anywhere. Just talk to me to take your mind off the nerves and you'll be fine."

"I can't think straight right now. You start the conversation."

He chuckles and as he continues to draw circles with his thumb he says, "So did you make Cannon guess what Circle you'll rule when you told him?"

"No. I just blurted it out."

"What's the fun in that? Make the man work for the information."

"What Circle do you think he would have guessed?"

Jace taps his finger on my knee. "Lust."

"Oh yeah?" I ask, raising one brow. "And why's that?"

He leans in closer to me, bringing his mouth to my ear. "I know that's the sin tempting me whenever I'm around you."

I turn my face to his so our lips are inches apart. "Me too. We've barely started this trip and you've already got me wishing you'd use that blanket you were so excited about to cover our laps and *really* take my mind off the nerves," I murmur, forgetting every line I've drawn, every wall I've tried to build.

"Is that what you really want, Desideria?"

Yes. No. Maybe. I'm treading close to forbidden territory, and I should know better. Jace is right; when we're together I'm consumed by lust. So much so that a part of me wants to say forget the blanket and guide his hand between my legs. I want him to touch me, to make me feel all the things only he can. And when I'm done losing myself to his touch, I want to return the favor. The only thing that holds me back is that small voice of reason in the back of my head. As much as I want to ignore it, that voice is vital to my self-preservation right now.

"It's a nice fantasy, like something I would read about in one of my steamy romances." It's the truth, but not the full truth. I give him just enough to keep the flirtation going.

He leans his head back and hums his approval. "I *really* need to skim through one of these books sometime."

"Well, it's your lucky day," I say, reaching into my purse and pulling out the latest in the series I've been binge reading. "I just read a pretty sexy scene if you want to take a look." I open the book to where my bookmark rests, right after a particularly spicy scene in which the two enemies just gave in and decided that they were done fighting and wanted to work out their aggression in a different way. Flipping back a few pages, I hand him the book. "Here ya go. Have a gander."

As the flight attendants demonstrate the safety procedures, I watch Jace. More than once he runs his palm over his brow, wiping away the perspiration gathering there. The speed with which his gray eyes move across the page is impressive, like he's devouring each word. I don't miss the way he lingers on a sentence or two before shifting in his seat. I almost feel bad for handing him the book. Almost.

Jace's expression keeps me entertained until we taxi onto the runway and the plane speeds down it. He's glued to the pages well past our ascent. It's not until the flight attendant stops at our row for our drink order that he sets the book down. On his lap. To cover the bulge pressing against his zipper.

"I'll have a water, please."

"A red wine," I say, and when they leave, I turn to Jace. "Did that scene make you thirsty?"

"Among other things," he says, sliding his hand between the book and his pants and adjusting himself.

I smirk and nod down at where the book rests on his lap. "I'd say I'm sorry, but you've been teasing me all morning, so I think you deserved it. You don't have to read any more." I reach over to take it back from him, and my fingertips accidentally brush against his zipper, the feeling of his rock-hard cock sending an instant pool of warmth between my legs.

He flinches and makes a small, pained noise. "You're going to be the death of me, Desideria."

"Am I?"

"I may have to teach you a lesson—the characters in your books aren't the only ones who can work out their aggression in creative ways," he murmurs, his gaze traveling up and down my body.

This plane is in real danger; I feel like I'm going to combust at any moment. "I may have to hold you to that, Jace Wilder," I whisper.

"Well—"

"Do you two need anything else?" The flight attendant's chipper voice breaks the spell between us and we split, nearly jumping out of our skin.

"No, we're good," we both chirp, and I stare daggers into her back as she walks away.

We're both silent a moment before I clear my throat. "Oh, there was another thing I wanted to tell you about Cannon. So you know, he and I are very much on the same page about us having no romantic chemistry, and yet he's still willing to be my backup plan. For eternity. Wouldn't he want a chance to meet someone, fall in love, all that good stuff? I know feelings can develop over time, but it's not a guarantee. Do you think it's weird?"

Jace remains silent, and I can practically see his brain working through what I just told him, so I take the time to think it over again. Everyone strives to be the best, and when they come up a little short they're grateful for second place because it shows that they worked hard and never gave up. But in a relationship, especially one that lasts for eternity, who wants to be second best? Especially with someone they aren't clicking with in the sex department.

Jace tips his head side to side and says, "It's weird and it isn't. You know he's motivated to succeed in business. You'd literally be making him a king. Can't get any more successful than that. And you're gorgeous, so coming in second as your arm candy is a sweet deal by itself."

I consider this and purse my lips. "True. I mean, about the career thing. As far as me being gorgeous . . ." I lift one shoulder playfully. "That's subjective."

"True, but it's my job to know when something is exceptional. I have an eye for the things that stand out. And nothing is more attractive than owning who and what you are. You are beautiful, Desideria. Very little in this realm compares to you."

Suddenly the air in the cabin isn't enough and I can't breathe. "I have to go to the bathroom," I blurt, unbuckling my seat belt. "Is that—is that allowed? Can I?"

"Yes." He points to the sign at the front of the plane and moves out of my way.

I practically run down the aisle and dive into the bathroom, locking the door and leaning against it, threading my fingers through my hair.

I have to get control of myself.

I'm this close to surrendering and letting Jace back in, even though I know it'll end in nothing but heartache. But honestly, why shouldn't I? I'm not deluding myself into believing that I'm going to find anyone else to take with me to Infernis. I know I'm going to end up taking Cannon. I'm not going to meet someone else and fall in love in the little time I have left. It simply isn't going to happen.

If Jace wants to tell me I'm beautiful and put his hands on me, why shouldn't I let him? Why shouldn't I enjoy the time I have left with him? It may hurt to know how things will end for us, but at least I am prepared. Looking in the mirror, I take a deep breath and fix my curls.

Straightening to my full height, I square my shoulders. I'm a princess, dammit. I may be a princess of Sloth, but I'm still a princess. I'm going to go back to my seat, get in the mindset that Jace Wilder is my boyfriend, and we are the happiest couple on this plane. Soon we will be in New York City, and if he wants to go the extra mile to convince Matt, Edmonds, and the mayor himself, then that's what we'll do.

I wash my hands and leave the lavatory, flashing him a bright smile as I return and take my seat, trailing my fingers along his shoulder as I pass. "Sorry about that. I felt like I was going to be sick for a second. I'm good now."

Jace follows my every movement like he's searching for a hole in my story. Looking back, I'm certain he sat here contemplating whether or not he did something wrong. My exit *was* pretty hasty.

"Do you want me to call the flight attendant?" he asks, like he's talking to a skittish animal. Oh yeah, he *definitely* thinks he did something wrong.

"No. I just needed to splash some water on my face. I felt lightheaded after the takeoff and the wine. Honestly." I turn in my seat after buckling back up and slide my hand onto the inside of his thigh. "I'm perfect now."

He laces his fingers with mine and flashes me a timid smile, but his words are sincere. "Good. I want you to have the time of your life on this trip, and when you think back on your time here, I want you to remember the next few days."

I rub my thumb across his knuckles. "I know I will. And I have to admit—I want you to have the best time you've ever had with me over the next few days. Like, not just *with me*. But *ever*. Before I go, I want to know that I gave you the best days of your life." My voice cracks and I don't even bother to hide the emotion in it. I'm trying to let him know that I've given in. I'm waving my white flag. This isn't just for show.

But if he doesn't see it now, he will. I'll make sure of it.

He leans in and presses a kiss to my cheek. "You're here with me for one of the most exciting moments of my life. I have a feeling it won't be hard to make these the best days."

"Same," I say, laying my head on his shoulder and spending the rest of the flight in comfortable silence.

TWENTY-SEVEN
JACE

I don't *mean* to sit and watch her as she sleeps. But the plane is silent and the lights are still dimmed inside the cabin. Her window is cracked, and rays of sunlight shine over her face. Her head is resting on my shoulder and I can smell her coconut shampoo. Desi is filling my every sense; even her hand is still entwined with mine as she snoozes, little sleepy noises escaping her lips every now and then as she shifts in her seat to try to get more comfortable.

She's trying to lean in closer to me, but the goddamn armrest is in the way. I don't know how to move it without waking her, so I just settle for the knowledge that she *wants* to be closer to me. At least in her dreams.

The familiar *ding* of the seat belt light rings, and I know we're about to start our descent. I don't want her to miss seeing Manhattan from the air, so I brush my fingertips against her wrist. Her eyelids flutter open and when that green gaze lands on me, I nearly melt. I hope my instincts earlier didn't fail me and she's reconsidering sharing her time with me.

Lifting my hand tentatively to her forehead, I push her curls away from her face. "Wake up, princess, we're about to land at JFK."

She sits up straight in her seat and bounces a couple of times. "Yeah? I'm so excited. I can't wait to see everything. What do we do first?"

I grin and reach over to make sure her seat belt is buckled. I try to ignore the pull in my abdomen at being so close to her and say, "There is a two-hour time difference between here and Denver, so it's already past one. We need to check into the hotel, get freshened up, and head over to Matt's office to meet with Edmonds. That is, if you want to. I suppose you don't have to go to the actual meeting to sign, you could just come to dinner after—"

"No," she interrupts. "I want to come to all of it. I want to be by your side every second." She slides her hand back into mine. "That's what a supportive girlfriend does, right?"

"Well, yeah, I guess so."

She leans back in the seat. "Then that's settled."

After a bumpy landing that has her cutting off circulation to my fingers, we grab our luggage and hail a cab to take us to the hotel. Just like the plane tickets, I *may* have gone a little over the top, booking us a room at a Manhattan boutique hotel.

Desi ducks her head into the bathroom, scoping out the enormous bathtub. "I'm using that later. Don't even try to stop me," she says, winking at me as she tries out the plush bed. Like a child making snow angels, she spreads her arms and legs and slides them back and forth.

"Why would I try to stop you? That gets you naked in my bathroom. I welcome that," I say without thinking, removing my suit from its garment bag.

I'm so blurring the lines she made clear. It feels like a dick move without knowing for sure she's changed her mind.

"Desi—I'm sorry, I shouldn't—"

She gets to her feet, saunters across the room to me, and I can't help but let my eyes roam over her long legs encased in those tight jeans and the V-neck sweater that reminds me so much of the one she was wearing the day we met.

"Now that I know that for sure, it's game on, Mr. Wilder," she whispers, trailing her fingernail across my chest before disappearing into the bathroom with her toiletry bag.

Well, okay then. It looks like my anxiety can fuck off for once. I was right. She wants to try again. My phone rings, interrupting the moment—thankfully, because I was about to be in a pretty embarrassing physical situation in a second.

"This is Jace."

It's Matt, checking that we arrived and are still on to sign the contract at four. I assure him that Desi and I will be there, then hang up and fall back on the bed. I can't believe this is finally happening. The dream I've spent years working toward is on its way to becoming my reality. My stomach somersaults with a mixture of nerves and excitement—a volatile combination that makes my hands shake. My eyes flutter shut as I try to center myself.

My breathing returns to normal just as Desi steps out of the bathroom in nothing but black lace panties and a push-up bra.

"Sorry. I forgot my dress out here," she says innocently, like she isn't standing there in front of me looking like pure temptation and sex with a side of sin.

She gives me a once-over and her eyebrows knit together. "Jace, are you all right?"

"I—" I shake my head, trying to break the spell she has on me. "I was until this fucker," I say, pointing down at my crotch, where the erection that deflated when the phone rang has returned in full force.

Desi laughs while walking to the closet and taking a purple dress off the hanger. "I should apologize, but it's good to know you still like me that much."

"That's the understatement of the year," I mumble, sitting up on the edge of the bed so I have a better view to watch her while she dresses.

Desi slides the sleek dress over her head, shimmying into the clingy fabric. She moves her arms behind her to zip it, and after a couple seconds, her eyes widen and her cheeks flush. "Oh, dammit."

"What? What's wrong?"

"My dress. Can you zip it for me? I think I ate one too many Zebra Cakes—damn Glen for introducing me to those—and now it feels too tight." She's clearly embarrassed and trying to deflect using humor. I know a thing or two about that.

I stand and guide her around until her back is to me. The smooth skin along her spine calls me to run my fingers over it. I picture sliding the strap down her shoulder and letting it pool on the floor at her feet. Again, I wrangle in my hormones and zip the dress. The way the silky, dark-purple fabric clings to her curves is sinful. She has me thinking all sorts of depraved thoughts.

"You look really good in this dress," I say, my lips close to her neck, and watch as her skin rises in goosebumps.

She turns her head just enough so she can see me over her shoulder. "Thank you. You're sure it's not too tight?"

"No, it's perfect," I whisper and take a chance that might backfire on me. I press my lips to the top of her shoulder, desperate for one small taste of her skin.

Her sharp intake of breath has me holding mine, but when she turns around, there's a smile on her face. I would do whatever I can to see it over and over again.

After I put my suit on and ask for a bit of extra assistance straightening my tie, possibly just to get Desi close to me again, we're on our way to Matt's office. The city is bustling, with people rushing this way and that, and the noise is overwhelming as always. My senses are overloaded, but I'm absolutely enamored watching Desi's reactions to everything around us. The smile on her face is wide and so are her eyes, trying to take in as much as possible.

"Jace, this place is amazing. It's even better than I thought it would be. Thank you for bringing me here. We haven't even gone anywhere yet and I am about to explode from excitement," she says, bouncing on the balls of her feet, her curls mimicking the action against her shoulders. "Where's Matt's office?"

"We're going to have to grab a cab." I lift my hand and flag the first yellow car I see, opening the door for Desi and then climbing in next to her. The drive itself isn't that far, but the traffic is horrendous. I'm starting to get nervous that we're going to be late, and the first impression Edmonds has of me will be a terrible one. He might decide to back out, that he can't count on me, that I'm irrespon—

"Downtown Denver is a grain of sand compared to this place," Desi says in awe. "Everything is so *tall*! And all the people . . . it reminds me of trying to fit a new outfit into my overstuffed closet," she says out of nowhere, completely oblivious to my inner spiral.

I can't help it; I laugh at that comparison. I swear, this woman is like a natural anti-anxiety medication. She can ease my worries without even realizing it, and there's just something so pure about that.

We stop in front of a high-rise office building and I help Desi out of the taxi. With her arm looped in mine, we enter the modern lobby and the woman at the front desk directs us to the fifty-second floor.

"Fifty-two floors?" Desi hisses. "That's a lot of floors to take an elevator for. What if it—"

"It won't," I assure her as we wait for the doors to open, and I usher her in. "I promise." Wherever she was going with that train of thought, I don't want to jump on for the ride. There's no worry she can voice that I haven't thought of at least once before.

The elevator stops at several floors as we travel farther up, and people pile in. The man next to us moves closer, and I notice Desi inch even nearer to me. Not that I mind, but she was practically standing on top of me to begin with. Glancing at the guy who's crowding us, I see him raking his smarmy gaze over her, snagging on her hips and chest.

My nostrils flare and I wrap my arm around her waist, pulling her back flush against my chest, even closer than before. My voice is a firm warning when I say, "Keep your eyes off my girl, man."

The older man straightens his tie, his hand adorned with a golden wedding band, and mumbles an apology before exiting on the next floor.

Desi's chest expands with a sharp inhale and when she exhales, I feel her whole body relax against me. I know she's all right when she looks up at me and teases, "Your girl, huh?"

I lift one shoulder in a casual shrug. "Saying my roommate seemed weak, and it was a moment where I had to pull some macho-man shit."

"Feel free to do it anytime—it reminded me of that night outside the club except this time I didn't have to endure the dude's hands on me, and I still got to hear you get all alpha-hole possessive."

"Alpha-hole? I don't think anyone has ever called me that."

"Too bad, because I think it's a turn-on."

I smirk. "Good to know."

The elevator signals our floor and I take Desi's hand as we scoot through the couple of people around us. If we thought the lobby was nice, Matt's office is the lap of luxury. Rich, dark furniture, amber light, and the scent of leather in the air. The young man at the front desk has perfectly coiffed hair and a slim-fitted suit. He guides us to a conference room and taps on the tall walnut door before entering.

Matt sits at the head of the conference table with an older man. They each have their hands clasped on top of folders and crystal glasses of water within reach.

Matt stands and gives Desi a once-over. It's the harmless flirtation we've both come to expect of him, and while it doesn't bother Desi in the least—in fact, I think she finds the attention amusing—I must admit I'm becoming slightly perturbed. Maybe I *am* an alpha-hole.

After an appreciative whistle, he says, "How do you do it? Four hours on a plane and you still manage to look like a million bucks. Why couldn't you get your man to clean up this good?"

She leans forward and kisses the air at both of his cheeks before turning back to me and tugging on the lapels of my suit jacket. "Thank you, but I think Jace not only looks phenomenal, but like he's about to sign the most promising young graphic designer in the business."

"On that, I will agree with you. Come take a seat." Matt points to the empty chair across from the other man. "This is Maxwell Cartwright, my attorney. Maxwell, may I introduce Jace Wilder and his better half, Desideria."

We shake hands.

"I apologize in advance if this all seems rushed. I just got a call about a last-minute will reading at my Connecticut office. I wasn't planning on heading out tonight, but getting this family to agree on a time has been the bane of my existence," Cartwright says.

"No problem at all," I answer with a smile. "I'm happy to get it all signed and taken care of sooner rather than later."

Mr. Cartwright double-checks the contracts, making sure it's the agreement that gives Matt a stake in my company. The attorney takes his time going through each section, ensuring we both agree on all the stipulations. He hands me the fountain pen and the contract, saying, "If there are no other questions, I just need your signature."

Emotions rise to the surface, and to my horror, *tears* fill my eyes. *Jace, get it together.* But there's no chance of that at all, not when Desi reaches over and places her hand on my thigh.

"All those countless hours working for this have paid off. I'm so proud of you," she murmurs, leaning toward me and placing a kiss on my jaw.

"Thank you, Desideria," I say, pressing my lips to her forehead. "I couldn't have done it if it weren't for you. Not like this. You carved this path for me, and I'll be forever grateful." I blink away the tears and she just smiles, shaking her head, and I know what she's telling me with that single look.

I didn't do anything, you did, but I'm not arguing with you right now.

The door opens and in walks a handsome young man with slicked back blond hair, a sprinkling of freckles across his nose, and lightly tanned skin, the Gen-Zer who is making all of this possible with his incredible talent.

Bryce Edmonds.

He is a hell of a lot more composed than I was the first time I met Matt in person, shaking his hand with a confidence I still struggle to convey.

Next to me, Desi stifles a strange noise that I recognize as her snort-laugh, and she taps my thigh. I snap my head toward her with a *what the hell* expression on my face.

"Sorry, frog in my throat," she says, scratching behind her left ear before taking a giant gulp of water, sliding her gaze from me to Edmonds.

I narrow my eyes as I follow her line of sight and nearly fall out of my chair when I see the telltale mark behind his left ear. A sun that is several shades lighter than his skin, that probably no one else would notice unless they were looking for it.

I'll be damned. Bryce Edmonds is an angel.

I jump to my feet, not wanting to create an awkward lull in the flow of things. I don't need to be overthinking right now. "Bryce. It's nice to finally meet you in person."

"You too," Bryce responds, shaking my hand. "Ever since our conference call I've been researching your work, and I already admire your style."

I place a hand on Desi's lower back, guiding her forward. "I'd like to introduce you to my girlfriend, Desi."

She flashes Edmonds one of her most charming smiles, and my chest warms at the sight of it. Thankfully, I don't have time to dwell on what that means because she's off on a roll. "It's so nice to meet you. I cannot tell you how often I've heard your name around the house. Jace was starting to talk about you more than his PlayStation games, and I knew then that if you didn't sign with him, he'd be devastated," she jokes, and everyone in the room laughs, including Edmonds, and I give her hip a playful pinch.

"It's a pleasure to meet you, and I apologize for taking up so much of Jace's time. I'm sure you'll be glad to have his undivided attention again."

She glances up at me and winks. "Oh, don't worry, he found plenty of time for me."

Little hurricane . . . I wrap my arm around her shoulder and kiss her temple. "Come on, let's get this paperwork signed so we can go eat dinner. If I know my girlfriend, and I think I do, she's starving right about now."

We all take our seats and get settled in. "You aren't wrong," she says, and I tap the tabletop twice.

"You all heard that," I say, pointing a finger around the table. "Mr. Cartwright, I'm going to need you to draw up a legal document stating that Desi admitted I wasn't wrong."

Everyone laughs, and the rest of the meeting carries on just as smoothly as it began.

When the last document is signed, everyone stands, and Mr. Cartwright wishes us fun celebrating. We head out of the office and the elevator takes us to the garage floor. A large, black SUV with tinted windows and a man in a black suit waits for us. He opens the back door and the four of us crawl inside. Desi remains quiet during the ride, while the digital design nerds talk about the latest trends and new technologies that will make our jobs easier.

She's looking out the window, presumably watching the hustle and bustle of the city, when I scoot in a little closer and slide my hand into hers, intertwining our fingers. When she turns her head toward me, I run my thumb over hers, letting it drift to the inside of her wrist.

"Are you okay, Desideria?"

"Yeah, I'm fine," she whispers, angling her head to mine so our lips are only inches apart.

She really is going to be the death of me.

I force myself to back up just enough that I don't end up making out with her in front of my new business partners. "Is this too much geek talk for you?"

"No. It's entertaining to hear how passionate you all are about your work. I'd go as far as saying you almost show as much enthusiasm as I do for shopping."

I chuckle. "That's a big claim."

"I know," she says, fighting to keep a straight face.

We reach the restaurant and file inside. The host greets Matt by name and leads us through the dining room to a booth in a quiet corner. Other than a few meticulously placed lights in the ceiling, the restaurant is illuminated by candlelight. Oil lamps hang from the walls, their light dancing across the crystals of the chandeliers. Our table is dressed in a black cloth with white napkins folded beside polished silverware. This is the kind of place where you need an *in* to get a table.

I start to sit so I can scoot in toward the wall, but Desi stops me.

"Wait, let me."

"But you're wearing—"

"I know, but I'm left-handed, remember?" She winks at me, and my entire body heats. "If I sit on the other side of you, we'll bump elbows all night."

"Fine, go ahead," I say, stepping aside.

After we all get settled, we peruse the menu as Matt orders wine for the table. Desi leans over and whispers, "Are you sure about this place? These prices . . . everything you've done for this trip has been so extravagant. I can help pay if you need me to."

"This meal is on Matt. He insisted, so order what you like. And trust me when I tell you that he can afford it. And even if he weren't paying, neither would you." I slide my hand over the top of her leg and brush my thumb over her thigh.

She shifts in her seat, and I swear, she spreads her legs just enough to allow me to slide my hand higher if I want to. And of course, I do. "All right, then," she says, her voice a little wobbly.

I behave for a few minutes, simply toying with the hem of her dress with my pinkie, sweeping against her skin every few seconds. But the more she shifts under my touch, the higher her skirt rides, and my fingers follow. I'm desperate to touch her, desperate to know if she's as wet for me as I'm hard for her.

This has been fun and all, teasing her with the little touches while at dinner in a public place, but I didn't think this all the way through . . . didn't count on the consequences for myself. That if I were to have to stand up right now, I'd be *really* embarrassed.

But I can't help myself. I slide my hand up another inch and glide my pinkie over the center of her black lace panties to find her soaked.

I glance at her, and she's politely listening to Matt and Edmonds talk about the newest Illustrator update. Her chin rests on her knuckles and her lips are tucked between her teeth. God, her neck and chest are so pretty when they're flushed. I'm getting to her. *Good. I want her to be as starved for me as I am for her by the time we leave this table.*

I rejoin the conversation like I never left, but I keep up the steady back and forth of my fingertip over her panties, and to her credit, she doesn't bat an eye. But I know Desi, and she is going to be ready to strangle me by the time we get out of here.

"Desi?" Matt asks, and I realize it's the second time he's said her name. I press my pinkie harder against her center, and she nearly drops her fork, shooting me a glare that's more of an aroused, pleading stare. I tilt my head toward Matt and her face heats as she turns to him.

"Oh, sorry, I was so zoned out. Just thinking about how good this risotto is," she says, lying through her teeth. My touch grows bolder, stroking her harder over the lace.

Matt laughs and takes a sip of wine. "Fair enough. I was just wondering what it is you do. I don't think Jace ever told us."

"Oh, I'm sort of in between gigs right now. Just taking some time to figure out what I really want. I have a position in my father's company, but I wanted to take some time to explore my options first before I take it."

"Smart. You're young and have time to make up your mind. I'm sure Jace will eventually need someone to keep him organized with all the accounts coming in. It could be beneficial to work together."

"I don't know about that." I trace the leg of her panties. "You know what they say about mixing business with pleasure. Desi would be a distraction for sure."

The distraction in question reaches for her glass of wine but finds it empty, then snatches mine and downs it. "You're a distraction yourself, mister," she manages as my finger hooks inside her underwear and grazes her wet skin.

I pull away, satisfied with how much I've frustrated her. "Far be it from me to distract you," I say. I don't know what's gotten into me, but I lift my hand to my mouth, pretending to swipe away something at the corner, slipping the wet tip of my finger between my lips.

I just tasted her at this table in front of everyone, and now I don't think my dick could be any harder. I really did not think this through.

It's probably good that when I slide my hand back onto her thigh she's crossed one leg over the other, denying me access. I pinch the skin on the side of her knee playfully, and she bats her eyelashes at me, saying, "Don't worry, I won't distract you back at the hotel if you have some work you need to get done."

Matt clears his throat with a hand over his mouth, and he and Bryce exchange an amused glance. When he moves his hand, his lips are curved into a knowing smile. "Are you two okay? Do you need a minute?"

"I'm perfectly content. Desi, do you need a minute?"

She flashes me a bright smile. "I'm one hundred percent good to go. I'm good for the rest of the night, in fact. I'll take another drink, if you don't mind," she announces, holding up her wine glass.

Oh. She's either really *not amused or she's just giving me a hard time. I'm going to try to go 2-0 against my anxiety today and hope I didn't just royally screw things up.*

"Far be it for me to deny the queen her wine," Matt says.

With all hands to oneself and the conversation back on track, we continue with our dinner. We talk about graphics, copyright, the dangers of AI, even movies and music, making sure to include Desi in every conversation. She especially impresses Bryce with her knowledge of *Star Wars*. A burst of pride fills me at that, and I wrap my arm around her and squeeze the back of her neck.

Finally, Matt waves the server over and asks for the check. While we wait, Bryce says, "I want to thank you both for bringing me on board. I can't wait to get started and really show you what I bring to the table."

I shake my head and say, "No, Bryce, I should thank you. It's an honor to have someone of your talent as the first designer on my team. I know we'll do great things together. You're a major part of why this is getting to happen for me, and I'm thankful for it."

It's true. I may have dived into work as a way to drown painful memories, but I do love it. Art makes me happy in a way little else does. That is, until a few months ago when I met someone who calmed my nerves and cared about me even when I was acting my worst. That new source of happiness is something I can't wait to drown in tonight.

Matt's driver drops us off at the hotel, and I hold tight to Desi's hand all the way through the revolving door and into the lobby, but as soon as we're out of Matt's sight, we both pull away as though our skin is burning.

It might actually be.

I try to clear my mind and will my heart to slow as we ride the elevator to our floor. I might as well be asking to fly on a spaceship and for Yoda to be real. I slide the key card into the lock and as soon as we walk over the threshold, we both start to speak.

"Jace, I—"

"Desi—"

A nervous laugh escapes her. "You go first."

"No, please," I insist, taking my suit coat off and tossing it on the couch.

She takes a deep breath and drops her purse onto the bedside table. "I'm sorry if I initiated something at dinner that I shouldn't have. I got a little out of control and that was probably really uncomfortable for you."

I freeze while loosening my tie and say in a low voice, "You've got to be kidding me right now."

"What do you mean?"

"You *barely* spread your legs to give me a little more room. I slid my hand all the way up to your panties and slipped my finger inside *and* licked said finger *all* at the dinner table. Now ask yourself again who was out of control," I say, taking one step toward her. "I *wanted* to touch you, Desideria."

Her chest is rising and falling with her rapid breaths, and all I want is to take her in my arms and kiss her until neither of us can breathe. "So much that you couldn't stop yourself, even in public? Even in front of your new co-workers?" she asks, stepping toward me and taking her hair out of the bun she'd pulled it into, letting it fall over her shoulders.

"I've never claimed that I can resist you, Desi. I just agreed to respect your wishes while you did what you needed to do." I slide my tie from around my neck and release the top two buttons of my shirt.

"Well, I'm done concentrating on that now. I've made my choices."

I pause, my fingers going still at the buttons on my wrist. My heart flutters in my chest. I'm not dense. I was adding up all the flirtations happening between us today. What they equaled was clear. Slowly lifting my gaze, I whisper, "What are you saying, Desideria?"

"I'm saying fuck resisting it, Jace. I'm tired of fighting what I want. And I want you. All I want is you."

I wait for her to take it back. For the moment when she says *Wait, no, hold on, maybe we shouldn't. Maybe it will hurt too much. I'm sorry. I'm so sorry, Jace. There's no possible way this can work out the way we want, so why are we going to hurt ourselves? It's for the best.*

But it doesn't come. She's walking toward me, her gaze never leaving mine. I meet her in the middle of the room, finish removing my shirt, and let it drop to the floor. I grip the back of her neck and she cups my cheeks.

Without another moment's breath, she rises to her tiptoes and pulls my face down to hers as she repeats my words from the first time I ever kissed her.

"Fuck it."

TWENTY-EIGHT
DESI

My entire being sparks to life as our mouths press together in a hungry kiss. It's been too long, and I'm starved for the taste of Jace. I've chased this feeling for weeks, wanting to feel the undying ache for more, the thought of attempting to lose myself to someone else. I knew it would be useless because no one can compare to him.

His hands drop to the zipper on my dress and he slides it down with ease, as if it wasn't difficult to get up *before* I ate my weight in gourmet food. He slips the straps off my shoulders, and it falls to the floor. His stormy gaze takes in the black push-up bra and thong, still soaked from our escapade at dinner, and my black stilettos before he hisses with an appreciative tone that sends my heart into overdrive.

He lays me back on the bed, his mouth colliding with mine before kissing down my neck and across my collarbone. I run my hands over his cheeks and into his hair, lifting his face into my view. "Jace, I—I don't want you to stop this time. *Please.*"

"You're the only force that can stop me, Desideria. All you have to do is say the word. No questions asked."

"I won't."

"Then I won't stop until I have you screaming my name."

The determination flashing in Jace's eyes is a complete turn-on. I know his fingers and mouth are magical, but I'm eager to discover what the rest of him can do. I don't doubt he'll make good on his promise more than once. Jace Wilder only does things to perfection.

He fishes his wallet out of his pocket and removes a golden packet.

I place my hand over his. "You don't have to if you don't want to. We aren't compatible in *that* way, and I can't contract any kind of human diseases, remember? Besides, I've only ever been with you, so . . ."

One side of Jace's mouth quirks and he tosses the condom over his shoulder. Pressing his lips to my neck, he says, "Now that I know I'll get to feel you around me with no barriers, it's going to be hard to hold back."

I thread my fingers into his hair and tug until he lifts his eyes to mine. "Who said anything about holding back? I meant what I said—I want you to give me *everything*, Jace. We've waited long enough for this." I lift my hips and press the damp center of my panties against the bulge in his slacks as I reach down and undo the button so fast I rip it from the material. "I can take every inch of you."

"Spoken like a true queen." He lowers the lace cupping my breast and drags his lips over the hard peak. "I suggest you not get ahead of yourself. You just might bite off more than this beautiful body can handle."

I arch my neck back and murmur, "Remember: I'm immortal. Nothing you do is going to break me." I bring my gaze back to his. "I want you to think about every time you wanted to be inside me and forced yourself to resist. Make up for all those times right now."

"I have a better idea." He bites my nipple. "Quit rushing this and let me savor you. I want to make this last."

I settle back into the pillow, raising my arms and crossing them behind my head. "Well, when you put it that way, why would I do anything else?" I eye his pants. "But can you at least take those off? I already ripped the button, so it should be easy."

He chuckles and tugs them down. "I'm second-guessing my plan. Maybe I should sit back and let *you* worship *me*. I have a feeling I would end up thoroughly ravaged."

I grin and bring one hand down to his cheek as if to tenderly stroke it, but instead I slide it to the back of his neck and pull him so our faces are inches apart. "It would be my distinct pleasure to thoroughly ravage you, and I think I could come just from getting you off," I say, my lips barely brushing against his.

"A theory I'd like to put to the test, but not right now."

Jace makes his way down my body, pulling the straps of my bra down my arms and lowering it to free my breasts. He pauses a moment to lavish each nipple with wet strokes of his tongue before kissing the moon on my sternum. When he reaches my soft stomach, his thumbs continue to the sides of my panties. They hook beneath the lace and drag it down my legs. Jace showers open-mouth kisses over each new patch of skin he reveals.

I shift underneath him, my body aflame with the insatiable need to touch him. Now that I'm here, underneath him, it's taking every ounce of my rapidly deteriorating self-control to let him continue his slow descent to my throbbing center.

When he finally slides my panties all the way off my feet and drops them to the floor, he leans back on his heels and admires me. Every inch of my skin tightens under his scrutiny. I let my own gaze roam over him—his smooth, tanned skin, hard abs, the strong biceps that I want wrapped around me, his chestnut hair mussed, and his gray eyes lit by lust, excitement, and something else I can't quite define.

My eyes drift to the scar on his chest. The reminder that Jace was once in mortal danger. To think that I might have never had the chance to know this beautiful, intelligent, witty creature . . . I'm absolutely smitten with him, every part, inside and out.

Jace lowers the band of his black boxer briefs. It follows the V at his hips and reveals the dark thatch of hair before the hard length of him is free. The last of his clothes end up on the floor and nothing remains between us as he covers my body with his.

He brushes the curls away from my face and says, "Are you sure this is what you want?"

One last attempt at giving me an out. His concern is totally unnecessary. My mind is made up, and I know what I want to happen from here.

"Yes, Jace. I'm surer of this than I have been of anything else in my entire existence. I need to be with you as much as I need my next breath. Don't make me wait any longer," I murmur, my heart racing against my rib cage.

I know what I'm getting with Jace. The passion we share, every kiss and touch are exactly what my body craves. I've spent too many decades chasing this feeling to fall short. It doesn't matter that we aren't forever or that he might not feel as intensely about me as I feel about him. I have the chance, even if it's only for one night, to give myself to someone who can satisfy me the way no one else can.

Jace places my hand around the back of his neck and curls my fingers in his hair. "You're in charge, little hurricane."

Little hurricane. I worried I'd never hear it again, but just now, hearing it from his lips, it feels like he never stopped saying it.

I tremble as he lifts my leg over his hip and aligns his body with mine. He runs his knuckles from my temple to my jaw and holds my gaze. My breath hitches as he rocks forward, and his fingertips dig into my outer thigh.

"Relax and stay right here with me. I promise I'm about to ruin every toy in the drawer next to your bed for the rest of your life."

I nod, and again he rolls his hips and his length glides through the seam of me. The tip of him touches my clit, rubbing against it in a way that makes my back arch. He plays with me until the need between my legs is a throbbing void desperate to be filled.

I grip his hair and brush my lips against his. "Please, Jace."

"Fuck, that's a pretty sound."

"What? Me begging for you? You like to hear that? My tongue dripping with those words, the pleas for your body to give me what I've wanted from you for months?" I tug at his hair and press my hips against his, a moan escaping my throat when I feel how hard he is against me. "You do realize how long I've wanted you, don't you?"

"I know, and I'm going to make the wait worth it."

Jace presses forward, stretching me open. He takes his time pulling away and dipping inside me again and again. Each movement pushes him deeper until every long, hard inch of him fills me.

He holds still and presses a kiss to my forehead. "Are you good?"

His lips brand my skin, and I know that even long after the sensation of his touch is gone, I'll feel their absence.

I meet his eyes and nod. "I'm more than good. I'm perfect."

He kisses my temple and down my jawline. "Yes. You are."

I stretch my neck back, and with each little open-mouthed kiss, he makes a contented sound in the back of his throat that makes me feel like maybe, just maybe, he *is* as smitten with me as I am with him.

He rolls his hips and the way he fills me up takes my breath. How goddamn *perfect*. "Jace," I gasp. "Tell me you feel that."

He laces his fingers with mine, pinning my hand above my head. "All I feel is you. Every curve." He pulls out and sinks back in. "Every inch of soft skin." Another thrust. "The tight, warm depths of you." This time he hits deeper. "I feel it all, and I want more." He lifts my leg higher, wrapping it around his waist. "Tell me I can take more, Desideria."

I meet his every move, clenching my walls around him, loving the groans he's breathing in my ear. "Jace, take it all. I'd let you have everything, forever, and you know it," I say without thinking, and I inhale sharply, hoping my words don't scare him away or cause him to back off. Not now. Not when I need him so close.

He takes my hand from his neck and pins it next to the other. Raw need burns in his eyes and the muscle in his jaw flexes. I hold my breath, waiting for this to all come to an end. Jace glides his tongue up the side of my neck and whispers against my ear, "Just give me now."

My reply leaves my lips as a moan as his body drives into mine over and over again. All tenderness evaporates into primal need. Jace takes me hard, fast, like he's just as starved for me as I am for him. I accept every gloriously rough stroke, letting them draw me closer to the edge. This is what I need, the hard push that sends me flying into euphoria.

"What are you doing to me, Jace?" I cry, struggling against his hold on me, not because I don't like it, but because I want him to scold me. I want him to dominate me. "I never thought it could feel like this."

"Only with me. It can only feel like this with me."

The truth of his words is harsh, but I don't fight it. I have no doubt he's right. This is us, and no one else will ever compare. His body was made to be buried deep in mine, his words are for my ears only, and the desire he feels belongs to me. I drink it up like fresh rain after a lifetime of blistering heat.

"Yes," I cry, tears slipping from the corners of my eyes as he lifts me off the bed, wrapping both of my legs around his waist so our bodies are flush together.

I squeeze until there's not even an inch of space between us. "Jace," I whisper, my lips brushing his. "I love what you're doing to me. It's everything I've fantasized about, but I want you to be rough with me."

His breath catches and he studies me before asking, "Are you sure, little hurricane?"

"Yes, I want you to be rougher with me than you've ever been before."

He groans. One hand grips my hip and the other slides up my spine and into my hair. He takes my curls into his fist and tugs. My head tilts back and he looks down at me with metallic eyes.

I hiss in response to the sting and my sex squeezes him. "Fuck, yes."

"No." My heart falters for a second, sinking like a stone to the pit of my stomach. His palm slides around my neck until he is gripping it from the front. "I think *this* is what you're aching for."

His hold is firm, constricting, but not enough to scare me. He lifts my face and hovers his lips over mine. Every inch of me threatens to melt under his dominant stare. Instead, I lock my eyes on his and move my hips.

I lean my head forward as far as I can, just enough to nip at his bottom lip with my teeth. I know I've bitten too hard when the coppery taste of blood hits my tongue, but instead of disgusting me, I am even more turned on. Especially by the thought that it might spur him on to rougher treatment.

Without missing a beat, he pushes me into the mattress and tightens his hold on my neck. The pressure at my windpipe does something to me. My body grips him tighter, and the light-headed feeling makes me feel like I'm floating.

His voice is husky as he demands, "Put your legs back the way they were."

With some effort I lift my legs around his waist and hook my ankles together, pulling him hard against me. I slide my hand down his chest, my fingertips trailing over every ripple and ridge of his abdomen before resting my palm at his waist, gripping his hip.

"Jace. Don't hold back," I manage.

"No chance."

And with that, he loses control. But this is more than sex, more than fucking. Yes, it's hard, fast, and rough. It is the intense joining of two bodies seeking the most basic kind of pleasure. But it's so much more. It's heightened emotions—a need to convey everything words cannot. It feels good—damn, does it feel good—but this moment is more than physical. This is a sacrament . . . it's spiritual.

Jace glides his hand between us and presses his thumb to my clit. "Come on, little hurricane. I want you to unleash that chaos inside you and rip me apart."

Jace Wilder means to make good on his promise to make me scream because when he pushes deeper inside me and pinches my clit, his name flows from my lips in an animalistic cry. The orgasm that rips through me is sudden, hard, and almost painfully intense. Wave after wave racks my body, my muscles tensing, legs shaking, stars flashing in front of my eyes.

And he doesn't ease up. He tightens his hold around my neck and leans over, closing his lips over mine in a kiss that takes every bit of breath that I have left.

"Fuck," he grunts through gritted teeth.

Jace shudders above me while he pulsates and fills me in a way I never knew was possible. It isn't just his release pouring into my body, but an overwhelming joy that runs soul deep. And as he thrusts into me for the final time, I know this moment will leave the most beautiful scar on my heart. I'll never forget when he was fully mine, and I gave myself completely to him.

With his mouth pressed to mine, he loosens his grip on my neck and rolls over, taking me with him, tucking me into his side. All the raw need is sedated for now, and he showers me with sweet, tentative kisses.

"Are you all right? I wasn't too rough, was I?"

I snuggle against him and shake my head. "I'm perfect. *You* were perfect." Running my fingertips down the center of his chest, I let them drift over his pecs and trace the scar from the wound that nearly claimed his life.

"Jace?"

"Hmm?" His lips are against my temple, and I'm so distracted by the way they feel on my skin that I nearly lose my train of thought.

"Are you going to miss me when I'm gone? *All* of me? Like, even my laundry when I leave it in the dryer too long and it's all wrinkly. Or when I forget and leave my blanket unfolded on the couch. Or when you're watching *Star Wars* and I'm not there to do my amazing R2-D2 impression."

"Yes, Desideria. I'll miss you. And all your little chaotic additions to my house," he teases. "It's been a long time since I've let myself get this close to someone, and it'll be hard to say goodbye."

I swallow over the lump in my throat and force the tears back. "Me too. I've never trusted someone like I trust you." I slide my hand up into his hair and rub my thumb along his jaw. "I want to spend every second I can with you before I go. Is that—" My voice cracks. "Is that okay?"

His gray eyes search mine and so quietly I almost don't hear it he says, "Yes. That's what I want too."

I'm torn in two by his confession. The upcoming weeks will give me more time to have moments like this with him. I'll get to curl up in his arms and tell him everything I want him to hear. I won't waste a minute. And when the time comes for me to leave, a gaping hole will run through my heart. I'll understand what it is to lose someone I love.

TWENTY-NINE
DESI

"I told you it was going to be cold by the bay," Jace says as he turns to me and slides the ticket for the ferry into the front pocket of my jeans. I can't take it because my hands are currently shoved into the sleeves of my jacket.

"I know, but the wind is *frigid*!" I say through chattering teeth as he wraps his arm around me and leads me into the throng of tourists boarding the boat that will take us to the Statue of Liberty. It's the first stop on our tour of slightly clichéd but necessary attractions in New York City. Of all the things on the list, this is the one I'm the most excited to see.

We step onto the ferry and instead of heading to one of the benches under the protective awning, Jace and I keep walking until we reach the far end of the boat. I place my hands on the railing, and he cages me in with his arms on either side of me. I savor the warmth radiating from his body, letting every muscled inch of him chase away the chill.

It's sunny today, and the rays reflecting off the water of New York Bay create a sparkling effect, making it look much warmer than it is. But the statue sitting in the distance is worth the cold air, and so is the man behind me.

"This is beautiful," I murmur, my eyes scanning the horizon, the midmorning wind whipping my hair across my face.

Jace doesn't answer right away, and I glance up to find him studying my face. "What? Why are you looking at me like that?" I ask.

"I've seen the statue before, but I've never seen you so captivated with something. You're breathtaking."

I turn all the way around to face him and brush my windblown hair from my eyes, but it's stubborn and keeps flying back across my face. "You say the nicest things to me, you know that?" I giggle, and when he cocks his head to the side, I say, "I was just thinking about how we used to be such assholes to each other all the time."

His arms slip around my waist, pulling me close. "I think you kind of like my asshole side. It can always make an appearance again if you want."

I raise my brows and press myself flush against him. "Actually, I think it's sexy when you're all dominant and tough. What about you? Did you like my bitchy side, Wilder?"

"Yes, but I enjoy all of your sides." He tucks a strand of hair behind my ear. "Particularly your sweet and sexually needy ones."

From across the bay, the Statue of Liberty looks so small, but standing at its base with my head craned back, I realize how very wrong I was. Even the sculptures of Lucifer and Lilith in Infernis aren't as impressive.

"Wow," I breathe, as we walk toward the pedestal where groups of people are taking photos in front of the statue and pointing and talking in countless different languages. "It's so much bigger than I thought it was going to be!" I look up at Jace only to see him staring down at me again. "What?"

"You levitate things and are going to rule your own Circle, and this is what impresses you?"

I shrug and look back up at the statue. "I've been levitating things since I was old enough to walk, and ruling my own Circle has been expected of me since I was born. This is just cool," I say, bumping his hip with mine. I open my mouth to say something else when my gaze falls on a familiar figure leaning against the flagpole. "Oh no." My voice is little more than a rasp above the wind.

"What? What is it?"

"There's my freaking brother," I say, my heart sinking.

"What?" Jace says again, louder and sharper this time. "Where?"

"Right there," I mutter, guiding us toward him.

"What is he doing here?"

"I have no idea." Avaros meets us in the middle of the walkway as tourists stroll past us. My brother is, as always, dressed to the nines in a blue pinstriped suit and wing-tipped shoes, his red hair somehow managing to stay in place whereas mine is *still* whipping around my head like a kite. "Avaros. What are you doing here? Is everything okay? Mom and Dad?"

He ignores me and holds out a hand to Jace. "How's it going, man? It's good to see my sister hasn't scared you off yet."

"Far from it," Jace replies as they shake.

I cross my arms. "Hello, Avaros! Over here. I asked you a question."

He gives me a pointed look, like I'm the one being rude when he was the one who ignored me. Brushing a speck of lint from his sleeve, he says, "I need you both to come with me. Father needs to speak with you."

My heart speeds up, and despite the cold, beads of sweat form along my brow. This is disastrous. Jace can't go back with us to Infernis. Not unless . . .

"But Jace can't go!"

Avaros stares at me like I've grown a second head. "He can't go to a pub in Manhattan?"

"Oh. I—yeah, a pub. I thought you meant—never mind, it doesn't matter. Yeah, right now?"

"Yeah, let's head over there. He's probably waiting for us by now."

In the dimly lit pub on Ninth Avenue, a few people in business suits sit around the dark wood bar, sipping their drink of choice. The music is lively but not overbearing and the red-bearded barkeep could be the eighth child in our family. We zigzag through the round tables to a large booth in the back corner. I trip over my own feet when my dad scoots out of the vinyl seat.

No leather. No boots. No ax hanging at his side. My father is dressed in a black tailored suit with a tie.

"Dad," I say as he pulls me into his arms for a hug. "Is everything okay? Avaros was short on details." I shoot my brother a glare as he sits in the spot next to the one my dad vacated.

Dad smiles and puts his palms on my cheeks. "Don't worry, Desideria. Everything will be fine. Just sit so we can talk."

My stomach sinks when I notice that he doesn't say that everything *is* fine, but Jace doesn't falter as he shakes my father's hand.

"Jace!" Dad exclaims. "Good to see you're still hanging in there with our girl."

"I don't think hanging in there is the right term. It makes it sound like being around Desi is difficult, and that's the last thing being with her is, sir."

Despite the stress of my father calling us to an urgent meeting, I want to melt out of my chair into a sticky puddle on the ground. Even if I spent forever in this realm, I'd never get used to hearing Jace say sweet things.

Instead of melting, I settle for intertwining our fingers under the table and squeezing. "Thank you, Jace," I say before giving my father a pointed look. "See? Not everyone thinks I'm difficult."

"That makes one being in the entire universe," Avaros mumbles.

"I personally enjoy a challenge," Jace says.

Something in my dad's green gaze softens. I've never seen him look at another being like that before. Apparently, Jace is the unknowing thief of many hearts.

"That's good to hear. I have a difficult challenge for the both of you. But I believe you'll be up to the task. I need Desideria to return home sooner than I was planning, which means, if you've chosen to be her eternal partner, you'll need to leave this realm too."

Jace's grip on my hand is like a vice cutting off all circulation. He's got to be lost for words.

But I have words—a lot of them. "What? Dad, what are you talking about? How soon? I'm supposed to have, like, a month left."

My father swallows, and I notice for the first time how pale he is. "I need you to come as soon as possible. Within the next three days."

Jace and I exchange horrified glances. "Three days? Wh—why? What for? I can't leave in three days. I'm supposed to have more time." Panic seizes me and I begin to tremble all over. I was supposed to have another month to spend with Jace. Not three days.

Dad leans over the table and folds his hands on top. His face is gaunt, and his shoulders don't appear as broad as they were before I left Infernis with Jace. Or maybe they were, but I was so caught up in the man beside me that I didn't notice.

Dad clears his throat and says, "Despite popular belief, it wasn't just your mother's and my robust sex life that led us to have seven children. We made a conscious decision to break the tradition of having only one. We never wanted to put the burden of ruling on just one child. There is power in numbers, and that is why the responsibility of Infernis is divided between you and your brothers."

"I know all that, Dad. That still doesn't explain why I need to come home early."

"I thought I could keep fueling the chaos in our realm for a few more weeks. But I was wrong, Desideria. Our realm has grown so much over the past decades, and it's draining me." He lowers his chin and watches his fidgeting fingers. "If you don't come home soon and take your Circle, I'll use the last of my power and our realm will self-detonate, and the freedom of human energies to choose their final destination will end."

I brush a tear away with the back of my hand. "You're dying?"

"For lack of a better word, yes."

"No . . ." I murmur, and Jace slips his arm around my shoulder and tucks me into his side. I lay my head on his shoulder and close my eyes, letting what my father said sink in for a moment as tears slide down my cheeks.

"I'm sorry to have to tell you like this, in a public place, but it was the only way."

I lift my head from Jace's shoulder and say, "Don't apologize, Dad. You have nothing to apologize for. I'm sorry I was a brat." I spring up from my seat, and Avaros, seeing what I intend to do, hops out of the booth and motions for Jace to scoot over. My dad moves down so I can sit next to him, and he wraps me in his arms, pressing a kiss to my forehead.

"Shhh, Desideria. It's okay."

"No, it's not okay. Is this my fault?" I ask in a small voice, sitting up and looking at him with wide eyes, the horrifying idea dawning on me. "If I had chosen an eternal partner before now, and the seven of us could have taken our places, would it have saved you?"

My dad starts to say something but to my surprise, it's Avaros who speaks up. "Sister, no. It's not your fault. And you know I'd tell you if it was. A hundred years ago, even fifty years ago, most people were choosing Pax as the final resting place for their energy. You know that. There weren't as many energies in Infernis for Dad to manage. No one could have predicted that this would become a lethal problem. Not to mention, Fier and Lux chose their eternal partners not so long ago. It's not like we've all been sitting here waiting for you for millennia. *Plus*, Mom and Dad had seven kids to make their lives *easier* one day, not to *save Dad's life*. They didn't know that would be necessary. Stop blaming yourself."

"See, my darling? You know your brother is a douche bag. If it were your fault, he would've taken the chance to berate you already. Even Jace knows that, and he's only met him once before," Dad says, planting a kiss on my forehead.

I can't help but laugh and look at Jace, who glances at Avaros and nods with a shrug. "Sorry, bro. It's true."

Avaros pinches the bridge of his nose. "You people act like I don't know I'm a dickhead."

We all chuckle and in the silence that follows, my dad adds, "And besides, if you had found a demon before you took a chance and came to the human realm, you never would have found Jace. And that, I think, would have been a far greater tragedy than an old geezer like me choosing to go to the In-Between a little earlier than expected."

My heart squeezes in my chest as I meet Jace's gaze across the table. That notion both crushes me and gives me an immense amount of joy. I should be bringing Jace back with me. Because after this weekend, I know how I feel about him. And it's not just lust. He's not just my best friend. Leaving him here is going to gut me. Losing my father is going to destroy what's left of me.

I should come clean and tell them that what they think Jace feels for me isn't as serious as they believe. That it's not strong enough for him to give up the life he's built in this realm. But I can't now, not when Dad is sick. I'm better off showing up without Jace and telling my family that I had a backup plan. The least I can do is spare them some worry.

I wish it didn't have to be this way, that Jace chose me, but I don't blame him for not doing it. I don't know that I could give up Infernis for just anyone, but I could for him. Or at least I could if my father's life didn't depend on me returning. I suppose I've found my limit as well.

"All right. I'll be home in three days," I say, sliding out of the booth.

My father pulls me into a hug and says, "I'm sorry I couldn't give you the time I promised. Thank you for understanding, Desideria."

After Avaros and my dad retreat to the back of the restaurant where I'm sure there is a portal, Jace and I step out onto the sidewalk, and I turn to him, my eyes filled with tears. "This fucking sucks," I blurt, an unexpected sob rattling my body.

He pulls me into his arms and smooths my hair. "I know. I'm sorry your dad is sick. I know how hard it is to learn that the man you thought was the strongest person in the universe has found his kryptonite."

"Yeah, for sure." A moment of silence goes by.

"You have no idea what kryptonite is, do you?"

"Not a clue."

He chuckles and tightens his arms around me. "That's okay, Desideria." He squeezes me one more time and we pull back just far enough so we can see each other's faces. "What are you thinking?"

"That all I want to do for the next three days is to be in your arms. That's it. Can we do that?"

"I'm all yours. Whatever you need, I'll take care of it. I just want us to make the most of the time we have left together."

I want that too. Even though I know it won't be enough, and it will rip my heart in two when I have to say goodbye. I want to spend the next three days lost in Jace Wilder, willingly handing him my breaking heart one tiny piece at a time.

THIRTY
DESI

The ride from the airport to the house is silent. Neither Jace nor I slept much last night. He held me as I sobbed and worried about my father's health and urged me to share some of my favorite memories of growing up in Infernis. I finally fell asleep for a couple of hours, and when I woke up his arms were still around me. Jace hasn't let go of my hand since we stepped out of the hotel room. He's been attentive, kind, showering me with hugs and kisses, doing his best to soften the blow of my father's news.

I know that it's only going to make what happens in three days even harder.

When the Uber pulls up in front of the house, Jace jumps out and runs around to open the door for me, extending his hand to help me out of the SUV. I take it and we each roll a suitcase inside. He stops me before I open the front door.

"Wait. What are you going to tell Cannon?"

My eyes snap to his. "What do you mean?"

"Are you going to—I mean—"

"Am I going to tell him that I definitely need him to come back with me in three days?" I ask, my heart sinking a little lower in my chest.

His nod is almost imperceptible, and he can't meet my eyes. I wish I fully understood. If he cares this much, if the idea of me leaving is so hard for him to imagine, why can't he just take the risk and go with me?

But I think I know the answer to that question. As much as I hate to admit it, maybe Jace *really* isn't capable of love at this point in his life. And if he doesn't love me—isn't *in love* with me—he could never take such a giant step. And to be honest, I know that it doesn't matter if I get it or not.

Jace is doing the best he can. That much I know is true.

"I think so," I say in a small voice. It isn't really what I want, but it's the next best thing. "And I think it's a conversation I need to have alone with him. Just in case it gets uncomfortable. Is that okay?"

He squeezes my hand. "Of course. I'll just take our bags upstairs. Come to my room when you're done?"

Leaning into him, I kiss the scruff on his jaw. "You couldn't pay me to be anywhere else," I say, opening the door. I take off my boots, pushing them under the bench in the foyer. My eyes linger on all my shoes lined up next to Jace's; it's such a silly thing, but I'll miss that sight when I go home.

"Cannon, are you here?" Jace calls, walking into the living room.

The man in question turns and smiles at us from his place on the couch. A bag of chips and two soda cans litter the coffee table. I don't miss the tick in Jace's jaw when he eyes what he considers a mess, but he doesn't say a word. I can see he doesn't have the energy.

Pausing the game on the flatscreen, Cannon stands and gathers his trash. "Sorry, man. I thought you two were coming back tomorrow."

"Change of plans," Jace grumbles, opening the cupboard housing the trash can.

I cross the room to our well-meaning roommate, the one whose world is about to be turned upside down by me and my chaotic mess of a life. "I got it," I say, giving Cannon a quick hug before taking the trash from his hands. "How are you?"

He smiles and thanks me before taking a seat at the island. "Fine, just holding down the fort. How was your trip?"

I force a smile and say, "New York City is magnificent. I got to see the Statue of Liberty, and Jace got Edmonds signed. It was a success."

"I'm glad you had a good time. Why did you come home early? You needed more than one day to see everything."

I open my mouth to tell Cannon everything from the beginning, but a gigantic lump rises in my throat, thwarting my ability to speak. I close my eyes and grip the edge of the counter, leaning forward and staring at the pristine tile floor.

Jace is right behind me in an instant. I didn't even realize he hadn't gone upstairs yet. He slides one arm around my waist and places the other around me, palm on the counter, caging me in. "Are you all right, princess?"

I take a deep breath, my eyes squeezed shut, and turn my head toward where his chin is resting on my shoulder. "No, but yes."

He nods his understanding and kisses my temple before running his fingers through my hair. "Do you need me to stay? I can help you through this if you need me to."

I shake my head once. "No. I can do it. I'll come up when I'm done, okay?"

"Okay." As Jace passes by Cannon, he squeezes his shoulder once. "Take her over to the couch. She's going to need your support through this."

Cannon's brows dip even lower as he immediately jumps to his feet and rounds the island to me. "Desi, come sit."

With one more grateful look at Jace, I hook my arm into Cannon's and move to sit with him on the couch. We remain in silence for a few seconds until he speaks.

"Desi, you're scaring me. Are you okay? What's going on? Why did you come home early? Why do you look like you're about to tell me the worst news on the face of the planet?"

Because I am. My father, the man who has loved me and taken care of me for over a century, is essentially burning out. And there isn't a thing I can do to stop it. Oh, and I have to leave behind the man I've fallen—grown very fond of.

I don't wait another second because my other best friend looks incredibly worried for me. I tell Cannon the whole story about my brother showing up on Liberty Island, meeting my father at the pub, and him dropping the news that I'd have to come home in three days instead of a month. But when I get to the part where I need to explain *why*, that lump returns to my throat, and I freeze.

He scoots closer to me on the couch and wraps his arm around my shoulders, and I lean into him, pulling my knees up and tucking them against my body. I'm basically a ball of quivering, fraying nerves, and Cannon just tugs me to his chest and holds me there. Quiet sobs escape from my throat, and he runs his hand over the back of my head, murmuring comforting words in my ear.

"Shh, Desi. You're safe. Whatever happened in New York, in this moment, you're okay." He rests his chin on top of my head and gently rocks me back and forth, letting me cry. I soak the front of his black T-shirt with my tears, but he doesn't even flinch.

Finally, I look up and wipe my face with the backs of my hands. "I've made a mess of you. I'm sorry."

He waves me off and reaches over to the end table, handing me a tissue. "Please. I don't care about that. I just want to make sure I'm here when my best friend needs me. Take your time. I'm ready when you are."

"Thank you. So the reason I had to come home early is that my dad is essentially . . . well, he's dying, Cannon."

His blue eyes widen, and I spend the next ten minutes answering questions about that and what it means for me and my realm. Cannon fidgets with one of the mini twists on his head as he listens, and when I'm done explaining, he loudly exhales.

"I am so sorry, Desi. I can't even imagine what you must be feeling right now. Especially thinking you'd have him for literally centuries longer."

I nod, staring at the floor and fiddling with a loose thread on my blouse. "I know. I still can't believe it—I keep hoping it's some kind of nightmare I'll wake up from, but with every minute that passes, I know it's real."

Cannon clears his throat. "So, I . . . I have to ask. You and Jace . . . you seemed . . . *close* in the kitchen just now. What's going on there?" He raises his brows.

I elbow him in the ribs and try but fail to hide the blush that colors my cheeks. "We . . . we're something, but I don't know exactly what that *something* is. I know what it isn't, though."

"It's not an eternal partnership." The way he says it makes me suspect that he knows at least the basics about Hannah and Jace's mother.

"He's opened up to you? And told you about—"

"Not exactly. I just found it obvious that he has some sort of block against commitment. I never thought committing to someone for eternity, even a woman who is perfect for him, would be something he could handle." Cannon's eyes narrow and he inspects my face like he's reading the guidebook to my soul. I feel raw, wide open, like everything about me is just bare right there for him to see.

"Why are you looking at me like that?"

"You're upset by this. Deeply. It bothers you almost as much as what's happening to your father," Cannon says, his tone matter-of-fact, like he's reading ingredients off the back of a soup can.

No point in denying it; the man is hopefully going to be with me for the rest of eternity. "What are you, some kind of mind reader?"

He smiles and leans back into the couch cushions. "No, just good at reading people. It's part of my job."

"Well, you deserve a promotion because that was right on point. But we've just decided to take these last few days and spend them together. That's the best I can ask from him. But that brings us to the next thing I need to talk to you about."

"I think I know what that is."

"I won't hold you to it, Cannon. It may have seemed like something that would never happen. But now it has, and the time is sooner than you—"

"I'll do it, Desi."

"You will?"

"Yes. I told you I would, and I meant it. You're my best friend, and I see no reason why I shouldn't spend the rest of my life doing something as amazing as running an entire Circle of Infernis with you."

My heart swells and I throw my arms around his neck. "Thank you, Cannon. Thank you. You're saving my life—and my entire realm—here."

"I'm happy to do it. I'll be ready when you need me. I'll start tying up loose ends tomorrow morning."

"Can you give me a day before you come through the portal? My family is going to be really confused if I come home with someone besides Jace. I want to explain everything to them and prepare them to meet you."

He nods in that accepting, patient way that is so uniquely Cannon. "Of course. That will give me time to go home and say goodbye to my family. Then I'll come to you."

"Thank you. I know I've already told you, but I can't say it enough. Everything else sucks, but at least you're going to be next to me through it all," I whisper, and Cannon leans over to kiss my cheek.

"It's all going to work out fine. You'll see, Desi." He pauses. "Wait—what's a portal?"

I laugh despite everything falling apart around me. "I'll explain it all to you later."

The room falls silent as Cannon makes his way upstairs to begin preparing for his departure from this realm. I try to fill my lungs with a calming breath, but the air is too thick. Everything is closing in on me and I can't move quickly enough to get out of its way. I'm going to suffocate to death, and there's nothing I can do about it.

But I can deflect the pain, and my best distraction is waiting for me.

THIRTY-ONE
DESI

I trudge up the stairs and make my way to Jace's room. After two light taps of my knuckles, he answers the door. He's traded his traveling clothes for joggers and a T-shirt depicting the evolution of humans into robots. His hair stands on end like he's run his fingers through it a thousand times. I feel very overdressed.

"I'm going to change," I say, pivoting to head down the hall again.

He grabs my arm and guides me into his room. "That won't be necessary."

It doesn't escape me that Jace has already unpacked; not an item in his room is out of place. I also don't miss the flickering amber glow coming from his bathroom.

"You didn't get a chance to use that tub in the hotel. I thought I'd make it up to you," he says, leading me forward with his hand on my lower back.

The calming scent of lavender fills my lungs as we enter the bathroom. Candles are placed around the bathtub, which is billowing with bubbles. Towels are neatly folded on the ledge. Jace has transformed his bathroom into a romantic spa.

Turning to him, I place my hand on his cheek and run my palm over his scruff. "How are you so perfect?"

Jace shakes his head and presses a kiss to my forehead. "I'm not. But you—that's a different story. So that makes me want to treat you like the princess you are." He slips his hands under the hem of my blouse and pushes it over my bra. "Here, let's get you undressed so you can relax. Lift your arms for me."

Jace taking care of me like this is exactly what I need right now, so I do what he says. He takes my shirt off and drops it in the laundry basket, then slides his hands down the curve of my waist. "These next." Popping the button on my jeans, he slides the zipper down and slips them over my ass, running his palm across the bare skin that's barely covered by my cheeky green lace panties. "These are new," he comments as he helps me step out of my pants.

My skin heats and I push a loose curl out of my eyes. "I bought them because I knew you liked the color on me. It's the first time I've worn them."

He grins and reaches behind me to unfasten my bra, letting it fall to the floor without bothering to pick it up. Pressing his lips to the valley between my breasts, he kisses a path down the center of my stomach until he reaches the waistband of said panties. I shiver when he runs his fingertip along it. "I love them. I wonder if they're ruined yet," he whispers as he slips his fingers underneath to pull them off.

"Oh yeah, you can bet on it," I breathe, reaching out to hang on to the towel rack for support.

He glances at the lace after I step out of them, and I'm certain my body temperature rises at least a hundred degrees when he gives me a wicked grin and puts them in the pocket of his joggers. "I think I'll keep these." With a featherlight kiss under my belly button, he stands to his full height. "All right, let's get you settled."

He takes my hand and helps me into the tub as if he didn't just turn me on to high heat. But when I sink under the bubbles, I forget everything. "Damn, this feels fucking good," I say, opening my eyes and meeting his scorching gaze.

"That's what I wanted. For you to feel good." He leans down and kisses the corner of my mouth. I try to capture his lips for a deeper kiss but he pulls back. "This is you time. I'm going to go check on a couple of other things while you relax. I'll come back in a few. Okay?"

My chest deflates. I thought for sure he was going to join me. But just as quickly, I remember how grateful I am that he did all this. Just for me. "Okay, I'll be here," I say, splashing the bubbles at him playfully.

"You better be." With that, he disappears into his room, leaving me with my thoughts.

It's surreal to think that my time in this realm is already up. I never forgot that it was ticking down day by day, but another part of me felt like I had all the time in the world. The thought of leaving this house feels like a foreign concept. Or maybe it's knowing that I'm leaving Jace. I hate it. Deep in my gut it feels so wrong.

Every woman who has held an important role in Jace's life has walked away without a fight. They never showed him that he was worth more than enduring pain. They had limits to what they would do for him, but I don't.

I care about him. So much that I'll fight for him but let him go if that's what he wants. Either way, I want him to understand I'd do anything for him. If I knew it wouldn't cause harm in the end, I'd even consider not returning to Infernis for him.

I sink lower in the tub and close my eyes. I picture every heavy emotion that plagues me turning into iridescent bubbles. My father's health. My pending eternity with Cannon. My self-doubt about ruling a Circle. My fear of leaving Jace. Each problem floats away until they burst into nothingness.

The calm of a presence I've come to know as if it were my own washes over me, and I inch my eyes open. Jace sits on the side of the tub, his eyes locked on me, as his index finger slides along his bottom lip.

"Did I doze off?" I ask.

"You did. I'm glad my plan to get you to relax worked."

I lift my lips in a halfhearted smile. "You look like you could use a little relaxing yourself. You could always join me. There's plenty of room."

Jace chuckles as he stands and pulls his shirt over his head. "Can't refuse that offer."

He strips down, and I take the opportunity to memorize every cut of muscle and little imperfection. I want the image of Jace Wilder seared into my memory for the rest of my existence.

He motions for me to sit up and slides his body behind mine. I relax against his chest and pull his arms around my waist. My body surrounded by his could easily be my favorite place.

We sit in silence for a few minutes, and Jace adds more hot water to the tub while I sprinkle in another handful of lavender bath salts. When we sink back under the water, he runs his fingers across my stomach and I'm resting my hands on his legs. It's nice, just being in his presence, but I have too many things on my mind to keep them all bottled up. I'm about to break the silence when Jace speaks first.

"Desi, I want you to know something."

I sit up and turn to face him, pulling my legs in close to my body and scooting between his thighs so we're as close as possible. "What is it?"

He wraps his arms around me and rests his hands on my lower back, his thumb drawing circles on my skin under the water. "That this has never been about you and me."

I cock my head to the side. "What do you mean?"

"I mean, it—it's never been a matter of whether or not I *want* to go with you. Or if I think we're compatible. I *know* we are. That's why this *sucks* so goddamn much," he says, his voice suddenly hard, anger bursting out of him like he's been holding it in for weeks.

I scoot in closer, wrapping my legs around him, placing my palms on his cheeks. I'm scared to say what I want to say, scared he'll direct that anger at me, and I don't want that, least of all in our last days together. But I need to say it. "But it doesn't *have* to be like this, Jace. I would *never* hurt you. Not in all of eternity, not for all the riches and wonders my realm has to offer."

"I wish it could be me. I wish I could look past my issues and the soul-splitting pain I felt putting my trust in someone else. What you're offering is forever, and I don't get how that's possible. Hearts change, unconditional love bends until it has conditions, sacrifices are easy to make until they demand everything. Forever always comes to an end." He slides the back of his fingers over the side of my face. "Not only do I wish it could be me, but I wish I had a heart like yours."

The heart he just spoke about is cracking, and I know I should stop before I break it right in half, but I can't. I can't let it go. "Jace, you *do*. You do have a heart like mine. I've seen it. What happened to you doesn't have to define who you are now. You've trusted me with your darkest secrets these past weeks. Why can't you trust me enough to let me make you happy?" Tears fill my eyes but I blink them away, refusing to break down. I need to be strong for him.

"This isn't about happiness! It's about the hard times. The moment everything doesn't go to plan. It's about love not being enough to keep a wife by her dying husband's hospital bed. It's about a mother bailing on her seventeen-year-old son and letting him figure out how to care for his dad. It's about learning your fiancé may never walk again, never make it to the altar, and running away. It's about love not being enough to sustain a person through the hardest times."

Jace drops his arms to his sides, gasping for breath. His eyes brim with tears and all the determination to fight has drained from him. His soul is naked before me, exposing every deep cut and scar. I've never seen him so vulnerable before.

He cradles my face in his palms and gives me the most painful glimpse of his truth as he says, "I *don't* have a heart like yours, Desideria. You give yours without a second thought. I'm holding on to the scraps of mine with clenched fists. Don't get me wrong. You're sliding those broken pieces out through my fingers, stealing them one by one, but I'm not giving them freely. I'm terrified to hand you even one piece. You'll be the woman who has the power to obliterate what's left of me. I'm begging you to keep what you've already stolen and leave me with what little I have left. Please."

The tears welling in his eyes break me. I know now that there is nothing I can say to change his mind. Nothing I can say to make him see that forever with me could be the happiest he's ever been. I may be immortal, I may have the power to levitate televisions across the room, but I don't have the power to heal the wounds that the most important women in his life inflicted before I came into it.

I lean forward and rest my head against his chest, listening to his rapid heartbeat. "I'm sorry, Jace. I'm so sorry. I wish I could make it better."

"You do," he says, wrapping me in his arms and kissing the top of my head. "I don't want to think about past hurts and the future. I just want to get lost in you while you're still here. Let me take your mind off everything but me."

I swallow and sit up to meet his gaze. "I don't want to think about any of that either. All I want is to be with you." I run a finger down the center of his chest. "I want . . . I want to put my mouth on you."

He slides a soapy hand over my breast and lightly pinches my nipple. His lips glide up my neck, and his breath is warm against my ear as he says, "And where exactly do you want to put your mouth? Say it, little hurricane."

I lean back so I can see his face and look him in the eye before saying, "I want to suck your cock." Moving back toward him, I brush my mouth against his, nip his bottom lip, and murmur, "And I want to do it now." He twitches underneath me, and I grin against his mouth.

"On your knees, princess," he commands, moving up the back of the tub until he is sitting on the edge. He grips his hard length and I watch in awe as his hand slides up and down. He is irresistible like this.

"Come put your mouth on me," he says, his words gravelly with desire.

Shifting to my knees, I slip between his legs, putting my hands on his thighs to hold myself up. "Damn, I know how big you are after the other night, but . . . I don't know if I can take all of you."

He smirks, grabbing a handful of my wet curls and tugging firmly. "I believe in you, little hurricane."

The slightly cocky tone of voice he uses with me in this moment is so hot, I have to take a second to inhale a breath of fresh air or I might hyperventilate. "Well, then I better show up for you, huh?" I say, and without warning, I lower my head and close my mouth over him, taking over half his length into my mouth in one go.

Sliding my lips back up, I swirl my tongue over the head and lick the bead of pre-cum that's already leaking out of the tip. "Fuck," I moan around his cock. "You taste so good."

He brushes his thumb near my mouth and thrusts his hips, pushing himself a little deeper. "That's it. Take me deep. Your mouth looks so pretty on me, making me feel so good."

His praise moves me forward and I take him deeper, inch by inch until he hits the back of my throat. I gag a little, and it isn't just to make him feel good, but because I can't help it. Dragging my fingernails up and down his thighs, I dig into his skin and glide my lips up his length before repeating the action and taking him all the way down my throat again.

Watching Jace find pleasure has become one of my favorite

things, but being completely in control of that pleasure, it's a power unlike anything I've ever known. I'm the reason he licks his lips as he watches himself disappear into my mouth. His blissful hums and surprised hisses are mine. He is at my mercy, and it's a total turn-on.

Jace takes my hand from his thigh and wraps my fingers around him, just below my mouth. He shows me how to pump him with a twist over his slick shaft as I continue to take him as deep as I can.

"Good girl. Keep going just like that, princess."

His words send a fresh wave of longing through me, and I'm wet all over again in a way that has nothing to do with the bath we've all but abandoned. I hum around him, a contented noise in the back of my throat that earns me a deep groan. When I do it again, he arches his back, pushing himself just a little too far down my throat. I gag again, but this time I recover by tugging up from the base of his shaft toward where my tongue now laps at the proof of his desire at the tip.

He grips the hair at the back of my head and thrusts his hips once . . . twice. "I'm going to come," he says through gritted teeth. He's holding back, warning me of what's about to happen. I appreciate him giving me that choice, but he didn't have to. The moment I put my mouth on him I knew I wanted it all.

I lock eyes with Jace and bat my lashes, wordlessly telling him to let go. His hold on my hair grows tighter, and his entire body tenses.

"Fuck, Desideria," he says, as his release washes over my tongue.

I don't let up, taking it all until his body goes limp. He sinks into the tub and pulls me into his arms. Holding my head to his shoulder, he kisses my forehead and says, "Thank you."

I angle my head back so I can see his face. "You don't have to thank me for that. Giving you pleasure feels just as good for me as it does for you. I love watching you fall apart like that. Especially knowing that I'm the cause," I say, running my fingertip down the center of his chest.

"Good to know, but a performance that good deserves a reward. Is there anything I can do for you?"

My stomach growls in response and my cheeks heat at the sound of it. "Feed me."

Jace's phone lights up on the counter across the bathroom. "I got you covered. Our food just arrived."

He helps me out of the tub and dries me off. After giving me one of his shirts to wear, he leads me into his room, where blankets and pillows are spread out on the floor. The setup reminds me of a people-sized nest. A lap tray holds a bucket of ice with a bottle of wine in the center and two glasses placed upside down. The small touch brings a smile to my face. It's a tiny show of surrender in Jace's very controlled environment. He grabs a bag of take-out food from outside his door. I assume Cannon put it there for us after it arrived. While I prepare our plates with what Jace has declared is the best Chinese food in Denver, he turns on the television hanging on the wall. Three of my favorite rom-com movies appear on the screen.

We spend the night in our little nest, arms and legs tangled, never missing an opportunity to steal a kiss. Wrapped in the blankets and buried between the pillows, we can pretend that the inevitable isn't inching closer. We can get lost in wandering hands and the warmth of skin on skin. I wish I could cling to him, body and soul, and keep him with me like this always. But the end of our time together never stops creeping closer.

THIRTY-TWO
JACE

I can't take my eyes off Desi. Between the way her lips remain parted as she sleeps and the gentle fluttering of her lashes above her cheeks, I can't look away. I memorize how every slope and curve of her face looks in the silver glow of the moon. The next sunrise I witness will remind me of her red hair wild against a satin pillowcase and the warmth of her skin in the golden rays of the sun. I have a little over twenty-four hours left to carve every detail of this beautiful demon into my brain.

After three movies Desi fell asleep, and I picked her up and put her in bed. It would sound chivalrous to say I didn't want her sleeping on the floor all night, that I did it for the sake of comfort. But the truth is, I wanted her in my bed. When she's gone I want to catch the scent of her in my sheets and remember what her skin felt like while she slept next to me.

I reach out and brush my fingertips over her lips and glide them along her cheek and down her neck. She's so soft. Her eyes open and I'm struck by how green they are when she first wakes up.

"Good morning," I say, my voice hoarse from lack of use.

"Good morning," she replies, easing out of her sleepy haze. "Did you sleep at all?"

I drag my finger down the slope of her nose. "Not a wink." I sigh and lean back against the headboard, fingers absentmindedly running through her hair. "Not to mention, it's your last day, Desi. I couldn't stop thinking about it." Saying it out loud makes it feel like the reality I've always known it would be.

Desi draws her bottom lip between her teeth, and I hate the tears in her eyes as she says, "I know. I don't want to miss a second."

I don't want her to be upset. Not for a moment. We can't waste this day, not when it's all we have left. "I don't plan on it." Twisting around to the nightstand, I pluck a strawberry off the platter I brought from downstairs. "A little bit of breakfast in bed?"

Desi's eyes light up and she parts her plump lips to take the piece of fruit I offer her, and all I can think about is her little gift to me in the tub yesterday. And when she lets out a moan that's borderline erotic, I have to adjust myself over my joggers. "Wow, that's delicious," she exclaims, completely oblivious to the effect she's having on me as she lazily points at the platter and wiggles her fingers until a piece of the red fruit lands in her palm. "Your turn," she murmurs, holding the fruit to my lips.

I take a bite and nod. "It's a good strawberry." I lean in and kiss her lips. It's innocent but the way it makes me feel is anything but. "I like the taste of you better though."

Desi flushes at the compliment, and just like that sets my plans for the day in motion. I can't let her leave without seeing her do that a hundred more times. For today, every smile, every bashful look, every moan of desire will be mine alone.

I cut into the eggs Benedict and hand her the fork. "I was thinking that in a few hours you should take some time to say goodbye to Meredith and prepare as much as you can."

Her happy expression fades into disappointment, and a stabbing pain pierces my chest.

"I just thought you should get it out of the way since I plan on consuming the rest of your evening. I need some time to put a surprise into place," I admit, hoping I can make her smile again.

At the mention of the word *surprise*, her demeanor perks back up and I thank whatever deity might be watching that her lips turn into a grin. "A surprise, you say? Well, in that case," she says, pretending to get out of bed right away.

"Hey, now, you need to finish your breakfast," I growl, pouncing on her and pulling her against me for at least one more kiss.

)))——————————— 🎮 ———————————(((

The sun is low in the sky when Desi's bedroom door opens and she descends the stairs. I've spent the last few hours pulling some strings and sneaking around the house to get everything just right. It wasn't easy. What does one give a future demon queen to thank her for her friendship? I couldn't let her leave with a cheesy trinket. No, I wanted her last night with me to be an experience she could never have in her realm.

I glance up from my second bowl of peanut butter puff cereal. My anxiety is running high and not even a shot of pure sugar to my veins can set it right. But the sight of Desi in an oversized sweatshirt and leggings seems to do the trick. She looks so innocent with her hair piled on top of her head and crimson curls framing her face. The puffiness around her eyes tells me she's been crying. Saying goodbye to Meredith and packing to leave were difficult for her. I plan on taking her mind off all of that.

"Go put on your boots and meet me in the backyard," I say, moving to the sink to rinse out my bowl.

"Is it time for my surprise?" she calls as she sits on the bench in the foyer, and I can hear her tugging on her waterproof boots, a cute little grunt escaping her before one of her feet slams onto the ground.

I walk into the foyer and lean against the doorway, crossing my arms over my chest and one leg over the other. "It is. Are you having trouble?"

She looks up at me and blows a stray curl off her forehead. "These boots are annoying. Glen bought them for me, and he got them half a size too small. Not to mention these socks I have on are so damn thick," she growls.

I kneel in front of her and pick up her other boot. "Here, little hurricane, let me help you before you tear down the house with your sassy attitude." Picking up her foot, I slide the boot on with very little trouble.

She huffs and watches me closely. "How'd you do that so easily?"

I shrug. "Magic, I guess. You aren't the only one with powers, ya know."

Rolling her eyes, she gets to her feet. "You're such a dork." Leaning into my chest, she takes a deep breath and whispers, "I'm going to miss that so much."

I place my index finger under her chin and lift it. "None of that. Give me tonight. Stay in this moment with me. Understand?"

She nods and tears pool in her eyes. I wipe them away with my thumbs before they can fall down her cheeks. When she's composed, I hold out my hand to her. Her delicate fingers curl around mine, sending a shock wave through my system. The simplest of gestures has my body reacting when Desi is involved.

I lead her back through the house and smirk at the confusion on her face. "This feels . . . odd," she says, watching her shoes leave imprints on the area rug in the living room.

I open the French doors to the back porch and say, "I've trained you well, young Padawan."

She shakes her head and rolls her eyes before she stops in her tracks. Snowflakes drift to the ground and cling to the trees at the edge of the yard. Steam rises from the surface of the pool as the lights gradually change the color of the water. Off in the far corner a fire crackles in a crude fire pit lined with river rocks. The flames reach for the darkening sky while illuminating a cream-colored, A-framed tent.

"What is this?" she asks.

"I figure this might be one of the last times you see snow for a while. And I wanted to give you an experience you can't have at home. We're camping for the evening. Minus the bugs, terrible toilet situation, and bathing with baby wipes."

She turns to face me, and when her eyes meet mine I know for a fact I will never in my life see another shade of green like that. And every time I see anything that even remotely resembles it, I'll think of her, this moment, and a hundred others when she looked at me with this kind of emotion reflected in them.

And for the five thousandth time since I've met Desideria, I wish that I could be what she needs.

"Thank you, Jace. This looks perfect. Come on," she urges, tugging me toward the tent. The snow falls faster, landing in her hair and sticking to her clothing. She holds out her palm and several flakes pepper her skin, melting almost as soon as they land. "It's beautiful."

Her pink tongue slips between her lips, and she turns her head to the gloomy sky. Her arms spread out at her sides like she is going to take flight as she spins in slow circles. I'm captivated by her every movement. Fuck angels; nothing is as beautiful as a demon queen.

When she's captured several snowflakes, she closes her mouth, and her lips form a playful smile. I'd sell my soul to her father just to relive that again.

"Are you ready to go inside?" I ask, tilting my chin at the tent.

She squats down so she can crawl through the tent flap, and I follow. Her round ass shimmies as she moves toward the pile of pillows stacked on a faux fur blanket. Unable to help myself, I slap it as she goes. "Hurry up, sloth queen. It's cold out here."

Desi squeals and kicks at me as she turns around to settle into one of the two large pillows I bought for us to sit on. "Hey! I'll levitate your ass right out of here!" she says, but she's laughing even as she crosses her arms over her chest.

I tie back the flaps of the tent before setting to work with the bag of camping goodies I got for the occasion. She watches me intently as I pull out two metal skewers and a bag of big, fluffy marshmallows. I stab one onto the end of the stick and hand it to her.

"Have you ever made s'mores before?" I ask.

She twists the skewer and stares at the marshmallow, clearly unsure about what to do. "No," she drawls.

I prepare a graham cracker and a slab of chocolate before moving in behind her and scooting us to the edge of the entrance. Extending her arm until the fluffy sugar-filled treat hovers over the fire, I say, "You're going to roast it. Just hold it right above the flames and turn it."

She follows my directions, holding the marshmallow a little too high above the fire. With her focus straight ahead, I drop my lips to her neck and leave a trail of kisses. She is so warm and soft. I could easily spend the rest of the night holding her like this.

"Oh. Oh! Jace, it's on fire!"

Desi swings her flaming marshmallow in front of us, trying to put it out. I grab her wrist and bring the skewer close enough for me to blow it out. She sighs while staring at the burned ball of goo at the end.

I laugh and pluck the marshmallow off the stick and pop it into my mouth, humming as the crispy outside gives way to the warm, soft center. "You had one job, Desideria."

"You distracted me," she says.

I set her up to try again. "It's not my fault that you're irresistible."

"You're pretty irresistible yourself, sir." She takes the skewer from me, and this time, even when I slide my arms around her waist, she keeps her eyes on the fire, rotating the marshmallow and keeping it out of the flames. And when I press my lips to the back of her neck and run my fingertips up and down her spine, she squirms against me and says, "Ya know, you didn't really think this through. We're sort of out here in the open and you're over here turning me on. Now what are we going to do?"

I nip at her earlobe and say, "I thought this through. Don't you think we could have just sat by the fire and done this? The tent does have a purpose. I have every intention of fucking you if that's what you want."

My hand at her waist moves to her thigh, my fingers brushing dangerously close to her center.

She yanks the skewer out of the fire and pulls the marshmallow off, setting it on the plate with the chocolate and graham cracker before spinning to face me. "It's only a tent, Wilder. You know I like to get loud."

I brush away a wild curl that falls over her eye. "Looks like I'm not the only one who put thought into this. I guess you're going to have to keep quiet for me, little hurricane." I take her hand and bring her sticky fingers to my mouth. One by one, I suck them clean while she makes the sweetest sounds. "Can you be quiet for me, Desideria?"

She whimpers and gives me a slow nod, her heavily lidded eyes traveling my body, sending a shiver up and down my spine. "Yes," she breathes as I take the last finger from my mouth.

I pull her to me and my lips meet hers in a searing kiss. Tracing the seam of her mouth, I coax her to open for me. There's no holding back as I'm consumed by the taste of her. She is the warmth of a lazy summer afternoon laced with addicting sweet spice. I can't get enough.

She groans into the kiss as I lay her back and rest my body between her legs. Every curve of her fits perfectly against me. I love the soft give of her stomach and the way her legs wrap around my hips. No other woman will come close to doing what she does to me.

We separate for air, and I kiss the tip of her nose. She stares up at me with long lashes framing her emerald-green eyes. I'm going to miss getting lost in her gaze.

"What?" she asks, her voice raspy with need. "What is it?"

I dip my head, planting kisses down her jawline and on her neck as I struggle with the truth. It's been a long time since I've accepted an absolute about a woman who wasn't just a friend. I've built high, impenetrable walls, guarding every possible way that someone could sneak past them. Desideria has slipped through them all and unleashed the most exquisite chaos inside of me.

My mouth drifts back up to her ear, and I freely give her a truth that rips me open from the inside. "No other woman will ever compare to you. Your humor, your compassion, your loyalty, your beauty, it isn't possible. No one will ever be as stunning as you."

Her brow furrows in disbelief. "Come on, Jace. There are plenty—"

I rest a finger against her lips. Running my hand down the curve of her waist, I say, "This body? These wild curls? All of that is unmatched, yes. But your beauty radiates from in here," I say, flattening a palm against her sternum. "Your heart and soul lured me in. They gave me a safe place to open myself up even if it was only a fraction. Those who know me would say it's impossible for a woman to get through my defenses, and they'd be right. But you aren't just a woman are you, little hurricane?"

She bites her lip, and it sends a stabbing pain through me to see her fighting tears and a smile at the same time. "No, I'm not. And that's part of the problem. I came here with the intention of finding a human who would keep me on my toes, keep me tame. I felt like I was *too* chaotic, too *much*, and that I would never find someone whose energy complemented mine. And here you are, encouraging me to let go, be myself, embrace the chaos within even though it's not always comfortable for you. And sometimes, you even join me."

She places her palm on my cheek and runs her thumb over my bottom lip. "Which I know isn't easy. Jace, you've taught me what it means to truly live, and I wish more than anything that I didn't have to say goodbye to you, that I could stay here, in this tent with you, forever. Because I would. I'd give it all up, just to stay in your arms."

Damn, what I wouldn't give for that to be possible.

"Your family is counting on you and the energies who crave your type of chaos need you too. I would never ask you to give up that calling. You were made to be a queen, not a girl who spends her days with a nerd who plays video games and makes cool graphic art."

"I know I have to take my place on the throne, but I just needed you to hear me; if it were possible, it would be enough for me, Jace."

I place two soft kisses on her lips. I hope that those kisses say the words I can't: if my heart were bandaged and on the mend, we wouldn't be saying goodbye right now. We'd be packing our books and movies and clothing in boxes together and despite whatever lingering doubts I might have, I wouldn't be so broken that I couldn't even try.

I've never cursed time the way I do now. "Just tell me I can be enough for you for one more night, Desideria," I whisper against her temple.

She turns her head so she can look at me when she says, "You've always been enough for me, Jace. Even more so tonight."

The force with which I pin her to the soft blanket beneath us leaves her breathless. Taking both of her wrists in one hand, I hold them above her head and whisper, "How do you want me to show you how much I'll miss your presence in my life, Desideria?" I run my free hand down her face, tracing her cheekbone with the utmost reverence. I'm going to worship her like she is my personal savior. Because she is. Desideria has kept me afloat these past months. She has been my life support, my anchor, a new reason for me to live a full life.

"Do you want me to show you by being soft? Vulnerable?"

Dipping my head to brush my lips against hers, I murmur, "Treat you like a princess?" She relaxes beneath me as my palm slides down and tightens around her throat. "Or rough? Demanding?" I nip her bottom lip and growl, "Like a queen."

She gasps and wraps her legs around me, pulling me closer. "Like a queen."

"You want me to leave my mark on you, so you never forget?"

"Even if you took me gently, I'd never forget, Jace."

I groan and roll my hips over her, my fingers gripping her throat and wrists tighter like she might slip away. She's so willing to bend to my desires, my willing captive, who craves everything I need to give her.

I release her neck and slide my hand to the hem of her sweatshirt. As my cold fingers brush over her stomach, her skin prickles with goosebumps. Palming her breast, my chilled thumb caresses her nipple.

"Take it off," she gasps, writhing against my hold on her wrists. "Please. I don't want anything between us."

I ease the warm fabric up her torso and watch in awe at how her body responds to the cold air. Sitting back on my legs, I toss her shirt to the side. The light of the fire dances over every soft dip and hill. I return to my task from this morning, sketching every inch of her in my memory. I never want to forget how she looks or the softness of her skin. Her scent will always be my favorite and her taste will leave me forever unsatisfied. She has ruined me to my core, and I've never been so happy to be a mess.

"*So* fucking beautiful," I whisper.

She sits up and slips her hands under the hem of my T-shirt, and I lift my arms, allowing her to pull it over my head. She doesn't take her eyes off me as she drops it to the ground next to us. Dragging her fingers up my bare chest, she leans forward, planting a kiss on the scar over my heart, the tough skin that has kept everyone from reaching it.

She lifts her eyes to mine and echoes my words. "So fucking beautiful. Every single inch."

I reach just beyond the entrance of the tent and scrape my fingers in the snow. I hold her gaze and bring the ball of ice to the tops of her breasts. She arches into my touch as I drag the ice over her skin. Droplets of water run over her nipples and stream down her stomach, glistening like priceless diamonds against her skin.

"Lie down, Desideria, and let me taste the snow on your body."

She lies back, her hair spilling over her shoulders and onto the pillows. I run my tongue across the swells of her breasts, lapping up the water, down to one hard peak. Her breath catches, a little yelp escaping her throat. I glance up at her and the most wicked thoughts slip inside my head. I know exactly what to do to have her turning to putty in my hands. Sliding one palm up her other breast, I circle her nipple in a slow, tantalizing motion, getting so close, but not quite close enough. She arches her back with each pass of my tongue, offering herself to me. I take and take because she is the only thing I crave.

"Jace," she whines, tangling her hand in my hair and pulling hard. "Please."

I deny her . . . for now. Lifting her leg, I remove her boots and fluffy socks. My fingers drift up her thighs and hook into the waistband of her leggings. It's so tempting to yank them off, but I want to savor the task of undressing her for the final time. Every inch of revealed skin makes my mouth water. I want to lick, suck, and bite until she's left with my mark on her body.

When she's naked, one side of my mouth tilts up. My fingers prickle with the need to touch. I want to make her understand without words the ache I feel seeing her like this. Taking another handful of snow, I press it to her sex. I'm captivated by how it melts against her, following all the lines of her body I want to trace with my tongue.

"That's a pretty sight. So wet and aching for me," I say.

Her neck stretches and her lips part at the frozen sensation. "Jace, that feels so good."

I could do this all night just to hear her moan my name. It's like hearing a song, feminine with a hint of rasp. I'd put it on repeat, losing myself to it over and over again.

"Please, let me make you feel good too," she begs.

I lean over her and brush her hair behind her ears. "All I need is you close and I'm hard. All the other things like kissing"—I press my lips to hers—"and touching"—my fingertips brush the seam of her—"and fucking, I do to watch you get wet. Knowing it's because of me that you're turned on makes me feel good."

She places her hand over her heart and her voice is shaky when she says, "You must feel good a lot then, because I'm always wet when you're around. You've ruined your fair share of my panties, Jace Wilder."

The stroke to my ego is real. Everything I've worked for tonight, she says I do naturally. How can I not be proud of myself? I cock a brow and say, "I guess I'll have to do the chivalrous thing and keep you naked to spare those sexy lace panties."

"That's so kind of you. How can I ever repay you?" she says, batting her eyelashes.

I pull at the rest of my clothes, tossing them haphazardly around the tent. "Get on your hands and knees. Let me see that sexy ass, Desideria."

She doesn't hesitate—no fear at the promise of what's to come and no shame in the vulnerable position we've never tried. There is only complete submission to my demand, and it's the sexiest thing I've ever witnessed.

She kneels with her back to me, and slowly, as if enticing me, she leans over, propping herself on her elbows. Her hair frames her face in crimson waves. She sweeps it over her shoulder and looks back at me. "You want me like this?"

I scoot closer and palm her ass. She presses back into my touch. The hum coming from her lets me know she welcomes it. I place a kiss at the lowest point of her spine.

"I'm going to regret for the rest of my life that I didn't have you like this more often," I say, opening her to me so I can see all the pretty pink parts of her.

I kiss one swell of her ass and then the other, drawing a blissful sound from her. My fingers drift lower until they play at her soaked entrance. I slide one inside and my eyes flutter shut as I'm greeted by her warmth. I bask in the feel of her for a moment before curling my finger and rubbing that sensitive spot inside her that makes her whimper.

"You're so tight like this," I say, kissing the middle of her back.

Needing her to feel me everywhere, I strum her clit a little faster. She presses down, taking my finger deeper. The sight of her like this is breathtaking. Each sound of ecstasy and every roll of her hips is just for me. Without a single word, her body tells me she wants more.

"Do you know how full I can make you feel like this, the depths I could reach inside you? Do you understand how hard I could fuck you?" I ask, wrapping her hair around my hand and pulling.

She is beautiful with her face tilted up and her lips parted. My fingers move faster, and her breath picks up with each thrust.

I lean in, pressing my chest to her back. "I could demand so much out of your body like this," I whisper, and bite the curve where her neck meets her shoulder.

My plans for tonight were sweet, almost innocent. I wanted to treat her with tenderness and give her a romantic experience. She was supposed to walk away with memories framed in rose petals with an amber glow. But she's awakened something carnal inside me and I want to show her passion in its rawest form.

"Show me, Jace. Show me exactly how hard you could take me. Demand anything you want from me because I'll give you anything you desire, every part of me. I'm completely open to you right now. Vulnerable. I'm yours. Take what you want. Because I want it too."

Her words spur me on, coaxing forward an animalistic part of me. I grip her hips, digging my fingertips into her plump flesh. She stops breathing, and I know she's waiting to see what she's unleashed.

I yank her back and her silken center meets my tongue. With one long lick, I'm addicted. I need to feast until I've taken every last drop.

"Jace," she groans, throwing her head back. "I love it when you do this. But you haven't gotten anything yet tonight . . . I haven't touched you, you haven't been inside me . . . this seems unfair."

"I just need one more taste," I say, desperate for her to let me keep my mouth right where it is.

She reaches back and grabs the hair on the top of my head and holds me to her. I moan in appreciation and plunge my tongue deeper inside of her. My fingertips find their way to her clit and rub, her body flexing around me with each tight circle. I don't let up, forcing her closer to the edge until she's in a free fall.

"Yes, Jace. Yes."

I groan as she shatters. She is sweeter than honey straight from the hive, more decadent than the richest chocolate. I lick and suck, taking care not to let a drop go to waste.

Desi rides my mouth until she has given me all she has. Her head falls to the pillows, her breathing labored. But I don't give her a second to recover. I bite her ass and flip her onto her back.

Running the back of my hand over my wet lips, I say, "God, I love seeing you like this, spread out for me with your hair like a flaming halo. It is hard to believe someone so perfect is a demon."

The corners of her lips lift in a wicked smile. "Did you know that the word *demon* comes from the ancient Greeks—*daimōn*, which means *deity*? So really, when you call me demon, you're calling me a goddess."

I move over her and brush my lips against hers, letting her taste how sweet she is on them. "Did you know that is exactly what I think you are? I'm going to worship you, Desideria."

I slide my hand under her thigh and lift her leg, opening her to me. I want to bury myself deep inside her, feel her tight grip on me. Instead, I dip the head of my cock inside of her and pull away. She is aching for me; I can feel it in the way her nails bite into my shoulder and her legs lock around my hips. I want to give in to her desire, but only when she feels like she can't take another breath without me inside her. I repeat my shallow thrust, leaving her with a taste of what's to come.

She moves with me—a sensual roll of her hips enticing me to plunge deeper. It's hard to deny her. It's a pain clawing at my gut. Unable to stand it any longer, I take her hand in mine and lace our fingers. With a thrust so deliberately slow, it might kill us both, I sink into her.

Her lips part and my name flows from them on a heated gasp. "Jace. How is it possible that you fit even more perfectly this time than you did last time?"

I brush my nose against hers and nip at her earlobe before saying, "Because our bodies are in tune with one another now. I know exactly what you need, and you know exactly how to make me hard to the point of no return."

She clenches around me and lifts her hips to meet my measured movements. All the wild tendencies I felt moments ago are tamed for now. It's a euphoric feeling, the way her body grips me, and I don't want to chase it away just yet. Nothing is more important than making sure this beautiful creature below me feels it too.

There are no words, heartfelt declarations, or unbreakable oaths. Nothing that would be enough to make her understand how I feel with her surrendering to me like this. She's everything. The beginning and end. Infinity. Eternity.

Wrapping her legs around me, she pulls me against her, forcing me out of my haze and reminding me that I'm here for her. She grips my hair and brings our mouths together, parting my lips with hers. Her quiet demands taunt the beast inside of me, urging it to come back out and play.

"I was trying to be gentle with you, Desideria, but my body is desperate to be buried deep inside you. I want to fuck you so hard you never forget how good we were together," I say through strained breaths and shaking muscles.

She squeezes my fingers, which are still intertwined with hers, and moves her free hand to my face, gripping my chin and holding it tight so we're eye to eye. "Stop holding back. I've felt your tenderness already. I know what that's like, but I want to feel the other side of that—the raw, unrestrained side." She runs her tongue up my jawline, and I shiver as she says the words I need to hear. "Fuck me hard, Jace. Treat me like a queen."

My mouth covers hers and I grip her hip and pull out of her. She only has a split second to miss the way I fill her when I slam back in. I go so deep that a whimper laced with pain and satisfaction escapes her. Everything stills, and my eyes widen with the fear that I've hurt her.

"Don't stop," she begs against my lips.

I grip the hair at her nape, and my hips move in long, fast thrusts.

She screams my name with absolutely no regard for where we are, that even though we're sheltered by this tent, we're still outside with neighbors on either side. I couldn't care less; I'm in heaven right now. Deep inside her with her hands on my skin and hair, inching closer and closer to the point of no return. The more we connect, both physically and emotionally, the more obvious it is that saying goodbye is going to rip me in two.

The pain that will haunt me tomorrow isn't enough to make me stop. I need this, even if it means living the rest of my life in some incomplete way. At least I had this moment, holding her in my arms, filling her body with mine. For this single night, I know what it is to be completely wanted.

Desi arches her back and rolls her hips with mine. "Jace, I am so close," she whispers. "But I want you to come too. I want you to fall apart inside me."

I groan as my hand slides between us, and my fingers touch her clit, demanding that she give in to the euphoria. She squeezes around me, and I moan before sinking my teeth into the curve of her neck. I pump into her, filling her up as she pulsates around me. Neither one of us holds back, filling the night with the sounds of our bliss. I don't let up on her until she goes slack beneath me. Exhausted, I rest my full weight on her and lower my head to her chest. Her heart thumps against my cheek as I catch my breath.

"No matter how many nights I had you, Desideria, it would never be enough," I say, the words slipping from my mouth before I can stop them. But I don't regret them. They are just more of my truth that I seal with a kiss to her chest.

She runs her fingers through my hair and kisses the crown of my head. "I couldn't have said it better."

THIRTY-THREE
DESI

We stay in the tent for I don't even know how long, the wind whipping around us, until I start to shiver even in his arms. He rubs my bare biceps and grabs my sweatshirt and leggings.

"Here, Desi, put these on so we can go back inside and get you warm," he says, pulling his own shirt over his head and placing his glasses on his face.

Nodding, I tug on the sweatshirt and leggings before shoving my feet in my boots and following Jace out of the tent. He offers me his hand and I take it like second nature, trying like hell to ignore the stab of pain that hits my chest when I think about the fact that, after tomorrow, I won't feel his fingers intertwined with mine ever again.

When we get inside, I glance at the clock over the microwave and gape at the time. "It's already after midnight?"

He grins and raises a brow. "We spent a lot of time out in the snow."

"True," I say, covering my mouth as a yawn slips out.

"You're tired," he says. It's a statement, not a question, and I can see in his eyes that he is too. We're both exhausted in more ways than one.

"Yeah," I say reluctantly, glancing up the stairs as I kick my boots off and slip them under the bench in the foyer. "I guess I better get to bed then. We both need a good night's sleep—big day tomorrow. Good night, Jace." I try to sound chipper, but I know that any second I'm going to burst into tears. I lean forward and kiss him on the cheek, turning to go to my room.

His fingers lock around my wrist, and his voice is rough with emotion as he says, "Stay in my room tonight. Please."

I turn around with wide eyes, questioning if I heard him right. Last night felt like an accident; I fell asleep on the floor, so he put me in his bed. I didn't expect him to extend the offer like this. This is a lot for him. An invasion of the space that is his and his alone in a house that he shares with two other people.

"Okay," I say, wrapping my fingers around his.

"Are you sure? Because you don't have—"

"Yes."

He scoops me up and throws me over his shoulder and I giggle, pounding my fists lightly against his back. "Put me down!"

"I will as soon as I get you where I want you," he growls against my hip as he ascends the stairs.

I grin, pinching the roundest part of his backside, and his palm promptly lands on my ass, sending shock waves all the way to my center.

My yelp echoes through the house. "Jace!"

"Oh, I know you can do better than that. Just wait until I get you in my bed."

He enters his room and kicks the door closed behind us. I brace myself to hit his mattress, but he gently lowers me to sit on the edge of the bed. He reaches for the hem of my shirt and pulls it over my head before working me out of my pants.

"Get dressed, get undressed, get dressed all so you can undress me again," I say while laughing.

"This time it's necessary. Let's get you into a hot shower."

The thought of that after being out in the cold—with snow and ice dragged across all my private parts, no less—has me practically salivating. I stand and run my fingers under the hem of his T-shirt.

"Tell me you're getting in with me, or I think I'll pass," I say, standing on my tiptoes and pressing my lips to his neck.

"You're going to pass even after the mess I made of you?" He shifts his hand between us and dips his finger inside me. His thumb brushes my clit and when I hiss, he smiles. "Although, I like knowing you have a piece of me deep inside you."

My knees nearly go weak, but I manage to stay upright. "Fine, I'll admit it. I don't want to be apart from you even long enough to take a shower. Sue me. Now, are you getting in or not? I'll do your back," I say with a wink.

Jace doesn't say another word. He disrobes and pulls me into the bathroom with him. When the water is warm enough to fog the mirrors, he guides me under the stream and sets to work lathering his soap between his hands. I groan when he massages my frozen muscles, starting with my shoulders. He works his thumbs along my spine and down my hips. His front presses to my back and he treats the front of my body with the same euphoric touches.

"We should have done this before today," he says, pressing a sweet kiss to my neck.

I nod. "Absolutely. We should've done this *every* day." I lean back against him, and he returns to my shoulders. "That is perfect. Don't stop doing that."

He doesn't, and before long I'm stifling a yawn, and his lips are next to my ear. "You're sleepy, princess. Let's go lie down."

I don't want to do that because lying down means bedtime, bedtime means sleep, and sleeping means our day is over and tomorrow will be here far too soon. But I just nod, step out of the shower, and let Jace dry me with one of his big fluffy towels.

After I slip into one of his oversized T-shirts, we hop into bed and click off the overhead light, leaving us in total darkness.

Turning over on my side, I reach out to touch him and find him in the exact same position, already facing me. I run my fingers down his jawline and whisper, "I don't want to go to sleep."

"Me either. Just talk to me about anything, I don't care how mundane it is."

"I always thought it was weird that humans domesticated animals. I felt bad that cats weren't allowed to climb trees and chase after rodents. But now I realize some animals have better lives than some humans. That's strange."

Jace chuckles and says, "I always wanted an owl as a pet, or an Ewok. They would have been fun to hang out with."

"Hades forbid that we go a day without a *Star Wars* reference."

His arms tighten around me and he kisses the top of my head, pulling me on top of him. "You'll miss it."

Tears fill my eyes and I try to swallow them back, but I can't, and they spill onto my cheeks and his bare chest. "I will. I'll miss everything about you, Jace. That's something I've known since the moment I realized you wouldn't be coming back to Infernis with me."

"I wish . . ." He clears his throat like he's stifling his emotions and tries again. "I wish I was as brave as you, Desi. You ventured into a realm you've never been to and opened yourself up to finding someone to be with you for eternity. I want you to know that I never thought your purpose for being here was a fool's errand. You took the leap to find love and believed it could last forever."

"But I—"

It's on the tip of my tongue to say that it *was* a fool's errand, that I *didn't* find it. But that's not true. I did. I found it.

I was too scared to admit it before, but I can't run from it. I'm in love with Jace Wilder. I've been in love with him for weeks.

But I can't tell him.

Why do it now when all it will do is make things harder?

"I'm glad you didn't see me as a fool," I murmur, nuzzling into his chest. "I respect you more than anyone in this realm or any other."

"Your people are lucky to have you. I would have gladly bowed to you as my queen."

"I would have happily stood by your side with you as my king," I whisper so quietly I'm not sure I said the words at all.

Jace stills under me and lets out a long, slow breath. I wait to see if he responds but the room remains silent. It feels like hours pass at a painful crawl. The room is too quiet and the darkness too deep to even pick up a shadow of him. I listen for even breaths or the sound of a snore, but I can't find any clue that he's dozed off. The tears well in my eyes and a sob builds in my chest. It burns, but I push it down.

"I'll regret letting you go for the rest of my life," he finally says, his voice hoarse with emotion.

Then come with me! The voice in my head is wailing, fighting to break free, but I won't beg him. I refuse. He has his reasons. And I have my dignity.

"And I'll feel the void you'll leave in my heart for eternity," I murmur, shifting on top of him, and even in the pitch dark, our mouths find each other like they're magnetized.

I put my all into that single kiss, knowing it's the countdown to our last. We stay suspended in that moment, speaking in whispers, stealing kisses, and touching our fill. It isn't until the dreaded sun beams through the window and the alarm shrieks that our time together officially comes to a heart-shattering end.

We retreat into silence as we get ready for the day ahead—the day that begins the rest of our lives without the other in it. The task of dressing is exhausting, and I can't so much as stomach a cup of tea. Jace carries my bags to the car my father sent for me. I hate the thought of driving away by myself. If only Cannon were here to help distract me from what's going to be the hardest thing I've ever done, but he left sometime yesterday, needing to tie up all his loose ends in this realm.

Jace leans against the counter, watching me arrange the last of my personal items into my oversized purse. His stormy eyes follow my every movement, and his jaw is clenched, like he's holding out on saying our final goodbye. I toss my purse over my shoulder and stand on the other side of the kitchen island.

"Are you sure you got everything?" Jace asks.

No. No, I don't have everything. I'm leaving half of my heart behind with the person who would make the perfect eternal partner.

I force a smile and say, "I think so."

He walks around the island and stands in front of me, placing his hands on my cheeks. "Will you ever be able to come back and visit?" His tone tells me it's a question he's been dying to ask but was too scared to do so.

I draw my bottom lip between my teeth. "Not for longer than a couple of hours or so. As queen I'll be expected to be in my Circle almost all the time. The only reason my brothers were allowed to come up like they did was because they were dealing with me, and they haven't taken full control yet." Cocking my head to the side, I say, "And don't you think it would make it harder? To see each other again for a short amount of time? Would you even want to?"

"I—" He clamps his lips shut and gives a curt nod. "You're right. It would be too hard."

I don't know what I expected him to say, but my belly clenches at his response. I push past the roiling in my stomach and say, "I mean, to go through this again sounds like hell." A tear slides down my cheek.

He wipes it away and pulls me into his arms. "Yeah."

On a deep inhale, he buries his face in the crook of my neck. His hold is so tight that I fight for my next breath, but I wouldn't want it any other way. I hope he holds me hostage and never lets me leave. But of course, he eventually has to let me go.

When we separate, I swear his eyes are misty, but when he blinks, they're back to their normal gloomy hue. I sigh and say, "I have to go. Walk me outside?"

He just nods and intertwines our fingers, leading us out the door and onto the sidewalk to where the car and driver wait for me. The driver opens the door, and I toss my purse onto the backseat, turning back to Jace.

Cupping his cheek in my hand, I bring my mouth to his and press a gentle kiss to his lips.

"Jace," I whisper against his skin. "I have one wish for you. I hope that one day you feel safe enough to open your heart and allow yourself to take a risk and let someone adore you the way you deserve. I want you to fall so deeply in love that you wonder how you ever went so long without it."

Saying these words hurts me to the depths of my soul because that's how I feel about him.

That's how I want him to feel about me.

But he can't right now. And I understand that. But one day, I want that for him. Even if it can't be with me.

He nods and tucks a curl behind my ear.

I can see it in his eyes; he doesn't believe he'll ever know a love like the one I want for him. It breaks my heart to think this man, who has so much to give, will never open himself up.

"I want the same for you. Cannon is a good man, and he'll be what you need. Don't give up on him and let the passion that smolders inside you burn out. That passion is powerful and transforming, Desideria."

You're what I need.

"I won't give up," is all I say, though, because it's time to go. I have to let this man go, let him live his life. I've already disrupted it enough, and even though he says it's been one of the best things that's ever happened to him, he deserves to move on. He has exciting, career-altering changes waiting for him, and I'm just the demon princess who crash-landed on his front porch.

"I'll never forget you. Ever," I whisper, pulling him forward until his forehead rests against mine.

He cups my face in his palms, softly kisses me, and says, "Goodbye, my little hurricane."

What's left of my heart shatters at his feet. "Goodbye, Jace Wilder."

And when I get into the backseat, I have no regard for the oblivious driver when I burst into tears.

THIRTY-FOUR
JACE

It's been nine hours, fifty-two minutes, and seventeen seconds since Desi climbed into the backseat of that car and drove away from me for the last time.

Since then I've eaten five bowls of peanut butter puff cereal, felt like I was going to vomit, watched two *Star Wars* movies, and I swear I teared up when R2-D2 slid on screen because she wasn't there to do her "beep-beep-boops." I tried to work on a project for a client but gave up when I realized it was terrible, and took a shower so long that the water ran cold. Nothing I do relieves the ache in my chest or makes me feel a semblance of happiness.

I am absolutely 300 percent miserable without her. The house is so quiet, so boring without her laughter bouncing off the walls. All I want is her right here next to me so I can reach over and touch her, brush my fingertips over her skin, surprise her with kisses . . . but she's so far away from me now and I'll never see her again.

It's so fucking depressing.

The only consolation I have is that Cannon will be with her, but even that is a stab to my gut. I'm so jealous of him I could punch something. But at the same time, I know it's for the best. I rub my temples and my attention turns to the door as I hear the knob rattle and Cannon walk through the foyer, kicking off his shoes.

I don't even bother to care that they're in the middle of the floor. I don't have the energy.

"Jace? You here?"

"Yeah, man, I'm in the living room," I call.

Cannon walks toward the couch and stops short when his eyes land on me. "You look like shit."

"That's exactly the look I was going for today—hammered shit with a side of what the fuck. I'm glad I pulled it off." I can't even bother to add inflection to my sarcastic tone because that takes too much energy.

He drops down on the opposite side of the couch and turns to me, leaning against the arm. "Desi left already, huh?" he says.

"Yeah, about nine this morning," I say, leaning my head back against the couch and staring at the ceiling.

Cannon sighs and props his elbows on his knees. "Are you okay, Jace? I know how much she means to you."

"It was just hard to say goodbye, but in my gut I know it's for the best. I mean look at you." I eye his tailored gray suit and thin black tie. He looks like he just stepped off a *GQ* cover ready to meet his future queen and spend the rest of his life with her. Everything about him is perfect. Hell, if I were into guys, he'd be perfect for me too. "You're the type of guy who was made for the kind of life Desi lives."

Cannon loosens his tie and sits back against the arm of the couch. "She doesn't feel the same way about me as she does about you, though. I know you know that."

"It doesn't matter what she feels for me. I can't give her what she needs; you can. She shouldn't have to wait patiently as I overcome my issues. It could take all eternity for that to happen."

It doesn't matter what I feel for her either. Because we both knew from the beginning that this was never going to last longer than ninety days.

Cannon shakes his head and gets to his feet. "Your issues must be pretty major, dude. For you to give up a woman like Desi—" He blows out a breath that rattles his lips. He paces the room, removing his tie and unbuttoning the top few buttons of his shirt. His skin is flushed and his movements twitchy; he's clearly anxious about this conversation. "I'm sorry. I shouldn't have said that. That was rude; I just consider you a friend, Jace, and I hate to see you miserable like this, and to know I'm leaving you in this state to take what I know should be yours. It makes me feel bad."

"It shouldn't. I made my choices, and I chose the route with the least risk."

Cannon flops back down on the couch, the frame groaning from the impact. "I need you to understand that what I feel for Desi is nothing but friendship. She's in a hard place and I hate to think she'll spend the rest of her life miserable with someone she didn't choose. I care about her, but I care about you too, man."

I tilt my head up to the ceiling and run my palm down my face. What do I say to that? *Thanks for settling for the woman I wish I could get my shit together for?* I won't take my feelings out on him. Cannon's been a good friend to me and Desi. He's giving up everything for her simply because she's his friend. Desi offered me the same chance in a thousand ways without saying it, and I declined because I'm a coward.

I take a deep breath and face Cannon again. "Promise me you'll take care of her. Draw her a bath on days when she's stressed and watch sappy rom-coms with her once in a while. Remember her favorite dinner is fettuccine alfredo and she likes red wine over white. Oh, and never put her jeans in the dryer. She likes to hang them."

Cannon laughs and says, "Why?"

"Something about they always shrink and then they're too short and too small in the ass and blah, blah, blah. You'll get a lecture about it if you do it, trust me." My stomach does some kind of painful turn and I add, "Oh yeah, and don't forget to put her cups face down. She'll just waste time turning them back over and explaining why you're wrong if you don't."

Cannon groans and leans his head back on the arm of the couch. "For fuck's sake, y'all and your cups. See, you know all these things about her. All I know is she loves fried pickles and likes to read smutty romance novels."

My heart squeezes like it's in a vise, but I press on. I need Cannon to have the confidence that he can take care of her. I have to know that he's ready. "You know things about her. You're her best friend. I bet you two have had all sorts of conversations I haven't been privy to."

"No, man. Most of my conversations with her were about you. She was an open book and never held back what she was thinking. You heard it all. In fact, I think she dived a little deeper with you than she did with me."

The lump growing in my throat makes it hard to breathe. My chest hurts like a motherfucker and my heart is racing. I can't get a firm grip on my emotions and that gut-sinking feeling is pulling me down. It's been weeks since I felt like this, but I never forgot what it signals.

I leap to my feet and stomp into the kitchen. My hands shake as I rip open the cupboard with my daily vitamins and push them to the side. I snag the orange prescription bottle from the back and rip off the cap. My nerves are so on edge that my hands shake as I cram the medication under my tongue. I glance at the stove, knowing I have at least twenty minutes of managing my anxiety on my own.

Cannon stands on the other side of the kitchen island with concern written all over his face. "Can I get you anything or would you like to talk? I can stay quiet and listen if you just need to ramble."

I shake my head and grab two bowls from the cabinet on the other side of the kitchen. With the box of cereal and milk in hand, I set to work. My mind is a mess, but the simple task gives me a slight peace of mind. It's familiar, predictable, and keeps me busy until my meds can kick in.

I hand Cannon a bowl of peanut butter puffs and slide onto the stool beside him. We don't say a word as we shovel spoonfuls of cereal into our mouths. Since the accident, no one other than Desi has witnessed one of my panic attacks. I wait for the judgmental stare and awkwardness to kick in, followed by the inevitable sense of shame. But those things don't come. Cannon remains a quiet presence, and I have to admit it's nice not to spiral alone.

Placing my spoon in my empty bowl, I say, "I'm not all right."

"That's okay. You don't always have to be all right. I just don't want you to *always* be not all right."

"I'm not, but I think I'm in a place where that *could* happen," I admit.

Cannon's eyes cut to me and he pushes his bowl aside. "What can you do to head those feelings off? Stop them before it's too late?"

I sigh and slide my fingers into my hair, gripping it at the roots. "I need to call my therapist."

"I didn't even know you—"

"Yeah. I don't talk about it a lot, but Desi knew." I stop and shake my head, looking down at the table. "Desi knew everything."

Cannon swivels his stool so he can look me in the face. "I'm sorry that you aren't in a place to take what you want. I promise I'll take care of her. You won't have to worry if she's okay."

I lift my head and meet his concerned gaze. "Thank you, Cannon."

"You're welcome." He nods and stands. "I've got to finish packing. Are you okay for right now?"

"Yeah, I'll be all right." I get to my feet and hold my hand out to him. He grips my fingers and pulls me into a hug. It is then that I realize that I not only lost Desi, but I'm losing someone who has been a great friend to me. I swallow down my emotion and release him. As I grab the dirty bowls, he straightens his shirt, covering the sharp points of a tattoo on his chest.

"If I don't see you before I go tomorrow morning, take care, Jace."

"You too, Cannon."

Cannon rushes up the stairs, taking them two at a time. As soon as he's out of sight I drag my hand over my face. The decision I made was with Desi's best interest at heart. It should give me some peace knowing I did right by her, but it feels so wrong. I haven't felt like this since I came home from the hospital and found Hannah's ring sitting on the counter with a letter saying *Sorry, Jace. I just can't do this.*

I pick up my phone and scroll through my contacts. My thumb hovers over Holloman's name. We cut down my visits to once a month shortly after I started my own business. I had decided I was fine with living my life just for me, with no romantic relationship. I was doing better, and I needed the extra time for work. We aren't scheduled to meet again for ten days, but I don't think I can wait that long. I meant what I said to Cannon; I'm scared that my mental state could take a turn for the worse if I don't talk to someone. I need a voice of reason as soon as possible. I press Dr. Holloman's contact, and within minutes I'm scheduled to meet with him tomorrow.

I already feel a little better. If anyone can help me through this, he can.

〉〉——————————— 🎮 ———————————〈〈

"Jace?"

I sit up in my chair and drop the *Psychology Today* magazine I'd been thumbing through onto the table next to me. A sigh of relief escapes me knowing I'm one step closer to working through this disaster.

Dr. Holloman stands in his office doorway, welcoming me inside with a sweep of his tattooed arm. "Jace, good to see you. Come on in, have a seat." He gestures to the fluffy, red armchairs and takes the seat across from them. I plop down in one with a heavy sigh. "Hey, Doc. Thank you for fitting me in."

"Of course. It was clear you needed to talk." He leans back in his chair and steeples his fingers in front of his mouth. "What's going on?"

I shrug, unsure where to start, so I just let my feelings flow. "I feel like I've made the biggest mistake of my life, and at the same time, I know I did the right thing. I'm not in a position to take on more responsibility. I'm focused on my career, and I don't want to give that up. But another part of me feels like that is so stupid when I really like someone. I haven't connected with someone like this in forever."

He raises a dark eyebrow. "You met someone?"

"Remember my roommates I told you about?" Dr. Holloman nods and I continue, "Desi. It's her. I know I said when they moved in that I was setting firm boundaries and there would be no drama, but things happened, and she and I ended up in this . . ." I tilt my head back and forth. "Fake dating scenario that sort of turned into a *real* dating scenario."

"Fake dating? People *actually* do that?" He holds up his hand and shakes his head. "On second thought, let's not go there right now. I don't need details. So, the *fake dating* turned into something more."

I swallow and lean back against the chair, staring at the ceiling before meeting his gaze. "That's an understatement. Doc, she's perfect. Smart, kind, funny as hell, beautiful. But even if I was open to a relationship, she has these over-the-top family responsibilities, and I just signed this talented designer to my firm. She had no choice but to move back home to take her place in her," I pause and choose my words carefully, "family business. So to even date casually, I'd have to move, and I just can't."

"Why can't you? You work at a computer screen and own your own business. I'm having a hard time seeing what's tying you down."

I went through a couple of doctors before choosing Dr. Holloman.

At first I was wary. He only has a decade on me at best, and he looks more like a rock god with his black hair and stubble than a psychiatrist. Then I saw the colorful tattoos of movie and video game characters on his arms. I knew then I was in the presence of a fellow nerd and my first connection with him was made. But the thing that hooked me with Dr. Holloman was the first discussion we had. I hated feeling coddled and treated like everything I was doing was a normal part of my healing process. He told me he didn't serve up shit sandwiches, that I wouldn't always leave feeling warm and fuzzy, but I would always know he'd told me the truth and given me the opportunity to tell mine. His straightforward approach spoke to me, and he's kept his word to this day.

"I just can't do it. I'm focused on the business, and you know I've come to the conclusion relationships aren't for me. It wouldn't be fair to either of us," I say, because I can't explain to him that I can't run a business in the human realm from Infernis.

"Even if it's with a 'perfect' woman? The business would still be your focus? You wouldn't reconsider your decision about relationships?"

"Yeah?" I say, cringing at how unsure I sound.

"That's your decision to make, Jace. But I wonder if you've considered how she feels about all this?"

Emotion builds inside of me and gets lodged in my throat. "She left yesterday morning."

He nods once, but infuriatingly, he presses, "That's not what I asked. How does she feel about it? Did you talk to her? Ask her what she wanted?"

"It doesn't matter what she wants because I'm not going there again. I can't."

He narrows his eyes. "That's what I thought. You're hiding behind your career and behind the first approach you mastered that kept you safe. What is this *really* about? Stop hiding."

"I've worked hard to get where I am. I can't give that up!" The anger in my voice is proof of my denial even to me, so I change tactics. "Her life is out of this world. She deserves a guy who's made for that. I'm not fancy parties and black ties."

He cocks his head to the side. "So, you can't give up *what* exactly? The wall you've built so high that you've given up a person who clearly brought you joy? Because you don't think you'd be a good date at parties or be comfortable wearing a tuxedo? Or because you had come to a decision that is most definitely reversible after you have clearly made progress with this woman? We've always been real with each other, Jace, so I have to say—I call bullshit." He points at his three degrees on the wall. "I know I look like I'm fresh out of undergrad, but you do realize I went to school for a long time to earn those pieces of paper. I know when a patient is in denial. It's Psych 101. And you are in it." He stands and comes to sit next to me in the other armchair. "Be honest with yourself: Are you happier with this woman or without her? And if it's with her, are those things you would have to 'give up' worth losing the chance to be with her?"

"I'm so happy with her, and that's what scares me. I'd be good for her, and she's so good for me. We connected because we complemented each other so well. But it's a risk. An emotional risk that didn't work out for me and Hannah, and it didn't work out for my dad."

"And whose fault was that?"

I drag my palms over my face. The excuse has me taking ten steps back in the progress I've made. The good doctor is about to make me put check *myself*.

"My mother's. It was her decision and her failure. I didn't make her leave and neither did my father. We did nothing wrong. I know that. I've known that for over a year now. The same with Hannah. She was selfish, unable to care about anyone but herself. I was never at fault for her shortcomings. I know all that is true, but sometimes it's hard to believe."

"This woman you care for is not them, Jace." The conviction in Dr. Holloman's voice is the same I found in Desi's when she told me the same thing.

"I know."

"Did Desi want you to go with her when she left?"

I give a curt nod, not trusting my voice to remain steady.

Dr. Holloman leans forward so I have no choice but to meet his eyes. "I need you to honestly answer this one question: *Why* didn't you go with her, Jace?"

"I'm scared. I've told myself for so long that I don't believe in forever. I'm always waiting for the moment when the true, long-lasting feelings come into play. They'll realize I was a mistake. That *we* were a mistake." I pause, remembering every moment Desi and I spent together. "But how could something that felt so right be a mistake?"

Dr. Holloman raises his eyebrows and says, "It's *not* a mistake, Jace. You and Desi are not a mistake, even if feelings were to change. It's the risk we all take when we open ourselves to that kind of love."

I suck in a breath and hot tears burn the back of my eyes. He's right. I was too scared to take that risk for her. I let another man take my place with the woman I love.

Love.

I love her. I love Desideria more than I could have ever imagined myself loving another person. I'm causing more damage to myself by letting her go than Hannah or my mother did put together. I'm denying myself the chance to be loved and return that love to someone deserving. But it doesn't matter now because she's gone, and there is *nothing* I can do to get her back. Ever.

I'll never again twirl her soft curls around my fingers or kiss her lips. My home won't be filled with her laughter and I'll never get unreasonably frustrated with the easy way she can do the most menial of tasks. My nights of staring into her dark room while she sleeps and holding her in my arms are over. The sweet lust-filled moans, the tight heat of her body, and her desire to please me in return will become faded memories. She won't wake beside me as I marvel at what a spectacular being she is.

I close my eyes and attempt to sear those memories deep into my mind. Her dayglow-green eyes, fiery hair, freckled skin—each part of her is perfect. Even the crescent moon marking her as a demon was flawless. I pause and picture the translucent symbol, slightly lighter than the rest of her skin. Since I've learned about the identifying marks of angels and demons, it's become second nature. And today, when I saw the same discoloration on Cannon's chest, it didn't register. Until now.

I stand as the sharp edges of his mark form in my mind. But those harsh lines didn't lead to a crescent moon like Desi's.

No, Cannon bears a full circle—a sun.

The mark of an angel.

Desi said an angel stepping into Infernis would set everything off kilter. Everyone—the energies, demons, Desi—is in danger.

I look at Dr. Holloman with wide eyes. "Fuck. I've got to stop him."

He stands and examines me like I might be on the verge of a panic attack. "Stop who?"

"Cannon. I have to stop Cannon before he hurts Desi."

Why would Cannon do this? He was so sincere yesterday evening trying to talk some sense into me, acting like he wouldn't go to Infernis if I chose to go instead. The three of us were friends, but he's putting all of us in danger. Not only will him being in Infernis be disastrous for everyone in the demon realm, but it will harm the woman I've fallen desperately in love with.

I race across town to the abandoned bus station and park my car haphazardly at the back of the lot before sprinting through the lobby.

When the hallway to the storage room comes into view, I swear I take my first breath since piecing this all together. I open the steel door and come face to face with the gum-smacking medium. They stop filing their nails and slowly look up at me.

"Access denied. You already spent two days in another realm," they say matter-of-factly.

I lean over and place my palms on my knees to catch my breath and then look back up at them. "You've gotta be kidding me. I have to get to Infernis, and I have to go *now*. It's vital that I speak with Desideria."

They raise a dark brow and tap a long nail on the desktop. "If I let you go, you'll never be able to come back to this realm. As in, like, *ever*."

"I understand, but you have to let me through. You let an angel go to Infernis."

"I know. He was given clearance."

I throw my hands in the air and shout, "Why would you do that? You know what happens if he stays there."

The medium doesn't so much as flinch at my outburst. "Who do we look like? Dex? Angel and demon affairs aren't our business. We don't make judgments. We watch the portals to protect humans. So as long as you're safe from physical harm, we've done our job. In fact, if I let you go, I'm putting you in danger. You've already spent your time in Infernis; if you go there again, your body will very likely give out. There are no guarantees that your energy won't leave you, and if that happens . . . well, humans and demons might make great sexual partners, but demons and energies with no bodies do not."

Pure panic and frustration boil within me. They've given me the speech, and I understand the risks. If I don't intervene, my everything, my reason to truly live again dies. I could let Desi go knowing she was safe within her own realm, but I can't stomach the thought of living in a universe where she no longer exists.

Through gritted teeth, I say, "Please, let me pass. I've made my choice, and I choose chaos. I choose the princess of Sloth."

"Wait!" The medium jumps up and slaps their palm over my mouth, stopping me from saying anything else. "Is this a declaration of love?"

I pull their hand away. "Yes! Yes, it is!"

For the first time since I entered their dingy space, they smile. With sure strides, they move to the broom cabinet and open the door. "Why didn't you say so? We have a soft spot for acts of love."

I can't even bring myself to shoot them a dirty look; I'm too worried about Desi. I step into the cabinet and as soon as the medium closes the doors and wishes me safe travels, that *whoosh*ing sensation fills my ears. My knees go weak and I reach out to brace myself against the walls, but they've vanished. I drop and drop and drop. Nothing meets my fall. The world tilts—all sense of direction is completely gone.

I hold my breath, remembering that it only takes seconds for the door to open to Infernis. But the fall doesn't stop, the door doesn't open. A heaviness like I've never known crushes me. My bones ache under the weight and a white, hot flash of pain courses through me, then . . . nothing.

THIRTY-FIVE
DESI

I'm sitting in front of my mother's vanity wearing an elegant, formfitting black lace dress. It's floor length with a train that extends nearly a foot and a half behind me. It may appear morbid to humans, but black is the traditional color of choice for bonding ceremonies in Infernis. In this realm, it represents unity and endless possibilities.

My mother stands behind me, braiding my curls into a giant French braid that she drapes over one shoulder, showcasing the back of my dress—the deep V going all the way down to the small of my back. On the vanity in front of me sits the crown that will symbolize my rule for eternity—rose gold with black diamonds, intricately twisted into a design that somehow looks both dark and dainty.

"You're breathtaking, Desideria," my mother says, bending down to check my makeup and ultimately deciding I look perfect. "A true queen."

I smile but I'm aware it doesn't reach my eyes. "Thank you, Mother."

She sits next to me on the bench. "Darling, are you all right? I know this isn't how you expected things to go. Everything changed so fast."

I can't hide the tears in my eyes. "It's strange to think I'm gaining something today when I'm losing so much. I don't know how I'm going to do this without you and Father. I'm going to miss you both more than you can ever know."

"You'll manage without us. And you're not alone. Your brothers and Cannon will support you."

It's true but it doesn't mean it feels right.

"I miss him, Mama," I murmur, calling her the name I haven't used since I was a little girl.

"Miss who?"

She knows, she always knows. But that doesn't mean she'll spare me from speaking my feelings. My mother has never let us hide from our emotions. No matter how painful the subject, she always coaxed it out of us. As soon as the words were said, my brothers and I felt a million times better. She always knew best, and she still does.

"Jace," I whisper, the word barely a breath on the tip of my tongue.

Placing her index finger beneath my chin, she lifts my face to hers. "Then why are you tethering your forever to Cannon? He's a nice man and very handsome, but you love another."

I shake my head and try to look away from her, but she won't let me. She has more strength in one finger than I do in my whole body. I have no choice but to answer.

"Because he doesn't love me in return. I thought he did. And maybe, somewhere inside him, in his own way, he does. But he won't allow himself to express it. I gave him a hundred chances to come with me. But he let me go. And Cannon agrees that what we have is platonic. He's a great friend and wants to stand by my side." I shrug. "I figured if I can't have a sweeping love story like you and Father, I might as well have the friendship of a lifetime."

"Oh, Desideria."

My mother pulls me into her arms, and I can no longer fight back the tears. Just this once I'll let myself cry for what could have been. If only I'd come into Jace Wilder's life earlier. If only he wasn't so deeply hurt. If only I was enough to heal him. Unfortunately, I'm another casualty in the wreckage he refuses to leave behind.

She runs her palm over my back and remains silent for several minutes, just letting me cry. I fight through that pain, battling it tooth and nail only to face another. My father is deteriorating and my time with him is quickly coming to an end. Like every epic love story, my mother will follow him, leaving my brothers and me to rule in their stead. I've always thought that it was strange how eternal partners follow each other into the In-Between. Until now. Now I understand why it would hurt too much to carry on without the one you love more than anyone else.

Finally, when I sit up and take a deep breath, she runs her fingertips under my eyes and smiles. "Thank Lilith for waterproof mascara, hmm?" I can't help but smile and she rubs her thumb over my cheek. "There's my strong girl. I know this isn't exactly what you want right now, but Cannon is your best friend, yes?"

I nod and sniffle, pushing my hair back into place. "Besides Jace, yeah."

"Time is a funny thing. It can help friendships bloom into love. All hope for your love story isn't lost. Your prince charming may be a different character than you thought."

"I know. I just wish you and Father would be here to guide me through all the new chapters."

"Me too, my sweet girl."

I get to my feet and smooth my dress, holding my arms out to my sides. "Well? Am I ready to be bonded?"

My mother nods and comes to face me. "You are the last piece of the puzzle, the final working part to make all this function the way it should. Your father will feel so much relief when he can finally let you all assume your roles. Thank you, Desideria."

I lean forward and kiss her cheek. "I'm ready to do my part, and I thank you both for letting me go find someone I'll enjoy spending eternity with. Even though it isn't true love, Cannon and I have a lot of fun together."

"Good. That's half of an eternal partnership right there."

A soft knock taps at the door and my mother glances at the clock on her bedside table. "Ah, it's nearly time. That must be Cannon."

My heart speeds up at the mention of his name, and I'm not even sure why. I still have this fear that he's going to change his mind or demand something more from me, even though that would be out of character. My nerves are ruling my mind, though, so common sense is taking a backseat.

"All right." I turn toward the door and clasp my hands in front of my abdomen. "Let him in."

With a nod my mother strides to the massive black door and swings it open, and with a peck on the cheek and a whispered exchange with Cannon, she disappears, and he enters, closing the door behind him.

He looks handsome in his black suit and bow tie. His hair is twisted into small spirals and his blue eyes are striking against his brown skin. He flashes me a wide grin and says, "You look amazing, Desi."

All my nerves melt away. This is my best friend; someone I can trust. I walk toward him and turn all the way around so he can see the whole dress. "Yeah? It's not too much?"

"No. I don't think it's possible for your beauty to be too much." Cannon reaches for my crown on the vanity and holds it up to me. "May I?"

I nod, my fingers nervously toying with the end of my braid. "Please."

With steady hands he places the crown on my head. The weight of it causes my knees to buckle, and Cannon grips my elbow to keep me upright. It isn't the metal and jewels that are too heavy, but the finality of the moment. I won't spend days roaming the human realm, I won't watch human science-fiction movies, or have to be conscious of my power. From this day forward, I will be bound to Infernis and the demons and energies in my Circle. They will be what I live for.

"It suits you," Cannon says, straightening the crown on my head.

I smile and reach up to run my fingers along the diamond encrusted crown. "Thank you. For everything. I could never express how grateful I am that you did this for me. Gave up *everything*."

"This is what I want, Desi. I'm gaining so much more than what I'm giving up. This is worth it."

His words carry so much conviction that my chest aches. Cannon is so sure of what he's doing. And I feel so unsure. I force a smile and try to mimic his certainty.

"We'll have a good existence together," I say.

He nods and pulls me into a hug, sliding his palm up to the back of my neck and holds me close against his chest. "We will. I'm going to make you happy, Desi," he murmurs in my ear.

Not as happy as Jace would have. I push the fruitless thought from my mind. "Promise?" is all I can manage.

"I promise. Things will work out the way they're meant to."

Cannon loops my arm inside his and leads me out of the room. Our footsteps click through the vast hallways, each step always off from the other's. It's as if my body is telling me that it will never sync up with Cannon the way it did with Jace. The man beside me will always live in the shadow of another. I would say it isn't fair to put him in this position, but he already knows the truth. Cannon wants this, which is more than I can say for Jace.

We reach the ornate double doors flanked by two occisor demons. They stand tall, the curved horns on their heads adding to their height. Flat black armor covers bulging muscles and rows of sharp teeth peek through gray lips. Cannon grips my hand at the crook of his elbow and his back straightens. I don't blame him for putting on an impenetrable façade. The warrior demons must be a horrifying sight for a human.

The guards bow as we draw closer, and I nod in acknowledgment before they open the doors. Demons of all shapes, colors, and sizes stand on either side of a golden runner. Some are dressed in their finest and others have opted to attend today's ceremony in their natural form. Glowing eyes, pointed tails, shiny hair, and skin in every imaginable hue—the beauty of demons is on full display.

Our royal family crest sways on crimson flags mounted on the floor-to-ceiling pillars. An iron chandelier hovers over the room, its scrolling arms holding countless candles that cast everything in a buttery glow. Cannon and I walk down the aisle, our focus on the enormous black marble dais in front of us. Sixteen thrones sit in two rows, the largest of them—my mother and father's—are positioned front and center. My brothers and their eternal partners sit upon all the remaining thrones but two. Soon Cannon and I will take our place among Infernis's future leaders.

The room spins as my father stands and descends the steps of the dais, and I'm certain that I'm going to pass out. I sway on my feet, and Cannon has to grab my hands to steady me.

"Desi, are you okay?" he whispers.

I nod, my eyelids drooping. "I—yeah. I think I'm just nervous."

"Are you sure? You're pale, and your hands are so clammy. You don't look well."

I squeeze his fingers but I can feel that my strength isn't where it usually is. "I'm telling you, it's just because everyone is staring at me, and I didn't eat today because I wanted to make sure I fit into this dress. I'm fine."

A dubious look crosses his face, but he lets it go. "I promise you have nothing to worry about. Soon everything will work out the way you hope it will. This is far from the end, Desi." He lifts his lips in a weak smile. "I'm going to keep hold of your hands just in case."

"Okay," I whisper, even though his words hit me as odd. How can any of this work out the way I hope?

My father smiles as he stands in front of us, clapping a hand on Cannon's shoulder and kissing me on the cheek. "You look fantastic, my darling Desideria. Cannon, you clean up well too."

My eyes fill with tears; I'm going to miss my father's terrible dad jokes. But I can see the toll that ruling has had on him. He looks weaker than he did less than a week ago. His light is dimming, and with it his physical strength.

A titter of laughter goes through the audience, and when everyone quietens down again, my father speaks, his voice loud, commanding, and somber. "Good afternoon, demons and energies of Infernis. Thank you for traveling from every corner of the realm to be here, to see my lastborn child bind herself to her eternal partner, followed by the coronation of each of my children to their Circles."

Applause breaks out for a few moments, but when my father holds up a hand to silence them, the hush that falls over the room is instantaneous.

"Over the millennia, Infernis has overcome many challenges. Our realm saw many decades without true growth, when humans believed only by obtaining peace would they find eternal happiness. You have worked tirelessly in their realm to teach them that not all energies thrive in what Pax can offer. You have helped them embrace their chaotic sides and filled our realm with their wild energies. Our kingdom has grown by leaps and bounds, and, as you all have likely deduced, it is no longer possible for only one to oversee the havoc you create. I am pleased to begin the process of passing my rule to my children, who will continue this new tradition."

Again, the crowd erupts into cheers.

"Never again will another ruler burn out too early. We will be a stronger realm from this day forward. But first, let us bear witness to the eternal bonding of Desideria and Cannon."

I take a deep breath, choosing to ignore the fact that I can hardly fill my lungs, and turn to face Cannon. He's looking at me with narrowed eyes, like he can tell I'm not feeling quite right.

"Desi. Are you sure you're okay?" he whispers, leaning in and gliding the backs of his fingers over my forehead.

I chew my lip and nod. "Yes. I told you, I feel a little light-headed that's all. Just hold on to me."

"I won't let go."

My father drags the back of his hand over his brow and releases a slow breath. He clears his throat once and then twice before saying, "The bonding of two beings should never be taken lightly. It is more than a promise to remain together until your dying day. You are swearing to always look after the other's well being and work together to better our realm. The words you speak today supersede you and extend to all Infernis's inhabitants." My father turns his attention to Cannon and holds his gaze. "Cannon Pierce, do you swear to serve this realm for the rest of your existence, to honor Desideria as your eternal partner, and exalt her as your queen?"

Cannon looks around the room and shifts side to side. His grip on my hand loosens and his words are softly spoken. "I do."

"Desideria, do you swear the remainder of your days to Cannon, to partner with him in your rule as a queen of Infernis, and to place his needs above all others?"

Time stops in that instant. My heart, which had been racing, slows to a crawl, and I swear, I can't breathe. Can I really promise this to Cannon, knowing that my heart will *always* belong to Jace? Even though I know I can never have him? Can I truly place Cannon's needs above all others?

"I—"

The doors to the throne room fly open and bang against the wall.

"Stop! Fucking stop! Cannon is an angel."

THIRTY-SIX
DESI

The two occisors chase Jace down the aisle but he hauls ass, and the bulky demons can't keep up. He charges past Cannon and me and grabs the ax hanging from my father's hip. The weapon breaks free of its restraints and Jace swings it in front of him at Cannon. The ax—specially made for my father—flies from his grip and somersaults toward the crowd as Cannon ducks, though the ax came nowhere near his head.

Screams echo off the vaulted ceilings and demons flee the weapon's path. Jace's gray eyes grow wide, his arms held out before him as if he still has control of the weapon.

"I saw that going differently in my head," he mutters.

My father shoves Jace to the side and grunts, "No one can wield my ax but me." He holds out his hand and calls it back to him. It stops and spins top over bottom until it lands in his palm. "What is this all about?" my father asks, securing the handle to his belt again.

The guards rush forward. "We're sorry, Your Majesty. The human is stronger and faster than we thought. We'll take care of him."

The occisors each take Jace's arms and pull him down from the dais.

"No!" I rush forward and attempt to pry the occisors' meaty fingers off Jace. "He needs to go. He doesn't belong here." When they don't release him, my panic morphs into pure anger. "Let him go. Now!"

"It's all right, Desi."

I glance up at Jace, realizing he was talking to me the entire time.

He holds my stare and again says, "I know what I've done, and it's all right."

"Jace?"

He looks like he hasn't slept—his hair's a mess and dark bags sit under his eyes, but he's as beautiful as always. I've never been happier to see someone . . . but also, I've never been more confused. How can this be all right when it isn't what he wanted? Jace doesn't give me a chance to wonder for long.

His features harden as he turns to our friend and repeats, "Cannon isn't who we thought. He's an angel."

Murmurs erupt and the crowd steps back, putting as much distance as possible between Cannon and them. Even my brothers lean back in their thrones. Saying an angel is in our realm is the equivalent of telling us the plague is sweeping through Infernis. If what Jace says is true, in a few hours Cannon will be tied to our realm and the energy flowing from him will affect every demon and those who have chosen to remain in chaos for eternity.

"Leave it to Desi to choose a damn angel as an eternal partner," one of my brothers says with a snicker.

Cannon holds up both hands and moves away. "I'm not—I mean I am, but . . ."

"His chest. His angelic mark is on his right pec," Jace says.

"What?" I whisper, my eyes darting between Cannon and Jace. "How could I not—I would have noticed . . ." No, I wouldn't have. We hadn't ever taken things that far because we didn't feel that attraction toward each other. Our energies clashed.

Chaos and peace.

Demon and angel.

We would have never connected on a deeper level than friends.

"How could I have been so—"

My father cuts me off, his voice weak. "You wouldn't know unless you saw his mark. Don't beat yourself up."

"Dad, you need to sit down," I say. Glen and Mandis immediately jump from their seats and help my father to his throne next to my mother.

Something is definitely wrong. My dad is already weak, but everyone in this room except for Cannon and Jace is starting to lose energy—we're sluggish, dazed, even some of their coloring is off.

"I saw his mark right before he left. It's been weeks now since I learned what they mean, and it was second nature to see it on someone else," Jace whispers in my ear from behind me, his hand gripping my hip.

"No," I breathe, my heart speeding back up, both at the prospect of everything falling into ruin in a matter of hours and Jace's proximity when I thought I'd never see him again. I step toward Cannon, and Jace shadows me, his palm lingering on the small of my back but letting me take the lead. "Why would you offer to come here? What's your real motive?"

Guards file into the room, closing in on Cannon. The angel has nowhere to go.

"My father sent me to distract you from finding an eternal partner. It was supposed to be my final trial to prove I was worthy of the throne," Cannon says, eyeing the occisors surrounding him.

"What? Trial? Your fa—" My jaw drops, and I look over my shoulder and catch my father's eye.

"He's Angelo's son," my father says, closing his eyes like I imagine one would when they get a headache.

Cannon bows his head. "Yes." He exhales and runs his hand down his face. "I thought it was a harmless plot for my father to get the upper hand in your bargain with him. It's been decades since Pax acquired more energies than Infernis. I just wanted to impress my dad." He lifts his gaze to mine and the next few words out of his mouth look like they pain him to say. "But we became friends and I felt how much it meant to you to do this for your family. It was the first thing I'd admired about you, and I genuinely wanted to help in any way I could."

With a scoff, Colére straightens upon his throne. "He's a stinking empath. You do choose winners, Desi."

I shake my head and lower myself to the bottom step of the dais. Jace follows me down and runs a soothing hand along my spine. This is all too much, and I don't have the strength to deal with it.

"What—why does everyone look like they're about to pass out?" Cannon asks, just realizing that all the demons and energies in here aren't doing well. He really has no clue that he's made a grave error by coming here.

That he is about to destroy us all from the inside out.

"That sly, greedy bastard Angelo wanted you out of the way," Avaros says.

Fier glances at our brother and cocks a brow. "He would sacrifice his own child if that's what it took to remain the ruler of Pax?"

"I don't trust the angel," Colére says, reaching for his sword. "If his daddy isn't giving up the throne, why not take ours? Kill us all off and he'll have his own realm to rule."

But the realm would be empty. He'd have to start all over, and even then, how could he be sure it would even sustain any sort of life? This isn't adding up.

Cannon shakes his head. "No. No, I didn't know this would happen." He looks at me and then at Jace, and he shifts from foot to foot. "In fact, I hoped that once I came here I could buy you and Jace some time. You guys belong together, but he's so hurt and not ready to take that leap. It wasn't going to be the perfect scenario, but I wanted it to have a happy ending for you guys. Chaos," he says, his gaze shifting to my father, "my motive was never to hurt any of you. I told my father my plan and he agreed. He *used* me to hurt you."

"If you didn't have ill intentions toward my daughter, why didn't you tell her the truth?" my father asks.

"My orders were to distract Desi. I was to make her believe I was human. If she found out what I was, I would fail. I was hoping that I could appease my father, and when Jace was ready, I'd reveal what I am and the bond would have to be broken. Jace and Desi would get to be together, and I'd return home to rule. I never thought my plan would lead to harming anyone."

Julius steps forward and glares at Cannon, jealousy saturating his stare. No doubt he's envious that everyone's attention is focused on the angel, not to mention how Cannon's muscular form fills out his tailored suit. "You're saying that you came up with this elaborate plan but didn't know what would happen if angels and demons were to invade each other's realms?"

Cannon shakes his head. "Our education focused on the principles of our realm and strategies to lure energies to Pax."

"I don't trust him," Mandis says, shifting in his throne and pulling a cellophane wrapped cake from his pocket. He takes a large bite and continues with his mouth full. "No way he didn't know. He was following Desi from the start."

Glen makes a disapproving *tsk* and says, "You aren't just saying that so your father will kill him, and we can go to dinner, are you?"

"Bitch, I might be," Mandis mutters, shoving the rest of the cake in his mouth.

I glare at my brother and say to my father, "What are we going to do?" I run the back of my hand over my forehead and lean back against Jace for support, my head spinning again. "Whether or not you believe him, we have to get him out of here before we all drop dead or melt or whatever the hell happens when an angel stays here for too long. I'm starting to feel really off."

"It is not our call to make," my father says, and his gaze cuts to Cannon. "Detain him."

Fear sweeps over Cannon's features. I'm not sure if it's his presence in Infernis or a hint of sympathy, but my stomach roils. I've spent hours upon hours with Cannon, and either he's a great actor or he's telling the truth. Other than his purpose for appearing at Jace's the moment I did, he's always been candid with me. It's hard for me to believe everything about our friendship was fake.

"What are you going to do to him?" I ask.

"This is a matter for Dex to judge. Take him to the portal."

The guards yank Cannon forward, and he twists his head and mouths *I'm sorry* to me. I wish I could know for sure if he's telling the truth. Thankfully, that isn't my call to make.

THIRTY-SEVEN
DESI

I'm swallowing the devil's claw root pill my mom handed me before we left the throne room, hoping that it works like it did for Jace when he left Infernis the last time he was here, when he finally speaks.

"Um, Desi?"

I look over at Jace as we walk toward the carriages my father had rushed around to the front of the palace. I cling to his hand, scared if I let go he'll disappear, and with the other, I fumble with my dress, nearly tripping on the train every other step.

I can't explain the feeling of relief I get every time I look over and realize that he's here, with me. Somehow, miraculously, I have a second chance. I don't know how, or what's going to happen next, but I know that I'm happier with him here than I was without him.

"Yeah?"

"Where are we going?" he asks as he picks up my train, clearing it from the path of my stilettos.

"Thank you," I say, flashing him a smile before continuing. "Dex's court. She's the one who makes all the decisions for both angels and demons. She's the final say, the judge for both Infernis and Pax."

His face pales. "We have to take a portal? Oh. God, Desi, I almost didn't make it through the last one. The medium from the human realm said I couldn't come back...that I'd remain in Infernis forever."

He doesn't even trip over the word *forever*. It's like it's second nature to him to be with me in the same place for eternity. Did he really choose this existence, choose me? Or was he forced to come here to save us? I'm dizzy with the thought, so I push it aside.

"No, going to Dex's court is different. It sits upon the In-Between. It's not in any of the three realms. It's neutral. Think of the In-Between as the border between Pax and Infernis. You'll be fine."

A look of relief passes over his face as we approach the carriages. "Oh, thank god."

I grin as I look at the drivers for guidance. "Which carriage should we take? The one with my parents or my brothers?"

The driver gives me a knowing look. "Neither. Your mother arranged for your own carriage with Mr. Wilder."

Jace and I exchange glances and a thrill runs through me, my cheeks, chest, and the space between my legs all heating at once. Only a day without Jace, and my body is reacting as if it's wandered the desert for decades and just happened upon an oasis.

"How nice," I say with a smirk, and Jace winks at me as we climb into the carriage.

I settle in next to the far window and watch as Jace steps inside. Instead of sitting on the bench opposite, he sits right next to me, our thighs flush against each other.

"Hi," I whisper, drawing my bottom lip between my teeth.

"Fancy meeting you here," he replies, and one corner of his lips tilts up.

I swing my knee toward his and bump him playfully. "Now that we have a moment alone, I—"

There are so many things I want to say . . . do . . . *touch* . . . but I don't know where to start. I suddenly feel shy, and I know that's idiotic, but I can't help it.

I try again. "Now that we're alone, I want to talk about . . . about what this really means, Jace. You came here. For me? You do realize what that means?"

"I know what it means. And I also know that I don't deserve you after the way I treated you." He looks away from me and his lips tense as his tongue swipes over his front teeth. A minute ticks by while he composes himself. Clearing his throat, he turns his attention to me again. "I hurt you. I assumed you were the same as my mother and Hannah, when you did nothing to justify that. I refused to believe you when you made your feelings for me clear, and I let my fear govern me. I'm so sorry for the way I treated you. And I understand if you need space and time to forgive me and figure out how I fit into your life." He shrugs. "My mortality lies in your hands, but I'm hoping you will grant me all the time in the world to wait for you, Desideria."

I turn to him and intertwine our fingers, meeting his gaze. "Forgiving you isn't even a question. Did you hurt me when you refused to come to Infernis? Yes." His eyes flick down to his lap, and I hook my finger under his chin and force him to look at me. "But for fuck's sake, I was asking a *lot* of you. I was asking you to leave your entire realm. Give up your entire existence. It would be a lot for anyone, let alone someone who's been through everything you have. And then you sacrificed *everything*, the dream you've worked so hard for, to come here and save my life—to save my entire realm. Do I need time to *forgive* you? Come on, Jace. I'm in love with you. I've been in love with you for a while, and I never thought I'd have the chance to tell you. But now I plan on saying it over and over again until you tell me to stop," I whisper, running my thumb over his knuckles, dying to kiss him.

"I knew you would wiggle your way into what was left of my heart as soon as you sat beside me to watch my favorite movie. How could I not be weak for a woman who came up with her own theories and spent the rest of the day beeping at me like R2-D2? But I was a goner the moment I saw you in that green dress and you spent the evening dancing with me, doing something for *me*." He slides his fingers along my neck and tilts my face up with his thumb. "It's like your laughter and goodness filled in all the holes left in my soul, and your touch mended my broken heart stitch by stitch. I'm so very in love with you, Desideria."

I've never believed anything as much as I believe Jace.

He loves me.

The corners of my lips tip up as I meet his eyes. "I'd only have expanded my movie tastes beyond rom-com for one person, Jace Wilder, and that's you."

"It's good to know your love has no limits. Neither does mine."

He kisses me then, not like the hungry kisses we've shared in the past. This kiss is slow and tender. His mouth is soft against mine and the glide of his tongue sure. This kiss seals his words and speaks of more promises to come. It is the start of our forever.

Everything falls back into place and it's like I never left him, like we've never been apart. I can't quite move the way I want to in this dress, but I do my best to pull it up as far as I can and shift onto his lap. "This isn't as close as I'd like to be," I whisper against his lips as I pull back for air, "but it's a start."

"It's a good start and more than I deserve right now."

The guilt Jace feels for letting me go will take time to dissipate, and I can give him that. The past will find its place behind him, and I'll continue to walk with him toward our future.

I slide my fingers into his hair and press a kiss under his ear and pepper them along his jawline. "You deserve everything in this realm and every other, and I have an eternity to give it all to you." Slipping the fingers of my free hand under the hem of his shirt, I sigh when my skin makes contact with his. I've missed this; simply being near enough to him that I can feel him against me. To know he's within my reach.

"I like the sound of that, and that I get to do the same for you," Jace says, gliding his fingertips down my spine.

Our lips meet again, and his grip tightens around my waist. I rock my hips over the growing length of him, and he moans into my mouth. Neither of us can get enough. Our hands search for bare skin and our tongues frantically lap for a taste of the other. It's more than I thought I'd ever feel again, yet it's not enough. I want my body naked and tangled with his, for his hard planes to press into my soft curves. Every inch of me is aching to be one with him again.

But time is an asshole, and the carriage comes to a stop.

I pull back, both of us breathing heavily, chests rising and falling in tandem. "Damn. We're here already."

He brushes his thumb over my cheek and asks, "What's going to happen to Cannon?"

I crawl off his lap and straighten my dress. "I don't know. It's up to Dex to issue the judgment. But I don't believe she'll go easy on him."

"Good. He could have killed you. He deserves a harsh punishment."

The anger radiating from Jace is so clear, from the tinge of pink in his cheeks to the harsh set of his jaw. But beyond the rage is a glint of concern deep in his gray eyes. He may want to see Cannon brought to justice, but that doesn't change that they were once friends.

I reach over and brush Jace's hair off his forehead and turn his face toward mine. "I know. But I really think we should get Angelo's side of the story before we judge Cannon too harshly. I just don't believe that he *actually* set out to hurt me. Before you busted in the room like the Incredible Hulk, he was asking me why I looked so sick, and what was wrong with everyone else. He was genuinely confused. Do you *really* believe he could hurt me?"

"I don't know what his intentions were, but I know what could have happened if he became your eternal partner. I'm struggling to see past that, Desi."

"But did *he* know what could've happened? I think he just thought he was going to screw things up for my dad regarding the bet and get on his daddy's good side. I don't think he would've come here if he knew it would harm anyone. Least of all me. I believe he cares about me, at least as a friend."

Jace tangles his fingers with mine and brings my knuckles to his lips. "And that is why you were made to be a queen. I can't be fair when it comes to your well being. I've discovered that I'm blinded by love." He flashes me one last charming smile before the coachman opens the door.

I squeeze his hand and we crawl out of the carriage, trying *not* to appear like we just got done making out, but of course, Lux is right there climbing out of the carriage in front of us, grinning like the asshole he is.

"Well, well, looks like our little royal couple got reacquainted on the ride over," he mutters, leaning toward me and Jace with a teasing smirk.

My face burns and I shoot him a glare, tucking myself in close to Jace's side. "Shut it, Lux."

"Come on, little sister. Own your lust because you two sure as hell can't contain it when you're around each other."

If I'm being honest, the thought of Jace and me acting affectionately in front of my family isn't as repulsive as it once was. I want them to know that I can't keep my hands off Jace, and it's another extension of the love I feel for him.

Jace surprises me by leaning in and nibbling at my earlobe. "I'll be happy to show everyone just how little I can contain myself around you," he whispers against my neck.

I grin and bump him with my hip. "You're naughty. We have *extremely* pressing matters at hand right now, sir."

"I can't believe you were going to bond yourself to this asshole for the rest of your existence," Colére says, pushing a restrained Cannon forward.

The remorse written on Cannon's face tugs at my heart. It isn't the type of regret someone has when they're caught doing something wrong. The sadness radiating from him is like a heavy weight causing his shoulders to slump and his face to contort in pain. Perhaps I'm mistaking his fear of punishment for something deserving of pity. Knowing that Dex may sentence him to the Perpetual Torment and set his soul on its final journey should trigger regret. It's hard to decipher what the true state of his emotions is.

"He's not an asshole," I mumble under my breath, and Jace looks down at me, squeezing my hip.

I resent the tears that fill my eyes as we walk toward the atrium where Dex presides. I don't want to shed a tear for Cannon, not knowing for sure what his true motives were, but I can't help it. All the memories we made together are rushing back to me—all the *Star Wars* movies we watched on the couch, the trips to eat fried pickles, ice skating, target shooting—was all of that a ruse and am I that foolish?

"I know," Jace says, placing a kiss on top of my head. "It's hard to believe that my little hurricane is a softhearted demon queen."

My lips lift into a reluctant smile and as we stop behind the rest of my family, I turn to him and press my body flush against his. Rising to my tiptoes, I whisper, "I may have some soft spots, but don't worry, I have plenty of rough patches that I save especially for my king."

"Rough patches?" One side of his mouth quirks. "I'm very interested in seeing what those parts entail."

"And I'm happy to show you."

Jace places a hand on either side of my face and presses his lips to mine. "You're all over the place right now. I think you can't figure out if you want to ravish me in the back of the carriage or do your duty and get to the bottom of what Cannon was up to when he came here."

I smile against his mouth. "Oh, no, I've figured it out. I want nothing more than to take the carriage back to the palace, ravish you in my bed, and then figure out Cannon's motivations in the morning. Unfortunately, that's not an option."

He shakes his head, and we follow my family.

My father leads the way up the white steps to the enormous stone doors. The moment we step inside, the atmosphere changes. It becomes lighter, as if nothing resides in the space. We are no longer in Infernis, or Pax, or the human realm. This is the gateway to the In-Between—the place the most powerful being in the universe calls home. Images depicting the creation of the realms are chiseled into the arched ceiling, which is held up by towering columns. The judicial building has no walls, giving a clear view of the billions of tiny lights zipping across a black backdrop. There is no beginning and no end to what lies beyond, just the In-Between. When my mother and father are ready to take their final journey together, they'll walk through this building and into the onyx oblivion.

A shiver runs down my spine as I take in a wide hole in the middle of the floor. It's the brightest white I've ever seen, but instead of all of the chaos and beauty of Infernis or peace and light of Pax, it's nothing but a meaningless reflection of the two. It's the embodiment of nothingness. The Perpetual Torment.

A woman sits behind a raised desk and peers down at us. Her eyes, such a dark shade of brown that they're almost black, rake over each of us. Her black hair is pulled into a tight bun, placing her sharp nose and round cheeks on perfect display. The golden robe she wears contrasts with her red lipstick but complements her brown skin.

"Chaos," she says, and her voice is steeped with authority, even more so than my father's. "My clerk has filled me in on the gist of the story here, but I want to hear directly from the parties involved—namely Desideria and Cannon." She looks around the room, her bottomless eyes landing on all of us before saying, "Where is Angelo?"

My father opens his mouth to answer, but his words are cut short when the doors to the atrium fly open and bang against the wall with an echoing thud.

"Who is that?" I ask whoever's listening.

"Angelo," my dad and Mandis answer at the same time, both rolling their eyes.

The ruler of all tranquil things looks as if he just came off a hard night with his rock band. His shaggy blond hair flows past his shoulders, and his beard is in desperate need of a trim. The attire he chose for today is more fitting for a day at the beach than to witness his son's judgment by the most powerful being in existence. He's out of place in his fringed shorts, tie-dyed T-shirt with a peace sign over the chest, and leather flip-flops. I expected a lot of things from the ruler of Pax, but this wasn't one of them.

"Sorry I'm late. I was in the middle of this relax fest and just chilling to some psychedelic tunes. Man, there is nothing like some shrooms and great music to help you find your zen."

Dex raises a sculpted brow and clicks her tongue on the top of her mouth. "If you're done enlightening us about your latest head trip, we have a problem that needs to be addressed. And why am I not surprised, Angelo, that it involves your son?"

The older angel flashes a look that makes Cannon flinch.

"Father," Cannon says, the normal certainty he speaks with muted into a timid greeting.

"How and why did you end up in Infernis?" Angelo's voice is so buttery smooth, and if I didn't know better, I'd think he was actually confused. "Do you want to kill every demon who lives there? Explain. Now."

Jace shifts beside me and crosses his arms over his chest. He lifts his brows and gives Cannon his undivided attention. The next words that come out of our friend's mouth will make or break them, these two men who have formed a tight friendship built on so many common interests. I don't think any of that was fake; at worst, it was a side effect of Cannon's ulterior motives.

Cannon's eyes harden with rage. "What do you mean *how did I end up here*? You sent me to distract her by, and I quote, 'Any means necessary.' And when I told you how well Desi and I got along and what a tough time I was having deceiving her, you suggested I should become her eternal partner. Where did you think I'd have to go to marry her, *Dad*?"

Angelo shakes his head and laughs. *Laughs.* "Cannon, you must've skipped school on the day they talked about what happens if an angel goes to Infernis. I would never suggest that."

Cannon's eyes narrow. "You know damn good and well I never missed a day of school. They never—"

"They did, you just weren't listening. Just like you weren't listening when I told you that you can't bond yourself to a demon in her realm. Why would you want to do this? You two aren't sexually compatible. All the headaches of marriage without any of the fun."

"Agreed," Lux says.

Julius whips his head around, his long red locks fanning across his face. He exchanges a glance with his platonic partner, Verte, and together they say, "Bullshit."

Angelo waves his hand like he's shooing away flies. "Maybe you don't care about the order of things. I raised you better than this, son."

"You were hardly there for my upbringing!" Cannon yells, fighting against his restraints and taking a step closer to Angelo. Like he's reining in an angry dog, my father calmly grips the back of Cannon's shirt and holds him in place.

Jace elbows me, and I look up at him to see his eyes as wide as saucers. "What is it? What's wrong?" I ask.

"He's lying."

My heart sinks. Everything's about to come to a head and boil over. Cannon played me. He was never my friend. He never cared. Even worse, he played Jace too. He made Jace think he *cared* about him, that he was his friend. Jace has already been abandoned by so many people in his life. Now, one of his closest friends?

"I think Dex will sentence Cannon to—"

Jace grabs my arm, leans down, and hisses in my ear, "No. Not Cannon. Angelo."

I rear back and my jaw drops. "What? How do you know that?"

"Three reasons. One, Cannon may have been up to no good, but he was diligent about it. He was 'dealing with business' just as much if not more than being with us. Two, why would something as important as the ins and outs of your rivals be taught only one day and never reiterated? I don't think it's ever taught at all. By design. Three, I have a strange feeling. A nagging deep in my gut that Cannon's telling the truth."

"But what reason does Angelo have to lie? He's the ruler of an entire realm, the long reigning king of Angels. To stand before Dex and concoct lies like this could lead to the end of his son."

Jace shifts side to side and his eyes lock on Angelo. He goes so silent watching the scene unfold that I question whether he's even breathing. It's like he's the lightning rod in the middle of this storm waiting for the blow that sets this all alight.

Finally, he whispers to me, "Is Cannon Angelo's only child?"

"Yes."

Jace's jaw ticks. "That's what he wants. The end of his line. Colére said something in the throne room that stuck with me. Maybe Angelo never *wanted* to give Cannon his throne but to get him out of the way. Then who could rule in his place? No one."

My breath catches. Angelo has never wanted to give up power. He's ruled Pax as long as anyone can remember while Infernis has gone through a reasonable number of rulers in the same time span. Father has always said Angelo is power hungry. I just never imagined he'd sacrifice his own son to cling to it.

"You're right. We have to stop this."

Jace nods and steps forward. He strolls through the room with his hands behind his back. As if he's speaking to himself out loud, he says, "What a shame that your only child committed such a breach of trust and put our entire realm at risk. The imbalance he would have caused to humans is unfathomable."

My emotions rip in two. Jace is claiming my realm as his own, but he's doing little to prove Cannon's innocence. If he isn't careful, Dex will have our friend thrust into the Perpetual Torment, and Angelo will get what he wants.

Angelo shrugs. "Kids. You do the best you can to raise them right, but they seem to always disappoint you."

Jace clenches his jaw so tightly his lips pucker. "I completely understand. Kids are such a burden. Now, you'll have to rule Pax for eternity."

Dex crosses her hands on her desk and sits forward. Something tells me she's waiting to see Angelo's reaction. And rightfully so. If my father was in Angelo's place, I know he'd be fighting to save us. He'd go as far as to take the blame and suffer the consequences if it meant sparing us pain. Angelo doesn't strike me as the type to do the same.

"I'll do what I must for my realm. My first responsibility is to the angels and energies I rule."

Dex turns her attention to Jace. "Who do *you* believe is the guilty party, Mr. Wilder?"

I am stunned into silence. Dex asking Jace for his opinion on the situation is *strange* to say the least. He's a human who's been in Infernis for only a few hours, and she's asking him for his opinion on a crime that is certain to end in extinction.

But Jace doesn't appear to be taken aback or scared. He looks strong, certain, and . . . kingly, if that's even a word. My chest is warm, and my body erupts into tingles when he speaks in a loud, clear voice.

"Angelo. He's lying about Cannon learning what happens when an angel or demon goes to another realm. I don't know how I know that, but I do."

The angel king scoffs. "So says a human. They can't figure out what's best for them without our intervention. I'd hardly put value on his opinion, Dex."

"You're really freaking out about my opinion for a being who cares so little for it. I take it that you don't like the idea of your son taking over your precious rule. You want Dex to kill him off so you can rule forever. Don't you, Angelo?"

Without any warning, Angelo shakes out of his hallucinogenic haze and charges at Jace. He slams his shoulder into Jace's center, knocking them both off their feet. They skid across the polished floor toward the gaping hole in the middle. They stop just short of toppling over the side, Jace's head hanging over the edge. Angelo straddles Jace with his hands around his neck, shaking him as his grip tightens. The movement causes Jace's glasses to slip from his face and vanish into the void.

I rush forward with my father and brothers, but Angelo's snarled words stop us.

"Touch me and we'll both find our final rest in the Perpetual Torment. I hear it's even worse for a human energy—the silence, the disconnect from all other beings. Don't make that his fate."

I continue forward but then Glen and Mandis are on either side of me, hanging on to each of my arms. "Don't move, Desi. You know he'll do it. This is a desperate angel we're dealing with," Mandis whispers, his usual sarcastic tone absent.

Rage bubbles inside me and hot tears fill my eyes. "We have to stop him." The idea of losing Jace *again*, and to the Perpetual Torment no less, makes my entire body shake with horror.

My heart is pounding against my rib cage, and Angelo is so close to me that I could shove him over myself. But it's too risky. His grip on Jace is firm, and Jace would end up going too, and I could never forgive myself.

"Desideria, stay back. Please," Jace chokes out.

Angelo turns to me. "You heard your *king*," he says, the last word dripping with sarcasm. "Don't put yourself in this, sweetheart. You'll be sorry."

Cannon moves beside me and rubs his shoulder to mine. He quietly says, "It'll be all right. My father doesn't want to give up his crown. Let Dex judge us, Desi. It's the only way to ensure Jace's safety."

I turn to him and meet his eyes. "What if your father pushes Jace over the edge before she has her say? Look at him, he's lost his mind!"

"Stop this nonsense! This is my courtroom not some damned wrestling ring. Get up. Before I sentence everyone in this room to the Perpetual Torment!" Dex's command halts all sound, and I breathe a sigh of relief as Angelo's hands loosen on Jace's neck.

Angelo stands, yanking Jace up with him. Neither of them moves far from the edge of the hole, doing little to calm my nerves. I won't be happy until I can hold Jace's hand in mine and know he's safe. He hasn't gone through the transition into immortality yet. Angelo could still end him without shoving him into the void.

"Never in my existence have I seen such a debacle in my courtroom. And I've dealt with my fair share of archaic rulers. What should have been a good-natured bet between rivals has spun out of control and put more than one realm in peril today. I should punish the lot of you," Dex says, dragging her gaze over each of us.

The room is eerily quiet. I'm not sure anyone is breathing any-more until the telltale crinkle of plastic draws my attention. Glen fumbles with a round chocolate cake, fighting to open it. I inch closer to him to put a stop to what sounds like a swarm of bees buzz-ing around us during this serious moment. We might all be tossed into the hole, and his insatiable sweet tooth could be what drives Dex to make that call.

Dex carries on chastising us for our behavior, either not hearing the racket or choosing to ignore it. "Cannon, I'm disappointed that you allowed yourself to become a pawn in this ridiculous bet. You used deceit to worm your way in with not only Desideria, but Jace Wilder as well. Angels and demons do not resort to these means. Your calling is to guide humans with truth."

"Glen," I growl out through clenched teeth.

He glances at me and clutches his snack for dear life. Taking a step away from me, he continues pulling on the wrapper.

"But I understand your desire to please your father," Dex con-tinues. "As an angel under his command, it is your duty to act upon his wishes. I believe you meant the demon realm no harm. In the future, I suggest you educate yourself on the realms and what might destroy their perfect balance. I would also suggest you educate the other angels in your realm. All of them need to understand the con-sequences of their actions."

"Yes, Your Honor," Cannon says, bowing his head.

"Angelo—"

I reach for the chocolate snack cake, and Glen moves to the side, furiously ripping it open. His elbow shoots back, jamming Angelo in the side. The king of Angels stumbles and reaches for Jace, but he jumps away from the side of the chasm. Glen turns with wide eyes and holds his cake to his massive chest. With flailing arms, Angelo falls into nothingness.

The entire room gapes at Glen.

He throws his arms to the side and says, "Sorry, I'm a nervous eater!" He looks over the ledge into the vast pool of blinding light and takes a bite of his cake. "That's sort of a tragedy."

If I weren't so scared for Glen's fate, I would laugh. But Dex hasn't announced her punishment yet, and Glen quite literally sent Angelo into the void. I don't have time to think for long because Jace rushes to me and folds me in his arms, and I tangle myself around him, breathing in his scent and convincing myself that he's really here. "Jace, you're okay," I murmur against his chest.

"I'm kind of feeling like a superhero after that."

"Too bad the same can't be said for Glen." I watch as he gingerly takes another bite of the cake, afraid it will be the last thing he ever eats.

Dex releases a long breath and tosses her hands in the air. "I guess that saves me from another long speech about inappropriate behavior. I was sentencing him to the Perpetual Torment anyway." She turns her focus to Cannon. "Congratulations, you're the new ruler of Pax. Please make better decisions than your father and stay away from the drugs."

My jaw unhinges, and everyone's heads snap toward Cannon. "Cannon!" I exclaim. "You—you're king!"

Cannon's eyes widen and a litany of emotions rush over his face— the sting of betrayal, grief at losing his father, shock at Dex's proclamation, relief that we know he was telling the truth, and joy that he's now the king of his realm.

"I—thank you, Your Honor," he says with a bow. "I vow to keep Pax guarded and to teach the angels everything they should know about the three realms. I know I have a lot to learn, and I swear I'll do just that."

Dex nods once and bangs her gavel. "Very well. Now, go so I can return to binge watching trashy human television and finishing my jewel art of a kitten wrapped in yarn."

My stomach flips and Jace's grip tightens around my waist. I look up at him, and when my eyes meet his, there's nothing but pure love reflected in them. No more fear, no more uncertainty, Jace Wilder is ready to open himself up to a life of being loved by me.

We file out of the atrium. My family is all smiles and boisterous recounting of what just happened as we make our way to our carriages. The driver holds the door open for us and before I climb in something urges me to look back. A lone figure walks with his hands in his pockets, heading in the opposite direction from us.

"Cannon," I yell and run after him. "Cannon, wait."

He turns toward me with a sad smile pulling at his lips. I reach him and we awkwardly stare at each other for a second, knowing it will be a long time before we see each other again.

"I didn't want you to leave without me saying thank you." I laugh, tears clogging my voice. Jace steps to my side and places his hand on my waist. "I know that may sound a little batshit after what you almost did by accident, but I want to thank you for showing me friendship. You didn't have to do that."

He clears his throat and blinks back tears. "I'm sorry I wasn't up front with both of you. I really thought I could work this all out in your favor in the end. It looks like that's the case, but not because of me. Just know that my friendship was sincere."

Cannon holds out his hand to Jace. A moment passes before Jace finally wraps his fingers around Cannon's and pulls him into a hug.

"I know what it's like to have a parent betray you, man. Take the time to feel that hurt. You hear me? But once you've felt it, deal with it, and move forward. Don't let it steal your joy for years, like I did," Jace says against Cannon's shoulder.

The tears Cannon had been blinking back slip down his cheeks and he doesn't even bother to wipe them away as he pats Jace on the back and they separate. "Noted. I'm glad you came to your senses. Keep the queen happy and let up a little on all the cleanliness stuff."

"No chance."

The two laugh, and Cannon sobers as he turns to me. "Good luck ruling your Circle."

I raise an eyebrow. "Good luck ruling *all* of Pax."

"Maybe one day we can have a friendly wager . . ." Jace begins.

"No!" Cannon and I exclaim in unison.

Cannon grins and his eyes soften. "Goodbye, Desi."

"Goodbye, Cannon."

With one final nod, he starts down the road toward his realm.

"That was commendable, Desideria."

I spin around and find my father watching us. He leans against one of the massive columns of the atrium, spinning his ax in front of him from its chain. Stress lines still mar his face, and his body isn't as bulky as it once was, but he looks better than he did when I returned home.

"I'll give you a minute," Jace says, kissing my temple and walking away.

I close the distance to my father, and he lets his weapon fall to his side.

"Dad." I don't even know what to say because I feel like no matter what words I choose, they'll never be enough. But I owe it to him to try. "I almost don't want to go back and do all the things we need to do. Because that means it's time for us all to step up . . . and I'm afraid you're going to lea—" My voice cracks and I look down and chew my bottom lip. "I'm afraid you're going to leave me right away. And I'm not ready."

"If I'm telling the truth, this feels like my weakest moment as a ruler . . . as a father. I have to let go and trust that I've taught you and your brothers everything you need to know to rule. That's hard for me to do when it's been my job for centuries to protect you. I'm good at that, but now I'm feeding you to the wolves. Or the demons."

"You've taught us everything you could. There are some things we'll have to learn for ourselves, but you've prepared us to deal with that. And you've never been weak. Not as a ruler, and *definitely* not as a father." I step forward and throw my arms around him, careful not to squeeze too tightly. "Thank you for letting me go to the human realm to find my partner—to find Jace. I can't imagine what would've happened or who I'd have ended up with if you hadn't loved me enough to give me that freedom."

He hugs me tighter and inhales like he's breathing me in for the final time. "You're welcome. Letting you go might have been the best parenting moment of my life." He pulls back and lifts an eyebrow, looking over my shoulder to where Fier and Mandis are in a brutal argument with my other brothers egging them on. "Your brothers could have benefited from living in a little less chaos for a minute."

I turn and follow his stare, laughing through the tears. "They're ridiculous." I shake my head and look back up at my father. "Did Glen really end Angelo with a snack cake?"

He nods with a disgusted expression. "Not the way I would have done it, but it got the job done. No one will ever deny that my kids aren't good at wreaking chaos. The same can be said for their partners. Except for yours." He hooks his finger under my chin and lifts it. "Jace is good for you, Desideria."

"I know."

"I need you to do one more thing for me before I let you go rule your own Circle."

My heart sinks with the finality of his request. "Anything."

"Tell me I was right about him and the way he feels about you. Let your old man win this last battle."

A grin spreads across my face. I'm happy to give my father this victory fair and square.

"You were right. Even when we came here the first time, and it was all a ruse to buy me a little more time, it was real. It was just that neither one of us was ready to admit it yet."

He nods and flashes a proud smile. "A good ruler always knows when to admit they're wrong. You'll make a great, lazy queen." Father gives me a kiss on the forehead. "I love you."

"I love you," I say, choking back tears.

He pulls back and nudges me in the direction of Jace. "Let's get your eternal partner home so we can complete the ceremony and bond him to his form. I'm guessing you want to keep him as he is."

"Yes," I say with a laugh.

I return to the carriage to find Jace leaning on the side, his arms crossed over his chest. He doesn't say a word, just pulls me to him, where I can safely let my emotions go. When I feel drained, yet a little lighter, I pull away and say, "Are you ready to face life in Infernis?"

His lips pull into that contented smile that always melts my heart. "If that entails being your eternal partner and sharing a bed with you, then yes."

I sweep my arm in front of me and bend at the waist, saying, "Then after you, my king."

EPILOGUE
JACE

One Year Later

The last thing I should be is the king of Sloth. Anyone who knows me would say it's asinine. I thrive on productivity, order, and most of all, control. The slightest change in my schedule sends my entire day into disarray. Yet here I am ruling the most laid-back of the seven circles of Infernis by my wife's side.

Desi cares for the energies under her rule in a way I can't. She understands what they need to feed their lazy natures. She is so attentive and kind, always striving to make them happy. And that is where she turns to me.

I know how to make her visions for our Circle come to life. Everything from the dark caves where some choose to live to the ice-cream shops with hammock swings in the center for naps, even the lazy river that winds through our Circle, were my creations.

We make quite the team, designing our little piece of forever together. I never imagined that chaos and order could create something so flawless.

But Desi did.

I was too stuck in my head but she saw what we could be together. She knew it when she accepted Cannon's offer to be her eternal partner, and when I let her leave. I was the idiot who almost let her slip through my fingers—a mistake I will never make again. And I think I've found the perfect way to prove it to her.

She fidgets with the scarf I tied over her eyes as I race down the road in my demon-made sports car—a perk of living in my new realm.

"Don't you dare peek, Desideria," I chide, fighting to keep a straight face. She is adorable when she's nervous.

"I'm not going to peek, *Daddy*," she teases, reaching over to squeeze my thigh.

I shift under her touch, hungry for more, but manage to keep the desire she invokes in check. "Keep it up and I'll pull this car over and show you just how *Daddy* I can be." She opens her mouth and I place my hand over it. "And before you say that's fine with you, I suggest you opt for the surprise over the spanking."

She licks my palm and laughs when I squeeze her cheeks. "Fine. But only because I *really* want to know what you've been up to. Just so you know, though, I might try to earn a spanking later anyway. How about that?"

"I wouldn't expect any less from you," I say with a chuckle, wiping my hand on my pants.

I must hand it to Desi; she has only hounded me for details about my secret project a few dozen times. That is the height of patience for her. I'll admit that it was tempting to give in when she offered sexual promises that made my imagination run wild. I'd managed to resist, which was difficult considering the chances have been rare lately; our grueling schedules have kept us busier than I'd like.

After Desi, my attention has gone to the demons who help us run our Circle. I listen to their concerns and work to find solutions that will best meet their needs. Every extra moment I've had, I've slipped away to ensure every detail of my gift to her was just the way I pictured it. The wait is finally over, and I can't wait to show her what I've been up to.

In a hurry to get to our destination, I floor it, and we speed down the tree-lined road. Immortality has given me the freedom to let go of some of the worries that used to weigh me down. I still have moments when ruling gets the better of me. My anxiety hasn't just gone away because I'm a king. The eternal happiness of countless energies relies on me and Desi, but I no longer fear what lies ahead. I've found safety and trust in the arms of a stunning demon, and death no longer has a hold on me.

"Are we almost there?" she asks, her knee bouncing rapidly in the seat, fingertips drumming on her thigh.

I reach over and grab her hand, clasping her fingers with mine and planting them on her leg, calming her nerves enough that she stops shaking her thigh. "Yes, Mrs. Impatient."

She grins and I know, even though I can't see them, her eyes are twinkling. "That's *Queen* Impatient to you, my king."

I squeeze her inner thigh and she squirms in her seat. "I still love hearing you call me that."

"Good, because you're going to hear it for an eternity."

I still don't think she has any idea how happy I am that I burst through those doors that day, outran those two occisor demons through the sheer power of adrenaline, and made sure that would be the case.

It isn't until we reach the destination that I'm brought back to the present by Desi's sharp inhale.

"You're slowing down. We're here, aren't we?"

Her wide smile is rounding her cheeks so much that they're practically begging for my lips to brush against one, to place a kiss on her soft skin and hold her close to me for a moment. I've never felt so at peace before in my whole life. And to know it'll be this way forever—I'm overwhelmed, and it's so nice that here, in Infernis, it can also be the *good kind* of overwhelmed.

"I love you, Desideria. I just—I want you to know that."

She tilts her head to the side and turns to face me, pressing her forehead to mine. "I do, silly. Always."

"Good. Don't move, I'm coming to help you."

I hop out of the car and rush around to her side, helping her out and hooking her arm with mine. Our steps click on the stone under our feet, and when the door creaks open, I move in behind her, placing my hand on the small of her back, ushering us a few steps forward.

Resting my chin on her shoulder, I wrap my arms around her waist. I take a final look at what I've worked so hard to create. Not a thing is out of place, yet my stomach still flips as if it is competing for a gold medal in gymnastics. I breathe through my nerves and say, "I know you don't dread the commute from the capital to our Circle, but I thought it was time we had somewhere to call our own."

"Jace, you didn't—" she starts, her body trembling against me.

I reach up, untie the blindfold, and let it fall away. Her shocked gasp and widened eyes when she glances back at me say it all.

"Jace . . . it's just like our old house," she whispers, taking in all the details. "Everything is here. The kitchen island, the TV, you even bought a blanket just like my old one. It's all the same . . . you redesigned it." She turns in my arms and looks up at me, with tears shining in her brilliant emerald eyes.

"I did, and all the furnishings are actually from the old house. Since I turned my share of the business over to Edmonds and helped Matt hire a new designer to take my place, I thought it was time to let it go and only focus on creating a life with you."

Desi's eyebrows knit together, and she gnaws on her bottom lip. "That house was the last thing that tied you to the human realm. Are you sure about this?"

It amazes me that this beautiful, intelligent being matches my love for her. Despite her lazy nature, she would go to any length to ensure my happiness. It's a wonderful feeling to know I am the center of her world. And she is solely the center of mine.

"The only other thing I've been surer of was the day I passed through that portal and knew I was giving up my human life for you. This is what I want."

"All right, but don't you think this house is too big for just the two of us? Maybe we should advertise for a roommate," she jokes.

"Absolutely not." I tip her chin up until we are eye to eye. "You know, the reason I put the ad out for a roommate wasn't so much to take the financial pressure off me as I started the business. I was tired of being alone and haunted by thoughts of Hannah and my accident. I wanted to make new memories in that house and for it to feel like my home again. The moment you set foot inside, everything changed. I laughed more, opened myself up to new friendships, and wanted more than a successful business. My house was filled with love and happiness because of you."

A whimper escapes her. She stands on her tiptoes and presses her lips to mine. "Jace Wilder, before I met you, I had this warped, black and white image of who I was. I thought I needed organization and someone to offset my chaos. You give me that calm I was thirsty for, but you also taught me that my chaos has its own brand of beauty." She slides her hands up my chest, wrapping her arms around my neck. "I love chaotic me with you. It feels right."

"It sounds like you found your home too."

"I did."

I press my lips to hers again. It doesn't matter if it's this realm or another, this house or a castle. Wherever Desi is, it's the place where my heart finds joy.

With bright smiles we pull away from each other, and I turn to the pantry, taking out a box of cereal. "Shall we christen the house with a bowl of peanut butter puffs?"

"I can't say no to that," she says, hurrying to the cabinet next to the sink. "I get—" She swings open the door and freezes, staring at all the cups turned upside down. "You put the cups in the right way."

I shake my head when she spins around with disbelief written all over her face. My new favorite expression of hers just might be surprise—her parted lips and eyelashes fanning the tops of her cheeks.

"I put them in the *wrong* way because I'm ready to give up a little control and surrender to the chaos," I say, placing the box and milk carton on the counter.

A smile spreads over her face as she curls her index finger at the bowls. They float out of the cabinet and come to rest side by side in front of me. Before I get the chance, she directs the cereal box to open. Sweet, round puffs fill the bowls, and the milk pours over them.

"Well, in that case, maybe I'll try to be less lazy, and, uh . . . not use my powers to do my chores every day."

I snort and grab two spoons from the drawer, handing her one. "No, you won't. But that's okay, little hurricane. I wouldn't have your chaos any other way."

ACKNOWLEDGMENTS

Thank you to every reader who fell in love with Desi and Jace's story. Whether you were first introduced to *UC* on Wattpad, within the pages of an ARC, or in this book, we appreciate the excitement and support you have given us. It's because of you that we are blessed to live out our dream as writers.

To our husbands, Richard and Tony, thank you for believing in us. You will never understand how grateful we are that you work so hard to allow us the chance to do what we love. We love you. Aidyn, Steven, Sara, and the rest of our families, thank you for not disowning us for our outlandish imaginations. Y'all are the best.

Sam, we could not have asked for a better PA. The time and effort you put into supporting us by caring for all the ways we reach our readers is priceless. You are a queen, making us friends with royalty.

Angie, Kacy, and Lee, thank you for being fearless and sharing your thoughts with us. It was your suggestions that helped put the finishing touches on this book.

To Fiona and the team of sensitivity readers and proofreaders, thank you for helping us produce the best story possible. Fiona, we know we get a little wacky and push the limits of what the human body can do. Thankfully, we have you to remind us that legs don't work like that when arms are bound behind one's back.

Sarah and the Literally Yours PR team, you all are top notch and have taught us so much about marketing. We would have been lost if it weren't for your guidance.

Of course, we wouldn't be where we are without Wattpad and the Wattpad Books team. We will forever have an orange *W* engraved on our hearts. A special thank-you to Maeve, who pushed us to go to the bar that night in L.A. Irina, thank you for always going to bat for us.

Frayed Pages team, you all are wonderful, and we're elated to be a part of your publishing family. Your listening ears have made this an outstanding experience for us.

Finally, to our friend Anna Todd. We can never thank you enough for believing in us and this book. Working with you is a dream come true. We love ya. Also, we are still waiting for our BTS PowerPoint presentation.

ABOUT THE AUTHORS

Crystal J. Johnson is a best-selling, award-winning author, Wattpad Creator, and half of the writing duo Crystal and Felicity. She has written and co-written seventeen novels, including *Kept in the Dark*, *Spellbound*, *Edge of the Veil*, and the Affliction Trilogy. Crystal lives in Phoenix, Arizona, with her husband, son, and a multitude of rescued animals. She is a self-proclaimed connoisseur of Ben & Jerry's ice cream and a lover of boy bands. When she is not writing, you can find her with her nose in a book or an audiobook in her ears.

Felicity Vaughn is an award-winning Wattpad Creator, author, and co-author of sixteen novels, including *Kept in the Dark*, *Spellbound*, *Edge of the Veil*, and *His to Steal*. Felicity is from Nashville, Tennessee, where she lives with her husband and spoiled-rotten cat. She loves the color pink, slip-on Vans, and sloth-themed items. When she isn't spending time with family or writing with her bestie, you can find her watching reruns from the '90s or crying over books that probably aren't even supposed to be tearjerkers.

PROLOGUE

People from all over the world flocked to the Reynard Hotel for one reason—ghosts. They charged their cameras, packed their families in minivans, and set off for a sleepy coastal town in Connecticut, exchanging the thrill of roller coasters and the excitement of meeting a beloved movie character for the chance to encounter the things that go bump in the night. People sacrificed the luxuries of fine hotels and crammed into small guest rooms with the hopes of catching a glimpse of the Hyde brothers.

The twin boys were rumored to haunt the grounds of the historic Reynard. Disembodied laughter, pounding footsteps, and glowing orbs of blue and purple had all been caught on video and attributed to the brothers. On occasion, keys and sunglasses would inexplicably fly across a room, and tapping would sound from inside the walls as the two souls cursed to live out eternity in the hotel made their presence known to the living.

Hazel Fox lifted a gnarled hand to the ruby pendant around her neck as she made her way through the empty narrow hallway. The light bulbs flickered, casting shadows over the golden outline of peonies etched into the peacock-blue wallpaper. With each step she took toward the staircase, the flowers appeared to sway with an unfelt breeze. Most would be unnerved by the groaning wooden floors and the squeaking of rusted hinges, but she found comfort in the settling of the colonial building. Especially on a night like this.

Winter Spirits was one of her favorite days of the year. For a single night, the brothers were free from the confines of the hotel's property. Legend had it they slaughtered animals and snatched babies from their cribs, but Hazel knew the truth. The twins wreaked havoc the way young men tend to do, but never with malice. So, when Hazel had taken ownership of the Reynard, she had dismantled the terrifying tales and turned the night into a celebration.

"Aunt Hazel! Wait!"

Hazel turned to find a blond, gangly preteen running toward her, buttoning her gray wool coat and skidding to a stop in her patent leather shoes.

"Someone looks ready for a festival." Hazel looked down at her favorite niece, and the brightness in the child's eyes filled her with pride. She hadn't had children of her own, so Gemma was the closest thing to a daughter she'd ever have.

"Yeah, but I was wondering if I could practice my ghost tour on you on the way out. You said I could lead them by myself next summer, remember?" The girl was practically bouncing on the balls of her feet.

"Of course. Show me what you've got," Hazel said, then stopped short, looking around the empty hallway. "Wait. Where's your cousin?"

Gemma didn't even bother to hide her eye roll. "Raven already went outside. She said she couldn't stand spending another minute in this creepy hotel, and the festival was the only reason she came." Hazel covered her mouth with her palm to hide her grin; Gemma's impression of her other niece was impeccable.

Where Gemma was free-spirited, Raven thrived on schedules and boundaries. One girl enjoyed her time at the Reynard, while the other saw the days there as nothing more than an obligation to spend time with her eccentric great-aunt. Gemma was open to all possibilities, but Raven was firmly grounded in tangibles. Which is why she would never be the one to cherish the Reynard as Gemma did.

"All right then, her loss." Hazel held out her hand, and Gemma wrapped her fingers around it. "I'm ready for the best ghost tour this hotel has ever seen."

"As the Fox family legend goes, it was the coldest night of 1886, and twin baby boys were left on the steps of the hotel. When they were found by Amity Fox, the hotel's first owner, they were blue, lifeless, dead. Their spirits are here roaming the halls of this hotel. Many see them in the form of the young men they never grew up to be."

"It's true. This is the only home Archer and Soren have ever known."

Gemma held her hands in front of her, brushing the air with her palms like she could feel their presence. She took big steps, lifting her knees to her chest and dropping her voice to a haunting whisper. "If you listen closely, you might hear them laughing in a hallway or knocking on the walls from the other side."

Hazel's big jeweled earrings dangled next to her cheeks, and her go-to fuchsia lipstick turned her thin lips into a wicked grin. She mimicked her niece's creepy stride. "The Hyde brothers never disappoint."

"They enjoy playing in the dark, and that's why every night at ten o'clock we turn out the lights and guide the ghost tour with nothing more than the light of lanterns."

Hazel couldn't fight her smile. While other girls Gemma's age were absorbed in social media accounts, celebrity crushes, and favorite TV shows, all of that fell off her niece's radar when she set foot in the Reynard. She spent every waking moment of her annual summer visits searching for the ghostly boys. Every year she begged her parents to book rooms at the hotel for Winter Spirits, and they compromised by bringing her every other January. Gemma's love for the Reynard was unquestionable.

"And where's the boys' favorite place to hide, Gem?"

Gemma didn't even have to think twice. "The bell tower. No one can go up there because the entrance is closed off. They like it there, because they're safe from curious eyes. But on this very night, they come out to play with all of Spelling."

Hazel squeezed Gemma's shoulder, proud that the girl clung to her every word. They would sit for hours in Hazel's suite, talking about the women in their family who had owned the hotel before her, and she gave her niece the necessary tidbits about the twins who were portrayed in a painting over Hazel's fireplace. Gemma studied the artwork and absorbed every story, eager to share the tales with those who wanted to hear them.

They descended the last flight of stairs and entered the lobby. Gemma skipped over the checkered tile and sat in the velvet wingback chair in the sitting room. She crossed her ankles and clasped her hands in her lap, staring at the fire crackling in the stone-carved fireplace.

Hazel rounded the antique mahogany counter, running her fingers over the hand-carved filigree along the edge. Her heart swelled at the sight of the girl so comfortably settled at the Reynard. It was quite the feat to gain Hazel's adoration; only two people had accomplished it before Gemma. Like them, her niece saw beyond the bright muumuus and collection of silver rings that adorned each of her fingers. She was one of the few who enjoyed Hazel's questionable humor and joined in with her boisterous laughter. Her niece loved her as she was, and Hazel adored her in return.

With the money from the register secured in the safe, Hazel stood and met the familiar gaze of a young man. A grin spread over her face; she would never grow tired of those unusual sparkling eyes, or how a dimple indented his right cheek when he smiled.

"Sun's just set. It's time for some fun, darling," he said, propping an elbow on the countertop.

His smooth voice, laced with a hint of mischief, echoed through the empty lobby and grabbed Gemma's attention. From the fit of his new slacks to the black button-down shirt, her wide-eyed gaze soaked in every detail. Hazel recognized the enthralled expression on her niece's face; it was the same one she herself had worn the first time she'd seen him.

"Is that—"

"It is," Hazel said to him.

"She's growing up."

"As are you, my friend." Hazel stepped out from behind the desk and held her hand out to her niece. "Come along, Gemma. It's time to celebrate with the spirits."

"Yes, *the spirits*," the boy repeated with a sly grin.

Gemma wrapped her fingers around her aunt's and tilted her head to the side, studying the boy through narrowed eyes. When they stepped out into the frosty winter evening, she asked, "Have you seen the Hyde brothers?"

He exchanged a glance with Hazel. A smile that held four lifetimes' worth of secrets pulled at his lips. "I guess you could say that."

"Do you think they're here now?"

Hazel didn't miss the calculated undertone of the question. If Gemma was anything, she was perceptive.

"I do. And I think it's quite probable that you'll run into at least one of them before the night is through," he said with a wink.

"Are you—"

"Let the young man be on his way, Gemma. There's so much to discover, and some only have this one night. And we have a tradition that awaits us."

Gemma followed her aunt down the hotel's front steps, eager to dance and play carnival games in the town square. "I hope you have fun tonight," she said, looking back at the boy, but her words fizzled when she found no one there.

"Where'd he go?"

Hazel put her arm around her niece's slender shoulders and led her toward the town square. "I'm sure you'll see him again."

The wistful look on the girl's face warmed Hazel's heart, and right then she knew—if anyone would be able to do what she herself couldn't, it would be Gemma Fox.

CHAPTER ONE

Of all the days for my chronic tardiness to kick in, it had to be today.

I crammed my keys into my purse and slung it over my shoulder. Slamming my car door, I caught my reflection in the dusty window. Wisps of golden hair broke free from my ponytail and crowned my freckled face like a lion's mane. I licked my fingers to tame the strands and cringed as it did little to better my appearance. With a sigh, I gave up and ran toward the sky rise.

Today was just another nail in my aunt Hazel's coffin. After years of battling breast cancer, my great-aunt had been in remission. Or that was the impression she'd given my family. It turned out Hazel had sugarcoated the truth in a thick, sticky glaze. She'd gone as far as concocting an active lifestyle of daily swims, Bunco every Tuesday, and a slew of renovation projects around the Reynard. When the disease claimed her, she had been alone, and I'd been living it up with no clue. Not only was I not at her side when she died, but I couldn't convince my family to forgo a traditional funeral. Hazel would have wanted a party to celebrate her life. Bright clothing, strong drinks, and cheesy '80s pop songs—a quirky gathering that she would have loved to have attended. Now, all that was left was this final meeting, which she would have hated too.

After the twenty-floor elevator ride, I burst into the attorney's office and asked the receptionist to point me to the conference room. My shoes beat against the tile floor, and I nearly tripped when I skidded to a stop in front of the double oak doors. Smoothing down my dress, I took two deep breaths to still my racing heart and walked in.

Everyone seated around the oval conference table fell silent. My skin prickled with embarrassment under their scrutinizing gazes. They were freshly pressed suits and designer shoes, and I was a broken-in pair of Vans and a red sundress from my senior year of high school. I avoided making eye contact, turning my attention to the window overlooking the Boston cityscape. It was bad enough that my parents and brothers were here to witness what I was sure they considered another irresponsible Gemma moment, but Raven's family was here too.

My uncle Kevin was the spitting image of my father, down to the silk ties and Italian leather shoes they wore to work every day at Fox Imports, the luxury-car empire they had built from the ground up. They weren't twins, but only eleven months sat between them, and they'd been inseparable since birth. The only discernible difference between them was their taste in women—while my aunt Deborah was pretentious and materialistic, my mother was a sweet, sincere woman, who was charmed by my father's charisma and stability.

"Nice of you to join us, Gemma," my father said, his tone dripping with sarcasm. His hazel eyes radiated disappointment—an expression I had grown to expect over the years.

My mom elbowed him, offering me a tight smile that didn't show off her new set of veneers, a gift from my father for their last anniversary. "Christopher, stop it. Come on in, honey, sit down."

I took the empty seat next to my brother Hunter. "You okay,

Gem?" he whispered, brushing his palm over the scruff on his jaw.

I appreciated Hunter's empathy. No one in this room understood just how much Hazel meant to me. She was just a kooky relative to them, a woman obsessed with ghosts who lived in a musty, old hotel. But Hunter was always sensitive to other people's emotions, especially mine.

I nodded, tears stinging my eyes. "Yes. I just—"

"I know today is hard for you. It'll be over soon enough," he said, squeezing my arm.

"That's right. I can finally shut down that outdated roach motel and do something useful with the profits," my cousin, Raven, said, flipping her long black hair over her shoulder.

Anger bubbled up in me, heating my cheeks and the back of my neck. Raven had always hated the Reynard, never wanted to spend the summer there, and never took the initiative to learn its history. Her ridicule and eye rolls were the only things I saw from her where the hotel was concerned.

"Raven, you can't—"

She shot me a glare across the table, and the air in the room seemed to chill. "I'm the oldest female Fox. I'll be able to do whatever I please."

Gritting my teeth, I clamped my hands down on the arms of the expensive leather chair, my pulse pounding in my ears. And I had no reply. None, because Raven was right. As soon as that will was read, everything I loved about being with my aunt Hazel would be in my cousin's hands. Hands that wanted to do nothing but destroy what our ancestors had worked so hard to build.

The door at the front of the room opened, and my great-aunt's balding, middle-aged lawyer, Mr. Cartwright, stepped over the threshold. "Are we all here now?"

"Sorry I was late," I said with a sheepish smile.

His face was warm and open, and he wore an expression that made me feel like maybe I wasn't the most irresponsible person ever to exist. "It's all right, Miss Fox." He sat at the head of the table and opened the folder in his hand, pulling out a packet of papers. The will.

"Let's get started. The will isn't very long, and it's relatively straightforward." He cleared his throat and began to read.

It was all the standard wording about sound mind and last will and testament. My thoughts drifted as he droned on, thinking, *This is it*. Hazel's will was her last act on this earth. Never again would she walk the halls of the Reynard or lead a ghost tour. We would never sit together in her hotel suite and talk about what it was like to own the hotel or our plans for the future. I would never pull her close in a hug and melt against her as she embraced me back. She was gone.

"'I hereby bequeath the Reynard Hotel and all its assets to my great-niece Gemma Diane Fox.'"

"Wait, what did you say?" I blurted out, snapping my gaze to Mr. Cartwright. "Did you say my name? That can't—"

"That can't be right!" Raven sprang from her seat and slapped her palms on the table. "For one hundred and fifty years, the hotel has been passed to the oldest girl with the Fox name. *I* am the oldest. Hazel can't break tradition."

It was my brother Trevor who backed her up. "She's right, there was only one incident when it didn't pass from an aunt to her oldest niece. What's going on here?" His dark, perfectly coiffed hair without a strand out of place only added to his *I'm better than you* attitude.

I shouldn't have been surprised at Trevor's reaction. He and I may have gotten along when we were younger—he used to take up for me on the playground when the older kids picked on me—but in our later teen years, he became more and more critical of me and my life decisions. He didn't like my friends, my boyfriends, my choice of extracurriculars. When I'd dropped out of college two years ago, he'd laughed and told me that I would never make it in this world. He had no mercy when it came to me, no forgiveness. He had become a carbon copy of our father.

"Hazel had every right to break tradition. She had no legal obligation to follow it, and she made no mistake in her wishes. We discussed it at length, and Gemma is the one she left the Reynard to. There's no question about it," Mr. Cartwright said.

"It doesn't make any sense; Gemma doesn't know anything about running a hotel," my father said, and my aunt and uncle grumbled their agreement. Of course they did. They wanted their daughter to inherit it so she could shut it down.

"I can learn," I started, but everyone spoke over each other, pushing me out of a conversation that had nothing to do with them and everything to do with me.

Raven raised her voice over the others, her attitude one of utter disdain and condescension. "Not to mention that I have my degree in hospitality and am currently the manager of a five-star luxury hotel in downtown Boston." Her eyes darted to me on the word *degree*, as if to rub it in my face that she had graduated and I hadn't.

"Hazel was very clear that even though Gemma is not the oldest girl, she was the one she wished to leave the hotel to as she showed the most interest in it throughout her life," Mr. Cartwright replied.

The attorney's words warmed my heart. Hazel had gifted me the thing that meant the most to her. The Reynard was mine because the oldest girl hadn't given a shit about Hazel or the hotel. The only reason Raven ever came to visit was because her parents saw it as an obligation. *I* was the one who took the time to get to know Hazel, helped her with ghost tours, spent weekends repainting the porches, and took afternoon tea with her when it seemed like no one else valued her presence. Hazel didn't care that Raven had her bachelor's degree in hospitality or managed a cookie-cutter chain hotel. She wanted someone to run the Reynard who *loved* it.

And that was not Raven. My cousin hated all things paranormal. Where I was intrigued by and open to the inexplicable, she was disgusted by it. I was the one who embraced it with Hazel. No one else in this entire world saw me like my great-aunt did. And I saw her too.

Mr. Cartwright held up a hand to silence everyone. "It is worth noting that the hotel will remain the property of the trust, as it has for over a hundred years. The person who it is handed down to will keep any profit made during the time it is under her care. If Gemma either does not want the hotel or is proven unfit to run it, Raven will take over, but there is a caveat."

"This should be rich. What outlandish stipulation did Hazel put in place for my daughter?" Kevin asked.

"Your aunt was not a foolish woman. She recognized that Raven has more experience in the industry. Therefore, Raven must put forth every effort to help Gemma learn to run the business. Christopher and Kevin, since you are the oldest surviving members of the Fox line, Hazel has given you authority to determine if Gemma is unfit to manage the hotel. You may check the physical state of the building and its finances at your discretion within the first year of her ownership. Once the first year has passed, the hotel and its assets will be fully assigned to Gemma in accordance with the terms of the trust. If you should choose to remove her, your reasoning must be based solely on her performance."

Trevor scoffed and said, "You might as well just give it to Raven now because Gemma isn't capable of tying her shoes, let alone running a business."

I glanced at my slip-on Vans, and anger and embarrassment heated my skin. "Shut up, Trevor."

"If we're done acting like children," Raven said, directing her attention only to me, "I'd like to understand what exactly is expected from me to fulfill our great-aunt's last wishes."

I fought the urge to roll my eyes. "Why? You couldn't even stay in the rooms by yourself. Every summer you threw a fit about going to spend time with Aunt Hazel."

"You know I was traumatized in that hotel as a child. Whatever is there liked to pick on me. It was evil."

"I know, I know. Things pulled your hair while you slept, and shadows chased you down the hall during a ghost tour." I gave in to the eye roll. "Funny, but it sounds like even the spirits never wanted you there. I had no problem."

"Whether you like it or not, Gemma, this is what Hazel wanted. When you fail—and you will—I want to be prepared to take over."

Raven couldn't care less about Hazel's final wishes. She wanted to get her perfectly manicured claws into what was left of our family legacy and rip it apart from the inside out. By the time she was done with the Reynard, the property would house an upscale boutique hotel. The guests would feast on caviar and schedule afternoon pampering sessions. All signs of Hazel and the Fox women before her would vanish.

"I'll schedule a meeting with you to discuss what actions you need to take to secure your place as owner if Gemma should forfeit or not meet the terms," Mr. Cartwright said, sliding a stack of papers across the table in my direction. "Right now, all I need is for Gemma to sign."

Deborah spoke up, her nasal voice piercing my ears. "There really is nothing else we can do? No recourse? Raven just has to wait for what is supposed to be her birthright?"

Hunter released a lip-rattling breath and ran a hand through his dark-blond hair. "Please. Everyone at this table knows that Gemma is the *only* one of us who gave a damn about the Reynard. And anyway, the will is final. Aunt Hazel is gone. Gemma is in charge of the hotel. Just let her sign so we can move on with our lives."

It amazed me how Hunter and Trevor were both my brothers but so different from each other in every way. Where Trevor couldn't get enough of insulting me, Hunter would always come to my rescue. I could have hugged him, but I settled for reaching over and squeezing his hand where it rested on the arm of his chair.

Mr. Cartwright handed me a pen, and my heart stuttered. This was the biggest kind of commitment I could make, and even I could admit that my track record wasn't exactly spotless.

"Can I—can I have some time to think about it?" I asked.

"Of course she can't make up her mind; it's just like ballet classes, piano lessons, and lacrosse." My father sat back in his chair and looked at my mother. "Libby, do you remember that summer she begged us to send her to space camp and then called us a week and a half into it to come and get her because she was bored learning about stars. What did she think *space* camp was going to be about?"

Just when I thought I couldn't feel smaller, my father knocked me down yet another peg. "We get it, Dad. I'm a total flake."

Before he could respond, Mr. Cartwright spoke again. "You

have seven days. The trust has some stipulations. Call me and let me know what you decide, and the two of us will meet again to go over the terms."

"Thank you, Mr. Cartwright. I'll give you a call this week." My skin was crawling with the need to get out of this room, away from my father's disapproval, my cousin's wrathful stare, and the final, stark realization that the one adult in the world who *really* understood me was gone.

When the lawyer dismissed us, I didn't waste a second, springing from the chair so fast I nearly knocked it over. I pushed open the heavy double doors and rushed to the elevator.

"Gem!" The pounding of footsteps came from behind me. "Gem, wait."

"What is it, Hunter? I just want to go home and forget that entire meeting ever happened. Especially the part where Dad made me look like an idiot."

Not only did Hunter and I look the most alike, but we were also the ones who didn't live up to our parents' high standards. The dark-blond siblings who didn't aspire for riches. We were the ones who preferred a beer over wine, and the wallflowers at the ritzy parties my parents threw for Christmas and New Year's. While they were talking politics and the stock market, we exchanged inside jokes and talked about trash reality TV. They were Gucci, and we were Target. And we liked it that way.

He pressed the Down button for the elevator, and we stepped on, trying to force the doors shut before the rest of our family could barge in. "He was just pissed things weren't going 'to plan,'" Hunter said, making exaggerated air quotes around the last two words.

"I wish he would pick on someone else for a change. Trevor

is long overdue for some parental humiliation," I said, earning a laugh from Hunter.

"Trevor is the golden child. You know that. Anyway, I was coming to offer my help. I'll go down to the hotel with you and take a look at it. With things having been worse than we thought with Hazel, there is no telling what you're getting yourself into."

I could use the extra set of eyes, especially when it came to the hotel's physical condition. While our father would have preferred that Hunter spend his days behind a desk and run his company from there, my brother enjoyed working with his hands and getting a little messy, and he had created a thriving construction business. I couldn't think of a better person to accompany me to the hotel for my first visit since Hazel had passed.

I bumped him with my hip. "I suppose I could use a passenger with impeccable taste in music during the two-hour drive."

"Just say it; I'm your favorite brother." He pulled me into a headlock and rubbed the top of my head with his knuckles. "Besides, I wouldn't let you drive your Honda; that thing is almost as old as you. You would just have to call me to rescue you from the middle of nowhere, and I have a date I can't miss this weekend."

I pinched one of his love handles until he yelped and let me go. Brushing my hair down with my fingers, I followed him to his brand-new truck with wheels so big that I almost needed a ladder to climb inside. Hunter turned on a playlist that the two of us had added songs to over the past few years, and I rolled down the window, kicked off my shoes, and watched the Massachusetts coastline fly by.

A NOTE FROM THE AUTHORS

While most of this book is fun, spicy, and fluffy, *Unleashing Chaos* does contain some sensitive topics. Jace, our hero, is a man who lives with anxiety and panic attacks. In representing this, there are a few scenes with potentially triggering content, including on-page panic attacks along with mentions of a potentially fatal car accident, parental abandonment, and death of a parent (all of which happen in the past and therefore off-page).

There is also a club scene in which our main character dances with a stranger who somehow thinks it is his right to grope her without permission (don't worry; he finds out quickly that he is wrong).

As always, we did our absolute best to handle these topics with supreme care. For a detailed list of trigger and content warnings, please visit our website at www.crystalandfelicity.com.

With all our love,

Crystal and Felicity

SPECIAL NOTE FROM FELICITY

While I am a woman and our main character who lives with anxiety is a man, I wanted to note that all anxiety representation in this book is influenced by my lived experience. I was formally diagnosed with generalized anxiety disorder over a decade ago, but I've lived with it since I was a preteen. Obviously, everyone's experience is different, so to ensure we represented anxiety from the man's perspective as respectfully as possible, we utilized sensitivity reading, something we highly recommend when you're broaching sensitive topics that are different from your lived experience.

But it was very important to us that you all know that I've been there, I live this, and I see you if you're here too.

Love,

Felicity